The Treasure Hunt Club

A Novel

By Michael Scott Clifton

To: Megan

The Treasure Hunt Club
ISBN: 10-1985854031
13-9781985854031
Michael Scott Clifton
Fiction, Action & Adventure

DEDICATION

For Melanie

Proverbs 31:10 says it best: "A wife of noble character who can find? She is worth far more than rubies."

Also

For my children, Brett and Holly

ACKNOWLEDGMENTS

As a first-time author, I actively sought the advice and opinion of others who I felt would give me an honest appraisal of my "literary" efforts. I have many friends, family members, and colleagues to thank. Not the least of these is Sandi Miles (the "Comma" Lady!), who has read virtually everything I have ever written, and Helen Thompson, a dear friend and librarian extraordinaire, whose advice and encouragement has proven invaluable to me. A special thank you to the Northeast Texas Writers Organization (NETWO) for providing a vehicle for aspiring writers.

Chapter 1

"Dunk him again!"

Struggling mightily, Nick Hollister futilely tried to prevent his head from being submerged a second time in the toilet. With water streaming down his face and his wet hair plastered to his head, he was held upside down by four hulking football players. Their leader, Carter Cannon, stood off to the side smirking.

"I told you, *JV*, that the varsity locker room was for varsity players! Since your dimwit brain doesn't get the message, I guess we will have to teach you a lesson even *you* won't forget!"

With his head poised just above the toilet bowl, Nick said, "Damn you, Carter, I was just cleaning out my locker!"

Laughing, Carter gestured with his hand, and Nick was dunked again. Striding over, Carter flushed the toilet as Nick's head was held under the swirling water. Dropping

Nick, the football players stepped away as Nick flopped wetly over on his back, gasping like a fish.

"Last warning! Stay out of the varsity locker room, Hollister!" Carter growled. With that, he and the football players left, their derisive snickering slowly fading as they walked away.

Tears of anger and frustration mixed with the commode water dripping from Nick's face. Slamming his fist repeatedly against the stall divider, Nick finally stood unsteadily. Kicking the door of the stall open, Nick stalked to his locker where he hastily stuffed the remaining items of clothes and personal possessions into his bag. Slamming the locker door shut, he left without a backward glance.

"Wonder where Nick is?" Mark Chambers asked his girlfriend, Patti, as they sat together in the Pleasant Mountain High School cafeteria. "He's never late for lunch."

"I don't know, but Nick promised me he would turn in his senior profile sheet for the yearbook today. Even though I'm one of the editors, the deadline is tomorrow and can't be extended. I explained that to him!"

Mark mumbled something unintelligible in response as he continued to chew on his turkey and cheese sandwich. Bringing the sandwich up to his mouth in preparation for another bite, he froze as he saw his friend, Nick, suddenly enter the cafeteria. Nick's face was red, and water dripped from his hastily slicked- back hair. Spotting his friends, Nick stormed over to their table and threw himself into a chair beside them.

"Nick! What … what happened to you?" Mark asked, shocked at his friend's appearance.

Fuming silently, Nick tried to compose himself so he could answer. Finally, and with great effort, he managed to rein in his temper.

"Well, let's see, the festivities all started when Coach Gaffney told me that I didn't make the varsity baseball team and that I would be on the JV team … again!"

"Oh no! I'm so sorry, Nick," Patti said, squeezing his arm gently.

"Anyway, as I was cleaning my stuff out of the varsity locker room, Carter and four of his Neanderthal buddies walk in on me, and the next thing I know, I'm upside down and getting a toilet bath!"

Mark, his sandwich forgotten, couldn't believe his ears.

"Carter's gone too far this time, Nick! You've got to go to Mr. Bostick and tell him what he's done!"

"And what good would that do, Mark?" Nick asked, his voice rising. "Carter's the star athlete, the scholar student, and his dad owns all the premier car dealerships in a five-county area! It'll be his word against mine, plus that of his four thick-necked friends! I'll be laughed right out of the principal's office!"

Before either Mark or Patti could respond, Nick pulled a piece of paper and a pen from the book bag he had slung down beside him. Writing furiously, he stopped abruptly and shoved the paper toward Patti.

"Here's my senior profile sheet, Patti!" Nick said, his voice shaking in anger. "Where it says 'what are my plans for the future,' note that I've said I want to be as far from this stinking town as possible! The day I graduate, I'm outta here!"

With that, Nick slung his book bag over his shoulder and stormed out of the cafeteria.

Little did Nick know just how difficult that would prove to be.

Chapter 2

Fifteen Years Later

"Strike one!"

Nick Hollister stepped out of the batter's box as the umpire behind the plate adjusted his mask. Idly, he brushed back the sandy blond hair that had fallen across his pale blue eyes. Freckles graced the bridge of his nose and cheeks, and a square chin jutted from underneath lips now pursed in concentration. Tall, he stood about six-foot three inches. Unfortunately, despite his best efforts, he had never gained enough weight to fill out his frame, and soaking wet, he only weighed a mere 160 pounds. When his skinny frame was combined with hands and feet that were unusually large, it gave him a gawky, ungainly look. Taking a deep breath, he stepped back into the batter's box.

The pitcher toed the rubber and grinned insolently at Nick. Nick's team was behind 35–0 in this Division I, City Recreation League slow-pitch softball game, and they were only in the third inning. None of their games so far had proceeded past the third inning, since the fifteen-run mercy rule took effect then. To add insult to injury, the opposing team's players had all been batting left-handed since the second inning, and they were *still* scoring runs at will on them! These beatings were depressingly common, and Nick's team hadn't come close to winning a game the entire summer. In fact, they hadn't scored a single run in the past five games combined. However, with a runner on third and two outs, all Nick had to do to break the scoreless streak was hit a single to score the runner.

The pitcher released the ball, and it looped upward in a lazy arc before coming back down into the catcher's mitt, just wide of the plate.

"Ball one!"

Nick stepped out of the box again and wiped the sweat from his eyes with his jersey. It was almost the middle of July, and the day was a typically hot East Texas day in the city of Pleasant Mountain, population 19,983 souls, with the temperature hitting the high nineties and over 50 percent humidity. Located roughly halfway between Dallas and Texarkana on I-30, Pleasant Mountain sat squarely in the Piney Woods region of East Texas. "C'mon, Nick, get a hit!" a voice said halfheartedly from Nick's dugout.

It was noon, and the sun was a blazing yellow ball in the cloudless blue sky directly overhead, with not a breath of wind stirring. Looking back at his teammates sitting in the dugout, Nick saw a mostly dispirited lot fanning themselves with their gloves in the unrelenting heat. Nick had known most of them since they had all graduated from high school years earlier. He could tell that, like him, they just wanted to get this game over and go someplace (preferably at least twenty degrees cooler) other than the softball field.

That they were playing in a Division I softball league against semi-pro players was, of course, all Nick's fault. They normally played in Division II, the lowest league, and one made up of the least-skilled players. More importantly, most teams and players in Division II were looking to have *actual fun* while playing softball. Nick had been responsible for turning in the application for the team, and unfortunately, time had slipped away from him, and he had turned it in after the deadline had passed.

The only softball league still taking applications was the super-competitive Division I. He had been forced to turn in his team's application for Division I, and so now, they were playing ex-high school and college jocks, who treated every contest as if it were the seventh and deciding game of the World Series.

Nick had also been part of his team's second softball-related disaster, in that he additionally had been responsible for the uniforms his team was now wearing. Rather than obtaining the uniforms from a reputable sporting goods store in town as they normally did, he had convinced the team instead to order them from a cut-rate, out-of-town wholesaler to save money. The wholesaler had gotten both the name and color of the uniforms wrong, later claiming he couldn't read Nick's scribbled writing on the order form. So instead of their team being named the "Bombers," the name on each softball jersey was the "Boogers," and the color, instead of Carolina Blue, was Guacamole Green. The wholesaler had refused to return their money or change the jerseys, so they had been forced to wear the jerseys. The natural result was that in addition to being massacred at each softball game, Nick and the rest of the team also had to endure a litany of nose-picking jokes.

"Ball two!" the ump cried, as the next pitch was again slightly wide of the plate.

"C'mon, JV! Are you afraid to swing at the ball?"

Nick's eyes narrowed as he honed in on the source of the voice. It came from the opposing team's first baseman, Carter Cannon. Like everyone else on his team, Carter was impeccably dressed in a new crisp Cannon Auto Group softball uniform, which did not conceal his bulging muscles underneath.

Although he had the looks of a Southern California surfer with piercing blue eyes and sun-bleached blond hair, Carter and his family had actually moved to Pleasant Mountain from Atlantic City, New Jersey, when Carter was in first grade.

How the Cannon family had acquired their wealth was the subject of much whispered speculation in Pleasant Mountain. Some said Carter's father was somehow connected to the mafia back in New Jersey, while others said he had made most of his money through shady deals, kickbacks, and shakedowns.

As the proverbial thorn in Nick's side, Nick's introduction to Carter had been in grade school when Carter had walked up to him and shoved him, face first, off the playground swing. Carter had taken great enjoyment in making life miserable for him ever since.

In short, Nick hated Carter Cannon.

"Take a swing, JV. Maybe you will get lucky and get a hit." Laughter erupted from Carter's team, which was made up mostly of employees from the Cannon car dealerships, and Nick felt his face begin to turn red.

Angrily, Nick stepped back into the batter's box. He would show Cannon a thing or two about hitting! Gritting his teeth, he waited impatiently for the next pitch. As the high, looping pitch came down over the plate, Nick swung as hard as he could, missing the ball and almost spinning himself completely around from the effort.

"Strike two!"

Carter almost fell down he was laughing so hard at Nick. "Way … way to go JV! Next time, make sure your bat actually *hits* the ball!" he said, gasping.

His face now beet-red in anger and embarrassment, Nick stepped out of the box and tried to control his breathing. He *would* get a hit, he thought, and his team *would* score and avoid the shutout. Finally, he managed to compose himself and stepped back into the batter's box. When the next pitch was delivered, he was ready. Swinging, he connected solidly with the ball, sending it sharply down the third base line. The runner at third took off for home as soon as Nick's bat hit the ball. Running hard for first, Nick risked a glance at the third baseman and saw him dive for the ball. Man- aging to knock the ball down with his glove, the third baseman bobbled the softball in his haste to pick it up and throw it to first.

Nick felt his heart leap! He was going to make it! He was going to be safe at first, and they were going to finally score!

Putting his head down, Nick ran for all he was worth for the first-base bag. Just as he was about to safely reach first, Carter stuck his leg out in front of the first-base bag. Nick tripped over Carter's outstretched leg and cartwheeled past first base before he finally came to a stop face down in the infield dirt.

Spitting dirt out of his mouth, Nick got up quickly. Enraged, he headed for Carter.

"You … you look like a moon pie, JV!" Carter crowed laughing as he pointed at Nick's face. Indeed, the red dirt of the infield was caked on Nick's sweaty face so that despite his obvious anger, it gave him a comical appearance.

"You bastard! You did that on purpose!" Nick yelled as he pointed a shaking finger at Carter.

"I can't help it if you are clumsy, JV. Next time, touch the base before tripping over your own two feet," Carter replied coolly.

This was too much for Nick, and he made for Carter. Before he got two steps, the Boogers' first-base coach interposed himself between Nick and Carter.

"Nick, stop!"

The Boogers' first-base coach was Mark Chambers. He and Nick had been best friends since elementary school. Mark's brown eyes looked up at Nick with concern as he strained to hold him back. At five feet ten inches and with a slender build, Mark was significantly shorter than Nick.

"You saw what he did, Mark! He tripped me on purpose!" Nick cried, his voice trembling in anger.

"What about it, ump? Did you see what happened?" Mark demanded.

The field umpire was a skinny, redheaded high school kid with a bad acne condition. He had a prominent Adam's apple, which bobbed up and down as he tried to form a reply.

"We need a call, ump! He's out, isn't he? I mean he completely missed the bag!" Carter pointed out smugly as he and the rest of his team slowly formed a semicircle around the umpire.

With his Adam's apple now bobbing frantically, the umpire looked around at the mass of muscle surrounding him and decided that the correct call required more than the twenty dollars he was paid per game.

"Er … he's out," the kid said in a quivering voice.

"What? That's crap!" Nick yelled. Ripping himself from Mark's grasp, Nick headed for Carter.

"You can't get away with … *oof!*"

Nick folded up like an accordion as Carter's right jab landed sharply in his midsection. Air exploded from his lungs, and he crumpled to the ground, fighting to breathe.

"Don't crowd me, Hollister!" Carter said with a dangerous smile on his face.

"Damn you, Carter! Leave him alone!" Mark cried angrily as he pushed past him and tried to help Nick back to his feet.

"Hey, Cannon! I got something for ya!" Through eyes still bleary in pain, Nick looked up and saw a figure from the Boogers' dugout heading toward Carter. As he fought to bring his eyes into focus, he finally saw that it was Steve Parsons approaching Carter.

After Mark, Steve was probably Nick's next best friend. His watery green eyes were flashing dangerously as he approached Carter. Steve had dropped out of high school his senior year and had eventually gotten a GED. To everyone's surprise, he had gone to a tech school at a nearby community college and had become a certified diesel mechanic, and he now worked as a mechanic at Dock's Auto Repair in Pleasant Mountain. Steve was only a trim six feet tall, but he was extremely muscular. He had removed the sleeves from his Boogers softball jersey, and one large bicep sported a tattoo of a flaming guitar with the words "*Born to Rock*" inscribed on the guitar. Steve was into heavy metal and played drums every weekend for a garage band.

Taking a pull from a Coors Light bottle in his right hand, Steve stopped a few paces from Carter, his eyes never leaving Carter's face. As long as he had known him, Nick had never known Steve to be very far from a can, bottle, or mug of beer. Although Nick had rarely seen Steve truly drunk, Steve drank enough beer on a regular basis that he wore the perpetual expression of someone with a slight buzz on. However, there was no evidence of that now as he gazed fearlessly at Carter.

"How 'bout it, Cannon? Me and you can go a few rounds here and now," Steve drawled casually.

Eyeing the beer bottle in Steve's hand, Carter smirked and said, "I doubt you'd feel anything, Parsons. As much as I'd like pounding your ass, I'm afraid my efforts would be wasted."

Before more could be said, the plate umpire shouldered his way past the knot of players and interposed himself between Steve and Carter. Not much older than the field umpire, he apparently was made of sterner stuff as he fearlessly announced, "The game's over! Break it up, or I'll call the cops!"

Sneering one more time at Steve, Carter nodded and jerked his head toward his team, and they began to walk away. However, he had taken only a few steps before he stopped and turned back toward Nick, who still lay on the ground, fighting to get his breath back.

"You're a loser and a screw-up, Hollister," he said. "Always have been, always will be. If you ever finish anything you start, please let me know so I can personally witness that miracle." Snickering, he walked off.

The ball game was finally over.

Chapter 3

After the game, Mark and Steve had helped Nick to his car. Humiliated and still hurting, he had declined their offer to go somewhere for a cold drink. Besides, he had to go to work. He worked as a forklift operator at a Home Depot distribution center, and he had just enough time to grab a quick shower and drive to work before his shift began.

Nick carefully folded himself into the '88 Chevy Sprint that he drove. The precursor of the Geo, the car was tiny and was only a three cylinder with an eight-gallon fuel tank. Steve had modified the front seat for him so that it scooted back far enough that he could get his six feet three-inch frame into it. At one time, the Sprint had been robin's egg blue, but now the paint was chipped and faded, and the front wheel section was a darker blue, the result of being replaced because of an accident by the previous owner. Nick had bought the car for a song, and although it used oil, it got close to forty miles per gallon.

With gas prices so high and Nick chronically short of cash, he could overlook the Sprint's shortcomings.

Nick considered going to his girlfriend Lisa's apartment on the east side of town to shower and change for work but decided his place was closer.

Nick had met Lisa at the Pleasant Mountain bowling alley two years ago. She worked as a hair dresser at Hair Creations in town, and they hit it off almost immediately. Their relationship had become more serious over time, and six months ago, he had moved some of his things into Lisa's apartment, and he lived there off and on. Their intention was to eventually get married as soon as Nick could settle on a steady, good-paying job. Unfortunately, that goal seemed to be as elusive now as it had always been in Nick's life. In fact, lately, it seemed Nick's inability to hold and keep a job was wearing thin on Lisa. She didn't seem herself around him, and he was beginning to sense a subtle yet still fundamental change in her attitude toward him. When a position at Home Depot had opened up, he had leaped at the opportunity and had worked there for the past several months. Compared to the length of time Nick had worked at other jobs, he had worked practically a lifetime at the distribution center.

Nick's place was located out in the country, five miles from town. Ten minutes later, he pulled off the paved farm-to-market road and onto a dirt road. Pines and sweet gums grew thickly alongside the road as Nick carefully negotiated the Sprint around ruts and potholes.

Finally, he pulled into a grass and weed-choked clearing and parked the car under a rusty awning. A twenty-five-foot Airstream trailer was located adjacent to the car awning. Electricity was provided to the trailer by a nearby utility pole stuck into the ground with a meter attached to it.

A ninety-by-fifty-foot prefab workshop was located just north of the trailer. Two of the buildings' large sliding doors stood ajar, providing a glimpse of the interior. Surplus oil field pipe had been used in framing the workshop, and the metal ribs of the pipe nearest the doors gleamed dully as sunlight reflected off of its rusty surface.

Nick stirred up a small army of grasshoppers and crickets that hopped and flew madly through the air as he strode through the overgrown grass from his car to the trailer. Stopping before the trailer, he stepped up onto a broken cinder block he used for a step and unlocked the trailer's door. Opening the door, he ducked and stepped inside. Like the Sprint Nick drove, everything about the trailer was cramped. The bed loft was located on the right side of the trailer, and when Nick slept in the trailer, he did so with his knees folded up to his chest. The tiny shower was on the other side of the trailer and barely accommodated Nick's frame. In fact, he had been forced to install a flex-a-shower hose on the shower head because there was no turning around in the shower. The only way to reach his back was with the hose. A small box refrigerator and two-burner electric stove were located on the west side of the trailer. On the east side was a small padded couch, which folded up or down, and in front of it was a square wooden table attached to a three-inch diameter metal pole. The pole fit into a bracket in the floor, and like the padded seat, the pole could be pulled from the bracket, the table folded, and both table and pole stored. Finally, a diminutive window unit air conditioner was set in a window above the table. Cranking it up to high, Nick attempted to cool the stifling interior of the trailer.

Flinging off his sweaty clothes, Nick stepped into the shower. Not bothering to turn the hot water on, Nick turned the cold-water faucet to its highest setting. As the water sluiced over him, he let his mind drift.

He had, by default, inherited the workshop and thirty acres of land when his mother had moved to Dallas to be closer to his sister and her family. His sister, Susan, was five years older than him and was married to a pharmacist. They had two children, and his niece and nephew were ten and seven. His mother had claimed her reason for moving was that she couldn't keep up with the land or buildings on it, but Nick knew the real reason: his father had left when Nick was thirteen years old. From that moment on, the home place had become an uncomfortable and alien environment to her.

As Nick recalled, there had been no warning, no signals from his father that he was unhappy with his marriage. His daddy, an electrician, had apparently met a woman, some twenty years younger than him, when he had gone on a job call to the woman's apartment to repair an electrical outlet. Two months later, Nick's mother came home from her job as a nurse at the local hospital to find all of Nick's father's belongings gone and a brief note explaining that he loved another woman. There was no other explanation, no further elaboration, nothing but the note to show for over twenty years of marriage.

His father now lived in Lubbock, married to the woman he ran off with. The only contact Nick had had with him since was an occasional card on his birth- day or at Christmas, and even those had stopped a few years ago. That was just fine, as far as Nick was concerned, because he had no desire to see his father ever again.

Nick's parents' divorce had almost destroyed his mother. She had loved his father deeply and had truly never seen it coming. Although she had repeatedly denied it when he had asked her, Nick knew she blamed herself for the divorce and his father running off with a woman young enough to be his daughter. His mother, a normally evocative and effervescent woman, had become withdrawn and sluggish. He had watched her age years in the span of mere months after the divorce was final.

Nick's father, eager for a quickie divorce so he could marry his young honey, gave Nick's mother the shop, the doublewide trailer they had been living in, and the acreage it sat on. She had waited until Nick had graduated from high school and then moved to Dallas, telling him the land, the trailer, the shop—everything— was his. Although she had never directly told him why, he knew it was because the place held too many painful memories. The sooner that part of her life was behind her, the sooner she could get on with the rest of her life.

Nick found that without his mother living there, the old double- wide trailer was too empty, and its very presence evoked memories he too would just as soon put behind him. Therefore, he had sold the doublewide and moved into the Airstream shortly after his mother had left. He had gone from a spacious trailer to a cramped one, but he found he now slept much better at night, and he had never regretted the move.

Shaking his head, Nick quickly finished showering. Exiting the shower, he found the air in the trailer was only marginally cooler. Dressing in front of the air conditioner, he pulled on a pair of jeans and boots and tucked his Home Depot work shirt in. Grabbing his wallet and keys, he exited the trailer, locked the door, and headed for his car.

The huge Home Depot distribution center was located on a spur just off the interstate highway. Covering some fifty acres, the parking lot, loading docks, and warehouse occupied an enormous amount of land. As Nick exited the interstate onto the service road leading to the main gates of the distribution center, he found himself behind a line of eighteen-wheelers waiting to enter the facility and unload at the warehouse. Night and day, there was a constant stream of them as they disgorged the contents of their trailers into the distribution center's warehouse. It was Nick's job to load and unload each of the trailers and place their contents in the proper location within the warehouse. Hour after hour, he and his trusty forklift worked at this tedious task. As with all his previous jobs, Nick didn't see himself working at this job one second longer than necessary until he found the job or calling he *really* wanted to do! Trouble was, at thirty-three years old, Nick *still* didn't know what that was!

Nick parked his car in the cavernous employee parking lot and walked back to the warehouse. Entering the building, he was just about to clock in when one of the secretaries working in the glassed-in administrative center poked her head out of a door and called out to Nick.

"Hey, Nick! Roger wants to see you!"

Puzzled, Nick put his time card back into its slot and walked back to the door the secretary had used. Roger Smith was the foreman of his crew, and Nick had liked him from his first day on the job. He was friendly, personable, and seemed to have an endless stream of jokes that made the repetitive job of loading and unloading the eighteen-wheelers seem to go by faster. What could he possibly want to speak to him about?

The door to Roger's small office was open, and as Nick entered, one look at Roger told him he was in for some kind of bad news. Roger normally wore a carefree grin on his face, but now his expression was a mixture of both serious and sad.

"Sit down, Nick," Roger said, indicating with his hand a chair in front of his desk.

As Nick took a seat in the chair, he asked apprehensively, "What's going on, Roger?"

Sighing, Roger stood up and walked from behind his desk and sat on the front of the desk next to Nick.

"We have to lay you off, Nick," he said sadly.

Stunned, Nick's mouth opened and closed several times like a fish before he was finally able to say, "What? Why? I've worked hard, never been late—" Nick stopped as Roger raised his hand, interrupting him.

"It has nothing to do with your job performance, Nick, because you're right, you're a good worker. Unfortunately, the company's quarterly earnings report just came out, and they weren't as rosy as expected. Therefore, he company bigwigs decided that a three percent reduction in employees was needed to fix it.

"You know the drill, Nick, 'Last hired, first fired,'" Roger said as he placed his hand sorrowfully on Nick's shoulder.

Nick's mind raced as he considered the implications of losing his job. It couldn't have come at a worse time! Lisa would kill him! How would he explain it to her?

"Roger, listen, I have to have this job!" he said desperately. "I'll work straight graveyard shifts! I'll do any of the grunt jobs that nobody else wants to do! I'll—"

Roger raised his hand again to forestall any further protests from Nick.

"It's out of my hands, Nick. I truly am sorry. I did manage to get you two-weeks severance pay, and I promise you that if and when we begin hiring again, your name will be at the top of the list." With that, Roger handed Nick an envelope. Dully, Nick opened the envelope. Inside was his severance check for $350.23. A short time later, Nick found himself trudging zombie-like back to his car. The same thought kept going through his mind over and over again.

How was he going to explain this to Lisa?

Chapter 4

Lost in thought, Nick almost missed the exit off the interstate to Pleasant Mountain. The job he had just lost was the best paying one he had had since meeting Lisa. She was going to flip! Even though it wasn't his fault, he was sure she wouldn't see it that way. He had lost or quit too many other jobs since he had met her, and he could just see her nodding her head as she told herself she had heard this all before. No, what he needed was a plan, something to soften the bad news before she blew her top. He snapped his fingers as an idea came to him. A gift! A peace offering of sorts was what was needed! *That* ought to do the trick! But what kind of a gift? Candy or flowers were too blasé, and besides, they were expensive. What he needed was a gift that would hit a home run for him yet still stay within his modest means to pay. Thinking hard, he remembered a new store that had opened recently in downtown Pleasant Mountain. It sold odds and ends, antiques, and garage sale stuff, but he just might find something unique there. More importantly, whatever he found, it was likely to be cheap! With that, he turned on the next road that led to the business route through the city.

Five minutes later, Nick parked in front of the new store. The freshly painted sign above it said "Harper's Hidden Treasures: Knickknacks and Antiques." It occupied one of the old, two-storydowntown buildings. The front of the store consisted mostly of huge plate glass windows, the old-fashioned kind you only saw in old buildings anymore. The rest of the building's exterior was composed of glazed orange brick, so typical of the Americana of fifty to a hundred years earlier. As had happened in so many small and medium-sized towns in Texas, the down- town merchants of Pleasant Mountain had gone out of business one by one, unable to compete with Walmart and other large chain stores. However, the city fathers of Pleasant Mountain had made a concerted effort to restore and refurbish the downtown area, and it had experienced a rebirth of sorts. This had included keeping as much of the original architecture as possible. Now, although there were still too many boarded up buildings, most of the downtown businesses had tenants that ranged from small cafés to gift shops.

Stepping to the curb, Nick saw a three-wheeled motorcycle parked in the alley next to the store. Looking closer, Nick saw the bike was a Harley, and it was painted a metallic purple. A black helmet, festooned with small stickers from all over the U.S., rested in the motorcycle's black leather seat, while polished chrome handlebars, backrest, and exhaust pipes glinted in the sun. All in all, it was an impressive ride! Tearing his eyes from the trike, Nick entered the store.

A bell located on the door tinkled pleasantly as Nick opened it. Looking around, he saw that unopened boxes and crates were scattered here and there throughout the store. Apparently, the store's merchandise had not yet all been unpacked and set on display. A broad stairway with a gleaming, dark-wood railing was directly in front of him and led up to the second story. A scarred, hardwood floor ran the length of the store, while the ceiling was made of old-fashioned, white ceramic tile. The store itself was much longer in length than width, and displays of everything from antique furniture to old quilts had been artfully arranged to fit the store's contours. As Nick continued his visual inspection, a baritone, masculine voice called to him from somewhere in the back of the store.

"Hold on! Be there in a minute!"

A moment or two later, the source of the voice walked from behind a stack of crates, wiping his hands on a well-used dust rag. Nick's eyes opened wide in surprise as he saw that the "man" was only about three feet tall! He was a dwarf—a midget! Thick, black hair was pulled back in a long ponytail that fell past the midget's shoulders, and both ears sported a trio of earrings, each with a tiny red, white, and blue feather dangling from them. He was wearing black jeans with black boots, and a black T-shirt was tucked into the jeans. A thick, gold chain dangled from around his neck. A broad smile creased his smooth, unlined face, and the age of the dwarf-sized man could have been anywhere from mid-thirties to late forties. Twinkling blue eyes looked up at Nick.

"I apologize for the mess," the dwarf said with a warm smile on his face. "We have been open for a week now, but I still haven't unpacked everything. By the way, my name is Hank, Hank Harper." With that, he extended his hand to Nick.

For a split second, Nick stood in frozen surprise before his brain registered Hank's greeting. Before he could stop himself, the question of *What kind of name was Hank for a midget anyway?* ran fleetingly through his mind as he shook hands with him.

"My … my name is N … Nick," he finally managed to stammer.

Hank apprised Nick with a wry look before saying, "Pleased to meet you, Nick. Is there something wrong? You have a funny expression on your face."

"No!" Nick said a bit too quickly. "No, there is nothing wrong!"

"Say, you're not one of those people who has a problem with height-challenged people, are you?" Hank asked Nick as he fixed him with an accusing stare.

"What? No, of course not!" Nick blurted out as his face turned red in embarrassment. "I don't have any problems with midg … I mean height-challenged people!"

"You said it! You said the 'm' word!" Hank shouted as he stabbed his finger at Nick.

"Huh? Listen, I'm sorry! I didn't mean to say … " Nick stopped suddenly as he saw Hank laughing so hard, tears were streaming down his cheeks. His mouth open in amazement, Nick waited until Hank could stop laughing long enough to catch his breath.

"Sor … sorry about that, Nick," Hank finally managed to gasp. "It's just, well, you should have seen the expression on your face!" With that, Hank reached up and clapped Nick good-naturedly on the back. Seeing the shocked and puzzled expression on Nick's face, Hank motioned for Nick to have a seat in a chair located by the stairway.

"It's just an icebreaker, Nick," he explained. "You see, so many times when I'm around customers for the first time, they behave as if they don't know how to act around me. First, it's the staring, then the looking at me furtively out of the corner of their eyes, and when they talk to me, it's like they can't carry on a 'normal' conversation. In other words, since I'm a midget, they feel they have to treat me differently for some reason." Hank saw Nick's eyes widen slightly as he said the word *midget.*

Chuckling, Hank said, "Yes, you heard me right. I said 'midget.' I've never been much of a PC person, so the word doesn't bother me. God made me the way I am, and I have never thought any less of myself than an individual of normal height. But to finish my explanation, I decided long ago that I'd put folks at ease as soon as possible around me. Therefore, I came up with the 'offended midget' act." As Hank's eyes sparkled merrily at Nick, he found he took an instant liking to Hank.

Clapping his hands together, Hank said, "Well, enough about that! What can I do for you? Is there any particular item you are looking for?"

Nick hesitated for a minute as he thought how to answer Hank. What was he supposed to say? That he just lost his job and he needed a good—no, make that a *great*—gift to mollify his girlfriend? Oh, and it needed to be reasonably priced!

Finally, he said, "I am looking for a gift for my girlfriend. She's, ah, likely to be angry with me over something that just recently happened."

"I see." Hank tapped his chin with his forefinger as he thought of what Nick had told him.

"Might I ask *how* angry your girlfriend will be with you, Nick?"

Nick shrugged helplessly. "We're talking catastrophic, ground zero-type anger, Hank."

"That bad, huh? Well, in situations like this, normally I would suggest a diamond necklace and intimate dinner at the Waldorf in Dallas. But since you seem to be a man of, er, modest means, we will have to take plan B. Come with me."

Hank led Nick to the back of the store. A small room was located to their left, and as they entered it, Nick saw paintings of every conceivable size and description hanging from the walls. Several crates were stacked in one corner, as apparently Hank had even more paintings that still needed unpacking. As Nick studied the paintings, he saw that they were all obviously antiques. Many had their original wooden frames containing beautifully carved scrollwork. The craftsmanship in the frames was something you didn't see in today's modern, mass-produced frames. Nick nodded in appreciation.

Nick's attention was drawn to one particular painting located near the center of one wall. The painting itself was of a sailboat on a lake at night, with high peaks and crags surrounding the lake. A full moon, high in the clear night sky, cast a luminescent, reflective glow on the black water of the lake that was so placid, barely a ripple showed. The dark hull of the sailboat contrasted with the stark white of its double sails. The sailboat was heeled slightly into the wind, and as Nick leaned forward for a closer look, he saw the name *La Princesa Sirena* etched on her bow. Two figures, a man and a woman, stood side by side next to the spoked, wooden wheel that controlled the boat's rudder. In a display of obvious affection, the man had one arm around the woman's waist, while the other held the steerage wheel firmly. The woman's head lay on his shoulder, and from the familiar way they seemed to hold each other, it was obvious to Nick they had gone on these midnight sailing trips many times together. They were dressed in clothes from a bygone era—the man in a topcoat, dark pants, and frilled shirt of some sort, while the woman wore a long, hooped skirt, a blouse cinched tightly around her small waist, and a dark cape tied about her neck, which covered her shoulders. It was a beautiful, peaceful scene of two people in love out for a midnight sail. Even though the painting was obviously old, the colors hadn't seemed to fade, and indeed, the images seemed so lifelike, Nick half expected to hear the sails flapping in the freshening breeze.

Nick reached out and carefully ran his hands over the wooden frame. It appeared to be made of hand-carved, aged oak. The wood had been meticulously stained and lacquered to a polished, amber sheen. Peering closer, Nick could find no imperfections in the wood finish of the frame. Whoever made the frame definitely knew their business.

"It's quite beautiful, isn't it?" Hank asked as he stood by Nick's elbow.

"It's perfect," Nick whispered.

Seeing no price tag, he asked, "How much?"

"Well, let's see. I was thinking a masterpiece like this should fetch at least one hundred dollars."

Seeing the panicked look in Nick's eyes, Hank hastily added, "But I could be talked into fifty dollars."

When the crestfallen look on Nick's face remained, Hank sighed. Finally, he asked, "Would twenty-five dollars be too much?"

When Nick nodded eagerly, Hank cried, "Sold!"

Standing on his tiptoes, Hank removed the painting carefully from the wall and carried it with him as they both walked back toward the front of the store. They stopped by a wooden counter with an old, manual cash register on top of it. A modern credit and debit card machine was next to the cash register. A platform of sorts was built into the side of the counter, allowing Hank to step up and be at more or less eye level with his customers. As he carefully wrapped the painting in brown paper, Nick studied pictures that had been hung on the wall behind the counter.

One picture showed a willowy blonde and Hank sitting at a table in what must have been an upscale restaurant. They were dressed in formal attire—Hank in a tuxedo, and the blonde in a clinging, cream-colored dress. She was stunning and beautiful. Another picture had them both on the purple Harley, with Hank driving the trike and the woman towering above him as she sat behind him with both arms intertwined around his waist. Finally, Nick blinked as he saw what had to be a family picture. It included Hank, the blonde woman, and a teenage girl and a boy, who towered over Hank.

Hank placed flat sections of cardboard on the front and back of the painting and tied them onto the painting with a piece of twine. He looked up and smiled mischievously as he saw Nick looking at the pictures on the wall with his mouth slightly agape in amazement.

"What's the matter? You've never seen family pictures before? Hey, you're still not hating on height-challenged people, are you?" he demanded.

Nick's scandalized look caused Hank to start laughing all over again. Pointing at Nick, he said, "Gotcha!" The look of relief on Nick's face was so palpable, Hank almost dropped Nick's painting he was wrapping as a fresh round of laughter erupted from him.

"You know, you really need to loosen up, Nick!" Hank gasped as he wiped the tears from his eyes. "You're wound as tight as a watch spring!"

Sheepishly, Nick shrugged and said, "You really know how to keep your customers on their toes, Hank."

"Don't I know it!" he said, grinning.

Hank turned and pointed to each person in the family picture, said, "That's my wife, Elena, my son, Hank Jr., and my daughter, Sophia. My son is an architect with a firm based in Austin, and my daughter is in her last year at the UT law school." The evident pride in Hank's voice as he pointed out the members of his family caused Nick to smile. Unbidden, the thought of how the three-foot Hank had met his tall, blonde wife crossed Nick's mind. The question must have shown on his face, because Hank smiled and nodded at Nick knowingly.

"I met Elena when we were both enrolled in the engineering school at the University of Texas. I'm a structural engineer, and she's a chemical engineer. At any rate, as luck would have it, we had several classes together and found we both shared a common problem; namely, that our classmates and professors had a hard time taking us seriously. Elena is a tall, leggy blonde, and, as you can see, extremely good-looking. Therefore, all the guys and not a few of the professors were constantly hitting on her. As for me, the best I can describe it is that I was patronized; you know, 'He's a midget, so we won't hold him to the same standard as everyone else.' It's something I've battled all my life."

"You see, it takes extremely good grades—not to mention high test scores on entrance exams—just to get into the UT engineering school. Neither Elena nor I wanted to be treated any differently than anyone else. So as we commiserated with one another, we found we both shared a lot of the same interests. One thing led to another, and before you knew it, we were married six months later."

"That's great, Hank," Nick said as he nodded approvingly. "It looks like things really worked out great for you."

"I can't complain. I worked more than twenty-five years for the Grumman Corporation and Elena, twenty years for Dow Chemical. We both decided that life is—no pun intended—too short, and when the kids graduated from college, we would 'retire' to some place where the pace of life is slower and do what we wanted to do."

"So you ended up here, owning an antique store in Pleasant Mountain?"

"Yep! Elena is in Houston trying to sell our house, and as soon as it sells, she'll join me here!"

As Hank put the finishing touches on wrapping the painting, Nick thought of Hank's remarkable story. He had had to overcome formidable obstacles, not the least of which was his physical size and appearance, and yet despite all of that, here he was, doing exactly what he wanted to do, living his life exactly as he wanted. It was a success story in stark contrast to his own. At almost thirty-three years old, Nick had been striving for the same goal, the same brass ring, his entire life, and he was no closer now than when he graduated from high school. He couldn't even keep a crummy job, and he counted it a successful day when he found enough loose change under the couch pillows in his trailer to buy at Coke at McDonald's! Bitterly, he shook his head.

Hank seemed to sense Nick's thoughts as he rang up the cost of the purchase and handed Nick the neatly packaged painting.

"You know, Nick, we all face adversity no matter what our station in life. The measure of a man or woman is not how many times they get knocked down to the canvas, but how many times he or she gets back up. It makes you appreciate that much more your accomplishments and successes. Believe me. I know!"

Waving his hands expansively at his shop, Hank said, "Elena and I decided to call our store 'Hidden Treasures' because we have discovered at estate auctions and garage sales that people are often throwing out or selling cheaply items of rare and expensive value. It's like the old saying, 'One man's trash is another man's treasure.' Life is like that too. Our most precious treasures are often in plain sight, and yet we are too blind to see them, many times until it is too late."

Nick had the odd feeling that his life was an open book and that Hank had read every page. It was an eerie feeling, and he hastily paid Hank for the picture, thanked him, and turned to leave. He hadn't gotten halfway to the door when Hank called out to him.

"Good luck, Nick! I hope the painting brings you what you seek!"

Nick nodded at Hank, waving good-bye to him as he exited the antique shop. *What an odd comment,* he thought as he got into his car and started it. *Didn't he mean to say something like, 'Hope your girlfriend likes the painting?'* Deciding it didn't matter, he started the car.

The eerie feeling remained as Nick drove away.

Chapter 5

Lisa's apartment was located in a newer complex on the east side of town. Not much more than an efficiency apartment, it had a small bedroom with a double bed, a bathroom, and a kitchen-den combination. Located on the second floor, it was accessed by a set of concrete and metal stairs. It was past five o'clock when Nick pulled into the apartment parking lot, and he could see Lisa's Toyota Camry parked in its usual spot. That meant she had gotten home early from work. He bit back a curse, as he had hoped to surprise her by having the painting hung on the wall before she got home. *Oh well, might as well get it over with,* he thought as he steeled himself for the angry verbal hurricane he was sure was to come.

After exiting the car, he opened the passenger-side door and removed the painting that was wedged there. Taking a deep breath, he started for the stairs.

Nick had just finished climbing the stairs and was turning the corner that led to Lisa's apartment, when he stopped suddenly, and his jaw dropped in surprise. There, stacked neatly outside her apartment, were boxes containing all his things. Getting over his momentary shock, he hurried over and gazed down at the boxes. Turning, he was about to enter the apartment, when Lisa opened the door and planted herself firmly in the doorway.

Lisa was a curvaceous five feet six inches, with long, brunette hair highlighted with blonde streaks. Blue eyes were located beneath perfectly plucked eyebrows that flashed angrily at Nick. Full lips covered teeth now furiously chewing gum, something Nick knew from unpleasant experience meant she was past the stage of reasoning with. Somehow, she must have found out that he had lost his job! She was still wearing her neon pink, Hair Creations smock with her name, "Lisa," embroidered on it. With a sinking feeling, he knew how she must have found out. In a small town like Pleasant Mountain, hair salons were the center of town gossip. Nothing was kept secret for very long before it found its way to a beautician or hair stylist. *The Department of Homeland Security could learn a thing or two about the at of intelligence gathering by studying such places of business!* he thought bitterly.

At any rate, someone, some patron of Hair Creations, must have had a friend or relative that worked at the Home Depot distribution center who knew Nick had been laid off, and that person had then told another person, etc., etc., all the way down the information food chain. Once she had discovered he had lost his job, Lisa must have canceled the rest of her appointments and come straight back to the apartment and packed up his stuff.

"Look, I can explain everything!" Nick attempted to say before Lisa angrily cut him off.

"That's it! We're through, Nick! I'm not listening to one more excuse! Just pick up your things and leave!"

"Lisa, it wasn't my fault! The company was laying off people, and they started with the last ones hired!"

"Exactly! And why were you the last one hired, Nick? Because you can't hold on to a job, that's why! I'm tired of supporting us both, and I'm not going to do it anymore!"

"Lisa, listen, I'll get another job, I swear! Just give me another chance!"

In reply, Lisa angrily held her left hand up, as if on display, and wriggled her fingers before Nick's eyes.

"Do you see this, Nick? Look at it carefully, and tell me what you *don't* see! You don't see a ring, as in a *wedding* ring, do you? Why? Because you can't afford one, even *if* you could work up the courage to make such a commitment! I'm twenty-nine years old, and I'm tired of waiting for you to grow up! I don't intend to waste one more minute of my life with you!"

As Nick opened his mouth to try and reason with Lisa, he saw movement in her apartment through the partially open door. Suspiciously, he reached over Lisa and pushed the door wide open. A bare-chested young man lounged on a love seat next to the kitchenette, dressed only in cargo shorts and flip-flops. Dark curls framed his handsome face, and his shirtless torso revealed tanned, muscular arms and a trim waist etched with six- pack abs. For some reason, the guy looked familiar to Nick.

"Hey, dude," the young man intoned pleasantly.

"Who's this?" Nick demanded.

Caught off guard, Lisa was momentarily at a loss for words before finally saying, "It's … it's none of your business! I told you, we're through, Nick!"

"Wait!" Nick cried as his eyes narrowed in recognition. "It's Tony, the waiter from Porter's!" Porter's was a steakhouse that was located in an old Victorian home within Pleasant Mountain. The two-story home had been refurbished and remodeled into the steakhouse. The prices were normally way out of Nick's reach, even with both he and Lisa going dutch, yet she had insisted that they eat there, especially lately. In fact, they had eaten at Porter's four times in the past month alone! Tony was the waiter that always waited on them.

"No wonder you always insisted I leave him a five-dollar tip!" he said accusingly. Rather than answer him, Lisa averted her eyes and looked guiltily away.

Suddenly, it all became clear to Nick. The odd way Lisa had been acting toward him lately, the trips to Porter's. They had all neatly coincided within the past month. The revelation struck him with the impact of a bunker-buster bomb, and he knew with depressing finality that Lisa was right—they *were* through! But it hadn't started today, and it didn't have anything to do with losing his job. No, the beginning of the end of their relationship had come the first time they had eaten at Porter's and Lisa had first laid eyes on Tony. Losing his job had just accelerated their day of reckoning. After a moment or two of numbed silence, Nick, robot-like, finally picked up one of the boxes and began carrying it to his car.

Halfway to his car, Nick realized he was still carrying the painting he was going to give to Lisa. Reaching his car, he unlocked the hatchback and propped the painting in the narrow space there. As he turned to go back and get the rest of his things, he discovered Lisa and Tony had followed him, carrying the rest of the boxes. No one said a word as he took them one by one and somehow managed to cram them all in the Sprint. As he turned to get in his car, Lisa placed her hand gently on his arm.

"Wait just a minute, Nick," she said softly. Glancing at Tony, she asked, "Can you give us a moment?"

"Sure!" he replied, grinning. Pausing, he looked at Nick and added, "No hard feelings, dude!" and began walking back to the apartment.

Watching Tony's retreating back, Nick found he really wasn't that angry with him. The kid was what, twenty or twenty-one years old? He was at the age where there were no responsibilities, just opportunities. Lisa was Tony's latest opportunity, and whether she realized it or not, Nick was betting that sometime in the very near future, it would be Tony making his good-byes to Lisa.

That still didn't make the hurt of his breakup with Lisa any less painful.

Sniffing back tears, Lisa said, "I'm sorry, Nick. I tried, I really did. It's not that you're not a good person, because you are. You really are! You just can't seem to focus on anything. It's … it's like you're searching for something, but you don't know exactly what it is. I mean, since I've known you, you have tried selling used cars, tried being a volunteer fireman, and even tried being an EMT. You've worked at jobs from being a fry cook to an insurance salesman, and none of it panned out! My God, Nick, as little money as you have, you *still* gave some guy five hundred dollars as an investment in an ostrich farm! At some point, you need to figure something out and grow up!"

Lisa's words washed over Nick like a particularly strong astringent, made all the more painful, because she was right, of course. His life so far resembled a connect-the-dots picture that formed no pattern anyone outside a sanitarium would recognize. Trouble was, he was no closer to figuring it out now than before he had met Lisa.

Sighing, Lisa took a deep breath before continuing. "Nick," she began, and Nick knew what was coming next. *Please,* he prayed. *Please don't say what I think you're going to say!*

"Even though we aren't together—you know—*intimately* like we used to be, I still want to be *friends.* Can we still be friends, Nick?"

There! She had said it! The cruelest words of all! The last words any dumped guy wants to hear! The words that took away any shred of dignity left! Why not, "I never want to see you again!" or even, "Stick it where the sun don't shine!" Anything but, "*Can we still be friends?*"

Nick was in numb disbelief. Within the space of less than four hours, he had been beaten up by Carter Cannon, lost his job, and now, lost his girlfriend! Just when he believed his life couldn't get any worse, the hole had been dug deeper. Something snapped inside Nick, and suddenly, all he wanted to do was get as far away from Lisa as possible.

"Sure, we can be friends," he managed to say. "Look, I'll see you, Lisa!" and with that, he got into the car, backed up, and drove away.

He didn't notice Lisa waving sadly to him as he exited the apartment parking lot.

Chapter 6

Nick did not immediately go back home but instead drove around blindly for a while. At some point, he found himself turning on the dirt road leading to his trailer. Pulling up under the car awning, he turned off the car and just sat there listening to the hot engine tick as it cooled. Finally, he got out of the car, but rather than going into his trailer, he made a beeline for the large workshop. Pushing open the doors, Nick flipped a nearby light switch. Several banks of dirty fluorescent lights hung by chains from the ceiling flickered on.

The fluorescent lights revealed a poured concrete floor. Here and there, sheets and pieces of unfinished wood were piled haphazardly on the floor. A lathe, scroll saw, drill press, and other woodworking machines were interspersed between the stacks of pine, oak, and cherry. Other woodworking tools, such as a router, plane, adze, chisel, and sander, lay on a workbench. A false second floor was located toward the back of the shop, and it was accessed by a set of wooden steps. Plywood had been nailed in place to provide the flooring for this second floor, which was actually more of a platform of sorts, and a four-foot wooden railing encircled the platform. Hanging by metal hooks from the ceiling above the platform were wooden chairs in various stages of construction. Some of the chairs were rockers, and some were formal, high-back chairs, while others were durable chairs one would find around a kitchen table. Below the chairs and resting on the platform was an assortment of tables that, like the chairs, were unfinished.

Putting on a pair of goggles, Nick turned on the lathe and let it run while slipping on a pair of leather work gloves. He listened to the lathe's hum as he took a piece of pine and expertly turned it on the lathe with the intention of forming a table leg from it. Working with wood was Nick's refuge, and he found a certain peace and contentment whenever he was constructing a table, stool, or chair. He always came here whenever a crisis arose in his life—which meant he spent a lot of time in the workshop.

Nick's father and grandfather had built the workshop, and almost all of the tools and machines in the workshop had been his grandfather's. "Papa Bill" was Nick's dad's father, and he had worked as a carpenter from the age of fifteen until he had retired at almost seventy. A small man at barely five feet five inches, Papa Bill had possessed a quick wit and a ready smile. He had learned his trade at a time when quality and craftsmanship were valued commodities in a carpenter, and despite the rise of the mass-produced, cookie-cutter mentality and architecture of the latter twentieth century, he had never lacked for a job. Papa Bill loved to work with wood, and he built furniture as a sideline to his regular construction work.

Every single stick of furniture in his grandparents' house had been made by Papa Bill. When he had died at eighty-three, people had lined up a block long at the estate sale to buy Papa Bill's handmade furniture, a fitting tribute if there ever was one to the quality of his work.

Nick's grandmother had died shortly before he had been born, and with an empty house to come home to, Papa Bill had spent a great deal of his time with Nick and his family. The workshop had been built when Nick was seven, and shortly after that, Papa Bill had moved most of his woodworking equipment there. Unfortunately, fidelity, as well as a love for woodworking, were things Nick's father had not inherited from Papa Bill. Undeterred, Papa Bill took Nick under his wing and taught him everything he knew about working with wood. Nick wasn't sure why he had enjoyed it so much. He just knew he enjoyed the company of his grandfather immensely and that he loved him deeply. He had a gentle, patient nature when teaching Nick how to read the grain of wood or how to measure as many times as necessary to get the cut right the first time. Perhaps it was simply because since Papa Bill loved it, *Nick* loved it! At any rate, when most kids his age were off riding bikes, swimming, or going to the movies, Nick was working with his grandfather. When he got home after school, if he saw Papa Bill's battered '66 Chevy pickup parked by the double-wide, he would throw his books on the bed in his room and run out to the workshop. There, they would work side by side for hours until it grew dark and his mother called them in to supper. Nick had been twelve when Papa Bill had died. Next to his parent's divorce, it had been the darkest day of his life.

Nick continued to turn the wood piece on the lathe, but unlike all the other times he had fled here, he could not find the peace of mind he sought. The events of the day kept coming back to him like a bad dream he couldn't wake up from. Abruptly, he turned off the lathe, ripped the goggles off his eyes, and took the gloves off his hands.

Gripping the partially finished wood so firmly in his bare hands that his knuckles turned white, he stood motionless as hot tears of anger and frustration welled in his eyes. Finally, he could stand it no longer, and screaming, he pounded the top of the lathe with the wood in his hand until it broke. Snarling, he flung the piece that remained in his hand at the prefab wall of the workshop, where it struck with a loud *clunk*. For long moments, Nick stood with his arms by his side, clenching and unclenching his fists. When he was finally able to gain some measure of self- control, he came to a decision.

He had to leave.

It didn't really matter where, and it didn't really matter how far. All that mattered was that he had to leave now. As in tonight. As in immediately.

It was as if all the bad experiences, all the failures, and all the screw ups he had been involved in down through the years had decided to come home to roost at once, and their accumulated weight threatened to suffocate him.

Nick hurried out of the workshop, pushing the two sliding doors together and locking them. Glancing up, he saw that the sun was on its downward arc in the sky. Looking at his watch, he saw that it was a little past six o'clock. Running to his car, Nick opened the passenger-side door and stacked the boxes of his things on the ground. Once the boxes were all out of the car, he picked them up and walked slowly toward the trailer. Arranged like building blocks, one on top of the other, the precariously balanced boxes swayed dangerously as Nick staggered toward the trailer. Once he reached the door, he managed to drop the boxes to the ground without any of them falling over. Then he unlocked the door and impatiently began tossing the boxes inside. Quickly, he entered the trailer and rummaged around until he found a duffel bag and began stuffing it with a change of clothes, toothpaste, and other toiletry items. Nick did a quick inventory, decided he had all he needed in the duffel bag, zipped it shut, and stood up with the bag slung across his shoulder. That's when an obvious fact suddenly dawned on him.

He didn't have any idea where he was going.

Dropping the bag, Nick dug around in some drawers until he found a dog-eared edition of a *Rand-McNally Road Atlas*. Opening the road atlas, he flipped through pages, scanning the names of each state listed. When he came across Mississippi, he suddenly stopped. He recalled a conversation he had had with a coworker at the distribution center. The guy's name escaped him, but what Nick did remember was that he had gone on and on about Biloxi, about how the beaches were great, that there were floating gambling casinos there, and that the food and accommodations were cheap, since the casinos wanted to attract gamblers. Most people from around here went to the gambling boats in Shreveport if they sought such distractions, Nick knew, but this guy had sworn that Shreveport didn't hold a candle compared to Biloxi!

Nick thought about it for just a few moments longer. He wasn't much of a gambler, primarily because he never had much money to gamble with, but the idea of cheap accommodations appealed to him. Going to a place like Biloxi didn't mean he necessarily had to gamble. He could just take advantage of the enticements meant to lure gamblers to the casinos there!

The decision made. Nick took a pen and quickly traced the most direct route to Biloxi on the road atlas. Grabbing his duffel bag and the road atlas, Nick exited the trailer, locked it, and made his way to his car. Tossing the duffel bag into the car, he started it and immediately made his way to a bank with a drive-through that stayed open until seven o'clock. He cashed his severance check there, placing the entire $350 in his wallet. Next, he stopped at a convenience store with gas pumps, filled the Sprint's entire eight-gallon tank with gas, bought some snacks and a bottled water, and he was off.

Nick had a destination, even if he still didn't know what he was going to do once he got there.

Chapter 7

Traveling east on I-20 through Shreveport, Nick's chosen route would eventually take him to Vicksburg, Mississippi, and then to Jackson. From there, he would take State Highway 49 on a straight shot south to Biloxi. He drove without really thinking, just letting his mind drift. On those occasions when he had to change lanes or otherwise negotiate through the traffic on the interstate, he did so robotically, with as little conscious thought devoted to the task as possible.

The sun was setting when Nick crossed the grandfather of all North American rivers—the Mississippi. The last vestiges of the sun's reddish-gold light glinted gently off the water of the wide river. From Nick's vantage point on the bridge that spanned the Mississippi, the view should have been particularly spectacular. It was wasted on Nick, however, as still preoccupied, he barely noticed the river as he crossed it. A "Welcome to Mississippi" sign greeted him as he exited off the bridge and into the Magnolia State. Taking the loop that circled Vicksburg and led to S.H. 49, he had only traveled a few additional miles into Mississippi when his cell phone trilled, startling him.

Nick was unable to afford the monthly bill of a regular cell phone plan; so instead, he had bought a cheap phone at Walmart and purchased minutes. He fumbled for the cell in a frantic effort too remember how many minutes he had left and decided he had approximately an hour or so. There wasn't a caller ID on the no- frills phone, so he was mystified as to who would be calling him.

"Hello?"

"Nick, where are you?" Mark's concerned voice asked over the phone. "You weren't at your place when Patti and I went by, and nobody has seen you since … since, well … since you left Lisa's." *So that explains the phone call,* Nick thought as he closed his eyes momentarily in dismay. Mark and Patti had somehow found out about Lisa kicking him out and were worried about him.

When they hadn't found him at his trailer, their worry had only increased.

"What did he say?" Nick heard Patti's concerned voice ask in the background.

Patti was Mark's wife. They had been high school sweethearts, and with Nick serving as Mark's best man, they had married at nineteen, despite both their parents' protestations that they were too young. Mark and Patti's parent's fears had quickly proved unfounded, as their marriage had been rock solid ever since. In fact, the two were inseparable, and when you saw one, you usually saw the other. Although Mark was his best friend in the whole world, Nick considered Patti a close second. In his opinion, she was the nicest, kindest, most patient person he had ever met. Short, at only barely five feet tall, Patti tended to be on the plump side and was constantly dieting. She wore her dark brown hair short and curled in beneath her ears and had sparkling green eyes. Her smile was her best feature, however, and Nick knew it could light up a whole room. Thinking of his friends and how happy they were together compared to his own disastrous personal life brought a lump to Nick's throat.

"Nick, answer me! Where are you?" Mark demanded.

"I'm … I'm on my way to … to Biloxi," Nick managed to reply.

"What? Biloxi? As in Mississippi?" Mark asked in disbelief. "Why?" In the background, Nick heard Patti demanding details.

Nick didn't know what to say. The fact was he wasn't sure himself why he had gone on this impromptu road trip. All he knew was that he needed time alone to do some long, overdue soul-searching. Finally, he said, "I … I just had to get away, Mark. I … I can't explain it any simpler."

There was a long pause over the phone as Mark considered what Nick had said. Abruptly, Patti's voice came over the phone. "Nick, listen, sweetie, we know you got laid off from your job and what happened to you and Lisa. I can only imagine how hurt and upset you are right now! The thing is, you don't need to be alone, especially now! It's not healthy! Why don't you come stay with us for a while? I'll make my famous chicken spaghetti you like so much! We can play cards, go to the movies, go bowling, anything you want!"

Patti's warm, concerned voice caused Nick to smile despite himself. Not for the first time, he thought of what a lucky man Mark was.

"Thanks, Patti. I might take you up on that when I get back. But … but I really need to do this for … for myself. I hope you understand."

Hearing the finality in Nick's voice, Patti sighed. "Promise me you won't do anything foolish or impulsive then, okay? And promise you will call us the second you get back to Pleasant Mountain."

"I promise," Nick said, chuckling. "Besides, you know me Patti; I *never* do anything foolish or impulsive!" From the sound of Patti's nervous laughter, Nick knew that was *exactly* what she and Mark were worried about!

Patti handed the phone back to Mark, and they talked a few moments more, with Nick promising to call again sometime after he got to Biloxi.

Saying good-bye, Nick clicked off his phone, and once more he was driving alone in the solitude of his car.

An hour later got Nick into Jackson, where he stopped to grab a bite to eat and fill up his car with gas. By the time he was on the road again, it was approaching eleven o'clock at night. The traffic was light as he left Jackson behind, and yawning, he concentrated on trying to stay awake. A half hour later, he slowed down as he entered a small hamlet. A sign announced the town's name as "D'Lo," and other than a blinking yellow traffic light and a post office with several other buildings clustered near it, Nick found scant evidence that a "town" existed there. Yawning repeatedly now, he sped up as he passed the D'Lo city limit sign.

Nick had traveled less than half a mile from D'Lo when a motel suddenly appeared alongside the road. A neon sign atop the motel identified it as the Poolside Motel, and Nick briefly considered stopping there for the night before discarding the idea. His funds were limited, and another hour would put him in Biloxi. Besides, he figured if he had made it this far, he could make it all the way. No sooner had he made this decision than he heard a loud *pop*, followed shortly by his car swerving.

Gripping the wheel hard, Nick fought to keep the car under control before finally slowing down and pulling to a stop by the side of the road. Leaning over, he pulled a flashlight out of the glove compartment, Nick got out of the car.

Shining the flashlight on the tires, Nick soon discovered the problem. His left rear tire had suffered a blowout. Cursing, he was in the process of opening the hatchback of the Sprint to retrieve the spare when sudden realization caused him to stop and pound the top of the little car in dismay. He had used the spare tire to replace a flat several months ago, and he had not replaced it. *He had no spare tire!* Slamming the trunk of the hatchback down in frustration, Nick looked up and down the road. A long black ribbon of highway stretched away in the murky dark in both directions without a single car's headlights to be seen. In fact, he now realized there had been little traffic since shortly after he had left Jackson. Looking at his watch, he saw it was almost midnight, undoubtedly the reason why there was no one on the road.

Nick stood beside the car, fuming, while he considered his options. Finally, he sighed in resignation and got back in the car. Starting it back up, he turned it back around and, flat tire and all, limped slowly back to the motel. Five minutes later, he pulled into the cracked asphalt of the motel parking lot. A single light was on in the motel's office. As Nick opened a glass door and entered the cramped office, he saw no one there.

An old, yellowed map of D'Lo and the surrounding county hung from the wall behind a counter with a cracked Formica top. An antiquated swivel chair sat on the floor behind the counter. Resting on top of the counter was a mason jar filled with small replicas of the Confederate battle flag. A handwritten sign taped to the jar said "50 cents each." A swivel rack stood next to the counter, and it was filled with bumper stickers. One of the bumper stickers said, "I Love GRITS: Girls Raised In The South," while another had a picture of the Confederate flag, which said, "Heritage, Not Hate!" Finally, a small brass bell was screwed to the wall right above the counter. A piece of nylon cord hung from the clapper inside of it. Nick was about to turn and search elsewhere for the night manager when he heard a snoring noise coming from behind a partially closed door just to the left and behind the counter. Reaching up, he tentatively pulled the cord a couple of times, the bell ringing loudly in the small confines of the office. Abruptly, the snoring stopped, and a thin, middle-aged man exited the door and into the office, sleepily rubbing his eyes as he did so. Mussed brown hair stood up from the top of his head, much like a rooster comb. Peering curiously at Nick, he asked, "Yes, suh. What can I do for ya?"

"I … I guess I need a room for the night. My car has a flat, and I don't have a spare." Nick replied.

"Sorry to hear that, but we can sure fix you up for tonight! The room's forty dollars a night, and I'll just need ya to sign here!" The night manager sounded impossibly chipper to Nick for someone who had just been awoken from a sound sleep. *Perhaps he had a lot of practice at it,* he thought as he signed the old-fashioned ledger the manager handed him.

"Is there a place nearby that I can get another tire?" Nick asked as he handed the ledger back.

The manager thought briefly before answering. "I got a cousin, Bobby Dale, who owns a tire shop not far from here. Actually, he's my second cousin, once removed, but he still gives me discounts on tires. Family's family ya know," he said with a wink aimed at Nick.

"Er, that's great. Uh, how far from here is it?"

Hearing the concern in Nick's voice, the manager snapped his fingers and said, "That's right! Ya can't drive your car since it's got a flat! Tell ya what, after breakfast tomorrow, I'll drive ya over to Bobby Dale's. He's got a wrecker and can tow your car to his shop. He'll have ya fixed in a jiffy, and then you can be on your way!"

"Hey, that's fantastic! Thanks, uh … "

"Name's Merkel, Jedidiah Merkel, although everyone around here calls me Jed!"

"Well, thanks, Jed! I really appreciate it."

"No problem. D'Lo may be a small town, but it's got friendly people!" With that, Jed gave Nick a large brass key to his room.

Nick exited the office and looked for room twenty-three, the number stamped on his key. Several security lights in and around the motel and its parking lot aided Nick with a dim illumination as he made his way to his room. He saw that the layout of the motel was relatively simple, as two blocks of rooms led from the office, forming a V shape. As Nick followed the numbers on the rooms in search of his own, he discovered a restaurant was located behind the motel. Too tired to do any more than simply note the presence of the restaurant, he finally found his room near the end of one row of rooms. Going back to his car, he gingerly drove it next to his room and parked it. Taking the key, he unlocked the door to his room and then returned to his car.

As Nick was taking his duffel bag from the car, he noticed the painting in the back of the car for the first time. He had already forgotten all about it! Tossing the duffel bag on the bed in his room, he went back and opened the hatchback of the Sprint. Reaching in, he picked up the wrapped painting and took it out of the car. Gazing at it, he was in the act of placing it back in the car when he felt something slide within the painting.

Curiously, Nick took the painting back out of the car and carefully shook it. There it was again! There was something sliding around within the painting!

Thinking that a piece of the frame must have broken off, Nick took the painting back to his room and, sitting on the bed, began to remove the cardboard and other wrapping material. When he had finished, he laid the painting on the bed and looked in puzzlement at it. The frame was whole, and there were no broken pieces he could see.

Picking it up, he began to turn it over, and he felt something slide inside between the frame and the painting. His curiosity now thoroughly aroused, Nick carefully inspected the back of the painting. Unlike most modern frames, Nick discovered the back of the frame was not made of paper or cardboard. Instead, it was made of a sturdy, laminate sheet of wood screwed into the frame itself. Pulling a pocketknife from the pocket of his jeans, Nick flipped out one thin blade and, using the blade's tip, began loosening each of the screws holding the back of the frame in place. When finished, he had a small pile of screws lying on the bed. Using the pocketknife's blade again, he carefully wedged it between the frame and the painting and began to pry the thin wood backing off. Without warning, the back of the frame popped off, and a flat, rectangular object fell out and into Nick's lap. Picking it up, Nick stared at it in amazement. It was a book!

Turning it over in his hands, Nick carefully examined the book The book was thin, about a foot long and half again as wide. It was bound in a dark gray, leathery material that was slightly abrasive to the touch. Peering closer, Nick could see no title on the book. Flipping it over, he examined the other side of the book. He soon saw it was just as blank, with nothing writ- ten on the cover to give a clue as to the book's name or subject. Sighing, he flipped the book over one more time and almost dropped it from surprise! There, on the front cover of the book in gold, filigreed writing was the words, *The Book of Lost Treasures.* There had been nothing there when he had examined it moments earlier, he was sure of it! Gulping, he set the book down on the bed, as if it were hot to the touch.

Finally, Nick picked the book back up and peered closely at the book's title, which had appeared, as it were, out of thin air. The letters and words were all written stylishly with exaggerated loops and whorls, and the writing style reminded Nick of a Puritan hymnbook of the early 1700s that he had seen pictured in his high school American history textbook. Shaking his head, he carefully opened the book and turned to the first page. It was completely blank, save for the words "*Your Name*" at the top of the page. Quickly, Nick flipped through the rest of the book and found without exception that each and every page was blank! Puzzled, Nick set the book down and began to pace about the room, thinking hard.

Someone had gone to a lot of trouble to hide the book within the frame, of that he had no doubt. The odds of it "accidentally" finding its way there were so farfetched, he didn't even consider that an option. So *who* and, more importantly, *why* had someone hidden the book within the painting? Immediately, he thought of Hank. He knew from experience that the antique store owner had a mischievous nature, and he wouldn't put it past the diminutive Hank to pull a practical joke on him. However, the more he thought about it, the more he doubted Hank would have done that. First of all, a prank such as this is something you might pull on an old friend, *not* a customer you have met for the first time! Hank also knew the reason why Nick had bought the painting, and a practical joke under the circumstances would seem … well, it would seem somewhat cruel. Even though Nick had only met Hank the one time, that was enough to convince him that Hank didn't have a cruel bone in his body.

At a loss as what to do next, Nick sat down heavily on the edge of the bed. Looking around, he noticed the interior of the motel room for the first time. An ancient chest of drawers sat against the wall in front of the bed with a small oval mirror hanging on the wall above it. A dark blue, indoor-outdoor carpet that looked equally as ancient as the chest of drawers covered the floor. A coin-operated TV with an obsolete set of rabbit ears antenna sat on top of a desk next to the chest of drawers, and a wooden chair was pushed under the desk. A small bathroom was located to the right of the bed, and Nick stood up to look inside it. Given what he had seen so far in the motel room, he half expected to see a claw foot tub. He was pleasantly surprised to see a modern shower-tub combination. That reminded Nick of how dirty and gritty he felt, and he immediately stripped off his shirt and tossed it on the bed in preparation of taking a shower.

Nick paused as he gave the motel room one final glance. Despite the age of the furnishings, he had to admit the room looked clean. As he was about to turn away to start the water in the bathroom, his eye caught the nightstand next to the bed. Resting on it was an old black rotary phone. Next to the phone was a pad of stationary with the name "Poolside Motel" printed on the top, with a green, plastic, ballpoint pen lying on top of the pad. On impulse, Nick quickly strode over to the nightstand and picked up the pen. Sitting on the bed, he picked up the mysterious book and opened it. Turning to the first page, he located the "*Your Name*" writing at the top of it. Hesitating for only a moment, he wrote grandly, "*Nick Hollister,*" next to it. Grinning, he was about to pitch the book back onto the bed, when suddenly, writing began to flow beneath his name, as if written by some invisible hand!

"What the … !" Nick shouted, dropping the book as if it were a bomb that had gone off in his hand.

His shower forgotten, Nick stared at the book lying on the bed like it was some sort of dangerous snake. Surely this was some kind of elaborate joke someone was playing on him, he thought! It had to be! He almost pitched the book into the trash then and there, but his curiosity got the better of him, and sitting back on the bed, he picked up the book and began to examine it carefully. With the miniaturization of computer chips and electronic components, anything was possible nowadays, Nick thought, and with that in mind, he began to search the book for any kind of embedded circuitry or power source, like a small watch battery. After five minutes of fruitless searching, Nick finally gave up.

Exasperated, Nick next turned to studying the mysterious writing that had suddenly appeared. It said:

Rules of The Book of Lost Treasures

Rule One: The book can have only one owner

Rule Two: The book may reveal the location of only one lost treasure at a time

Rule Three: The lost treasure must be found before the book may reveal another

Rule Four: The book will only reveal the location of a lost treasure that is precisely described

Rule Five: Only a treasure that is truly lost may be revealed by the book

Nick read the mysterious writing in silent fascination. Glancing down, he saw there was one more sentence beneath the rules. It asked:

What is the lost treasure which you seek?

Reading the last part caused a sudden shiver of excitement to run up and down Nick's spine. The book claimed to be able to reveal the location of "lost treasures!" That meant valuable stuff, didn't it? Nick's enthusiasm quickly waned as he realized that what the book purportedly claimed to do was patently impossible. It was crazy to believe otherwise! The sense, however, that there was something extraordinary about the book would not leave Nick, even after he closed the book and prepared to take a shower.

Later, as he lay in bed with the lights off trying to sleep, the same feeling persisted. Finally, he drifted off to sleep, but not before one last thought drifted through his consciousness.

Maybe, just maybe, the strange book *could* find lost treasures.

Chapter 8

Nick got up early the next morning amazingly refreshed. His stomach growling, he counted his dwindling supply of cash before deciding he could afford breakfast. Quickly dressing, he made his way to the restaurant behind the motel. Nick saw a smattering of cars in the motel parking lot as he closed and locked the door to his room. However, there was another parking lot adjacent to the restaurant, one he hadn't seen the night before, and it was full of cars and pickup trucks. A sign on top of the restaurant said "Poolside Restaurant: Home of the World-Famous Rotating Buffet!" Puzzled as to what "rotating buffet" meant, Nick pushed through the double glass doors of the restaurant. The raucous noise of many people talking immediately assaulted his ears, and his nose detected the mouth-watering aroma of frying bacon and eggs.

The noise momentarily abated as those within the restaurant looked up curiously at Nick before they returned their attention to eating and talking.

After standing for a few minutes, Nick decided the patrons here seated themselves and took a seat at one of the few tables not occupied near the back of the restaurant. Looking around, Nick saw the place was packed. The motel, he decided, may not do a booming business, but its restaurant sure did! Curiously, he looked around the place.

The floor of the restaurant was covered in speckled linoleum tile. It must have at one time been white, but time and hard usage had turned it a dingy yellow. The furnishings, including the table and chair Nick sat at, were straight retro from the sixties and seventies. The legs of the tables and chairs were made of bright, shiny metal, and the chairs were upholstered in alternating colors of mustard yellow and forest green. The Formica tops of the tables were nicked and scarred and looked suspiciously to Nick like the same type or pattern of Formica that covered the motel office's counter.

A battered jukebox was located in one corner of the restaurant and was playing an old Brooks and Dunn song, "Only in America." Located above the jukebox and pinned securely to the wall was a large Confederate flag. However, what immediately caught Nick's eye was a contraption located roughly in the middle of the restaurant that looked, for all the world, like a Lazy Susan on steroids.

Peering curiously at it, Nick realized this must be the "famous" rotating buffet advertised on the restaurant sign. Oval in shape, the buffet had an open area contained within it much like a salad bar, while a flat, tread-like surface extended from it on the outside.

This surface was segmented and moved across rollers, with a chain-like track for propelling it located underneath it. It vaguely reminded Nick of a race car track set he had when he was a kid. Shaking his head, he pulled out a menu that was sandwiched between a bottle of ketchup and a bottle of mustard that were sitting on the table. The menu was a single-laminated sheet, with breakfast entrées on one side and lunch and dinner entrées on the other.

Nick was just beginning to study the menu when a feminine voice, edged with a rich Southern drawl, asked, "What can I get for ya, honey?"

Looking up, Nick saw the source of the voice was a waitress. She appeared to be in her mid-forties, and her waitress uniform was a skirt and blouse of the same color combination of yellow and green as the chairs. A white plastic nametag with "Lilly" etched on it in black letters was pinned to her blouse. Heavy makeup, applied pancake-like, covered Lilly's face, while blue eyes peered at Nick from under a set of false eyelashes.

Bottle-blonde hair with dark roots beginning to show was arranged in a beehive bouffant style on her head that hadn't been in fashion since Elvis was rocking in "Blue Hawaii." Realizing he was staring, Nick quickly averted his eyes back to the menu.

"Um, I'll take the breakfast special," he managed to say.

"For just fifty cents more, ya can get the Poolside Breakfast Grande. It comes with grits and an extra egg." Eyeing Nick's skinny frame critically, Lilly added, "From the looks of ya, honey, ya could use an extra helpin'."

Red faced, Nick sputtered, "Uh … sure. The breakfast grande sounds fine." Nodding, Lilly wrote the order smartly on her pad and turned on her heel to take the order back to the kitchen. Relieved, Nick idly studied a cheap paper placemat that sat on his table and was firmly anchored by a rolled-up napkin containing silverware. The placemat had activities printed on it that seemed to be geared for children.

It contained a word puzzle, a connect- the-dots drawing, and finally, a maze, with a big black "X" marking the end of the maze. Above the maze in bold print were the words "*Find Efurd Buckley's Hidden Gold!*" Looking at the maze suddenly reminded Nick of the book that had been hidden within the painting. This caused him to wonder anew about the book's ridiculous claim to be able to locate lost treasure.

Feeling foolish but thinking that he had nothing to lose, Nick decided he would work up the courage to question Lilly about this Efurd Buckley when she returned with his order. Ten minutes later, she appeared at his table and placed his plate full of bacon, eggs, toast, and a bowl of grits in front of him.

"Uh, I couldn't help but notice this maze about Efurd Buckley," Nick said rather lamely while pointing at the placemat. "Is he, uh, is he some sort of, you know … historical figure around here?"

Laughing, Lilly waved a hand in the air as if to swat at some invisible fly. "Oh, *everybody* around here knows the story about Colonel Buckley!" Pulling up a chair across from Nick, Lilly eagerly launched into the saga of Efurd Buckley.

"Ya see, Efurd Buckley was a colonel in the Confederate Army, and he was born and raised just a few miles from here. He led a group of Mississippi militia that fought in battles from Richmond to Vicksburg. Toward the end of the war, when it was apparent that the South had lost, Colonel Buckley decided to lead one last desperate raid against the Yankees. His target was a train carrying gold for the payroll of the Union forces occupying Vicksburg. Colonel Buckley and his men pried up sections of the track several miles out of Vicksburg at a point on the track that the train would be coming around a blind bend and the engineer couldn't see the missing sections of track until it was too late. The train derailed, and as soon as it slid to a stop, Colonel Buckley attacked. Unfortunately, the train was heavily guarded, and there were enough Yankee soldiers left uninjured to put up a good fight. Although Colonel Buckley managed to take the strongbox containing the payroll from the train, most of his men were killed, and he himself was mortally wounded. Days later, he stumbled home and died in his wife's arms, but not before he told her he had hidden the strongbox. No one has ever seen the Yankee gold shipment since."

"What about the men he led on the raid? Surely there must have been some survivors that helped him hide it," Nick asked curiously.

"Oh, there were some survivors all right! But they all claimed Colonel Buckley had taken the payroll strongbox off by himself. To a man, they denied knowing the location of where the gold was hidden."

"But what about Colonel Buckley's wife?" Nick persisted. "He must have told her something if he knew he was dying!"

"If he did, she took it to her grave She never admitted—even to her children—to knowing the strongbox's location. However," Lilly remarked wryly, "that hasn't stopped folks from looking. If I had a dollar for every hole dug in this county from someone looking for Buckley's gold, *I* would be the boss and *Donald Trump* would be the apprentice! In fact, legend has it that when

Colonel Buckley's widow died years later, the poor woman hadn't even grown cold in her casket before the colonel's home was taken apart, brick by brick and board by board, by some Yankee scalawags looking for the gold!"

Thinking of *The Book of Lost Treasures*, Nick asked, "So what do you think happened to the gold?"

"Honey, I haven't a clue!" Lilly snorted. "Life's too short to waste time chasin' that cat's tail. Besides, like I said, there's been plenty of fools who have already tried and failed to find it. However, I can tell you that the general thinkin' is that Colonel Buckley had to have hidden the payroll somewhere around D'Lo. It's an area he was familiar with, and in his severely wounded condition, he must have known he didn't have a lot of time left to hide the gold."

"So there you have it! The story of Buckley's gold!" Lilly said as she got up from the table. "Jed had the bright idea to print the maze on the placemats so that any tourist who stopped here on the way to the gambling boats in Biloxi would remember the motel and restaurant. He thought maybe we might drum up some more business that way."

At the mention of Jed's name, Nick suddenly remembered his promise to give him a ride to his cousin's tire shop.

"Do you know where Jed is right now?"

"Sure! He's where he always is this time of the morning. In the kitchen cookin,'" Lilly replied, jerking her thumb in the kitchen's direction.

Seeing the surprised look on Nick's face, Lilly chuckled. "Honey, this ain't no IHOP. In a small operation like this one, everybody wears a lot of different hats. After the breakfast rush is over, I gotta clean rooms." Hearing a customer call her name, Lilly turned and left Nick to ponder the story of Colonel Efurd Buckley.

Finding he was famished, Nick wolfed down his breakfast, paid his bill, and left, what was for him, a generous tip for Lilly. Making his way back to his room, he unlocked the door and closed it behind him. Picking up *The Book of Lost Treasures* lying on the nightstand next to the bed, he turned to the book's first page. Hesitating for a moment, he furtively looked around, as if to make sure no one was watching him. Carefully, he reread the rules of *The Book of Lost Treasures* one more time.

Then he took the pen lying on the Poolside Motel pad, and under "*What is the lost treasure which you seek?*" he wrote in the book:

> "Where is the hidden strongbox of Eferd Buckley?"

Holding his breath, Nick waited for something to happen. Not really knowing what to expect, he gripped the thin book tightly, as if afraid it would grow wings and fly out of his hands. Seconds passed, which, in turn, grew into minutes. When five minutes had passed, Nick impatiently leafed through the book's pages. Not a thing appeared to him, except the same blank pages as before. He closed the book with a loud *thump* and threw it on the bed.

"What did you expect?" he mumbled angrily to himself. "A tiny green genie to pop out of the book and grant you three wishes?" Stalking out of his room, he spent the next forty-five minutes wandering around the small motel and its grounds before finally ending up at the motel's swimming pool. He waited impatiently for Jed to exit the restaurant. Sitting under the shade of a table with an umbrella sprouting from the middle of it, Nick studied the pool. He was pleasantly surprised to see that the pool and the area around the pool were immaculate.

A white-washed, four-foot, wrought iron fence surrounded the pool, and colorful begonias and zinnias in colors of pink, red, yellow, and white were planted all along the fence. The pool itself was a throwback to the times when large pools were built at motels and had water depths that graduated from three-foot to twelve-foot depths within it. The mesh-metal chairs and tables around the pool had also been painted white, and overstuffed waterproof pillows were tied to their seats and backs.

The morning was already getting hot, and Nick was seriously contemplating taking a dip in the inviting blue water of the pool, when he spotted Jed exiting the front doors of the restaurant. Leaping up, he ran through the pool's gate and after Jed.

Jed spotted Nick and stopped to wait for him. A white grease- stained apron was tied around his waist, and he waved tiredly in greeting at Nick. As Nick approached Jed, he saw that his hair, amazingly, was still stuck up, cockscomb-like.

"Hey!" Nick said breathlessly as he skidded to a stop beside Jed.

"Hey," Jed said in return. "I guess you're ready to go see Bobby Dale so you can get your tire fixed?"

As Nick nodded eagerly, Jed suppressed a yawn. "It's gettin' harder and harder to keep these hours. Just as soon as I take you to Bobby Dale's, I got me an appointment with a soft bed and a feather pillow." Motioning for Nick to follow him, he led him to a candy apple red Ford pickup parked next to the motel office.

The Ford was an extended cab, and opening the door, Jed untied his apron and tossed it in the back of the cab.

A fishing rod, a bolt- action .22 caliber rifle, and a red, white, and blue NASCAR cap hung from a rack fixed to the back window of the cab. Motioning Nick to get in, Jed grabbed the NASCAR cap and jammed it on his head. He turned the ignition, and the truck rumbled to life. Moments later, they exited the motel parking lot and turned onto the highway in front of the motel.

As they drove back toward D'Lo, Jed kept up a conversation with Nick as he pointed out places of interest in and around the greater "metro" area of D'Lo. Nick, no stranger himself to a small-town environment, relaxed in the constant friendly banter from Jed. Coming to the intersection of the blinking yellow light in D'Lo, Jed turned the truck left onto another road, which led west out of the small hamlet. They had gone less than half a mile when they came to Bobby Dale's tire shop, located beside the road. Turning into the tire shop, Jed parked the truck and killed the engine.

Nick got out of the truck and looked around. The place looked to be an old gas station that had been converted into the tire shop. Tires of every size and description were stacked head high in an around the shop. There were two garage bays to Nick's right, and one was empty, while the other had a dark blue van suspended several feet off the floor by the garage's hydraulic lift. A dusky brown tow truck with "Bobby Dale's Tires" stenciled on both doors was parked beside the garage bays. An air-powered lug wrench lay on the ground next to the van, the air hose snaking from it to the compressor located at the back of the garage. There was no one in the garage bays, so Nick and Jed made their way to the office area next to the garage.

The large plate glass windows of the office were tinted black, so Nick could see nothing inside. Just as they reached the door to the office, Bobby Dale stepped out.

For a moment, Nick's mouth hung open as he stared at Jed's cousin, who looked like he had just come straight from a casting call of a *Pirates of the Caribbean* movie! Tall and rail-thin, Bobby Dale had a black do-rag tied around his head, which covered shaggy gray hair pulled back in a ponytail, while a matching black eye patch covered his right eye. A gold medallion of some kind hung from a heavy gold chain about his neck, while one ear sported a large, gold hoop earring. A black skull and crossbones with a dagger plunged through it was tattooed on his left fore- arm. Bobby Dale wore a pair of faded, blue, Dickies overalls stained here and there with oil. When he smiled at the sight of his cousin, Jed, he exposed two gold front teeth.

"Jed! What brings you here this time of the mornin'?" he boomed as he clapped Jed on the back.

"Well, I have a guest here who needs a new tire. Can you fix him up?" Jed asked.

"Why sure! How's your mama, by the way? I didn't see her at church last Sunday." The next few minutes were spent in small talk between Jed and Bobby Dale, as they apparently caught up each other up on family matters, large and small. Finally, Bobby Dale hopped into the tow truck and followed them back to the motel. Pulling up to Nick's car, Jed let him out while he drove back to his room next to the motel office to catch up on some much-needed sleep.

Bobby Dale had already climbed down from the tow truck and was examining Nick's tire when Jed drove away. A wry look of amusement was on his face as he carried out his inspection.

"They keep making these cars smaller n' smaller, don't they?" he commented. "Hell, I got a refrigerator bigger'n your car. If this keeps up, one day all we're going to need is bicycle tires for cars!"

"Well … it does get good gas mileage," Nick managed to say.

"Yep, I bet it does!" Bobby Dale said as he stood up and wiped his hands on an oil rag stuffed in the back pocket of the Dickies.

Looking at Nick, he said, "The tire is ruined, and you're going to need a new one. I don't carry tires that small in stock, and I'm going to hafta order it from a supplier in Jackson. Fortunately, the supplier runs a truck through here to Biloxi and Gulfport twice a week, and that truck will be through here tomorrow mornin'. I can get the tire then. The only other alternative is for me to drive to Jackson to pick up the tire, which will be expensive!"

When Nick asked how expensive, he gulped at the figure Bobby Dale gave him and quickly told him that tomorrow would be fine. It was cheaper just to stay one more night at the motel! As Bobby Dale got back into his tow truck and drove off, Nick sighed in resignation as he headed back to his room. At the rate he was going, he would have spent all of his money before he even reached the beaches of Biloxi! Reaching his room, he unlocked the door and threw himself onto the bed.

When is my luck going to change? he wondered bitterly.

Chapter 9

Nick changed into a pair of old shorts and spent much of the rest of the morning and early afternoon at the motel's swimming pool. For the most part, he had the pool all to himself with only a couple of children and their mother, who splashed around in the shallow end of the pool for a half hour or so to mar his solitude. Finally tiring of swimming, Nick went back to his room and took a nap.

It was early evening when Nick woke up from his nap. Going to the bathroom, Nick splashed water on his face to revive him- self. As he dried his face off with a towel, his stomach rumbled, reminding him he had had nothing to eat since breakfast early that morning. Grabbing his wallet and room key, he exited his room and headed back toward the motel restaurant. As he approached the restaurant, he saw the parking lot was again full of cars, and as he entered through its double glass doors, the place was, if possible, even more crowded than it had been for breakfast. Nick searched for several minutes before he finally spotted a small table open near the back of the room. Hurrying, lest someone beat him to the table, Nick reached it moments later and sat down.

The constant drone of dozens of conversations being carried out as people chatted while they were eating serenaded Nick's ears as he studied the dinner menu. He hadn't seen Lilly, and he wondered if Jed also had to cook at night. Putting the menu down, he looked up and was treated with the sight of the "World Famous Rotating Buffet" in action.

Ice had been spread out within the buffet's interior, and various chilled salads lay in large stainless-steel bowls resting on the ice. Moving and clanking like the treads on an Abrams tank, the buffet's conveyer belt-like surface rolled slowly around the buffet in a counterclockwise fashion. Steaming pans of meats and vegetables lay on the buffet's moving surface, each spaced an appropriate distance from the other. Hungry customers stood by the buffet, slowly shuffling along lemming-like with its moving tread as they loaded their plates with the entrées they desired. Most must have been regulars to the rotating buffet, as they seemed to know the drill in obtaining their food from its moving surface. It was an amazing spectacle, and one which Nick joined moments later, as he ordered the buffet from the waitress who appeared at his table.

Not as skilled as the regulars, Nick missed on a few attempts to spear or fork food onto his plate as it rumbled by him. He felt foolish following the food around the buffet, so instead, he was content to wait until it came around to the position he stood at. After a few minutes, he managed to load his plate and headed back to his table.

Spooning some mashed potatoes and gravy into his mouth, he had to admit that with or without the rotating buffet, the food was good. Soon, he cleaned his plate and went back for seconds. Ten minutes later, stuffed, he sat back contentedly in his chair and waited for the waitress to bring him his ticket.

Nick's eyes idly fell upon the placemat partially covered by his plate. Pushing the plate aside, he took his napkin and wiped a drop of brown gravy that had fallen from his plate off the paper placemat. Bored, he glanced at the maze on the placemat with its title of "*Find Efurd Buckley's Hidden Gold!*" Suddenly, his eyes opened wide, and he sat bolt upright. He had spelled it E-F-E-R-D in *The Book of Lost Treasures*! Thinking hard, he remembered that one of the rules the book listed was that a lost treasure must be "precisely" described! What if that included spelling? As his waitress approached his table, Nick practically grabbed the ticket from her hand as he jumped up and headed for the cashier. Paying for his bill, Nick sprinted for his room.

Fumbling for his key, Nick finally unlocked the door and ran into his room. The mysterious book lay on the nightstand by the bed, and Nick opened it to the first page. His heart pounding, he located what he had written earlier and carefully drew a line through "*Eferd*" and wrote above it the properly spelled name of "*Efurd.*" It now read, "*Where is the hidden strongbox of* Efurd *Buckley?*"

A golden glow immediately seemed to emanate from within the book, coming from behind the first page. With trembling fingers, Nick turned the page. There, before his incredulous eyes and where once there was a blank page, was a neatly drawn map!

The map was detailed with roads, landmarks, directional markers, and approximate distances. As Nick studied the map in disbelief, he found it reminded him of MapQuest directions printed from a computer. Only MapQuest directions didn't glow in a soft, ambient light!

A golden glowing line led from the Poolside Motel to a spot approximately three miles north of D'Lo. It ended abruptly with the words "*Here Lies the Lost Treasure*" that seemed to glow brighter than anything else on the map. As Nick continued to excitedly study the map, he was struck again by the highly stylized writing on the map that didn't seem to fit with the modern directions shown on it.

It was like someone installing a fuel-injected engine in a Model T car frame. It just didn't seem to mesh, as if the book itself was from a different age than Nick was currently living in.

Nick once again considered the possibility that someone was still trying to play a practical joke on him. However, if that were true, how had they known he was going to end up in D'Lo, the victim of a flat tire? They could have planted a GPS device in his car, he supposed, but why would anybody want to go that trouble and expense for a stupid joke? Even if *that* could somehow be explained, and even if Hank Harper was in cahoots with … with *whomever* it was playing this game, how would Hank have known which painting to plant the book in? Nick hadn't known *himself* what he was exactly looking for when he entered Hank's shop! Besides, he had already carefully examined the mysterious book and found nothing on it or in it that could produce the glowing writing and map that abruptly appeared in the book! That left only one possibility: that *The Book of Lost Treasures* was possessed of some sort of … of *mystical* powers!

If he could have, Nick would have left then and there to search for the location of Efurd Buckley's gold as shown on the map in the book. However, he had no car, at least not until the next morning. Until then, he had to be content to bide his time. Nick studied the map long into the night until his eyes became heavy and sleep finally overcame him.

His last thoughts before he slumbered were on the gold and riches that might be found in the strongbox of Efurd Buckley.

Chapter 10

When Nick woke up the next morning, he was so excited over the map in *The Book of Lost Treasures* that he couldn't eat breakfast. Impatiently, he waited for Bobby Dale to show up and replace the ruined tire on his car. Finally, Bobby Dale arrived just past ten thirty in the morning. Attaching the tow truck's hitch to the Sprint's small bumper, Bobby Dale raised the little car's rear end a few feet in the air. It was just a few minutes work from there to take the ruined tire off. Using a portable tire changer anchored to the bed of the tow truck, Bobby Dale forced the ruined tire off the rim before placing the new tire on it. Removing an air tank from the cab of the tow truck, he quickly filled the small tire with air. Nick paid Bobby Dale cash for the tire, thanked him, and then watched him drive off.

As soon as Bobby Dale's truck had driven out of sight, Nick sprinted to his room and retrieved *The Book of Lost Treasures*. Closing and locking his room behind him, Nick took the book and ran to his car. Getting into the car, Nick carefully placed the book so that it lay open in the passenger seat, showing the map. Starting the car, he drove out of the Poolside Motel parking lot, following the map's directions.

It took Nick almost forty minutes before he finally pulled to a stop on a dirt road that lay next to an open field, maybe a pasture. As unfamiliar as he was to the area, he had had to backtrack numerous times, even following the meticulous directions on the map, before he had finally reached the location where Efurd's gold was located. Along the way, he had made another amazing discovery about the map in *The Book of Lost Treasures*: a bright, blood-red spot had appeared mysteriously on the map the moment he had pulled out of the motel parking lot and had started the hunt for the hidden strongbox! The red dot appeared to move, and after puzzling over it for a few moments, it had suddenly occurred to Nick that the red dot was *his* location on the map! That was why he was certain he had arrived at the proper location. The red dot's position on the map was almost on top of the "*Here Lies the Lost Treasure*" in the book.

Nick carefully studied the large open field before him. It was obviously a hay meadow, and it had been recently cut. In fact, Nick could see two tractors at one end of the field. One was pulling a hay rake that raked the loose hay into neat rows.

Following this tractor was the other one, which pulled a hay baler as it followed the rows of hay. Periodically, this tractor would stop, a gate at the back of the baler would rise, and a large roll of hay would be disgorged from the baler. The field was dotted with rolls of hay that had already been rolled by the baler. Nick experienced a brief moment of panic, as he worried that one of the large, heavy bales of hay might be lying on top of the hidden location of the strongbox.

Looking to his right, Nick saw that a house and barn were located a little over a hundred yards from the field. A barbed wire fence encompassed the entire field, and a gate between the house and pasture provided entry into the hay meadow. Trees had grown up thickly along this side of the barbed wire fence, effectively screening anyone from the house from having a clear view of the pasture. On the left side of the field, a heavy forest of hardwood hardwood trees bordered the hay meadow. Across the road opposite of Nick were more scattered fields bounded by patches of forest. Grazing cattle appeared here and there in some of these fields. The dirt road stretched out before him in more or less a straight line before disappearing over a small hill or ridge, and there didn't seem to be another house or home along this remote stretch of road.

Puzzled, Nick studied the rather unremarkable hay meadow. It looked no different than the hundreds in and around Pleasant Mountain he had seen growing up. There were absolutely no landmarks that stood out, no rocky outcropping, no gigantic oak tree, not even a nearby creek or stream. What had Efurd Buckley been thinking when he buried the strongbox in this field? How could he hope to retrieve or find (or have somebody else find) the location of the strongbox? The fact that Buckley *must* have buried the strongbox in the ground was a detail readily apparent to Nick. There simply wasn't anything else he could have done with it, because there was nowhere else he could have put it. Besides, even if there had been something else here over 140 years ago—like a cabin, barn, or even the hollow bole of a huge tree—they were gone now, and the map in the book *still* showed the strongbox to be here!

Nick thought back to the story of Efurd Buckley. Lilly had said he had been severely wounded in the attack on the train carrying the Union payroll. In fact, she said he had died days later in his wife's arms. So putting himself in Buckley's place, Nick tried to imagine what he would have done. Wounded, bleeding, perhaps even delirious, Buckley would have eventually reached a physical condition where he could no longer be too choosy where he hid the strongbox. In his mind's eye, Nick could well imagine Buckley, just a few short miles from home, finally realizing he had to hide the Union payroll before he was too weak to do so. At that point, he must have struggled off his horse, dug a hole, and simply dropped the strongbox in it before covering it back up. By the time he reached his wife, he was probably so near death that he never had the opportunity to tell her where it was. It was as plausible an explanation as any, but whether or not it was true was unimportant to Nick. What *was* important was that the location of Efurd's hidden gold was *here* in the field across from Nick! Grinning in anticipation, Nick started the car, his mind already formulating a plan.

He would come back tonight!

The day crawled by; minutes seemed like hours. When he had informed Jed he would be staying another night, the manager of the motel had been surprised, but fortunately, he had not asked any questions. Nick had spent most of the rest of the day by the motel pool unsuccessfully trying to keep his mind off the hidden treasure. Early evening arrived, and even though he still wasn't hungry, Nick forced himself to eat, since he hadn't eaten since the previous day. The meal went by in a blur. He didn't remember what he had even eaten, as he speared and spooned the food dishes that clanked and rattled by him on the moving buffet. Going back to his room, Nick lay on his bed, periodically getting up to impatiently look through the curtains on the window to see if it had gotten any darker.

Blessedly, night finally fell, and Nick left his room and got into his car. Consulting his watch, he saw it was after ten o'clock. Then he checked the little pile of equipment in the passenger's seat that he had put together to help retrieve the buried strongbox. One item was a collapsible shovel he had bought the previous year at an army/navy surplus store in Texarkana. He always kept it in the little car, just in case he ever got stuck in mud. Another was the flashlight in the glove compartment, and he had bought fresh batteries for it from Jed, who kept a supply of them in the motel office.

Finally, he had his empty duffel bag in preparation of carrying whatever was in the strongbox, along with a pair of leather gloves he had used when driving the forklift at his former job. He was as ready as he was ever going to be, and taking a deep breath, he started the car and drove to the spot he had scouted earlier that day.

Since he already knew where he was going, it took Nick less than fifteen minutes to reach the field where the strongbox lay buried. Killing the lights, Nick pulled as far off the dirt road as he could without going into the ditch. Turning off the car, Nick sat in silence. Besides someone from the house next to the field noticing his car and coming over to investigate, his greatest fear was another car coming by while he was engaged in trying to find and dig up the strongbox. However, that afternoon, not a single car had driven by in the half hour or so that he had been studying the area. Hopefully, the same would apply tonight.

Getting out of the car, Nick grabbed the duffel bag and stuffed the shovel and flashlight in it. Shoving the gloves in his back pocket, he picked up the duffel bag and laid it softly on the top of the Sprint. Taking care to make as little noise as possible, he grabbed *The Book of Lost Treasures* with one hand while easing the car door shut. Looking around, he saw in the distance the lights of the house through the screen of trees and heard a dog barking from somewhere around the house. A symphony of chirping crickets serenaded his ears, and from somewhere in the distance, he heard the deep bass croaking of a bullfrog. A three-quarter full moon provided dim illumination for Nick, and as he looked up, he saw scudding clouds as they drifted by and temporarily obscured the moon.

From the northwest horizon, lightning flickered, and even as Nick reached he barbwire fence, the wind picked up, portending a coming storm. Pulling out his gloves, Nick put them on. Dropping the duffel bag on the other side of the fence, he pulled two strands of barbwire apart and gingerly eased his body through them. Picking up the duffel bag, Nick pulled *The Book of Lost Treasures* from the duffel bag and, studying it, began walking into the pasture.

Since the map in the book glowed with its own light, Nick found he didn't have to use his flashlight to see it. Zigzagging through the open field, Nick tried to get a fix as to where the strongbox was buried. A few times, he had to detour around the large, round bales of hay that were in his way. Finally, the red dot on the map was centered directly on the "*Here Lies the Treasure*" words on the map, which were now pulsing like a neon sign, and Nick knew he had reached the location of the buried strongbox. As he put the duffel bag down and dug the shovel out of it, he heard a low rumble of thunder, and the wind was now blowing steadily out of the northwest. The dog at the house was barking constantly as Nick hurriedly unfolded the collapsible shovel and locked it into place. Tentatively at first, and then with greater gusto, Nick began to dig.

Not really knowing just how pinpoint the accuracy of the map's location of the buried strongbox, Nick made the hole he dug wide. After a short time, even with the stiff breeze that was blowing, Nick's shirt was plastered in sweat as he continued digging in the hot, humid night air. After about fifteen minutes, he had managed to dig a hole approximately five feet in diameter and about three feet deep. Breathing heavily, Nick stopped for a rest as he sat on the edge of the hole. The dog was barking frantically, and even though it was becoming difficult to hear over the strongly blowing wind, Nick thought he heard someone from the house yelling at the dog to shut up. A lightning flash from the approaching storm illuminated the area, and Nick realized he had to hurry if he was going to beat the storm.

As Nick redoubled his efforts, a sudden sense of foolishness came upon him. His life had been spent chasing dreams down rabbit holes, with each and every one leading to dead ends; yet, here he was at it again! What kind of idiot would be out in the dead of night, digging for hidden gold in the middle of a hay meadow, pointed there as it were by a mysterious map found in an equally mysterious book? *Only Nick Hollister, the king of fools,* the answer shouted in his mind! Angrily, he dug faster. "Not this time," he told himself. "Not this time!"

So intent was he at digging that he almost missed the *clunk* as his shovel struck something solid. Pausing, Nick gingerly stuck the tip of the shovel again in the soft dirt. It struck something solid, and Nick, using the shovel's tip, quickly outlined the object's diameter. Frantically, he began to dig, and dirt flew out of the rapidly expanding hole. Soon, he partially uncovered an object that was about two and half feet long by one foot wide. It was covered by some sort of canvas or oilcloth, and as Nick pulled at it, the covering separated in his hands with a rotten ripping sound. His heart pounding in excitement, Nick gripped the canvas and pulled as much of it off as he could. In its decayed state, the canvas peeled off easily in Nick's hands. Underneath was what looked to Nick like a small, ironbound, wooden chest. It had to be the strongbox!

So giddy he almost started hyperventilating, Nick dropped the shovel and began digging dog-like, with his bare hands around the still partially buried strongbox.

Moments later, the strongbox lay completely exposed. Taking the flashlight from the duffel bag, Nick shone it on the strong- box. The wood on the strongbox was dark and water stained.

A rusted metal hasp with a large antiquated padlock held the strongbox's wooden lid shut, and equally rusting hinges were located on the back of the lid. What appeared to be moldy leather straps were screwed into the sides of the strongbox. Turning off the flashlight and tossing it back into the duffel bag, Nick bent over and grasped the leather handles and tried to pick up the strongbox. After a moment's resistance, both handles broke off in Nick's hands with a sodden tearing noise. Gingerly touching the wooden box with his hands, Nick discovered the wood was soft and spongy. He had to be careful, or the entire thing would fall apart in his hands! Digging with his hands again, he carefully excavated an area around the base of the strongbox. When he was finally satisfied, he gingerly placed his hands under it and gently lifted. The strongbox lifted easily in his hands and was not nearly as heavy as he had thought it would be. "Wasn't gold supposed to be heavy?" he mused to himself. Fighting the impulse to shake the wooden strongbox to see what rattled around inside, Nick placed it softly on the ground at the top of the hole. Collapsing the shovel and placing it in the duffel bag, he pushed it to the side of the duffel bag before carefully picking up the strongbox and placing it in the duffel bag. As soon as the strongbox was placed in the duffel bag, a bright flare of light came from *The Book of Lost Treasures* Nick had laid on the ground next to the bag. Curiously, Nick opened the book, and there, under the map in large fiery letters, were the words, *"Treasure Found!"*

As Nick was sighing in relief, two things happened almost simultaneously. First, a bolt of lightning struck nearby, followed almost immediately by an earsplitting clap of thunder, and rain began coming down in blowing sheets. Second, even over the noise of the breaking storm, Nick heard the hysterical barking of the nearby dog reach new heights.

"What the hell are you barking at, you mangy critter?" Nick managed to hear, as a man's voice shouted over the blowing wind and rain. "No one can get a wink of sleep with the racket you're making!"

Frozen in consternation, Nick realized that the dog's barking was getting closer. The dog's owner must have untied it! That realization broke Nick's paralysis, and he vaulted out of the hole. Grabbing the duffel bag's straps, Nick stopped only long enough to make sure the book and strongbox were securely in the bag before he took off and sprinted across the field for his car. The rain was coming down so hard now that Nick could see only a few feet in front of him, even with the aid of the flashlight he had pulled from the duffel bag. A sudden flash of lightning revealed the barbwire fence a mere five or six feet from Nick, and as he tried to stop to prevent himself from running full tilt into it, his feet squirted out from under him on the muddy, slippery ground. Up in the air he went, landing with a wet *plop* on his back! Fortunately, the ground was soft from the rain, but even so, the jolting force of landing flat on his back knocked the breath out of him. As Nick lay there stunned, he heard the excited dog's barking now very close by. If the volume of the dog's barking was any indication, it had to be a large dog!

Fear forced Nick to roll onto his knees on the muddy ground. Trying to breathe, he cast about until he located his flashlight, which had rolled from his hand when he hit the ground.

Somehow, he had managed to hold on to the duffel bag, despite landing on his back. Desperately, he stood unsteadily on his feet and dropped the duffel bag on the other side of the barbwire fence. Pulling the barb wire apart, Nick attempted to push through the fence once again. However, this time, his shirt caught on one of the strands, and after a moment or two of trying to free it, he gave up, the fabric ripping as he frantically pulled it free. Picking up the duffel bag, he splashed through a ditch and onto the road, looking around wild-eyed in the darkness and pouring rain. Where was his car? He couldn't see it! Standing in the middle of the dirt road in the pounding rain, he pointed the flashlight up and down the road trying to find his car. The rain was still coming down so hard, however, that the flashlight's beam only penetrated a few feet into the darkness.

The barking howl of the dog once again galvanized Nick into action. It came from somewhere near the fence, so close that the dog would be on Nick in moments if he didn't find his car!

Stumbling down the dirt road, Nick swept the beam of the flashlight back and forth in front of him, like a blind man would swing a cane. Suddenly, a flash of lightning revealed a dark object in front of Nick. It was his car! Running to it, he placed the duffel bag on top of the car and tried to open it. The door wouldn't open! He had forgotten he had locked it! As Nick fumbled for the keys in his pocket, the frenzied barking of the dog now came from some- where in the blowing rain and darkness close by the road.

Ripping the keys from his pocket, Nick tried to locate the car key before the keys suddenly slipped from his rain-slick hands. Getting down on his hands and knees, he groped blindly on the muddy surface of the dirt road for the keys. Suddenly, another flash of lightning lit up the night sky and surrounding area, even as Nick's fingers closed triumphantly on the keys. Looking up as he grasped the keys, the flash of lightning briefly revealed an image of his worst fears to him! A huge, black Mastiff was staring at him no less than fifty yards down the road. Moments later, the triumphant howl of the large dog echoed through the dark, rainy night.

His teeth chattering in fear, Nick practically danced a jig as he desperately tried key after key in the car's lock. It was too dark to see, and he had shoved the flashlight in his pocket to fumble with the keys. He had only moments before the dog was upon him, and he could almost feel its teeth sinking into the soft flesh of his calf! Abruptly pulling the flashlight from his pocket, Nick shone it on the keys. There! There was the key! Almost sobbing in relief, he managed to get his shaking hands to push it in the lock.

Turning the key, he heard a *click* as the car door unlocked. Grabbing the duffel bag, Nick hurled it and the flashlight into the passenger seat. Slamming the door shut, he locked it and tried to get his wildly beating heart to slow down.

After a moment or two, Nick was able to breathe normally as he listened to the steady drumbeat of rain on the top of the car. Leaning forward, he was putting the key into the ignition to start the car, when he felt the little car lurch as a thumping noise came from the car's hood. Looking up, another flash of lightning revealed a nightmare image to him! Sharp white teeth from a pair of snarling jaws were mirrored in sharp relief on the other side of the windshield by the lightning flash! Nick shouted in terror at the sight. The dog had jumped onto the hood of Nick's car and was barking and snapping its jaws madly at him!

After several frantic tries, Nick managed to start the car and, engaging the gear, rolled down the road. Still barking furiously, the dog jumped off the Sprint's hood when it felt the car begin to move. Switching on the headlights, Nick began to drive down the road. Splashing through ruts and puddles, it wasn't until he was safely on the solid black asphalt of the highway leading back to D'Lo that he began to breathe easier.

The giddiness that Nick had felt when he first uncovered the strongbox returned to him, as it replaced his rapidly ebbing fear. By the time he turned into the Poolside Motel parking lot, his excitement was again at full throttle. He had done it! He had used the map in the book and found Buckley's gold!

His luck had finally changed!

Chapter 11

The rain was still coming down hard when Nick pulled into the Poolside Motel parking lot. He struggled out of the Sprint and went to the passenger-side door to open it and retrieve the duffel bag. Already thoroughly soaked, Nick paid the rain little heed. Fumbling around in his sodden pocket for the brass room key, Nick grabbed it and unlocked the door to his room. Entering his room, he turned on a light and kicked the door shut behind him. Placing the muddy, dripping duffel bag on the floor, Nick stripped off his wet clothes and tossed them on the bathroom floor. Standing in only a damp pair of boxer shorts, he grabbed a towel from the bathroom and attempted to dry off the best he could. Nick had left the air conditioner going full blast when he had left the room earlier to search for Efurd's gold, and the cold air brought goose pimples to Nick's wet skin. Nick had earlier emptied the duffel bag by dumping his clothes in it on the bed, and now he pawed through them with chattering teeth until he found an old T-shirt and sweat bottoms. Pulling them on, he immediately went to the duffel bag and dragged it over to where he sat on the edge of the bed.

Barely able to control his excitement, Nick pulled the sides of the duffel bag open. The shovel, book, and strongbox rested in a muddy puddle of water at the bottom of the bag. Seeing the book lying in the muddy water jolted Nick with the sudden realization that the water could ruin it! Quickly, he grabbed the book and held it aloft so he could examine it. Nick's jaw dropped as he saw not a drop of water or speck of mud marred the surface of *The Book of Lost Treasures*! Opening the book and flipping through the pages, he expected to find them water-stained. Instead, they were as crisp and clean as the first time he had opened the book and examined them! As for the map that had shown the directions and location of the hidden strongbox, it had disappeared, leaving nothing but blank pages. Nick's scrawled question, "*Where is the hidden strongbox of Efurd Buckley?*" had also disappeared. Shaking his head, Nick decided nothing about the strange book surprised him anymore, and he turned his attention to the strongbox.

The strongbox had cracks in its wooden sides, evidence of the hard landing from Nick slipping and falling in the rain by the barbwire fence. As Nick attempted to pull it from the duffel bag, its rotted and decayed base finally gave, the contents of the strongbox spilling from inside it to the room's carpeted floor. Wads of sodden, mildew-stained paper fell with a watery thud to land on the carpet. A metallic clinking came from two small leather bags that split as soon as they hit the floor, exposing coins that scattered from the impact.

Nick sat frozen for a moment, staring in disbelief at the pile of damp paper and coins. This … *this* was Efurd's hidden gold? *This* was the payroll Colonel Buckley had given his life and that of many of his men for? In bitter disappointment, Nick picked up a wad of paper and looked at it. Though damp and blackened with mildew, it took only a moment's inspection to determine it was paper currency.

Pulling a bill from the middle of the stack of currency, Nick saw that the surrounding bills had preserved it some- what. It was a twenty-dollar reserve note, and one side appeared a green color. Although history was not Nick's strong suit, he recalled from his high school U.S. history class that during the Civil War, paper money had been printed by the U.S. Treasury to pay for the war. Called "greenbacks" because the reverse side of the bills was printed in green ink, he had no doubt what he was holding in his hand were, in fact, greenbacks. The payroll for the Union soldiers at Vicksburg was made up of greenbacks! Even if the greenbacks were perfectly preserved instead of the mildewed, water-soaked mess before him, the paper money was worthless, nothing more than interesting historical artifacts of the long-ago tragedy of the Civil War!

Morosely, Nick turned his attention to the small pile of coins that had scattered on the carpet. Picking up a handful, he inspected them carefully. Darkened with age and corrosion, he saw the coins ranged from penny-sized shapes to dollar and even half-dollar sizes. Because the coins were so discolored with age, Nick had difficulty making out much detail from them. Pulling out his pocketknife, Nick used its sharp tip to scrape the surface of some of the larger coins. He was pleasantly surprised to see a silver-colored sheen on most of them, and on one coin, a yellowish- metallic glint resulted from the pocketknife's scraping!

Sitting back up on the edge of the bed, Nick considered the contents of the strongbox, as well as the results of the night's events. The paper money was, of course, useless.

However, the coins might prove of value, especially to coin collectors. Until they were properly cleaned, he had no way of knowing *how* valuable! *Who knows,* he thought to himself, *maybe there's at least one rare coin in the bunch I could sell that could make this a* very *profitable night!*

Looking at *The Book of Lost Treasures* lying beside him on the bed, it suddenly occurred to Nick that the book had successfully led him to a lost treasure! In fact, according to Lilly, the location of Efurd Buckley's hidden strongbox survived countless attempts down through the years to find it, and none had discovered it until Nick had stumbled across the strange treasure book! That meant … that meant that it could be used *again* to find the *next* lost treasure! This realization caused possibilities to rush into Nick's mind in such a torrent that he could only blink in dumbfounded shock.

When finally he was able to gain some measure of control of his racing thoughts, one thing became certain to him.

He was going to be rich!

The next day, Nick rose early and ate a hearty breakfast. Lilly waited on him and commented approvingly about his appetite. Grinning from ear to ear, Nick nodded at Lilly and, picking up his ticket, paid the cashier for the meal. Before he left the restaurant, he poked his head in the kitchen and spotted Jed in his apron, frying eggs and sausage. Thanking him for his help in getting his tire replaced, he told Jed he was checking out. Wiping his hands on the greasy apron, Jed shook Nick's hand and told him to come back soon and visit them in D'Lo. Promising that he would, Nick went to the motel office, turned in his room key, and paid for the two nights he had stayed at the motel. Pulling out of the parking lot, rather than turn south on the highway that would take him to Gulfport and Biloxi, Nick turned north and back toward Jackson.

He was going home.

Six hours later, Nick turned onto the dirt road leading to his trailer. Looking at his watch, Nick saw it was three o'clock in the afternoon. Parking under the car awning, he hopped out of the little car and waded through the calf-high grass to the door of the trailer. Unlocking the door, he was greeted by a blast of hot, stuffy air. Turning the little window unit air conditioner on full blast, he left the door open to let the trailer air out while he retrieved his things from the car. The coins, paper money, book, and clothes he had stuffed all together in the duffel bag, which he placed on the small kitchen table. The painting he leaned against the wall in the small hallway leading to the bed loft. Digging around in a nearby drawer, he managed to find a box of Ziplock bags. Taking the coins and greenbacks, he separated them and placed them in the Ziplock bags. Satisfied with his handiwork, he pulled the mysterious treasure book from the duffel bag and, tossing the bag on the floor, sat behind the little table and studied the book.

In truth, Nick had thought of little else other than *The Book of Lost Treasures* as he had driven back to Pleasant Mountain. He had lost count of how many plans he had created and discarded in his mind on how to best to use the book. The problem was, he knew so little about the book's capabilities that he didn't know where to go next with it!

All he had to go on were the rules governing the book that, even now, were still glowing within it! His worst fear was that the book had been a one-shot opportunity and that it wouldn't work for him again. What he needed was another test of the book's ability to find the *next* lost treasure! Then, and only then, could he be sure of the book's reliability.

Lost in thought, Nick abruptly sat up and snapped his fingers. He knew of the perfect test for the book! A small portable TV rested on the counter in front of him, and he had lost the remote for it several months ago. He knew it *had* to be in the trailer somewhere, but despite looking everywhere for it, he had never been able to find it. Opening *The Book of Lost Treasures* excitedly, Nick considered momentarily how he would frame his request. Finally, he carefully wrote, "*Where is the lost TV remote in Nick Hollister's trailer?*"

Immediately, a glow appeared from behind the page Nick had written on. Turning the page, Nick's eyes were once again treated to the sight of a map. This one, however, showed in immaculate detail the inside of his trailer. A glowing line led from a blinking red dot located exactly where Nick was sitting at within the trailer. Pulling the map closer to his face, Nick perused it carefully. It seemed to lead to one of a series of three drawers built in stair-stacked fashion next to the tiny kitchen sink directly across from Nick. Looking at the map, Nick saw it was, in fact, the *top* drawer indicated on the map. Quickly, he put the book down on the small table and, getting up, pulled the drawer open. Inside the drawer was an untidy pile of dishtowels that Nick had crammed in there. Pawing through them, he began pulling them out one by one until his fingers brushed against a solid object located at the back of the drawer. Eagerly, his fingers closed on the object, and pulling it out, Nick held triumphantly aloft an oblong object made of black plastic in front of him. It was the remote he had lost months ago! Somehow it had fallen into the drawer, one of the few areas he hadn't searched within the trailer! Immediately, a bright light issued from *The Book of Lost Treasures.* Picking the book up off the table, Nick saw—glowing in a light so bright it caused him to shade his eyes—the words *"Treasure Found!"* beneath the map.

Giving a whoop of exultation, Nick danced around the trailer. He had done it! The book had revealed another lost object to him! After a while, the excited rush left him, and he sat back down behind the table, still holding the remote. Putting it down on the table, he picked up *The Book of Lost Treasures* and looked upon it in wonder. There was still so much he *didn't* know about the mysterious book! There was, however, one person that might be able to give him some insight about *The Book of Lost Treasures.* Pulling out his wallet, Nick dug around and found the business card Hank Harper had given him when he had purchased the painting from him. Locating the phone number of *Harper's Hidden Treasures* on the card, Nick pulled his cell from his pocket and turned it on. He had left it off the entire time he had been staying in D'Lo, afraid that Mark or Patti would call checking up on him. Looking at his watch, he saw that it was after four o'clock in the afternoon. *Hank should still be in*, he thought to himself as he punched in the number of the antique store on his cell.

Listening to the phone ring, he wondered just exactly what he would say to Hank. He couldn't just say he had found a book that had mystical powers to find lost treasures, or Hank would think he was crazy! Before he could think on it more, a familiar voice came over his cell.

"Harper's Hidden Treasures! How may I help you?"

"Hank! This is Nick, Nick Hollister … you know, the guy who was in your store a few days ago. I bought a painting from you."

"Nick! Of course! How did your girlfriend like the painting?" Hank's cheerful voice asked.

Nick blinked at Hank's question. He suddenly realized he hadn't thought of Lisa at all over the past few days.

"Er, well, the fact is, we broke up, Hank. I still have the painting."

"I'm so sorry, Nick. I was hoping you two could smooth things over. Look at the bright side, however. There are plenty of fish in the ocean, as they say, and you did get a *great* deal on the painting!"

"Thanks, Hank. I appreciate that. As a matter of fact, it's the painting I wanted to talk to you about."

There was a momentary pause. Finally, Hank said, "I see. Is there something wrong with the painting? You're not wanting to get your money back, are you? All sales are final, Nick. It says so right on the sales slip—"

"No, no!" Nick interjected hastily as he interrupted Hank. "I don't want to return the painting! You see, there … there was something … something *inside* the painting. As I was moving the painting from my car, I felt something sliding around within the frame and the painting. When I took the back off the frame, a … a book fell out!"

There was another momentary silence over the cell, and Nick could hear Hank's smooth, even breathing.

Finally, Hank said, "What kind of book? Can you describe it for me?" Quickly, Nick described the book in as much detail as possible. However, he deliberately left out everything else about the book—from the glowing writing, to how a map had appeared that had led him to the stolen payroll Colonel Buckley had buried in an open field.

When he had finished describing the book, Nick asked, "Do you know anything about this book, Hank?"

"Not really," Hank admitted over the phone. "However, I know a few rare book collectors and dealers I can ask, and if all else fails, there is always the Internet that might provide some clues about the book." Pausing, Hank continued, "You say the name of this book is *The Book of Lost Treasures?* Tell you what. I'll do some checking and get back with you as soon as I find out something."

Nick thanked Hank and clicked off. Sitting at the table, he considered his conversation with Hank. Although Hank had offered to try and discover all he could about the strange book, Nick couldn't shake a nagging feeling he had gotten from their conversation.

Why … why did he feel Hank already *knew* all about *The Book of Lost Treasures*?

Chapter 12

Nick spent the next hour cleaning up the small trailer and piling his dirty clothes in a plastic trash bag to take to the washateria. By the time he had finished, the tiny window unit air conditioner had lowered the temperature in the trailer to a tolerable, although not cool, level. Stripping off his clothes, he took a cold shower and changed into shorts, flip flops, and T-shirt. Sitting back by the table, he called Mark to let him know he was back in town. The phone rang a couple of times before Mark answered it. "Nick!" Mark said immediately. "What's going on? Where have you been? You said you would call! Patti and I have been trying for the past two days to call you, but you had your stupid phone turned off!" The questions and comments tumbled out of Mark in a pent-up rush, and by his accusatory tone, Nick knew he and Patti had been extremely worried about him. He felt guilty that he had caused such worry and consternation for his friends, and he vowed to himself to somehow make it up to them.

"I … I'm sorry, Mark. I just needed to be alone for a while. I … I just needed to sort things out. I hope you and Patti can forgive me."

"Are you kidding? Of course, we forgive you! Just don't do it again, or we'll have to break both your legs!" Mark said jokingly. Relieved, Nick could almost hear the tension drain from Mark's voice.

Nick had given a great deal of thought on what to do with the treasure book. Grand schemes had flown in and out of his mind like birds in a rookery. What he needed was a second opinion from someone with a more ordered and logical mind than his and from someone he could trust. Mark, his best friend, fit the bill on all counts.

"Mark … can you … can you come over to my trailer? I … I have something I need to … to show you."

"Sure. I'll just tell Daddy I'm leaving work a little early today. Is something wrong?" Mark asked, as concern began to creep into his tone of voice. Mark's father owned the local State Farm Insurance franchise, and Mark had joined his father once he had graduated from college.

"No, no! Nothing is wrong!" Nick said hastily. "I … I just need your advice on something. That's … that's all." Nick finished lamely.

"Okay. I'll call Patti and tell her you're back and everything is fine, and then I'll run right over. Are you sure … there's nothing wrong?"

"Mark, nothing is wrong!" Nick said exasperated. "In fact, I have something … *wonderful* to show you! Just get over here as soon as you can!"

His curiosity aroused, Mark assured Nick he would leave immediately, and the connection went dead. Putting his cell on the table, a vestige of a smile played across Nick's face.

Was Mark going to be surprised or what!

Less than a half hour later, Nick heard Mark's car arrive at the trailer. Pulling the curtain aside from a window, he saw a late a late-model Ford Expedition roll to a stop beside the trailer. As Mark got out of the dark blue SUV, Nick met him at the door, the two clapping each other on the back enthusiastically before settling around the small table in Nick's trailer.

"Okay, Nick, what's up?" Mark said curiously. "All the way over here, I've been trying to imagine all the things you could possibly want to show me. When I told Patti, she wanted to leave work and come with me! In fact, she probably would have if she hadn't scheduled to take a deposition from a client." Patti worked as a paralegal in a local law firm, a job she had acquired shortly after she and Mark had moved back to Pleasant Mountain.

"Just keep an open mind, Mark," Nick said firmly. "What I'm about to tell you … what I am about to *show you* defies rational explanation!"

A groan escaped from Mark's lips. "Not another wild scheme, Nick! How many times do you have to be burned? Do you remember the so-called 'millionaire' you met at Walmart? The one who claimed to have cornered the fresh chili market in New Mexico and was willing to let you buy in to it? You gave him $3,000 from the sale of your mother's doublewide trailer! Have you seen or heard from him again? No, please don't—"

"It's not like that, Mark!" Nick said as he cut Mark off. "I'm not talking about giving anybody money! Look … just hear me out, okay?" Reluctantly, Mark nodded.

Taking a plastic shopping bag from underneath the table, Nick took out the Ziplock bags containing the paper currency and coins he had retrieved from the strongbox and arranged them in a neat row before Mark's astonished eyes.

"Where … where did this come from?" he demanded.

"Before I answer that, I want you to take the money and coins out of the bags and examine them," Nick said firmly. Nodding, Mark took a stack of greenbacks out of one of the Ziplock bags and started looking at them one by one. Then he took the coins out of another bag, spreading them out on the table's flat surface as he peered closely at each of them. After examining the coins and paper money for five minutes or so, Mark looked up in puzzlement at Nick.

"All this money … the currency, the coins, it's … it's all *old.* I mean really old! It's hard to make out much detail on a lot of the coins, but on the ones I can make the date out on, they're all … they're all dated *before the Civil War*! Where … where did you find them?"

"I found them buried in a strongbox in the middle of a hay meadow in D'Lo, Mississippi. I was led there by a map that appeared in this book!" Nick replied as he picked up *The Book of Lost Treasures* and pushed it across the table. Dumbfounded, Mark picked up the book and began to examine it.

After leafing through the book, a confused look appeared on Mark's face. "I don't see any map in this book. In fact, except from some writing on the first page, all the pages are blank. Where's the map you said was in the book?"

The moment of truth had arrived. Taking a deep breath, Nick related to Mark everything that had happened to him since he had bought the painting at Harper's Antiques and had found the mysterious book inside it. He told him how he had discovered the book's mystical ability to find lost objects or treasures while at the Poolside Motel in D'Lo and how a map had appeared within the book that had led him to the lost strongbox of Colonel Efurd Buckley. He left nothing out, and when he had finished, Mark ran a nervous hand through his hair.

"You … *believe* this … book led you to … to this money, which you claim was found in a buried strongbox?" Mark asked in a tone of voice that one would use when talking to a child that just claimed to have an invisible friend over to play.

"I don't 'claim' anything, Mark! I *know*!" Nick replied heatedly. "It all happened; it's all fact! Look! Look at this!" Nick exclaimed as he held the TV remote aloft. "I lost this remote months ago! I asked the book to find it for me and it did! It had fallen into a kitchen drawer, and a map in the book led me straight to it!"

"Nick, this is crazy! Do you hear yourself? Do you know what you're saying? This is me, Mark, your best friend you're talking to! If it was anybody else, they would already have you committed! C'mon man, what *really* happened? Where did you get this money?"

"Crazy, am I?" Nick shouted at Mark, his face growing red. Turning *The Book of Lost Treasures* to the first page, he gestured to the glowing writing that listed the rules of the book's usage. "Then how do you explain this! Look at the writing! It's glowing, Mark, glowing as if it had its own inner light! How do you explain *that*?"

Gesturing helplessly, Mark said, "It could be written in some sort of phosphorescent substance like they put on watch faces, or it could be like one of those Hallmark cards that lights up and sings to you when you open it, or—"

"No, I've already thought of that, and I have examined every inch of the book, every inch, I tell you!" Nick said, his voice steadily rising in anger. "There is nothing on or in the book that can cause the writing! Besides, I already told you that once I wrote the lost treasure I was searching for in the book, a map to the treasure appeared on the next page! The proof is right in front of you! Where do you think that old money and coins came from? If you were any kind of friend like you claim to be, you would believe me!" Seeing Mark's stricken face, Nick, with great effort, managed to get his emotions under control.

"Look," he finally said softly, "I know it sounds like crazy loony tunes stuff. But it's true, and I have no one else I can talk to, no one else I can trust! It all happened *exactly* the way I told you, Mark, I swear! I mean, maybe there is another explanation for how a treasure map appears inexplicably on request in this book, but I have racked my brain, and *I can't come up with a reasonable explanation*! If *you* can, please be my guest!"

For several moments, they both sat in silence. Finally, Mark sighed and said, "All right. Just for the sake of argument, let's say this book *does* have some sort of … of *mystical* power to locate lost objects or treasure. What is it you want me to do, Nick?"

Eagerly, Nick hunched forward. "I want you to help me plan on how to use *The Book of Lost Treasures*! Don't you see? We could all become rich beyond our wildest dreams! Think about it, Mark! Think! How many valuable things, how many priceless objects have been lost down through the years? Jewelry, money, works of art, buried treasure, the list is endless! But where to start, and how do we prioritize the list of things we ask the book to reveal the location of? It boggles the mind!"

"If that's all you need, Nick, why do you need my help? I mean, you listed some pretty good things already you could ask the book to locate for you. Your imagination is as good as mine!"

Nodding, Nick said, "You're right, Mark. But I've given it a lot of thought, and I've decided it *isn't* that simple! For one, there are the rules the book lists that must be followed. I misspelled one letter in Efurd Buckley's first name, and no map appeared until I realized I had misspelled his name and changed it. That drove home to me that the rules must be followed precisely and that any request of the book must be carefully and painstakingly considered. For example, one rule states that before you can request the location of the next lost treasure, you must have found the previous lost treasure requested from the book. What happens if the lost treasure you request happens to be in a location where it is impossible to recover? Like maybe a shipwreck full of gold located in depths so great, no one can get to it, or maybe a lost gold mine buried under tons of rocks from a landslide! If a mistake is made in the request, you could be stopped before ever beginning!"

Although he still didn't believe the book possessed any "unusual" powers, Mark found himself beginning to be infected by Nick's enthusiasm, and he began to warm to the task presented by the book. "What would happen if you asked for the location of a lost object or treasure that didn't exist?" he asked Nick.

"Exactly!" Nick blurted exuberantly. "I mean, I've thought of that, and it isn't really covered by the rules of the book, so I assume nothing would happen, just like when I misspelled Efurd Buckley's name, but its stuff like that where two heads are better than one, you know? That's why I need your help!"

Mark nodded thoughtfully. Checking his watch, he saw it was after five o'clock. "I need to get home, Nick. Patti's probably already there and is bursting at the seams with questions about you."

"Just don't tell her about the book or anything," Nick pleaded. "At least for now. I don't want her thinking I'm crazy too."

Laughing, Mark said, "It's too late for that, Nick. She already *knows* you're crazy! But I'll keep this our little secret for the time being." Hesitating, Mark picked up one of the Ziplock bags of coins, a thoughtful look on his face.

"Daddy is an amateur coin collector. He bought a metal detector a couple of years ago, and now he goes all over the place searching for old coins. There's a coin dealer in Texarkana he has bought coins from and sold coins to. Why don't you let me take these coins you found and a bundle of this paper money and see what that coin dealer thinks of them? Maybe he can give an appraisal of their worth. I have to drive to Texarkana tomorrow to see a client, and I would be glad to take them by his shop."

"Thanks! That would be great!" Nick gushed.

"In the meantime, let me think about what you told me about the book. I'll try to come up with some ideas of my own, and then I'll run them by you."

Both men got up, and Nick saw Mark to his car. After Mark's car disappeared down the dirt road, Nick returned to the trailer and sat down again at the table, reflecting on his conversation with Mark. It hadn't gone as well as he would have liked, but then again, what did he expect?

Were he in Mark's shoes, he probably would have reacted in the same way, not to mention that Nick's checkered past when it came to wild schemes practically begged for healthy skepticism toward any ideas of his.

Sighing, Nick picked up the strange book. Looking at it, he turned it over and over in his hands. This was his ticket, his ticket to finally making something of himself! With Mark on board, albeit reluctantly, he just knew the sky was the limit! *Brighter days are definitely ahead,* he thought as, whistling, he put the book down and got up to make himself a sandwich.

Brighter days indeed!

Chapter 13

The next day dawned sunny and glorious as Nick, yawning, got up. He had slept like a baby, and for the first time in years, he looked forward to the coming day and, indeed, the coming week eagerly. Eating a hasty breakfast of cereal, he quickly went to the car awning, where an old Sears Craftsman riding lawn mower was located next to his car. Usually a job he dreaded, he tackled mowing the high grass cheerfully without a second thought. With over an acre of grass to mow in and around the trailer and workshop, it took Nick the better part of two hours to finish. After weed eating the hard-to-mow areas, it was almost noon and time for lunch. Stowing the weed eater back into the work- shop, Nick headed for the trailer, intent on shedding his sweaty, grass-stained clothes and taking a shower before eating lunch.

As Nick opened the door, he heard his cell phone ringing. Wiping the sweat out of his eyes with his sleeve, he picked his phone up where it was lying on the table and answered it.

"Hello?"

"Nick!" A cheerful voice sounded over the phone. "I managed to dig up some information on that book you found."

It took a moment or two before Nick's brain registered that the voice on the phone was Hank's.

"Hank! What did you find out?" Nick asked eagerly. Briefly, he puzzled over how Hank had managed to uncover information about the mysterious book so quickly, especially since he had only spoken to him about it the day before. Then, Hank interrupted his musings.

"Your book, it seems, has quite a history! I have a buddy on the East Coast whose bookstore deals exclusively with rare and, er, what you would call, 'unusual' books. I called and described the book to him. He called me back less than an hour later with the legend of *The Book of Lost Treasures*."

"Legend? You mean this book is … is like *famous*?" Nick asked incredulously.

"Well, I don't know if you would describe it as famous," Hank said chuckling. "It's not like there are many people who even know of its existence. I was lucky that one of the first people I asked about the book actually had some knowledge of it."

"Oh," Nick said, crestfallen.

"Anywho, as I said, the book has quite a history; one, in fact, that dates back to the mid 1700s. You want to hear it?"

"Are you kidding? Of course!" Nick blurted. Hearing Hank's laughter over the cell, Nick realized the diminutive antique dealer was baiting him again.

He could almost hear him saying, "Gotcha," and pointing at Nick as he had done at his store. All of this Nick quickly forgot as Hank launched into his story.

"In the mid 1700s, Spain, France, and England were involved in a struggle for supremacy in Europe, as well as on the high seas. Although alliances could and did change continuously, at this point in history, England and France were allied against Spain. Enter Captain Augustus McGregor. McGregor was the fifth son of a minor Scottish noble and, with no inheritance or future to look forward to in Scotland, took service in the British Navy.

A man of unquestioned valor and courage, his leadership skills led to his rapid rise in the ranks until he captained his own ship. Officially commissioned as a 'privateer' in the British Navy, McGregor's ship was given letters of marque to prey upon the Spanish galleons that plied between Spain and the Spanish possessions in the New World.

Much of the gold and silver that Spain was using to finance their intrigues in Europe were transported on these treasure ships, and the British hoped to choke this off through the use of privateers.

"Over the next few years, McGregor's ship and crew had minor successes but nothing spectacular, as the few Spanish ships they managed to capture and board contained little gold or silver. One morning, however, they came across a huge galleon escorted by two smaller Spanish warships. In a sea battle that lasted most of the day, McGregor displayed the fearlessness and cunning that had led to his rapid promotion, and he managed to sink both Spanish warships.

With his own ship severely damaged, McGregor was still able to catch up with the much slower galleon that was attempting to flee. Avoiding the galleon's cannons,

McGregor and his crew approached the aft side of the galleon and, in an unheard-of maneuver, managed to get close enough to throw grappling hooks over the aft side of the galleon and board her. Fierce hand-to-hand fighting ensued until finally, the remaining crew and officers of the galleon surrendered.

"Tying his ship alongside the galleon, the victorious Captain McGregor began an immediate inspection of the contents of the galleon. What he saw staggered him: the ship's holds were literally bursting with gold, silver, and precious gems mined or stolen from the initiatives of Spain's New World possessions! McGregor had gone from the penniless younger son of a minor noble to being wealthy beyond his wildest dreams! So caught up was he over the enormous wealth before him that he almost missed a small door covered by a thick curtain at the back of the hold. Locked and bolted shut, McGregor had to retrieve the key from the body of the slain captain of the galleon in order to open the door. As he unlocked and opened the door, the sight his eyes beheld rivaled even that of the king's ransom of treasure in the hold! A naked, young woman lay partially submerged in a large wooden tub of seawater!

"The woman was stunningly beautiful. Her eyes were the aquamarine blue of the sea, waist-long hair as white as sea foam, and skin as pale as milk. As McGregor moved closer, he was shocked to see that the 'normal' body of the woman ended at the waist. Instead of legs, a fish tail grew from the woman, complete with scales that glinted in the dim light of the room with an iridescent sheen! The young woman was a mermaid! However, as McGregor peered closer in incredulous fascination, he saw that some of the scales had begun to fall off the mermaid's tail, and there were patches here and there totally devoid of scales.

These areas barren of scales were raw-looking and covered with a ragged, mucous-like tissue. Abruptly, McGregor realized the mermaid was dying. Although a battle-hardened ship's captain, McGregor's heart went out immediately to the beautiful young mermaid. Angrily, he returned to the deck of the galleon and questioned the prisoners there about the captive mermaid.

"Most of the galleon's officers had been killed in the fierce fighting that led to its capture by McGregor, and none of the remaining crew seemed to know what McGregor was talking about. Finally, the first mate, who had survived the battle, came forward and told McGregor the tale he had been told by the captain concerning the mermaid. The captain had said that the mermaid had been washed up on shore in Hispaniola after a particularly fierce storm. Unconscious, she had been captured by natives, who presented her to the Spanish authorities on the island. Carried onto the galleon in the dead of night so that none of the superstitious crew could see her, the mermaid was to be transported back to Spain, where she was to be presented to the Spanish king and queen. Amazingly, the ship's captain had been able to talk and converse with the mermaid, who, he claimed, could speak fluent Spanish. The first mate had overheard the captain refer to the mermaid on several occasions as *La Princesa de las Sirenas*, or 'Princess of the Mermaids.' Whatever she was called, the first mate had spat, the mermaid had brought them nothing but bad luck since coming aboard the galleon.

Sudden storms, mysterious illnesses, freak accidents—the galleon had suffered them all—and he begged McGregor to kill the mermaid for all their sakes.

"McGregor considered what the first mate had said, and although he was no believer in curses or ill luck, he had seen fear in the first mate's eyes. Mariners as a whole, he knew, were a superstitious lot, and he feared his own crew would react as the first mate had if they knew a mermaid was aboard the ship. He decided no one would see or interact with the mermaid but himself. Returning to the mermaid's room, he locked the door with the dead captain's key and went about the business of completing the securing of the ship. When all of the Spanish prisoners were finally chained and manacled, McGregor ordered a celebration, and rum flowed freely. Around midnight, with most of his crew snoring in a drunken stupor, McGregor took the dead captain's key and, once more, unlocked the door to the mermaid's room. Covering the mermaid's tail with canvas sacking, he picked her up and carried her out onto the galleon's deck. Pausing only long enough to make sure he was unobserved, McGregor gently placed the mermaid in a dinghy, secured by a block and tackle to the side of the ship. Climbing into the dingy with the mermaid, he grabbed a rope and lowered the boat to the water's edge. Once in the water, McGregor rowed a short distance from where the huge galleon wallowed in the sea, and then stopped.

"It was a clear, moonless night, and a million stars cast their dim light as McGregor removed the canvas from the mermaid's tail and then helped her into the water, telling her she was free as he did so. Expecting her to immediately flee, he was surprised when, instead, the mermaid remained in the water next to the dingy. Then, in perfect English, she told him that he had saved her life and that she owed him a life debt that must be rewarded. Surging abruptly out of the water, the mermaid grasped the side of the dingy and kissed McGregor on the lips before returning to the sea. With a final flip of her tail, the mermaid disappeared from sight. The kiss tasted of salt, wind, and sea, and its memory would remain with McGregor the rest of his life.

"Returning to England, McGregor was hailed as a hero, and when he retired from the British Navy less than ten years later at the relatively young age of thirty-two, he was fabulously wealthy. McGregor spent the next several years acquiring estates in the Northern Highlands of Scotland, as well as near his beloved sea in southern Scotland by the Firth of Lorne.

Deciding to demolish the old homes on these estates, McGregor built for himself large ornate manors: one on the shore of a loch in the Highlands, and one overlooking the Atlantic Ocean by the Firth of Lorne. All of thirty-six years old when his estates were finished, McGregor was unmarried and restless, the mermaid's kiss never far from his thoughts.

"One morning in late spring, McGregor was strolling alone along the sand and rock-strewn beach near his estate by the Firth of Lorne. A storm had blown through the night before, and all manner of seaweed, shells, driftwood, and other debris from the sea had washed onto the beach. The storm had cleansed the air, and it was one of those rare days in Scotland where the sky was clear and crisp with not so much as a stray cloud to mar the unbroken march of blue. Appreciating the sight, McGregor slowly made his way along the beach, negotiating around the larger rocks and boulders. One particularly large boulder the size of a building blocked his way, and he found he had to practically step in the water lapping from the ocean to skirt around it. As he finally edged around the boulder, he saw a sight that stopped him in his tracks: by the water's edge, was the mermaid princess sitting on a water-smoothed rock! With her long white hair blowing in the gentle breeze—she was more beautiful than before—he ran to her. Without hesitation, he pulled her to him, and once more, they kissed. When they finally broke apart, she held up an object she was holding in her hand. It was a book, bound in sharkskin and titled *The Book of Lost Treasures.*

"The mermaid princess explained to McGregor that the book was his reward for saving her life. She further explained how the book had magical properties to find lost treasures. She finished with a cryptic warning to be careful what he asked for, saying that while the book would always deliver what was asked of it, the results were not always what were wished for or expected. Puzzled, McGregor questioned her about the warning, but all she would say was that human desires, including greed, sometimes misplaced that which *should* be valued most highly, a lesson mankind never seemed to learn, despite the repeated conflict and heartache it had caused. With that, they shared one more lingering kiss, and the mermaid princess slipped off into the water. He never saw her again. A few years later, McGregor married and started a family, and the book became something of a family heirloom and conversation piece before it inexplicably disappeared in the late 1700s. From time to time, it has been said to resurface in various places around the world, thus renewing the legend of the book."

Pausing to catch his breath, Hank said, "Of course, a book that can reveal so-called lost treasures is nonsense, but it still makes for quite a fascinating story, wouldn't you say? By the way, my buddy said he would pay you a handsome price for the book, should you want to sell it."

So caught up was he in the story Hank was telling him, Nick almost missed this last part.

"What? No, no, I don't want to sell the book!" Nick said. As he thought about what Hank had told him concerning the legend of the book, he was struck by how … by how *familiar* Hank seemed to be with the tale. It was almost as if Hank was giving him a first-person account of what had happened.

"You know, you seem to be pretty knowledgeable about the legend or story of the book, Hank," Nick commented curiously.

"Well, I guess I would since I have the personal account of Captain Augustus McGregor before me!" Hank said chuckling. "You see, McGregor wrote the whole story down in an old ship's logbook that he kept. He presented it to his wife and children on his deathbed, and now it's part of the McGregor Clan's historical archives. My East Coast friend e-mailed the entire account to me last night, and I can tell you, it makes for an interesting read! You are more than welcome to come by my store, and I'll give it to you."

"I might take you up on that sometime," Nick replied. "Hey, thanks for finding all this stuff out about the book for me. I owe you one."

"Happy to help, Nick! Well, don't stay a stranger. Come by the store and see me sometime!" Nick promised he would, and Hank clicked off.

Nick sat in the trailer, listening to the little window unit air conditioner blow while he thought about what Hank had told him of the legend of the book. Getting up, he pulled open a drawer where he had hidden the book and looked at it. The grayish, abrasive surface would fit with Hank's description that it was made of sharkskin. The highly stylized type of writing, with its exaggerated loops and whorls within the book (which had always struck him as rather old-fashioned or odd), now made sense to him. It was writing from almost three hundred years ago! But if *that* part of the book's legend was correct, was *all* of McGregor's account true also?

Did he really save the life of a mermaid princess, and did she really present him *The Book of Lost Treasures* as a reward for saving her life?

As Nick mused over these questions, his cell phone rang again. Thinking that Hank was calling him back about some detail he had forgotten about the mysterious book, he was surprised when answering the cell, he heard Mark's voice.

"Nick!" Mark's excited voice practically shouted. "I'm on my way back from Texarkana. You have *got* to meet me at my office! I'll be there in about forty-five minutes!"

"What's going on, Mark?" Nick asked curiously. "You sound like you just won the lottery or something!"

"Not me, Nick, you! You remember the coin dealer I told you I was going to show those old coins to? Well, he took one look at the coins and offered me *ten thousand dollars for them*!"

"No!" Nick cried, as it was his turn to shout into the cell.

"I'm not kidding! I possess a cashier's check for ten thousand dollars, and all you have to do is endorse it, and it's all yours! Listen, just meet me at my office okay? Oh, and one more thing."

"What?" Nick asked in giddy excitement.

"Bring *The Book of Lost Treasures* with you!"

Chapter 14

Nick set a personal record for the fastest shower he had ever taken in the Airstream's tiny, cramped shower stall. Throwing on an old T-shirt and faded jeans, he didn't bother with socks or tennis shoes and, instead, crammed a pair of flip-flops on his feet. Hurtling out of the trailer, he slowed only long enough to grab *The Book of Lost Treasures* and to lock the door. Then he sprinted to his car, managing to lose one of his flip-flops in the process. Cursing, he hopped on one foot before finally managing to slip the offending flip-flop back on his foot and make his way to the car. Starting the Sprint, he backed out from under the car awning and drove the little car down the dirt road as fast as he dared. Once on the paved county road, he floored the accelerator and drove to Mark's office.

Fifteen minutes later, Nick pulled into the parking lot in front of the State Farm Insurance office, which was located in a newer business section on the south side of

Pleasant Mountain. The building was actually a large house that had been remodeled into a suite of offices, complete with a reception area. Modern brick facing had been added to the house's façade, as well as large picture windows that overlooked the parking lot. Two white wooden columns flanked the oversized front door, which was itself painted a brilliant white. A shiny, old-fashioned brass knocker was fixed to the middle of the door, and a matching brass doorknob provided entry. Neatly trimmed shrubs, oleanders, and dwarf crape myrtles were planted around the office building, and a sign beside the road read "State Farm Insurance: Agents Larry and Mark Chambers."

As Nick got out of his car, he saw that despite his haste, Mark had beat him to his office, as his Expedition was already parked in its customary spot. Hurrying through the door, Nick was greeted by Susan Wolfe, a petite brunette in her late thirties who served as the receptionist for Mark and his father, Larry.

"He's waiting for you in his office, Nick," she said warmly. Nodding, Nick hurried toward the suite of offices located behind Susan's desk. Stopping before a partially closed door, he rapped on it once before entering.

"Nick!" Mark said as he looked up from where he was seated at his desk. "Have a seat!" he added excitedly as he motioned toward a comfortable-looking leather chair next to his desk.

Sitting down, Nick looked around Mark's office. The large desk Mark sat behind was, as usual, immaculate, with not a pen, piece of paper, or paper clip out of place. The desk's wooden surface was polished to a rich sheen, with desk accoutrements, such as tape dispenser, stapler,

Post-it notes, as well as a pen and pencil holder, all strategically arranged for maximum efficiency.

Several family pictures in silver frames were grouped in triangular fashion next to the phone on Mark's desk. Mounted on the wall behind Mark's desk was a montage of pictures of him and Patti, with each picture and its frame perfectly aligned with the picture next to it. Although not anal to the point of becoming irritating, Mark *definitely* liked things neat, clean, and orderly. As he continued looking around Mark's office, with its dust-free curtains flanking spot-free windows, Nick wondered for the umpteenth time about how he and Mark had ever become friends. Mark's life was like his office—neat and orderly—while Nick's life was unpredictable and chaotic.

"Look!" Mark said, interrupting Nick's thoughts. Excitedly, he held a cashier's check up before him. Practically snatching it from Mark's hands, the breath caught in Nick's throat as he saw the total of *$10,000* printed on the check. It was true! The coin dealer had offered $10,000 for the old coins he had found in the strongbox!

"What … what should I do, Mark?" he was finally able to ask, his voice barely above a whisper.

"Do? With the check? That's easy! You take the money, Nick!" Mark said laughing as he took a pen from his pocket and handed it to Nick. Nodding, Nick forced his hands to stop trembling as he endorsed the check. When he had finished, he stared dumbly at the cashier's check, still not quite believing he was now $10,000 richer. Vaguely, he saw Mark consult a business card before he called the coin dealer and told him the transaction for the old coins was complete.

When he hung up, Mark got up and, walking to Nick, clapped him heartily on the back.

"Congratulations, Nick! You're now the proud new owner of a ten-thousand-dollar check! Any ideas what you are going to do with the money?"

Shaking his head, Nick managed to say, "I don't … I don't know, Mark. I can still hardly believe it!"

"Well, it's your business, I suppose, but Nick, please take my advice and put the money in the bank. Don't spend it on any wild schemes, like emu farms, worm farms, or Tabasco pepper crops."

"Don't worry, Mark. I've learned my lesson," Nick replied, grinning.

Although Mark nodded, Nick knew he was far from assured.

Rubbing his hands together, Mark changed the subject by asking, "Did you bring the book?" Nodding, Nick pulled *The Book of Lost Treasures* from a small satchel he was carrying. As he handed it over to Mark, he saw him begin to study the book with a newfound interest.

"What's going on, Mark? I thought you didn't believe what I told you about the book?" Nick commented smugly.

Idly, Mark nodded as he turned to the page that listed the rules of the mysterious book. "It's just … it's just that I've had a lot of time to think about the story you've told me, Nick. Mind you, I'm still far from convinced, but I can't come up with an explanation of how you found those greenbacks and old coins. The coin dealer said there were Liberty Dollars, Seated Liberty Half Dollars and Dimes, and even a few Coronet Gold Dollars and Gold Indian Head Dollars in the old coins you found. In fact, the coin dealer said he hadn't seen such an impressive collection of coins since the last coin convention he attended in St. Louis! In other words, there is absolutely no way you could have 'accidentally' stumbled across those coins!"

"Then you *do* believe me!" Nick crowed.

"I didn't say that!" Mark said hastily. "However, just … just for the sake of argument, let's say this book does possess some … some *latent* ability to find things. What I propose to do is to *test* the book's capabilities in locating lost objects."

"But I've already done that!" Nick protested. "Remember, I told you it found my lost TV remote!"

"Yes, I know that, Nick, but *I* wasn't there when the book supposedly found the remote, and *I'm* the one that needs to be convinced! I need to see with my own two eyes this book of yours in action!"

"Well, … all right," Nick grumbled. "What do you want to do?" Eagerly, Mark sat behind his desk and pulled a legal pad from a briefcase by his chair. He consulted it for a few moments before looking up at Nick.

"The story you told me on how you had used *The Book of Lost Treasures* to find the old coins and money reminded me of a conversation I had with my granddaddy before he died a few years ago. He grew up during the Great Depression, and he told me money was extremely scarce back then. Banks were failing left and right, and anybody who put money in a bank usually lost all their savings. So he said folks back then developed a healthy and well-deserved distrust of banks, and any money they had left, they took to hiding. When I asked him where they hid their money, he laughed and said virtually everywhere. Some dug holes in their yard and buried coffee cans full of money, some stuffed it in their mattresses, some even put it in the hollows of trees. But the point I'm trying to make is that regardless of *where* they hid their money, there has to be a certain percentage of this money that is *still* hidden! People died all the time back then of sudden strokes and heart attacks, and I bet some of them never had a chance to tell their loved ones where they hid their money! The book can help us find some of this lost money!"

"But how?" Nick asked confused. "During the Depression, almost everybody grew up on farms, and most of those farms are long gone."

"You're right, Nick. That's why we have to phrase the request of the book carefully and according to its rules. The more precise we can be, the easier it will be to locate any of this lost money, should any of it still exist." Nodding, Nick and Mark spent the next half hour discussing the wording that they would use.

Writing, rewriting, and often scratching completely through sentences he was scribbling on his legal pad, Mark finally wrote the completed version of what they would ask of the book. Showing it to Nick for his approval, it read:

> Locate any money hidden and lost during the Great Depression within a one-mile radius of Nick Hollister's Airstream trailer.

Both Nick and Mark knew it was unlikely there was any such money that had been hidden and lost within such a small area close to his trailer. However, that was precisely the point; they didn't want to have to search multiple locations for the lost money. The book's rules stated that any lost treasure *must* be found before the next could be requested. If that were true, the last thing they wanted to do was create unnecessary hardships for themselves in locating the lost money. The fewer sites they had to search, the better! Therefore, if no map appeared within the book, Nick would erase and change the mileage or diameter of their request one mile at a time until they got a "hit" in the book.

Taking a deep breath, Nick wrote their request in the book. When nothing happened, they waited a few minutes before Nick erased the "one" written in the book and replaced it with the number "two." Still, nothing happened. Sighing, Nick changed the "two" to "three." Again, there was no response from the book.

Nick was beginning to fidget and get impatient when after writing "four" in the book, there was still no response. Taking a furtive glance at Mark, he saw doubt begin to creep onto the face of his friend. Gritting his teeth, he quickly erased the word "four" and wrote "five." Suddenly, light flared from the pages of the book. With shaking hands, Nick turned the page, and there before them was a detailed map leading from his trailer! Only a single location was indicated on the map, with the words "*Here Lies the Lost Treasure*" glowing brightly above it on the map.

Nick looked triumphantly over at Mark. His friend's mouth was open in amazement, and his eyes glazed over slightly, as if he couldn't believe the sight they were showing him.

"How … how did you do that?" he managed to whisper.

"Not me, the book, Mark! You saw it yourself!" Nick said, laughing in relief. Letting Mark stare at the map in disbelief for a few moments longer, Nick finally asked, "What now?"

"Huh? Oh, I guess … we try to find this … this lost money," Mark replied. Shaking his head as if to rid it of cobwebs, Mark got up and went to a file cabinet. Rooting around through it, he finally located what he wanted and returned to his desk.

Unfolding what proved to be a county map, he spread it out flat on the desk. He and Nick pored over the map until they found the precise location as indicated by the book's map. Writing down the county road number indicated on both maps, Mark picked up the phone and made a phone call to county clerk's office. Ten minutes later, Mark hung up the phone.

"The owner of that plot of land is a man named Cornelius Jones." Tapping his fingers thoughtfully on the top of his desk, Mark added, "That name seems awfully familiar. I think he is one of our clients."

A computer was located next to Mark's desk atop a wooden computer cabinet. Rolling his chair over to the computer, the black flat screen monitor flickered to life as Mark booted up the computer. A picture of Mark and Patti, faces cheek to cheek and laughing, appeared as a screen saver on the monitor. Entering his password, Mark's fingers flew over the keyboard, and soon, a list of clients began to scroll down the screen.

"There!" Mark cried triumphantly as he pointed at a name on the screen. Squinting, Nick saw Cornelius Jones's name listed as one of Mark and his father Larry's State Farm clients.

Mark's fingers clicked keys rapidly, and Cornelius Jones's account appeared.

"We have his home and car insurance," Mark commented. "He must be one of Daddy's clients because I know he's not one of mine." Consulting the information on the screen, he found a phone number and, picking up the phone, began to punch in the numbers.

"What … what are you doing?" Nick asked anxiously. When he saw Nick's scandalized expression, Mark sighed and put down the phone.

"Nick, we can't just drive over to Mr. Jones's property and search it without his permission. In case you have forgotten, that's called trespassing."

"Then what are you going to tell him?"

"The truth … or at least a version of it," Mark admitted. "Look, there has to be an old home, an old farmhouse or barn, or something that still exists either standing or in ruins. Otherwise, nothing would have shown up on the map in the book. I'm going to borrow Daddy's metal detector and ask Mr. Jones if we can search for old coins on his land."

"But what if he says no?" Nick protested.

"That's a chance we are going to have to take. I am not going to sneak onto someone's property without their permission!" Mark replied heatedly.

Looking at Nick, Mark saw he now wore an expression akin to that of a spooked rabbit. Seeking to allay his friend's fears, Mark said, "You're just going to have to trust me on this, Nick. I work with clients all the time, and if I can't get permission for us to search this old home site, nobody can!"

Seeing Nick's reluctant nod, Mark picked up the phone again and placed the phone call to Cornelius Jones. After several rings, someone picked up the phone, and after introducing himself, Mark spent the next few minutes in friendly conversation with them.

Finally, he got around to asking permission to search for old coins on the Jones's property.

Nick held his breath as he saw Mark smile. There were a few more moments of friendly banter before Mark thanked Mr. Jones and hung up the phone. Pushing back in his chair, Mark leaned back with his hands behind his head, smiling.

"What?" Nick blurted, unable to contain himself any longer.

"We're in! He said we could come over today if we wanted to!"

Chapter 15

After much backslapping, and shouts of self-congratulation, Nick and Mark finally settled down long enough to plan their next step. After gathering all the tools they believed they would need, they made a last stop to collect Mark's father's metal detector.

By this time, it was almost three o'clock in the afternoon. Going back to Mark's office, Mark changed out of his coat and tie into a pair of old jeans, T-shirt, and tennis shoes, hanging his good clothes up on coat hangers and placed them in a closet. Apparently, Mark had stopped at his house for a change of clothes while on his way back to Pleasant Mountain from Texarkana. Peering at Mark's clothes, Nick saw a sharp crease in the pant legs of the old jeans, as if they had been ironed, while the T-shirt didn't contain a single wrinkle anywhere that he could see. As for the tennis shoes, they were a pair of white Nike Runners without so much as a smudge or discoloration on them to indicate they had been used.

Grinning at his friend's fastidiousness, Nick followed Mark out of his office. Stopping only long enough to tell Susan he was leaving early today, Mark and Nick exited the office and went to Mark's Expedition in the parking lot. Climbing in, they briefly consulted the county map before Mark started the SUV and they pulled out onto the road.

Although *The Book of Lost Treasures'* map made the county map unneeded, it led from Nick's trailer, not the State Farm Insurance office, so they spent the next fifteen minutes or so using the county map to get their bearings before finally settling on the route diagrammed in the book. Leaving town, they followed a farm-to-market road for ten minutes or so before stopping before an overgrown meadow or field. A barbed wire fence enclosed the field, and an ancient gate, leaning on its hinges, provided entry. A rutted dirt road, itself overgrown with weeds and grass, led from the gate. Winding its way snake-like through the meadow, the road disappeared behind a grove of oak trees. Looking at the book's map, Nick and Mark determined they were at the right place, so Nick got out of the SUV to open the gate.

A strand of wire attached to a wooden post and looped over a metal strut on the gate proved to be the only thing holding the gate shut. Slipping the loop of wire off the gate, Nick pulled the gate open, and Mark pulled the SUV through. Closing the gate and looping the wire back onto the gate, Nick climbed back into the Expedition, and they slowly made their way down the dirt road. Pausing now and then to negotiate around a particularly deep pothole, Mark eased the SUV down the road and past the grove of oaks. Located approximately one hundred feet due east of the oak trees were the remains of an old house and barn. Stopping the car, Nick and Mark got out and studied the ruined structures.

The barn's roof had completely collapsed, leaving only the walls, which were themselves leaning precariously. A wild rose had taken root within the barn; its thorny canes grew in a wild profusion as they thrust through the rusted tin of the collapsed roof. Brambles from a blackberry bush grew thickly on one side of the ruined barn, competing with the wild rose for sunlight and space. An old persimmon tree, its branches heavy with unripened fruit, cast a long shadow on the west side of the barn. The old farmhouse was built in dogtrot fashion, with a breezeway in the middle of the structure separating the two main sections of the homestead. Its condition was little better than that of the barn, with large sections of the roof containing gaping holes.

Where windows had once existed, all that remained were empty, glassless window frames, the dark interior they revealed cloaked in black shadows. Of pier and beam construction, jagged holes could be seen by Nick and Mark in the wooden floor of the homestead's breezeway. The front porch, its foundation rotten, leaned drunkenly toward them. A chimney thrust upward from the east side of the house. Made of the native rust-colored rock found so commonly in the area, thick layers of masonry cemented the rocks of the chimney together. A trumpet vine had grown up the chimney's exterior, its orangish-red flowers hanging in clumps here and there from the clinging vine.

"Doesn't look very stable, does it?" Mark said doubtfully to Nick as they both continued to gaze at the old house. Nodding, Nick opened *The Book of Lost Treasures,* and both he and Mark spent the next several minutes studying the map within it. It soon became apparent to both of them that the map indicated a section of the chimney contained the hidden money they were looking for. Returning to the SUV, Mark retrieved a thick pair of gloves and a small crowbar he had brought from home. Then they both stepped up onto the porch and entered the breezeway.

The old wood groaned and creaked beneath their footsteps as they gingerly made their way, with both Nick and Mark half afraid that at any moment, their feet would plunge through the rotten flooring. Stopping before an open doorway, they stepped into the room containing the chimney.

The room's gloomy interior revealed that at one time, this must have been the kitchen. A pantry had been built to their right, its shelves empty now of anything but a thick layer of dust. A sink with a pump handle for drawing water was to their left, with the chimney directly across from them. An old table, one of its legs splintered in half, was balanced precariously on its remaining three legs in the middle of the room. If chairs had once complemented the table, they were now nowhere to be seen.

"The map shows the location of the money to be about four or five feet above the fire grate and almost exactly in the middle of the chimney," Nick commented as he squinted at the map in the dim light. Nodding wordlessly, Mark made his way to the chimney, with Nick following close on his heels. Leaves, which had blown in through the open doorway, formed scattered drifts on the floor. A dry crunching sound filled the room as Nick and Mark walked across the leaves toward the chimney.

Stopping before the chimney, Nick ran his hand along the rough masonry and rock of the chimney's surface. Taking the crowbar, he tapped the chimney with it, slowly moving upward as he did so. He was rewarded moments later when instead of a solid tap, a hollow sounding *thunk* resulted from striking the chimney with the crowbar. Excitedly, Nick and Mark looked at each other before Nick attacked the masonry with the crowbar. A short time later, Nick had excavated all the masonry around a rectangular piece of the reddish-orange rock that made up the chimney's facing. Carefully prying it loose, Mark helped him lower the rock to the floor.

A dark hollow or cavity was revealed behind the stone. Taking a small penlight from his pocket, Mark turned it on and pointed it toward the hollow. As he and Nick craned their necks and jockeyed with each other for the best view, they both saw almost simultaneously a small metal box nestled in the cavity.

Coated heavily with dust and cobwebs, it gave off a dull metallic gleam as the flashlight's beam played across it. Mark reached in with one gloved hand and pulled out the metal box. It was heavy in his hand, and something inside slid around loosely, making a *clinking* sound as he set it on top of the old table in the middle of the room. Mark brushed the dust off the box with his gloves, revealing that the money box was painted gunmetal gray.

Studying the metal box, Nick saw it was about a foot long and half that in width, with a height or depth of three inches. It reminded Nick of an old-fashioned cashbox a business might keep loose cash, change, and receipts in.

A single latch held the lid of the box shut, and Nick pushed the latch open. The hinges gave a rusty squeal as Nick pulled the lid open. A thick roll of bills was revealed lying on top of a pile of what looked to be loose change or coinage. As Mark breathlessly directed the flashlight's beam on the money, the scattered coins glinted with a metallic sheen.

"It's too dark in here. Let's take the box somewhere outside in the sunlight!" Mark said enthusiastically. Closing the lid, Nick picked up the cashbox, and he and Mark hurried outside.

Walking into the bright sunshine, Nick opened the lid, and once again, they stared into the box. Strewn loosely within the box were old coins of various sizes and in colors of copper, gold, and silver. Seizing one of the coins, Mark held it aloft, studying it. He said, "Nick, this is a Morgan Dollar! Do you know what that means?" When Nick shook his head no, Mark blurted, "It means it's made of gold!" Hurriedly sifting through the coins, Mark collected half a dozen more of the Morgan Dollars.

"This is unbelievable! There are seven Morgan Dollars among these coins! Depending on their mint date and their series, they could be worth thousands of dollars!"

Nick, caught up in Mark's excitement, still managed to grab the roll of bills with shaking hands. Untying the string that held the roll, he carefully counted the money. When he had finished, the bills totaled $323.

Although the total amount of money in the metal cashbox was small by today's standards, Nick knew it represented a king's ransom and probably the life savings of a farmer struggling to make ends meet during the Great Depression.

Nick looked up just in time to see Mark sit heavily on the ground. "What's wrong?" he asked, alarmed.

"Noth … nothing," Mark said as he stared vacantly at the gold coin in his hand. "It … it just occurred to me that your crazy book

… it can *actually* find lost treasures, just like you said it could! I mean, even after that map appeared in the book at the office, I … I still didn't believe it. I just knew that somewhere, somehow, a logical explanation would present itself. But the map led us straight to where this money was hidden, straight to it!" Standing up, Mark began to pace back and forth. Finally, he stopped and gazed at Nick, a look of wonder on his face.

"I don't know how, and I don't know why, but for once, you're right, Nick. *The Book of Lost Treasures* can find hidden and lost money, valuables, treasures, and who knows what else!"

Grinning, Nick put his arm around his friend's shoulders. "Don't forget the most important part I *also* told you, Mark!"

"What's that?" Mark asked, puzzled.

"That we're gonna be rich!"

Chapter 16

Nick and Mark stayed at the old homestead and talked until long shadows began to form in the late afternoon sun. When finally they got into Mark's Expedition and began the drive back to the State Farm office, it was decided they would meet again the next day at Nick's workshop. Mark felt strongly that they would need the skills and talents of other people to maximize the book's potential. The problem was whom could they trust? Indeed, who would *believe* them—much less join them—in their endeavor? The short list they had finally produced included three names besides Nick and Mark's: Patti, Steve, and Kenneth Langston. Kenneth was a friend of both Nick and Mark, and besides being a computer expert, he was also an avid collector of baseball cards and vintage comic books. The only area of disagreement between Nick and Mark had been what to do with the money they had found. Mark felt they should give at least some of it to Cornelius Jones, as it was his property they had found it on, while Nick felt just as strongly it was theirs to keep. Repeatedly, Nick had argued to Mark that had they not found the money box containing the old money and coins, Cornelius Jones certainly wouldn't have, and it would have forever remained lost. Although Mark agreed with Nick on that point, he maintained that the right thing to do would be to at least share some of their discovery with Mr. Jones.

When Mark dropped Nick off at his car, they finally agreed to disagree on the subject.

Nick's mind barely registered the drive back to his place. His thoughts were so full of the events of the day and the possibilities that now lay ahead that they claimed his complete attention and crowded out all else. Turning onto the rutted dirt road that led to his trailer, the little Sprint rolled to a stop under the car awning, and Nick sat for a few moments before turning off the engine and exiting the car. Rather than going to his trailer, he headed straight for the workshop. Rolling one of the doors to the side, Nick turned on the lights and walked in. Switching on the lathe, Nick lost himself in woodworking as he let his mind drift. When he finally switched the lathe off, he had a fully assembled chair made of white pine resting on the floor before him. The smell of wood glue and sawdust drifted in the air as he squatted beside the chair and gave it a critical inspection. It needed to be stained and varnished, but besides that, Nick could find no imperfections or mistakes in his craftsmanship. Nodding in satisfaction to himself, he picked up the chair and carried it up the flight of stairs to the false second-story platform.

There, Nick found a long iron hook and hung the chair from the ceiling to join the other chairs hanging suspended from the ceiling.

As Nick made his way back down the stairs, he looked up, and his face registered surprise. Through the open shop door, he saw it was completely dark, and night had fallen. Glancing at his watch, he was shocked to see it almost ten o'clock! It had been around six o'clock when he had arrived home, and he had worked nonstop for four hours, the time passing like a slipstream. A sudden sense of exhaustion came over Nick. However, it was a pleasant tiredness, one born of accomplishment and purpose, an unusual feeling for Nick. Deciding he rather liked the feeling, Nick yawned one more time as he turned off the lights, locked the workshop doors, and headed toward the Airstream trailer. Later, after he had showered and eaten, Nick lay in the trailer's bed loft with a small overhead light switched on. In one hand, he held *The Book of Lost Treasures*; in the other hand, he held the cashier's check for $10,000. Gazing at both of them, the whirlwind series of events by which he had obtained them flashed like a video loop through his mind.

Who would have believed it? he thought to himself. Who would ever have believed that a world-class screw-up like him could ever have stumbled across such good fortune? Gripping both book and check harder, Nick vowed he would make good on this opportunity, no matter what! His old life was behind him now, and he would *never ever* go back to it! With that grim determination in his mind, Nick placed the check in the book, switched off the light, and went to sleep.

The next day, a Saturday, dawned bright and cloudless as Nick rolled out of bed and fixed himself a cup of coffee. Eating a breakfast of cereal and milk, he changed into old shorts, T-shirt, and a beat-up pair of tennis shoes. Exiting the trailer, he went to the workshop, unlocked the doors, and pushed them wide open.

Switching on the lights, he put his hands on his hips and surveyed the shop's interior. It was a mess! Sawdust was everywhere, with mounds of it lying beneath the various woodworking machines. Tools and various cuts of wood were scattered haphazardly throughout the shop. Chairs, stools, and tables in various stages of completion were distributed throughout the workshop's interior, with no apparent rhyme or reason as to their placement.

A groan of resignation escaped from Nick's lips. If they were going to have a meeting here tonight, he had a major cleanup job ahead of him. Shaking his head, he eyed a whisk broom leaning against a corner in the shop. Cobwebs stretched from it, giving mute evidence of how long it had been since the last time the broom had been used. Deciding that the sooner he got started, the sooner he could get the worrisome task behind him, Nick strode over to the whisk broom, grabbed it, and got to work.

Nick worked all morning, stopping only for a brief lunch, consisting of a bologna sandwich and chips, before tackling the cleanup task anew. By early afternoon, he was finally finished with the job. The sawdust had been swept up and disposed of, the tools put back in their proper place, the wood stacked neatly, and the unfinished furniture placed and stored in some semblance of order. As a final act, Nick dragged an unstained and unvarnished table to the middle of the workshop's floor. Oval in shape with a drop leaf in the middle to expand the table's size, the table was soon joined by a half-dozen chairs that Nick placed strategically around it. Like the table, the chairs were also unstained and unvarnished. The unfinished furniture gave off a pungent but pleasant odor of sanded wood.

Surveying his handiwork, Nick nodded in satisfaction, a slight smile playing across his face. It had been years since his workshop had been this neat and clean! A sudden thought struck Nick, and he laughed out loud. Although it had been unintentional, *The Book of Lost Treasures* had worked its magic yet again: Nick had cleaned up and put his workshop in order, a task he had put off forever, and he had the mysterious book to thank for it! Still chuckling to himself, Nick headed back to the trailer.

The rest of the day crawled by as Nick waited impatiently for the seven o'clock meeting that he and Mark had agreed on. In addition, Mark was to contact all the other participants who were to attend the meeting. Although no one was going to be told the exact purpose for the meeting (other than it was a great new investment opportunity) until Mark and Nick had a captive audience, it was felt Mark's "credibility" would ensure everyone's attendance, rather than Nick calling them. Since Nick hadn't heard from Mark, he assumed all were planning on coming. How Mark had so far managed to keep any of this from Patti was a mystery to Nick. The married couple were connected to such a degree that they sometimes took turns finishing each other/s statements. If they were not such close friends of his, Nick might have found this psychic linkage eerie.

With time on his hands and not much else to do, Nick spent the afternoon in the trailer, thinking about the upcoming meeting and all the possibilities that lay ahead. The day had grown hot, and the small air conditioning unit struggled to keep the trailer's interior cool enough to be bearable. Lying in the bed loft, Nick eventually fell asleep, his nap filled with dreams of undiscovered gold and precious jewels. When he awoke, it was after six o'clock. Stumbling out of the loft, he went to the tiny bathroom and splashed water on his still groggy face. After changing into a pair of jeans and a T-shirt containing only a few wrinkles, Nick spent a few minutes combing his hair. Scrutinizing his appearance in the bathroom mirror for a few moments, he gave a satisfied grunt, turned off the light, and left the trailer. The day had cooled little as Nick walked to the workshop.

Although the sun was low in the horizon, it was late July, and Nick knew there was at least an hour of sunlight left. Pushing both doors of the workshop as wide open as they would go, Nick flicked on the lights and then a second set of switches next to the light switches. A rumbling noise filled the workshop's interior as a pair of large exhaust fans came to life. Located near the ceiling on the opposite end of the shop, Nick felt an immediate breeze as the exhaust fans pulled the hot air out of the workshop.

Returning to the trailer, Nick retrieved *The Book of Lost Treasures* before walking back to the shop. Heading for the table and chairs he had arranged in the middle of the floor, he chose one and sat down. Checking the book to make sure it still contained the cashier's check, Nick settled down to wait for his friends to arrive.

A little before seven o'clock, Steve's car drove slowly up the dirt road and came to a stop in the grass in front of the workshop. The car, a banana yellow 1968 GTO that Steve had meticulously restored, was his pride and joy.

Duel chrome exhaust pipes thrust from the GTO's jacked-up rear, which also featured wide competition tires. Chrome rims graced all four tires, and a chrome air scoop thrust from the GTO's hood. Not a scratch or a ding marred the paint job on the body of the GTO. The windows were down, and Nick heard AC/DC's "Back in Black" jolting from the oversized speakers Steve had installed in the car. The powerful engine, a 350 horsepower V-8 that Steve claimed could go from zero to sixty in less than eight seconds, growled into silence as Steve turned the car off.

As Steve got out of the car, Nick saw he was wearing a Mötley Crüe T-shirt with the sleeves removed. The ever present can of beer was balanced in one hand as he pocketed his keys and shut the car door. As Steve was doing this, Kenneth Langston got out of the passenger side of the car. Apparently, Kenneth had ridden with Steve from town.

"Hi'ya, Nick!" Steve called out, grinning, as he walked into the workshop.

"Hey, Nick!" Kenneth said, echoing Steve. He managed to lever himself up and out of the GTO's bucket seat and followed after Steve.

Greeting both of them with handshakes and backslaps, Nick showed Steve and Kenneth to the table he had set out in the shop, and they all took a seat in one of the chairs to wait for Mark and Patti.

"What's this all about, Nick?" Kenneth asked. He was unable to contain his curiosity.

"Well, I'd rather not say, Kenneth, until Mark gets here. We want to make the presentation to all of you at once," Nick replied. Nick and Mark had discussed the matter, and they had mutually concluded that the less Nick said, the better. Nick's well-deserved reputation for wild schemes notwithstanding, it was felt Mark was their best bet in what was definitely going to be a hard sell in the category of a "willing suspension of disbelief." In other words, with the proof he and Mark were going to show their friends, while they might believe Mark about *The Book of Lost Treasures*, they almost certainly wouldn't believe Nick!

Kenneth nodded in disappointment. Nick studied his friend as they chatted amiably with Steve. Kenneth had been part of their circle of friends since junior high. A computer nerd, Nick was convinced Kenneth represented every cliché or trait associated with the breed. A plastic pen guard jutted from the pocket of his buttoned and checkered short-sleeved shirt and was filled with a precisely arranged line of pens and mechanical pencils. Pudgy and just under six feet tall, Kenneth wore jeans that were in the high-water category, as they ended an inch or two above his ankles.

As if to emphasize this fact, Kenneth wore white socks (and for reasons known only to him) with black tennis shoes. Around his waist was a kind of utility belt from which a variety of electronic devices and tools were attached; this included an iPhone, palm pilot, a small can of compressed air, a tiny kit containing specialized computer tools, and of course, a ring of keys.

Kenneth's complexion was a doughy white, as if he never got out into the sun, and pale blue eyes peered from behind a pair of glasses with thick black frames. His hair was a dirty, dishwater blond color and was so wiry, it often reminded Nick of the Brillo pads his mother used to clean the oven with. Kenneth's hair grew thickly, and he wore it cut short and parted on the side. With the consistency of steel wool, Nick doubted a hurricane could have disturbed a single hair on Kenneth's head.

Kenneth, to Nick's knowledge, had never been on a single date. While relaxed and outgoing around his friends, he was pathologically shy around girls. He became tongue-tied and couldn't utter a coherent sentence around them. Kenneth had brought his mother as his date to his senior prom, which Nick was certain had to be a first in the annals of Pleasant Mountain High.

The fact that at thirty-two years old he still lived at home with his parents was testament that the ties that bind still had Kenneth firmly attached to his mother's apron strings.

However limited Kenneth was in appearance or around the opposite sex, he had few peers when it came to his computer skills. Kenneth could take apart and rebuild a computer from scratch, repair anything with a hard drive, write programs, design software, track down and eliminate viruses, add memory—you name it. If it was computer-related, Kenneth was an expert at it. In fact, Nick couldn't think of a single thing concerning computers Kenneth *wasn't* good at! He had worked at the local Radio Shack franchise in Pleasant Mountain since he had graduated from high school, and Kenneth had a thriving side business he ran from home in repairing computers. While other people might read books or magazines for pleasure, Kenneth devoured software and computer manuals like a starving man would devour a steak dinner, and he was constantly surfing the Net for new upgrades or information.

Mark's Expedition coming up the dirt road interrupted Nick's musings, and a little later, it came to a stop beside the workshop. Nick, Steve, and Kenneth got up from the table to greet Mark and Patti as they got out of the SUV. As Mark and Patti opened their doors to exit the Expedition, Nick saw a third per- son emerge from the backseat. Looking on curiously, he saw it was a young woman—and a pretty one at that!

The woman had a vague familiarity about her that Nick couldn't quite place. As she drew closer with Mark and Patti, the feeling he had seen her somewhere before deepened. She was tall—around five feet ten inches or so, he guessed—with long honey-brown hair. Her face, while not beautiful in the classic sense, was still pretty enough that most men would stop and take a second glance were she to pass by them.

She had warm liquid-brown eyes, and Nick had to force himself to look away to avoid the appearance of staring. However, moments later, he found himself glancing at her once again. Dressed in tan-colored capris and complimented by a pair of white, open-toed sandals, the young woman also wore a light cotton blouse tucked neatly into the capris. The blouse was V-cut, exposing a modest amount of cleavage, while a dark, even tan covered her skin. The young woman had a healthy vibrancy about her, and as if somehow sensing Nick's scrutiny, she looked in Nick's direction, and for the barest of moments, their gazes locked. As she flashed Nick a dazzling smile, Nick found himself staring again and quickly looked away. When finally he worked up the courage to glance back in her direction, he saw she was regarding him with a bemused expression on her face. Smiling weakly, he was spared further embarrassment when Patti came up to him and gave him an affectionate hug.

Pulling away, Patti winked at Nick and said, "I understand you and Mark have been up to some *interesting* things! I'm just dying to hear about it!" With that, Patti grasped one of Nick's arms and guided him to the table the others were gathered around.

Releasing Nick's arm, Patti motioned the young woman over and put her arm around her shoulders.

"Everybody, this is Abby—Abby Summers. Abby is my cousin, and she is going to be staying with Mark and me while she takes classes at Texas A&M-Texarkana."

With that, Patti introduced Abby to everyone at the table, and and they all took a seat around the table, with Abby sitting next to Nick.

When Patti introduced Abby, Nick suddenly recognized who she was! Although Abby had lived in another town, he recalled that throughout their junior high and high school years, he had often seen Patti and Abby together during week-ends, summers, and vacations. Even after Mark and Patti had gone off to college and married each other, Abby was still a frequent guest at their home or apartment. Nick had asked Mark about this once, and he had explained that both Patti and Abby came from families of brothers where they were the only girls. Because of that, they had formed a bond more closely akin to that of sisters than of cousins. That was why they were so close, he had explained. It didn't seem to bother Mark, so Nick hadn't really thought much more about it until today.

Abby was a couple of years younger than Patti, he knew, and she sure hadn't looked then like she did now! Nick remembered Abby as a skinny, gangly girl with braces, not the grownup woman with long legs and soft curves that sat beside him now. *My, how she had filled out!* he thought to himself. Abruptly, he remembered something else about Abby: she was—or at least had been—married. He knew that to be true, because Patti had been her maid of honor at her wedding, and the reason she was here now, staying with Mark and Patti, probably meant she was now separated or divorced from her husband. As a matter of fact, he remembered now Mark making a comment to him several months ago about Abby having marital difficulties. He hadn't given it much thought then, since he hadn't seen Abby in years.

For some reason, this realization caused Nick's heart to leap before he guiltily pushed the emotion aside.

By this time, everyone was seated and looking expectantly at Mark. The hum of the exhaust fans boiled over in the workshop as Mark took a deep breath. Despite the artificial breeze created by the fans, the air in the workshop was warm, and a trickle of sweat made its way down the side of Mark's face as he opened his mouth to speak.

"What I am about to tell you and, in fact, what I am about to *show* you, strains credibility. I didn't believe it myself at first, and all I ask is that you hear me out before you pronounce Nick and me as being crazy."

That got everyone's attention, and even Patti looked at her husband with undisguised curiosity. As Nick suspected, he had managed to keep the existence of *The Book of Lost Treasures* from her.

Starting from the beginning, Mark related how Nick had bought a painting from Harper's Antiques and how he had found a strange book inside it. Mark explained how Nick had eventually discovered the secret of *The Book of Lost Treasures* and how he had used it to locate the hidden strongbox of Colonel Efurd Buckley. From there, Mark recounted how Nick had come to him about the mysterious book and how, by using a map that appeared in the book, they had subsequently located the cashbox secreted inside the old farmhouse chimney. There was dead silence when Mark finished, as if those who had listened to the fantastic tale were afraid to speak. At last, Kenneth cleared his throat.

"You … you really don't believe this, do you, Mark? This is some kind of a joke, right? I mean, no offense, Mark, but this is something Nick might have cooked up, not you."

"I *do* believe it, Kenneth! And it's not something Nick 'cooked' up. I've seen the book in action, and I was there when we pulled that cashbox from the chimney. Look," Mark said, holding up his hands to forestall any further comments from Kenneth, "I don't expect you to just take my word for it. We have proof!" And with that, Mark reached down and picked up his briefcase. Clicking it open, he pulled out the wad of greenbacks from the stolen Union payroll and the metal cashbox and placed them on the table. Opening the cashbox, Mark indicated they should examine its contents, as well as the greenbacks. For the next ten minutes or so, the greenbacks and cashbox were passed back and forth between Kenneth, Patti, Steve, and Abby. Finally, Kenneth looked up and said, "Okay, I'm convinced that the money and greenbacks are genuine. However, that doesn't prove anything. I could have accidently dug them up in my own backyard and claimed to have found treasure! Besides, where are the old coins found in the strongbox and this so-called 'book?' Why aren't they here for us to see?"

Anticipating just such a question, Mark nodded at Nick. It was time for the coup de grace. Pulling *The Book of Lost Treasures* from his knapsack, Nick placed the book on the table. Opening it, he removed the $10,000 cashier's check he had placed within it and laid it out flat next to the book. Leaning back in his chair, he folded his arms across his chest and tried not to look too smug as gasps of surprise rang out from his friends as they spotted the check.

Kenneth picked up the check and held it up before the light, squinting at it, as if to determine if it was a forgery or not. His face a mask of confusion, he passed the check over to Steve and then turned his attention to the book. As he was scrutinizing the book, Mark spoke again.

"The check is legitimate, I can assure you. I took the coins from the strongbox myself to a coin dealer in Texarkana, and he gave me the check for the pre-Civil War coins. Until then, I didn't believe in the book's power either. I thought it to be just one more example of Nick's, shall we say, 'flights of fantasy.'

But the coin dealer's reaction to the coins I showed him convinced me that something was extraordinary about the book. It was at that point that I decided to give Nick a chance to 'prove' to me that the book indeed had the ability to find lost treasures." Standing up, Mark looked at the assembled friends sitting at the table before him. "When the map appeared in *The Book of Lost Treasures* at my office detailing the whereabouts of the hidden cashbox, well that … that sealed the deal for me. Believe me when I tell you I have thought of every reasonable explanation, every possible alternative, as to how this book can have a mysterious map suddenly appear and lead us to a cashbox hidden well over seventy years ago. I just can't come up with anything, and therefore, I must conclude that the book *works,* as Nick told me it did in finding lost treasures."

There was a momentary silence before Patti got up and slipped her arm around her husband's waist. "I believe you, sweetie." It was a simple enough statement, but it spoke volumes to the rest of them.

"Rock on, man, rock on!" Steve cried excitedly as he took a healthy gulp from the beer in his hand. Patti giggled at Steve's reaction, and soon everyone around the table was laughing and talking animatedly.

Finally, during a lull in the conversation, Kenneth held up his hand to catch Mark's and Nick's attention.

"Yes?" Mark asked curiously.

"Okay, even though I'm not saying I *completely* believe you, I'm willing to give you and Nick the benefit of the doubt. So *why* did you tell us all this, and *why* are we here?" It became quiet again around the table as faces looked over at Mark.

Smiling, Mark said, "Good question, Kenneth! Nick and I talked about it, and we decided that in order to take advantage of the book's potential, we needed the help and talents of others. What better place to start than our friends?"

"So … what is it you and Nick are proposing?" Kenneth was persistent.

"We want to form a … a corporation of sorts, one in which we are all equal partners and receive equal benefits or shares from whatever lost treasures the book helps us discover."

"Here, here!" Steve exclaimed, pounding the tabletop with his beer can and managing to slosh beer all over his hand.

"I can get one of the lawyers at the firm I work at to draw up an article of incorporation for us," Patti volunteered. "But what would we call our … our business?"

The next ten minutes were spent selecting and then discarding various names for their proposed business partnership. Finally, Abby, who had remained conspicuously silent through- out the night's proceedings, tentatively raised her hand.

As heads swiveled toward her, Abby gave an embarrassed shrug. "I know it's really not any of my business, but how about calling your new partnership 'The Treasure Hunt Club?' I mean, you're all friends already, so it's like a club, and from what I understand, you're going to use the book to try and find lost treasures and stuff, so why not 'The Treasure Hunt Club?'"

"I like it!" Nick blurted before he could stop himself, and soon, everyone else joined in a chorus of affirmation. Abby rewarded Nick with a warm smile as Mark rapped his knuckles on the table to get everyone's attention.

"The Treasure Hunt Club it is then! Thank you, Abby, for your suggestion. Now, we need to elect a board of officers for our corporation. Do I hear any nominations?"

Immediately, Kenneth nominated Mark for president, but Mark shook his head emphatically "no."

"I won't accept the nomination for president. In fact, I want to nominate Nick for president. It was Nick who found the book. He first discovered the book's ability, and Nick who had to convince me that it could indeed find lost money and valuables. I can't think of a more qualified person to take the position of president!" Nick looked up at Mark in surprise. Mark winked at him as Steve seconded the nomination. It left a warm feeling inside Nick knowing that his friend had such confidence in him. A slate of officers was nominated and voted on, with Nick as president; Mark, vice president; Patti, treasurer; and Kenneth as secretary.

One of Nick's first acts as president was to move that Abby be included in the Treasure Hunt Club. Despite her protestations, the measure passed unanimously.

"Call it fate, Abby, but depending on your point of view, you happened to be in either the right place at the wrong time or the wrong place at the right time tonight," he said jokingly to her.

The next item of business was the unresolved disagreement between Nick and Mark as to compensation for property owners on whose property any "lost" treasure was found.

Both Mark and Nick gave their sides of the argument, and it was discussed for the next half hour without coming to any conclusion. Finally, Patti raised her hand, and Nick recognized her.

"I can get a contract drawn up that we could get a property owner to sign. In return for their signature, we could offer them ten percent of the value of any discovery we make. Then we could legally claim any lost valuables we find on their property." Although the rest of the club thought it was a good idea, Nick raised an immediate objection.

"What happens if they refuse to sign, Patti? The book's rules state that we must find *and* recover any lost treasure before we can move on to another! If they refuse to sign, we can't look for another lost treasure!" Mark grudgingly agreed with Nick, and more discussion immediately ensued on the topic. Kenneth, who had *The Book of Lost Treasures* open and was studying the listed rules intently, raised his hand.

"The chair recognizes Kenneth!"

"One of the rules says to be as specific as possible about the lost treasure sought. What if when we write a request in the book, we include a statement saying it must be a lost treasure on the property of someone who would willingly sign the legal contract Patti described?"

"That's it! You're a genius!" Nick cried.

Steve pounded Kenneth on the back enthusiastically, and Kenneth's cheeks grew red at Nick's compliment. Everyone else quickly agreed, and so the statement and contract were voted in as part of their normal operating procedure.

"I guess it goes without saying that no one here can reveal the book's secret or how we use it to find lost money and other things," Nick warned. "None of us, no matter how tempted, can tell anyone—not family, not friends, not even your pastor or clergy. It must remain our secret! Do we all agree?" One by one, Nick went around the table until each and every person agreed to keep the book's existence a secret.

"Good! It's unanimous! Let's take Sunday to think of all that we have discussed here, and let's meet again Monday night to decide how to use the book next." A motion was made by Patti to adjourn, and it was seconded by Mark.

The first meeting of the Treasure Hunt Club came to an end.

Chapter 17

As the meeting broke up, Kenneth and Steve followed Patti and Mark to the workshop's doors, where they continued to talk about the night's proceedings. Nick had picked up a couple of the chairs and was carrying them up the stairs to the second-story platform when Abby's voice stopped him.

"Did you make this table and these chairs?" she asked.

Stopping, Nick put the chairs down and turned around to face Abby. She was looking at him inquisitively.

Smiling, he nodded. "I've made pretty much everything you see in here."

Running her hand over the table's smooth surface, Abby said, "I'm no expert, but you obviously do good work."

"Well, I don't know about that … but thanks."

"I've never met anyone who could make furniture before. How did you learn how to do it?" she asked curiously.

"That's kind of a long story, but my granddaddy taught me."

"Really? He must have taught you well. Your workmanship is fantastic! I wish the furniture at my old apartment was half as well made." Abby's compliment caused Nick's face to turn red, and she laughed at his reaction. It was a rich, easy laughter, and Nick soon found himself chuckling along with her.

"Surely, I must not be the first person to ever tell you that your craftsmanship is superb, Nick."

"Well … no, but I guess my friends are just used to seeing everything in here."

"Do you mind me asking why you haven't finished any of the pieces you have made? It looks like all they need is to be, you know … stained and varnished."

"That's a long story too," Nick admitted.

Abby laughed again, and Nick felt a pulling at his heart toward her. It was a different kind of feeling, and one he hadn't felt for anyone in a long, long time.

"Tell you what, Nick Hollister. Why don't you come to church with me tomorrow, and afterward, you can tell me these long stories of yours. Is it a deal?"

Nick blinked. He hadn't been to church in years—not since his mother had moved to Dallas, in fact.

"Well … sure," Nick finally managed to say.

"Good! I'll pick you up at ten thirty in the morning!" With that, both of them walked toward the workshop doors, where Mark and Patti were looking at them with undisguised curiosity.

As they stopped at the doors, Abby turned and took one more glance at the shop. "You know, this has possibilities, Nick—your furniture making, that is. Who knows? If you put your mind to it, you could probably make a pretty good living at it." With that, Abby turned, and she, Mark, and Patti got into the Expedition and drove off. Moments later, the throaty roar of Steve's GTO filled the air, and he and Kenneth also drove off, leaving Nick standing alone at the workshop doors.

Although from Nick's standpoint the establishment of the Treasure Hunt Club should have been the night's crowning achievement, Abby's last words kept coming back to him. Nobody, and that included all of his friends who were here tonight, had ever suggested to him that the woodworking and furniture he made as a sideline or hobby was good enough to make a living at—or even to sell at all! It was like they lacked confidence in him, while Abby had no such doubts.

The feeling—the tugging at his heart—returned as he thought of Abby, and he found himself looking forward to going to church with her tomorrow.

Nick turned out the lights and locked the workshop doors, and as he made the short walk through the night air to his trailer, his thoughts were not on the potential riches to be had through use of *The Book of Lost Treasures* but on Abby Summers.

Nick slept much later than he intended the next morning, and it was almost ten o'clock when he awoke. He had to scramble to take a quick shower and then look for something appropriate to wear to church. Rooting around in his tiny closet, he finally found an old tan-colored pair of Dockers. They had been in his closet so long that he had to clean a thin film of dust off of the pants crease where it had hung from the hanger. Further searching produced his one and only polo shirt, as well as a pair of brown shoes and socks. One of the socks had a hole in it, but as he didn't own another pair that color, he was forced to wear it. Once dressed, he looked at himself in the bathroom mirror. The polo shirt and Dockers were wrinkled, but not as badly as he had feared. He was in the process of combing his hair when he heard a car honking outside the trailer.

Taking a look through the window, Nick spotted a maroon Toyota Corolla that had pulled up to the trailer. Abby was behind the wheel, and she honked again as he scrambled to get his wallet and keys. Exiting the trailer, Nick locked the door and got in the passenger side of the Corolla.

"You look very nice, Nick!" Abby complimented him as he slid into the seat.

"Well, it's been a while since I had to wear anything but work clothes or jeans, and I was lucky to find this," Nick admitted. "By the way, you look very nice too," he added as he glanced over at Abby. She was wearing a white wrap-around skirt and matching blouse. It was a rather simple outfit, one which could be thrown on in minutes, but on Abby, the effect was stunning. The skirt fell to just above her knees, but had hiked up somewhat as she had sat down in the car seat, thus exposing more of her long, tanned legs. Her light brown hair fell to just below her shoulder blades, and it gleamed in the morning light. What little makeup Abby wore served to simply emphasize the natural beauty she already possessed. Nick found himself so mesmerized with Abby that he didn't hear her speaking to him.

"Nick!"

"Huh?" he managed to say.

"I said, don't you want to know where we are going to church this morning?"

"What? Oh … yeah, where are we going?

"We are going to First Baptist, where Mark and Patti go. They are going to save us a seat next to them in the pew."

"Hey, that's great!" Nick replied as they turned off the dirt road and onto the farm-to-market road.

Fifteen minutes later, they pulled into the First Baptist Church parking lot. Nick felt somewhat self-conscious as they walked through the doors and into the church foyer; after all, he hadn't darkened the door of any church in years. He was sure the second he walked into the church auditorium, heads would swivel in total disbelief at the sight of him. Fortunately, they were a little early, and the pews were only sparsely filled. It was with great relief that he slid in next to Mark and Patti without incident.

"Good to see you, buddy! See, the sky didn't fall, and the ground didn't crack open." Mark ribbed Nick good-naturedly.

"Yeah, very funny!" Nick managed to mumble.

"Congratulations, Abby! We've tried for years to get Nick to go to church with us, but he always had some excuse!" Mark said, grinning.

"I guess you just have to know how to ask, Mark," Abby said, smiling impishly at Nick. Fortunately, the church organist and piano player began playing, thus sparing Nick further ribbing from Mark.

The service went by faster than Nick thought it would, and soon they were exiting the church and walking back to Abby's car. They met Mark and Patti at Tres Pesos for lunch, a Mexican restaurant in town known for its great fajitas, and they talked, laughed, and shared ideas on what to first ask *The Book of Lost Treasures* to find. Nick found himself disappointed when they finally left the restaurant and Abby began to drive him home. He didn't know the last time he had had such a good time. While he always enjoyed Mark and Patti's company, Abby had made going to church, and then to lunch, a special experience for him. Besides being pretty and obviously intelligent, she was a good listener, often sitting with her chin cupped in her hands and her complete attention on Nick as he spoke. It wasn't so much that she waited breathlessly on what he had to say next, but simply that she had an *interest* in what he said! It had been a long time since a girl took a serious interest in anything that Nick Hollister had to say.

The Corolla pulled onto Nick's dirt road and, a short time later, rolled to a stop before the trailer. There was a moment or two of uncomfortable silence before Nick invited Abby in. To his surprise, she accepted, and they both got out of the car. Instead of walking to the trailer, however, Abby walked around to the back of it. Holding her hand up to screen the sun from her eyes, she gazed at the land and trees that surrounded the trailer.

"What's that?" Abby asked, pointing to a scummy pool of water some one hundred yards away that was surrounded by weeds and bushes. Nick, who had followed Abby around the trailer, squinted in the bright sunlight at what she was pointing at.

"Oh," he said recognizing the sight, "that's a stock pond. I was going to try and hire a bulldozer to expand it and make it bigger, but I just haven't had the money to do it."

Nodding her head, Abby asked curiously, "How much land do you own, Nick?"

"About thirty acres, counting the land my shop and trailer are on."

"What are you going to do with it?"

The question took Nick by surprise. No one had ever asked him that before, and he wasn't sure how to answer her.

"Well, er, to be honest with you, I haven't … really thought about it that much," he stammered.

"That's too bad, because your place here has possibilities," Abby commented. That was the second time Nick had heard Abby use the word "possibilities." She had said the same thing the night before about his shop.

"What do you mean?" he asked with a puzzled expression on his face.

"I mean your whole place here has potential and, you know … *possibilities*!" Abby's face was so animated when she said this that Nick started laughing before he could stop himself.

"Okay, I'll try to explain so that even *you* can understand!" Abby said in mock anger. Grabbing Nick by the arm, she pulled him around so that he faced his workshop.

"Now, imagine that you take all the tables, chairs, footstools, etc., that you have made and you actually *finish* them! Then you advertise and begin to sell a few pieces. Then, the people who bought your furniture begin to tell others until your reputation for quality craftsmanship has spread all over the county. Then you get *more* business! You decide to diversify by learning how to upholster, and before you know it, you are selling couches, love seats, and divans. Soon, you have more business than you can handle, and now *you* begin to choose your customers!"

Turning Nick back toward the scummy pond, Abby said, "Can't you just see a five-acre lake? Next to it would be a pavilion for having cookouts and picnics on nice days.

Of course, a small dock or pier would have to be built on the lake. Then you could sit on the edge of the dock and fish or just sit barefooted, splashing your feet in the cool water. Around the lake, you would plant wildflowers, like Bluebells and Indian paintbrush, so that in the spring, the land around the lake would be a riot of color."

Spinning Nick back toward the trailer, Abby continued, "Instead of a trailer, envision a grand country home standing in its place! And not just any home, but the one of your dreams! It will be two stories tall with an old-fashioned winding staircase leading to the second floor.

The kitchen will be huge with a walk-in pantry, a breakfast nook, and a serving island. The cabinets will, of course, all be made of hand-carved oak, and the kitchen floor of a rose-colored porcelain tile. The doors and doorways throughout the house will be oversized, with enormous picture windows on the front of the house. The den will have a polished hardwood floor, wood-paneled walls, and contain a fireplace with an antique mantle placed over it. The bedrooms will all have four-poster beds with canopies. Of course, each bedroom will have a different theme and color scheme, but the master bedroom will have a small balcony accessed by French doors, his and her walk-in closets, and a bathroom that's to die for!

The bathroom will contain a wall-to-ceiling mirror and a marble vanity, with two sinks with gold fixtures, a modern glassed-in shower, and an old, but beautifully restored, antique claw-foot tub. Finally, the house will have a large elevated porch that completely encircles it. It will be filled with comfortable rockers, wicker furniture, and of course, a wooden porch swing for two."

"Well, what do you think?" Abby asked as she turned toward Nick. Smiling broadly with arms crossed on her chest, she looked at Nick expectantly. Her cheeks were flushed slightly, as if the act of describing her "possibilities" had caused a sudden rush of adrenaline in her.

"Wow!" Nick said. "And I've been told *I* have an overactive imagination!" Giggling, Abby punched him playfully in the shoulder.

It was hot outside, and even in the short time they had been standing behind Nick's trailer, sweat had begun to trickle down his face. Motioning to Abby, Nick led them both into his trailer. Fortunately, he had left the little window unit air conditioner on, and it was reasonably cool inside the trailer. Fishing a couple of soft drinks out of the refrigerator, he handed one to Abby, and they both sat on the seat behind the tiny kitchen table. Like the rest of the trailer, it was cramped, and they both sat squeezed in next to each other.

"What improvement suggestions do you have for my current 'mansion?'" Nick asked tongue in cheek as he waved expansively at the trailer's interior.

"I'm afraid I'm going to have to get back to you on that one!" Abby said, laughing. Grinning, Nick laughed along with Abby. They shared small talk for a few more minutes as they each asked about the other's family, with Nick telling Abby his mother and sister were both living in Dallas, while Abby said most of her family still lived in and around the Tyler area.

At that point, the conversation seemed to dry up until Nick, clearing his throat, finally asked the question he had wanted to ask Abby since she had picked him up earlier that morning.

"Why … why did you ask me to go to church with you, Abby?" The question sounded blunter than he had intended, and quickly, he added, "Not that I didn't want to go or that I didn't have a good time!"

Abby turned her head and gazed at Nick. Gone was the smile she had worn earlier, and in its place was an uncertainty, as if she herself didn't know how quite to answer him.

Thinking he had blown it and crossed the line in asking the question, Nick was red faced as he sputtered, "I'm … I'm sorry, I didn't mean to be rude or anything. I—"

"Nick, it's all right," Abby said softly as she interrupted him and placed her hand on his. "The truth is, I … really don't know myself. It's just … it's just that when you insisted that I be included as a member of the Treasure Hunt Club, I … I thought that was a sweet and unselfish thing to do. The way my life has been lately… well, I could use a little sweet and unselfish for a change."

"At any rate," Abby said as she gave an embarrassed shrug, "if we are going to be business partners, we need to get to know each other, wouldn't you agree?"

"Right … partner!" Nick said, immensely relieved.

"Well, now that we've got that settled, I'd better be going!" Abby said, smiling, as she looked at her watch. For a moment, Nick just stared at Abby, noticing how her smile completely transformed her face. It made her warm brown eyes seem to come alive, and he found himself becoming lost in them.

Abruptly realizing what he was doing, Nick blinked and turned away. Squeezing out of their seats, Nick and Abby made their way out of the trailer and to Abby's car. As they made the walk, Nick knew he wanted to see Abby again, and he tried to frame the words in his mind on how he would ask her. As they drew closer and closer to the Corolla, Nick desperately tried, and then discarded, different ways to casually ask Abby out without seeming to be too eager or too forward.

Reaching her car, Abby said good-bye to Nick and opened the door and got in. As Abby started the car and put it in gear, Nick suddenly tapped on her window. Powering the window down, Abby looked up questioningly at Nick.

"I, er, I was, you know, wondering, if you would like to go out for … for dinner or something next week?" he stammered. *Idiot!* he thought as he mentally kicked himself. So much for the cool and casual approach!

"Why, that depends, Nick. Is this for business or pleasure?" she asked him coyly.

Nick froze like a deer in headlights, and his tongue felt thick in his mouth. It was only after he saw Abby begin to giggle that he knew she was teasing him.

"I, ah, I was thinking pleasure. Yes, definitely pleasure!"

"Well, in that case, I would love to! We can talk more about it tomorrow night at the meeting. See you then!" Waving, Abby backed up and then pulled away.

Nick watched Abby drive away, he pumped his fist in triumph and cried, "Yes!"

Turning and practically skipping back to the trailer, one word seemed to repeat itself over and over as it described his feeling toward her.

Possibilities …

Chapter 18

Nick spent Monday morning depositing his cashier's check at his bank and then opening up a checking account complete with a debit card. He had closed his old checking account years ago when he finally came to the conclusion, after overdrawing his account yet again, that he didn't possess the fiscal discipline to keep his checking account balanced. In fact, more than once, Mark had had to lend him money to pay off the overdrafts plus the penalties levied on them.

It had been a particularly humiliating experience and not one he was eager to repeat. Since then, he had paid for everything in cash or money orders. However, with the discovery of *The Book of Lost Treasures*, Nick's life had taken a definite turn for the better. He planned on having lots of cash to deposit in the future when being fifty to a hundred dollars off on his balance wouldn't register a blip on his bank account. Besides, with $10,000 to deposit, he now had plenty of cushion to cover any faulty accounting of his checkbook.

The meeting was to be held at Mark and Patti's house at seven o'clock that evening, and after running several errands in town, Nick went home and decided to pass the time by working in his shop. He found himself pausing every so often and pulling off his goggles; he would look around the shop, thinking as he did so about what Abby had said. "What … what if she was right?" he mused. What if he *could* sell the furniture he made? Shaking his head, he decided it didn't matter anyway. He was going to be *much* too busy spending the money *The Book of Lost Treasures* was going to bring them!

The time passed quickly, and before he knew it, it was time to leave for the meeting. Washing his face and hands, he combed his hair before throwing on a pair of cargo shorts and a T-shirt. Flip-flops completed his ensemble as he hurtled out of the trailer and to his car.

Mark and Patti's house was located in a subdivision on the south side of town, and Nick arrived there a short time later. As he pulled alongside the curb and parked in front of their house, he noticed he was the last one of the club members to arrive. Steve's car was parked in the driveway, and Kenneth's car, a blue Honda Civic, was parked behind Abby's. Getting out of the cramped confines of the Sprint, Nick took a few minutes to stretch and work the kinks out of his muscles. Then he strode toward the front door.

Mark and Patti's home was a three bedroom, two bath red brick affair with a two-car garage, and was a scene straight from suburbia, with only the backyard barbeque (which Mark had plans to build in the very near future) needed to complete the picture.

Having been to Mark and Patti's house numerous times, Nick didn't bother knocking and instead let himself in through the front door. A short hallway led from the front door, and as Nick entered it, he heard voices coming from the den. Turning right off the hallway, he entered the room and saw everyone already seated and waiting for him. The den was the largest room in Mark and Patti's home, with a couch, love seat, and two Queen Anne chairs arranged facing a walnut entertainment center complete with a flat screen TV.

In addition, a brick fireplace with a mahogany mantle was adjacent to the wall nearest the entertainment center. A tray containing a pitcher of iced tea and glass mugs was set on a coffee table in front of the couch. Helping himself to a glass of the tea, Nick plopped himself into one of the Queen Anne Chairs and looked around. Mark, Patti, and Abby were sit- ting on the couch, while Kenneth sat in the love seat and Steve in the other Queen Anne Chair. Nick's gaze stopped on Abby, and he felt his heart skip a beat. She was wearing a denim pair of crop pants with a yellow mandarin collar shirt. Barefooted, she had one leg tucked under her as she sat on the couch. To Nick, she looked prettier each time he saw her.

"Well, I guess now that Nick has *finally* arrived, we can begin!" Mark quipped.

Refusing to be baited, Nick grinned and immediately said, "I call this meeting of the Treasure Hunt Club to order. If there are no objections, let's skip the reading of the minutes and go straight to new business." Hearing no objections, Nick continued, "Who has suggestions concerning how we next use *The Book of Lost Treasures*?" Immediately, hands shot up from all the club members. Going around to each person in turn, Nick let them give their suggestions, followed by debate on the merits of each suggestion.

These ranged from asking the book to locate buried pirate treasure to Steve's suggestion that they find a rhythm guitar purportedly lost by Jim Morrison of The Doors shortly before his death. However, it was Patti whose idea they all agreed had the most merit. She had proposed that they search for valuable antiques, reasoning that they were much more likely to find them closer to the Pleasant Mountain area than other lost items of value. Nick then asked her to elaborate further on her idea.

Blushing slightly at the attention now focused on her, Patti said, "Well, I was trying to think of lost objects not necessarily common but, at the same time, not *uncommon* to where we live That way, we don't have far to travel to find them once their location is at last revealed by the book. Also—and this is very important—when I say 'lost,' I don't mean 'lost' in the sense that something is hidden and needs to be found. Rather, I mean 'lost' in terms that the owner of an antique doesn't know that their piece is extremely valuable. When approached like this, someone may literally have a 'lost' treasure right before their eyes and not be aware of it! If so, *The Book of Lost Treasures* might be able to locate these kinds of antiques as easily as those that are truly missing!"

Seeing confusion on some of the faces around her, Patti elaborated further. "I got the idea when I was flipping through the channels on the TV and came across a PBS program called *Antiques Roadshow.* It hit me, as I was watching the show, that practically *everybody* owns antiques of some kind.

But as evidenced on *Antiques Roadshow,* many people often aren't aware of their value! That started me to thinking that maybe *The Book of Lost Treasures* can reveal valuable antiques to us that are up for auction at estate sales or even garage sales. I mean, if I understand the rules of the book's usage, we could phrase the request to it like, 'Locate an antique at an estate sale or garage sale that unbeknownst to the owner is worth over one thousand dollars.' We could even add that it be located within this county or the nearby surrounding counties.

"What do you think?" Patti asked anxiously as she scanned the faces around her.

"Wow! Can you believe I'm married to such an intelligent woman?" Mark asked, grinning.

"Brains as well as beauty!" Nick agreed. Blushing furiously now, Patti wore an embarrassed smile as the club members applauded—all except Kenneth, who was strangely quiet. When the commotion quieted down, Kenneth raised his hand and was recognized by Nick.

"But how do we know the book will honor a request like that?" he asked with a skeptical look on his face. "As Patti mentioned, these antiques aren't really lost!"

"We won't know until we write the request in the book," Nick admitted. "I guess the worst that can happen is that … well, that no map appears in the book."

"Then I move that we write Patti's request in the book right now! That way we can immediately see if the book delivers as we've been told it can. I don't know about the rest of you, but I am still going to need proof this book can locate lost items of value." Kenneth's pudgy chin jutted out stubbornly as he said this, as if daring anyone to challenge his statement.

Mark, seeing Nick's eyes flash with anger, quickly interjected, "I don't think anybody here would disagree with you, Kenneth. Neither Nick nor I expect you to fully believe anything until *The Book of Lost Treasures* produces a map or directions to the next lost treasure."

"Okay, so what's wrong with right now? Let's write the request in the book and see if it produces a map!" Kenneth persisted. Puzzled, Nick studied Kenneth. He seemed almost angry, his normally pallid complexion flushed.

Nick wasn't surprised that Kenneth needed proof of the book's ability, but his reaction was way beyond that. Suddenly, it struck Nick as to the possible reason why: Kenneth's world was an orderly one of electronics, microchips, and logic based on software programs. *The Book of Lost Treasures* upset this predictable world, and it introduced a variable Kenneth neither understood nor could control. It wasn't doubt that he was observing in Kenneth, but *fear*! Kenneth was scared!

"What do you think?" Nick asked as he turned toward Mark.

Mark didn't answer immediately. Drumming his fingers on the couch's upholstered arm, he considered the question carefully. Finally, he said, "I think we should wait. In fact, I think we should wait until this Saturday to begin our search."

"But why?" Kenneth protested.

"For one or all of the following reasons. First of all, we have no working capital. Whose money are we going to use if we have to buy any of the antiques we discover?"

No one, it seemed, had considered that point. The question went unanswered.

Plunging on, Mark continued, "I was going to take the old coins we found in the cashbox to the coin dealer in Texarkana and see what they are worth. With any luck, he'll buy them from me, and we will have some money to deposit in the club's account. Of course, right now we don't have an account, which means we will have to set one up. That takes some time, as does driving all the way to Texarkana. I have meetings with clients scheduled throughout this week, and I'll be lucky to be able to find the time just to make it to the coin dealer.

"Then there is the legal establishment of our business. As a favor to Patti, one of the partners at her firm has offered to draw up an article of incorporation that establishes the Treasure Hunt Club as a business, as well as the contract offering ten percent to the owner of anyone whose property we find valuables on.

However, he is doing this on his own free time, and these legal documents won't be ready until sometime toward the end of the week. I don't think we should proceed until our business has legally been established and we have that contract in hand.

"Finally, as I alluded to earlier, I have to work, as do most of you. I just can't take off and go searching for whatever the book leads us to. It's liable to be time-consuming, and I'd rather not start a search I can't finish."

Turning to Nick, Mark said, "I would like to make a motion we meet here again at promptly eight o'clock this Saturday morning, write our request in the book, and begin to search for the antiques it leads us to." Patti quickly seconded the motion, and when Nick called for a vote, even Kenneth reluctantly raised his hand.

"I still don't see why we can't see if the book produces a map," he mumbled after the vote.

Hearing Kenneth, Nick spoke up, "We have to be careful about the *timing* of any request, Kenneth."

"Why is that?" Patti asked with a questioning look.

"Well, think about it. If the book produced a map based on a request we made tonight, circumstances might change between now and this weekend! What if someone at one of these estate sales buys the very antique revealed by the book and drives back to Dallas with it? What then? Would we be forced to approach this person and offer to buy the antique from them? What if they refuse? Then we couldn't make another request of the book until we obtained that antique!"

Standing up, Nick began to pace back and forth. "There is so much about *The Book of Lost Treasures* we don't understand! We don't need to make any kind of a wrong move that compromises the book's value to us until we know more of how the book operates."

"I agree with Nick. Let's just hold tight until Saturday. Then we will go from there," Hearing no further objections, Mark made a motion the meeting be adjourned, which was seconded by Abby. At that, the meeting ended, and the club members began to drift out of the den and to their cars.

Nick took his glass of tea to the kitchen and emptied it before rinsing it out. Placing it in the sink, he returned to den, empty now except for Abby, who stood with arms crossed, looking at him expectantly.

"Well?" she asked.

Looking around to see if he had missed anything, Nick finally glanced back at Abby, a confused expression on his face.

"Wh … what?"

Rolling her eyes, Abby said, "Don't you remember? You asked me Sunday about going out to dinner sometime this week! Or did I imagine it?"

"Oh … *that*! Of course! Where … I mean when …."

Nick stopped when he saw Abby giggling.

"Did anyone ever tell you that you look cute when you get that panicked look on your face?"

"Huh? Well, uh, no actually," he managed to stammer. Wait! Did she call him cute?

Before he could process that bit of information further, Abby looped her arm through his and began to steer him to the front door. "Here's what I think we should do," she carried on conversationally as they walked. "I think we should go to Longview Friday night. Patti told me about this new café that just opened that she and Mark went to. She said it was fabulous! We might even get to do a little shopping before we eat. What do you think?"

"Uh, that would be … great!"

"Good! I'll take care of making the reservation, say around eight o'clock?"

"Sure … eight o'clock sounds fine."

By this time, they had walked out the front door and were standing by Nick's car. Mark, Patti, Steve, and Kenneth were standing by Steve's car and looked over at them curiously.

"Oh, one more thing," Abby said to Nick as he opened the door to the little Sprint. "Do you mind if we take my car?"

Grinning at Abby, Nick said, "My car is really a lot roomier than it looks, but … if you insist!" Abby laughed, placing her hand on Nick's arm as she did so. His skin tingled where she touched him, and he was struck once again by how easy the sound of laughter seemed to come from her. For a moment or two, they stood in awkward silence knowing they were being observed by their friends. Nick finally got into the car, folding himself in carefully. The engine sputtered to life as he turned the key. Before driving off, he rolled the window down and said good-bye to Abby.

Watching her image in the rearview mirror, he gazed at her until he was forced to turn at the end of the street and she finally disappeared from sight.

Chapter 19

The week flew by quickly as Nick busied himself with various tasks. He spent one afternoon in the Pleasant Mountain public library poring through reference books on antiques. Writing notes on a legal pad, he was amazed at the variety and the value of antiques, large and small.

To his untrained eye, many of the valuable pieces pictured in the reference book looked rather ordinary—something he might pass by a hundred times at a flea market or estate sale and never suspect were priceless. For example, there was a copper tray, rather crude and ugly looking to Nick, pictured in the reference book that had an estimated value of $6,000, while a nineteenth century carved wooden mask made by Alaskan Eskimos, something that looked to him like a cheap souvenir, had a value of over $30,000!

By the time he left the library, Nick was convinced Patti's plan would work. Most people, the overwhelming majority, were just like him—they couldn't tell a valuable antique from garage sale junk! If so, these treasures were truly "lost" in the fullest sense of the word! It just remained for them to phrase their request to *The Book of Lost Treasures* carefully enough that it achieved the desired result. It left him with such an intense sense of anticipation, Nick felt sure if he were a dog, he would be salivating all over himself by now.

Friday morning dawned clear and cloudless, the precursor of another hot July day. Nick spent that morning at the Verizon office ditching his old cell phone and buying a new one. His new cell plan had unlimited minutes and text messaging, a significant upgrade over the paid minutes of his cheap Wal-Mart cell. He called Mark, Kenneth, and Steve and gave them his new number. While he had him on the phone, Mark told him that he had dropped the coins from the hidden cashbox off at the coin shop in Texarkana the day before. Unfortunately, the coin dealer had an out-of-town trip planned that weekend and wouldn't be able to give them an estimation of the coins' value until sometime next week. Without any money, Mark had not opened a bank account for the Treasure Hunt Club. Nick had told him he would use the money he had received from the cashier's check, and the club could just pay him back, something Mark readily agreed to.

Clicking off, Nick hesitated and then called Mark's home. He had not talked to Abby since Monday, and he found he was disappointed when no one answered the phone. Shrugging, he clicked off, reminding himself to get her cell phone number that night.

Nick headed back home and doodled around in his workshop until it was time to get ready, Nick returned to the trailer, where he showered and shaved. Standing in only his boxers, he opened the sliding door to his closet and considered what to wear. Unfortunately, his options were few; he had worn his only good pair of pants and shirt to church with Abby, and he couldn't just wear them again so soon.

All that was left was an eclectic selection of various blue jeans, T-shirts, and shorts—most of which were wrinkled from being jammed in his tiny closet.

Sighing, he finally chose a pair of khaki shorts and a T-shirt. Hunting around at the top of his closet produced his mother's old iron—something he had used exactly once in his life—and, plugging it in, used the top of the kitchen table as an ironing board in an attempt to iron the wrinkles out of the T-shirt.

A few minutes later, he held the T-shirt up before him and scrutinized it. Most of the worst wrinkles were gone. However, the smaller wrinkles had defied his best efforts to iron them out. Shrugging, he put the T-shirt on.

Next, Nick searched for a pair of shoes to wear. All he owned were tennis shoes and flip-flops besides his one pair of brown shoes. Arraying the tennis shoes on the floor before him, he eyed them critically. Most were scuffed and stained and were off-brands he had bought in the bargain bin. Choosing the least scuffed pair, he took a wet rag and tried with limited success to remove the worst of the dirt and stains. Putting them on, he finally headed to the bathroom, where he pawed through bottles of cologne lying jumbled in the bathroom drawer. Selecting a bottle Lisa had given him last Christmas, he sprayed some in his hands and rubbed it on his face, neck, and chest. The thought of Lisa caused him to pause.

Although they had broken up only two weeks ago, it now seemed like a lifetime! Given the time and level of commitment he had spent with her, he thought it odd that now he couldn't even summon faint feelings of regret. *Perhaps that was a direct reflection of just how shallow our relationship had always been,* he thought sadly to himself. Shaking his head, he took one last look at himself in the mirror before exiting the trailer and walking to his car. A few minutes later, he was on the road.

Nick pulled up and parked once again alongside the curb in front of Mark and Patti's house. As he walked up to the front door, Nick was startled as it was suddenly jerked open, and Mark and Patti were standing there with broad smiles on their faces.

"I want you to know that my cousin has a midnight curfew!" Patti tried to say sternly. Unfortunately, the effect was ruined because Patti couldn't keep the smile off her face.

"Yeah, and no funny business!" Mark chimed in, although he had no better success than Patti in keeping the grin off his face.

Holding both hands up before him in surrender, Nick said, "The perfect gentleman. I promise!"

"Well, in that case, it's liable to be a boring evening," a feminine voice said behind Mark and Patti. Looking up, Nick saw Abby walking down the hallway toward them. His mouth dropped open at the sight of her. She was wearing a black and white two-piece print dress. The top of the dress was a V-neck, with cap sleeves and a mock button front that hugged her small waist and bosom, while the flared skirt was mid-calf in length. A pair of black sandals completed the ensemble. A black hair band held Abby's long, shimmering hair behind her ears, and a pair of earrings made of tiny black and white pearls dangled from her ears. Abby's full lips glistened with the pink lip gloss she had applied to them, while she had added just enough rouge to her cheeks to bring out their natural color.

Nick was spellbound and convinced Abby was the loveliest woman he had ever seen!

Mark gave a low whistle. "Abby, if only I wasn't married to your cousin!" This earned him a good-natured jab from Patti's elbow.

"Well, what do you think?" Abby asked as she did a pirouette in front of Nick.

"You look … fantastic!" he finally managed to say.

Scanning Nick critically, Abby said, "It's nice to see you dressed up for the occasion also." Stammering, Nick tried to formulate an answer until he heard Abby's tinkling laughter.

Looking over her shoulder, Abby winked at Patti and said, "See, I told you! He does it every time! Isn't it cute?"

Turning, Abby looped her arm through Nick's and steered him toward her car parked in the driveway.

"Nick, you are *so* gullible! You need to lighten up!" she said, giggling. Relieved, Nick wondered if Abby had taken lessons from Hank Harper.

Handing her keys to Nick, she waited while he opened the passenger side door for her. Walking around to the other side of the car, Nick looked up and saw Mark giving him a big thumb's up. Grinning, he waved at Mark and Patti before getting in and starting the Corolla. Backing up, he pulled out onto the street, and a short time later, they were on their way to Longview.

Longview was a city of almost eighty thousand residents, approximately fifty miles southeast of Pleasant Mountain. Many people in Pleasant Mountain drove to Longview when looking for shop- ping, eating, and other distractions not found in their own small town. Not really knowing what to expect, Nick was pleasantly surprised when he and Abby chatted amiably the entire hour-long drive. She was easy to talk to, and Nick found himself, as before, immediately comfortable in her presence. He wondered if she was as comfortable with him.

They reached the city's outskirts a little after six o'clock. Abby had politely suggested that they do a little shopping at some clothing stores for Nick. Never much of a clotheshorse, Nick had reluctantly agreed. Stopping first at the mall, they made their way through Penney's, Sears, and Dillard's. By the time they made their last stop at Old Navy, Nick had three new pairs of pants, four new shirts, one new pair of tennis shoes, and one new pair of dress shoes. Although he had a man's natural aversion to trying on clothes to see if they actually fit, Abby had insisted he try on each and every article of clothing. At first, he had felt extremely foolish as he stood on display with tags sticking out of his collar or pant leg. However, as this process wore on, he found he enjoyed the attention Abby was giving him. Standing before him, she would purse her lips, as if in deep concentration, while asking him to turn this way and that. Occasionally, she would even tug at his shirts as if to adjust them for a better fit.

Old Navy had clothes that were more in line with the ones he usually wore, namely shorts and T-shirts. As such, he had looked around with greater interest than he had at the other stores. A clerk had assisted them shortly after they had entered the store, and Abby had asked him several questions before being pointed by the clerk to a display of clothes near one corner of the store. Rather than follow Abby, Nick chose to stay with the clerk, since the changing stalls were nearby.

"Been shopping long?" the clerk asked sympathetically. Nick nodded wearily as he looked over at the clerk. The young man looked to be in his late teens or early twenties, the stereotypical employee of this kind of clothing store. His brown hair had been moussed outward into long stringy spikes that would have made Don King proud. A wispy goatee struggled to grow from his chin, and he wore the standard, employee-issue, brown pants and white polo shirt. A plastic nametag hung at a crooked angle from his shirt with the name "Jordon" on it.

"Well, your girlfriend seems to know what she is looking for, so maybe it won't be too much longer."

"She's not … " Nick started to say before stopping himself. The clerk had called Abby his *girlfriend*!

The young man's mistaken interpretation of their relationship caused a warm feeling to blossom within him, and he found he didn't want to correct him. When Abby returned a short time later with several pairs of shorts and shirts for him to try on, he thought it was a feeling he could *definitely* get used to! By the time they left the store, he had another pair of shorts, and they headed for the café where Abby had made reservations.

The café turned out to be an upscale bistro that doubled as a book and gift shop. Called Lofton's, it was located in a strip mall close to the loop that encircled Longview. Lofton's, Nick soon discovered, had seating both inside and out. The outside dining area looked like a photograph out of a French or Italian tourist guidebook. A dozen small tables covered with starched white tablecloths were arranged cozily, and each had a covered candle to provide dim illumination. Ceiling fans turned lazily above the tables, providing a constant artificial breeze. Abby asked Nick if they could be seated outside, and he readily agreed. The setting sun was only a reddish glow in the western horizon as they were shown to their table by the hostess. Surprisingly, it had cooled considerably, and the movement of air provided by the ceiling fans made the atmosphere quite comfortable.

The hostess asked for their drink order, and Nick ordered a beer, while Abby requested a white wine. As they perused the menu, more couples began to drift into the bistro, although only a few chose to be seated outside. By the time their waiter appeared to take their order, there were only two other tables occupied besides their own. As they had on the drive down to Longview, they talked and chatted amiably, with none of the stiffness or moments of awkward silence that often occurred on first dates. Nick learned that both of Abby's older brothers were married and that she had two nephews and two nieces, with one sister-in-law expecting again in December. Her oldest brother, Sam, lived in Tyler, a city of one hundred thousand that was sixty miles south of Pleasant Mountain, and was an associate professor of math at Tyler Junior College, while her other brother, Brandon, lived in Rockwall, just east of Dallas, and was a CPA.

She and her brothers had grown up in Lindale, a community just just outside of Tyler. She had run cross-country and track while in high school and had graduated from Lindale High School in the top 10 percent of her class.

Nick told Abby his mother and sister lived in Plano, a suburb of Dallas, and that he too had a niece and nephew. Abby asked about his father, and Nick's face darkened. Thankfully, their food arrived providentially at that point, sparing Nick any comment about his father.

The food, although expensive, was as good as advertised. Nick had blackened snapper, served on a bed of brown rice and a baked potato, while Abby's entrée was chicken cordon bleu, served with steamed vegetables. For dessert, they shared a bread pudding drenched in a warm, buttery rum sauce. The waiter returned to clear their dishes, and while Abby ordered another glass of wine, Nick declined another beer since he was driving. By this time, it was after nine o'clock, and they were the only couple still in the outside dining area. Sitting at the table with only the flickering candle to provide a muted illumination, Nick and Abby listened to the distant traffic on the loop as a constant stream of cars drove by.

Fiddling with the saltshaker, Nick kept screwing the lid on and off as he tried to work up the courage to ask Abby a question he had wanted to ask her all night. Finally, he put it down and turned toward her.

"Abby, why did you go out with me? You're smart, beautiful, and talented, while I'm … well, I'm *me*—not the best catch in the world, if you know what I mean."

In the soft light, Nick saw Abby studying him, her expression unreadable. Finally, she looked away and said, "You already asked me that question, remember? I thought I had answered it."

"C'mon, Abby!" Nick said, uncomfortable in persisting but, at the same time, determined to get an answer from her. "You know what I mean! You've known Mark and Patti most of your life, and I'm sure you've heard all about my … my life and all the stupid screw-ups and crazy schemes."

Abby did not answer Nick for a long time, and he began to fear he had hurt her feelings. Finally, she turned to him and placed her hand on his. Her hand was smooth and warm, and she squeezed his own hand gently as she gazed into his eyes.

"Is that what you think of your life, Nick?" she asked softly. "That it is a series of one disaster after another? Well, let me give you another point of view." Nick swallowed hard, unable to tear his eyes away from her face.

"There's nothing wrong with dreaming, Nick. Most people have dreams, wishes, goals—whatever you want to call it. The difference between you and them is that you've tried to fulfill your dreams and followed the path less traveled, while they settled for the more stable, but less satisfying, niches of life. Believe me, I know. My ex-husband was a dentist, and I was the receptionist at his office for several years. I got to see all kinds of people: housewives, teachers, doctors, lawyers, businessmen, accountants—every type of professional you can imagine, and by normal standards, they were considered successful. They had the big houses, membership in the country club, and weekend cabins on the lake. However, the conversations I had with them showed me that too many simply weren't happy!

They were always complaining about the long hours, the tight schedules, the constant pressure they were under. Not all of them, mind you, but enough to make me see that too many had traded their own dreams for someone else's."

Abby paused and absently adjusted her hair band. "I heard on the news not too long ago that people who live in metropolitan areas—like Dallas—spend, on average, thirty-eight hours of their life each year stuck in traffic. Think about that, Nick.

Thirty-eight hours! How's that for a productive use of your time and your life! Now, compare that with your so-called screw-ups. Whose time, whose *life,* has been wasted now?"

Gripping Nick's hand harder, Abby continued, "You see, I think it takes courage to try and follow your dreams. Maybe you haven't found yours yet, maybe you never will, but despite all of that, you can truly say you had no regrets. You won't be one of those people who one day look at themselves in the mirror and wonder about what might have been."

Abby looked away from Nick momentarily, as if trying to choose her next words carefully. Finally, she turned back, facing him. "When I first saw you in your workshop, you had such an excited, intense look on your face, and you had such … *energy*! I thought, 'Here's someone interesting, someone who is not like most people.' That's why I asked you to go to church with me, and why I wanted to learn more about you."

Nick had never had anyone describe him in such a way as Abby had. It was like she understood him at a level that even his friends couldn't approach, despite knowing him for years. In fact, other than his grandfather and perhaps his mother, no one had even attempted to try and learn what made Nick Hollister tick. A lump arose in his throat, and it was at that precise moment he knew that Abby was unlike any person he had ever met.

For a long time, they said nothing, with only the whir of the ceiling fans and the bustle of the distant traffic disturbing their silence.

Finally, Nick asked softly, "What about you, Abby? What are your dreams?" Looking at Abby, Nick immediately regretted the question as he saw a sense of sadness seem to come over her.

Taking a sip of the wine as if to fortify herself, Abby glanced over at Nick and said, "I … I don't know. I used to think I knew what would make me happy, but now I don't know anymore." Nick considered her answer, and he began screwing and unscrewing the lid to the saltshaker again as an uncomfortable silence fell between them. Putting the saltshaker down with an audible *thump*, Nick looked over at Abby.

"Why? Why don't you know? I mean, you don't have to talk about it if you don't want to, but I'd really like to know."

Abby said nothing and graduated from the task of adjusting her headband to turning the wineglass round and round in her hands. She did this for several moments, as if unsure of how or even if she wanted to answer Nick's question. Finally, she gave a deep sigh and put the wine glass down.

"I met Rob, my ex-husband, when I was a sophomore at the University of Dallas," she began without preamble. "He was a senior and had already been accepted into dental school. He was handsome, charming, intelligent, and I fell for him almost immediately. We were married the day after he graduated. We didn't have much money, and I had to drop out of college in order to work and help Rob get through dental school. It was a long four years, and we lived pretty much hand-to-mouth, but I was happy, convinced that in the end, it would be worth it—Rob would establish his practice, we could buy a house, and we could raise a family.

"Rob finally graduated, and he opened his first office in an old building in McKinney that used to be a shoe store. The first year was difficult. Rob struggled to establish his practice.

Gradually, he began to build a patient base. Since we couldn't afford office help, I did practically everything, from answering phones to scheduling appointments. I even paid the bills and balanced the books each month. Finally, we were able to afford a full-time receptionist and a dental assistant. Things were looking up, Rob had all the patients he could handle, and I began to draw up floor plans of our dream house in my mind.

"After a year in McKinney, Rob moved his office to a brand new medical complex in Frisco, an area north of Dallas that was booming with new houses, strip malls, and subdivisions. He actually had to start turning down new patients, and he hired a dental hygienist to clean teeth. I no longer had to work, so I began to make plans to go back to college. I thought it also a good time to try and begin to start a family, but Rob wouldn't even discuss it with me! I thought that odd, since he had told me repeatedly while were dating and after we were married that he loved kids and wanted a family as soon as we could afford it. At any rate, his hours became longer and longer, and he was getting home later and later."

Nick rubbed his eyes, and remembering his parents' divorce, he thought he had a good idea of where this was going.

"One evening, Rob was working late, and I thought I would surprise him by going to his office so we could go out to dinner after he had finished. The duplex we were renting was close by, and it only took me ten minutes to reach the medical plaza. It was almost seven o'clock by then, and instead of just Rob's car, there were *two* cars parked in front of his office! As I parked and got out of my car, I noticed all the lights were out. Puzzled, I used my key to unlock the front door and went straight to Rob's office, which was adjacent to his dental suite. The door was shut, but I could see light coming from the crack at the bottom of the door and heard voices coming from behind the door. When … when I opened the door, he was on his couch with the dental hygienist. Her … her blouse was off, and he … he was ….” Unable to continue, Abby's voice trailed off, her eyes brimming with tears.

"That's all right. I don't need to hear anymore," Nick said quickly.

Abby took a napkin from the table and dabbed her eyes as she tried to compose herself. Putting it down, she patted Nick's hand.

"Thank you, Nick. But I *want* to tell you all of it, if you don't mind. It's … it's kind of like therapy," Abby said, laughing nervously.

"Of course, I don't mind. But don't feel you have to tell me everything, especially if it brings back memories you would just as soon forget." With that, Nick gave her hand a gentle squeeze.

Taking a deep breath, Abby continued, "It turned out he had been having an affair with the dental hygienist—Tiffany, I think her name was—for the past several months. That was why he was always 'working late.' I … I didn't know what to do at first; I didn't know what to think. I know I didn't scream, I didn't shout, I didn't even cry. All I can remember is closing the door and walking back to my car, like I was in a trance. I kept thinking I must be dreaming and having a nightmare and that I would wake up and everything would be all right. I was numb, so literally numb, that I don't remember getting in my car or even driving home. Somehow, I made it back to the duplex, and when Rob came home later that night, I wouldn't let him in the bedroom. He told me through the locked door that he was moving out, and I found out later he had moved in with Tiffany. He never told me he was sorry, and he never even tried to explain why."

Abby's voice cracked, and the tears returned to her eyes. "You know the worst part?" she whispered. "*He* was the one who had the affair! *He* was the one who moved out and left me! But I was convinced that somehow it was *my* fault and *I* was the one to blame! For the next month, I never left the duplex except to buy food, which wasn't often since I never felt like eating. I had no energy, and I slept all the time, and when I wasn't sleeping, I was crying. Sleep and cry, cry and sleep, that's all I did for weeks. I was so ashamed that I kept Rob's affair and our separation a secret from my parents, my brothers, and even Patti. Then one day, barely four weeks after Rob moved out, someone knocked at the door. When I opened it, a skinny, pimply-faced process server handed me divorce papers from Rob. I couldn't believe it! The bastard didn't even have the decency to call me and let me know he was filing for divorce!

"Something inside me snapped, and I snatched the papers from the kid and slammed the door in his face! I started throwing anything within reach as hard as I could until I was too exhausted to throw anymore. The inside of the duplex was a wreck, with shattered dishes, broken lamps, and holes in the wall. But it served to finally clear my head, and for the first time, I realized I had done nothing wrong and that my life could and *would* go on! I spent the rest of the day packing and renting a U-Haul. I left that evening, but not until I had taken a hammer and put a lot more holes in the walls."

"Why would you do that?" Nick asked, puzzled.

A faint smile crept across Abby's lips. "Because the lease was in Rob's name."

Nick couldn't help himself and laughed, with Abby joining him. The sadness of Abby's story and the somber atmosphere it had created was soon dispelled as they continued to laugh together. When the laughter finally died away, Abby glanced at Nick with an abashed look on her face.

"Thanks for listening, Nick. I … I don't normally unload those kinds of details about my personal life to … well, to just anyone. I'm sorry if I made you feel uncomfortable."

"Forget about it!" Nick said as he waved his hand dismissively. "There's nothing to apologize for. Besides, it was me, remember, who asked you!"

"I guess you're right," Abby said with a relieved look.

"Anyway, you know what I think?"

"No, what do you think, Nick Hollister?" Abby asked as a hint of playfulness returned to her voice.

"I think your ex-husband must be the biggest fool on earth! Anybody who's been around you for even a short period of time knows … well … knows what a special person you are!"

Turning his chair so that he faced Abby, Nick gazed at her and slowly said, "I mean, if you had been mine, I never would have let you go."

Abby stared at Nick, her eyes softening at what he had said. Hesitating for a brief moment, she then leaned toward him until her face was just inches from his. Her breath, warm on his cheek, smelled of wine as she kissed him. Nick pulled Abby toward him and returned her kiss with an urgency that surprised and exhilarated him. They kissed for a few moments longer before finally pulling apart.

Abruptly standing, Abby caught hold of Nick's hand.

"Let's go."

Surprised, Nick managed to ask, "Where to?"

Abby gazed at Nick as if an internal struggle was raging inside her. Finally, she smiled and said, "Let's go to your place."

Chapter 20

Nick lay in the bed loft of his darkened trailer with Abby's head on his chest. He listened to her breathing, her breath tickling his bare skin. Tiny as it was, they had both managed to fit into the bed loft, although it had made things *interesting* at times. Jammed together, Abby laid snuggly against him out of necessity, and he reveled in the feel of her soft skin against his.

Staring at the ceiling not two feet above his head, Nick thought of the remarkable sequence of events, the roller-coaster ride that had occurred in his life over the past couple of weeks. He had once heard a talking head on television, a so-called "expert," say that everyone had "markers" in their life, or events that profoundly and permanently changed the course of their lives. If so, over the course of the past couple of weeks, Nick had picked up a pocketful of these so-called markers. He had gone from having no job, no girlfriend, no money, and no prospects to discovering *The Book of Lost Treasures* and having Abby enter his life with the suddenness of an exploding bottle rocket.

Thinking of Abby caused Nick to unconsciously pull her closer to him, despite the already tight confines of the bed loft. Since he had met her, everything he knew or thought he knew about love and relationships had been cast into doubt. He *thought* he had been in love with Lisa—no, make that *convinced*—and yet, what he was feeling now for Abby was so far removed from that of Lisa, he found it laughable he could have ever believed he was in love with her!

As if sensing his thoughts, Abby stirred against him and began lazily tracing her finger in circles across the skin of his chest.

"Why aren't you sleeping?" she purred. "I thought that's what men were supposed to do after making love?"

Grinning in the darkness, Nick replied, "That's a vicious rumor probably started by women who watch too much Dr. Phil."

Abby giggled and propped herself up on one elbow, her soft breasts brushing against his arm as she did so. A security light mounted on the utility pole outside the trailer caused a small amount of light to leak through the curtained windows of the bed loft. The muted light provided just enough illumination for Nick to make out the contours of Abby's face and body, and the thought flashed through his mind of what it would be like to wake up to that vision every morning.

Tracing circles on his chest again, Abby said, "I know this sounds like a cliché, but I'm not the kind of girl who falls in bed with someone after the first date. In fact, you're … you're only the second man I've … well, I've ever been with."

"I'll take that as a compliment!" Nick said, grinning even wider. Pinching Nick hard until she elicited a loud "Ow!" from him, Abby said, "I'm serious, Nick! I just don't do something like this! I … I can't unless …" Her voice trailed off, and Nick, sensing an emotional change about Abby, strained to see her face in the darkness.

"Can I ask you a question?" Abby asked softly. Seeing Nick nod his head, she continued, "Do you believe two people fall in love, or … or do you believe they *grow* into love?"

The question was simple. although Abby had attempted to ask it whimsically, Nick suspected his answer was very important to her. Taking his time, he closed his eyes and thought of how to reply. His parents, his mother and father, had been happily married until his father had met the young bimbo, and suddenly… he was gone! Abby had thought she was happily married; then suddenly, she discovers her husband's affair. He had thought he was in love with Lisa, and then she shacked up with a waiter! The concept of love, at least in the traditional sense, seemed to be a disposable commodity with too many people these days, often stretching a mile wide but only an inch deep. The realization struck him that he was just as guilty, just as much to blame, for treating love in such a way. That he had met Abby, someone who *truly* knew and believed in love, made him a lucky man indeed!

"I … I guess it's a little of both," Nick finally said. "You fall in love … then that love grows deeper over time. At least, that's the way it's supposed to work, isn't it? But then, what do I know? I never believed in love at first sight; at least, not until tonight."

Nick heard Abby's breath catch in her throat. Then, still propped on her elbow, she leaned over and started kissing Nick slowly but with a passion that left him breathless.

Stopping, Abby gazed at him, their eyes only inches apart. "I love you, Nick. I know it sounds crazy, but I can't help myself," she breathed.

Pulling her tightly against him, Nick whispered, "Then I guess we're both crazy, because I love you too!"

"Promise me one thing."

Gently stroking Abby's cheek with his fingertips, Nick said "Anything!"

Brushing her lips up against Nick's ear, Abby murmured, "Promise me … promise me that, no matter what, I will always be the most important thing in your life."

Nick placed both hands on Abby's face and gently pulled her toward him. "You already are."

The morning came much too quickly, and Abby was the first to rise, climbing down out of the bed loft over Nick. Nick turned and watched as Abby dressed, unable to keep his eyes off of her. Noticing his scrutiny of her, Abby tiptoed around their jumble of clothes lying on the floor and kissed him.

"Got anything that passes for coffee in here?"

Yawning, Nick pointed toward a cabinet directly above a small automatic coffeemaker. Ten minutes later, the smell of freshly brewed coffee filled the inside of the trailer. Reluctantly, Nick swung his legs out of the loft and began to get dressed. Abby handed him a cup of coffee, and they sat together at the tiny kitchen table.

Glancing at his watch, Nick saw it was almost seven o'clock. The Treasure Hunt Club was due to meet at

Mark and Patti's at eight to begin their first search for lost treasure.

"Are you worried?" Abby abruptly asked him.

Taking a sip of coffee, Nick glanced at Abby. "A little," he admitted. "*The Book of Lost Treasures* has worked for me three times now, but you never know. When it produced the map to Colonel Buckley's hidden strongbox, I substituted an 'e' instead of a 'u,' which misspelled his first name. It wasn't until I corrected the spelling that something appeared in the book. It's quirky things like that, things we don't yet understand about the book, that concern me." "But I thought the rules of the book's usage were clearly stated."

"They are, but it's the *interpretations* of the rules that can cause us to make a mistake. That's why we have to be careful."

"Everything will be fine, you'll see," Abby assured him.

Leaning over and kissing him on the cheek, Abby said, "We'd better go. I'm already way past my 'curfew.'"

Grinning, Nick said, "I just hope you're not grounded!"

Laughing together, they walked out of the trailer, got into Abby's car, and drove back to Pleasant Mountain.

Arriving at Mark and Patti's, Nick and Abby walked hand in hand to the front door. It was unlocked, and they let themselves in. Immediately, their senses were assaulted by the rich aroma of biscuits baking and sausage frying. Following the smell, they came to the kitchen, where Patti stood over a stove, and Mark was sit- ting at the kitchen table sipping coffee and studying something he had written on a legal pad. Several large books lay on the table, and on closer inspection, Nick saw they were reference books on antiques.

Dressed in khaki shorts, brown Sketchers loafers, and a bright blue Hawaiian shirt with white palm trees printed on it, Mark looked more like a tourist just off a cruise ship than someone pre- pared to do battle at garage sales and flea markets. Looking up, he smiled as he saw Nick and Abby enter the room.

"Lucy, you got some 'splaining to do," he said jokingly to Abby in his best Ricky Ricardo imitation. Blushing, Abby turned to Patti, who had looked over her shoulder when she heard Mark talking. One look passed between the two women as if it were a silent communication that spoke volumes. Wiping her hands on a dishrag, Patti hugged Abby, tears forming in her eyes.

"What's wrong?" Mark asked, concerned.

Swiping at her eyes, Patti gave Mark a withering look. "Oh, Mark, I love you, but you are so dense at times!" she scolded him. "What?" Mark said, looking at Nick for support. Nick, feeling his own cheeks start to grow warm, quickly looked away from his friend. Then, as if scales had been lifted from his eyes, it suddenly became clear to Mark that something extraordinary had occurred between Nick and Abby, and his lips formed a silent, "Oh." During the momentary silence that followed, Abby took the opportunity to escape from the kitchen and go to her room to change. Nick hastily sat down at the table as Patti brought him a cup of coffee.

Eager to deflect the attention from Abby and himself, Nick gestured toward the reference books resting on the table. "I see you have been busy."

"Actually, Patti bought these at the bookstore yesterday, and we've been trying to study them to get a sense of what we are looking for."

"They'll come in handy when we try to identify whatever antique the book leads us to," Nick agreed. All conversation stopped at that point, as Patti set a platter stacked high with homemade sausage biscuits before them. The aroma made Nick's mouth water, and he immediately helped himself to one. Taking a huge bite, the sausage and warm, flaky biscuit practically melted in his mouth. Quickly finishing the sausage biscuit, he grabbed another one.

Mark watched Nick wolf down the sausage biscuits with a wry look of amusement on his face. "Your metabolism has always been on speed dial, Nick. If I ate like you did, I would weigh over three hundred pounds!"

"What can I say? It's a gift!" Nick replied, grinning.

A commotion came from the direction of the front door, and moments later, Steve and Kenneth trooped into the kitchen. They spied the platter of food, quickly sat down and began helping themselves as Nick had done earlier.

"Mark, can you save Abby and me a few of those hot sausage biscuits?" Patti called out over her shoulder as she was rinsing the skillet in the sink. "I'm afraid if I reach in there myself, I might pull back missing an appendage!"

Mark put several on a napkin as Nick, Steve, and Kenneth engaged in a fierce contest to see who could eat the most in the shortest amount of time. The platter was soon empty, much to the disappointment of those seated around the table.

"Patti, you make the best sausage biscuits in the county!" Nick said as he unsuccessfully tried to stifle a belch, which was quickly seconded by both Kenneth and Steve.

Studying his friends, Nick saw a look of excitement, He knew they were eager to test the book and get the day's proceedings started. Kenneth had changed for the occasion, and instead of the usual checkered buttoned shirt he usually wore, he now sported a plaid buttoned shirt of a green color. Peering closer, Nick saw even his plastic pocket protector looked new! Steve, on the other hand was, well, Steve. A black sleeveless Aerosmith T-shirt adorned his frame, and although Nick was sure he had entered the kitchen empty-handed, Steve had somehow produced a can of beer, which he opened and began to sip.

Abby reentered the kitchen, having changed into navy blue shorts, a white crewneck T-shirt, and tennis shoes. She had pulled her hair back into a long ponytail, and her face had a pink glow from the cold water she had scrubbed it with. Sitting down next to Nick, she nibbled on one of the sausage biscuits Mark had saved as they waited for Patti to join them.

"Well, I guess the moment of truth has arrived!" Mark said half in jest as Patti finally took a seat at the crowded table.

"Here's what I think we should write in the book," Mark said as he handed the legal pad to Nick.

Studying it, Nick saw that Mark had written.

> Reveal the location of any antique within the county at an estate sale or garage sale that, unbeknownst to the owner, has a value of at least $1,000 or more.

Nodding, Nick handed the legal pad to Abby, who studied it before handing it to the next person. In this fashion, the legal pad made it around the table and back to Mark.

"What do you think?" he asked. A chorus of "Looks good" and "Let's do it!" greeted his question.

"We won't need the contract agreeing to give the owner ten percent of what we find, since we're actually *buying* the item from them!" Mark explained. "However, we need to make sure we get a receipt of some kind to prove our ownership."

Seeing that everyone understood him, Mark looked over at Nick. "You ready, buddy?"

Taking a deep breath, Nick nodded and pulled *The Book of Lost Treasures* from his satchel and placed it on the table. Turning to the first page, under "*What is the lost treasure which you seek?*" he carefully wrote their request, copying it word for word from the legal pad Mark held up before him.

The pencil Nick was using had barely left the book's page when bright light flared from the book, startling all those around the table, except Nick and Mark. A deep sense of relief washed over Nick as he turned the page and saw not one, not two, but *three* maps etched in precise detail on three successive pages in the book! Now they had to believe him!

Looking around, Nick saw a range of emotions displayed by his friends, from open-mouthed amazement to shock. Steve, beer forgotten, was standing up and leaning over for as close a view as possible, while Kenneth sat with a stunned expression, as if his mind couldn't quite process what his eyes were telling him. Even Patti, normally unflappable, was making little waving motions in front of her face and said repeatedly, "Oh my, Oh my!" Mark's expression was much like that of Nick's, a mixture of relief and excitement.

Abby, a broad smile on her face, reached over and squeezed Nick's hand.

"Congratulations. You did it!"

Unable to stop himself, Nick pulled Abby to him and gave her an enthusiastic kiss before raising his hands in euphoria above his head.

"Yes!" he shouted.

An excited babbling broke out as everyone seemed to want to talk at once For a few minutes, a happy pandemonium reigned. *The Book of Lost Treasures* was passed around, and everyone took a turn staring at the maps within it.

"Brook Street! That's just two blocks from here!" Patti exclaimed as she pointed at one of the maps. "And look! Edwards Avenue is on here too! Mark, that's close to you and your daddy's State Farm office!"

"Where's this?" Steve asked, pointing at the third and last map. Patti saw it was a location out of the city and in the country. Mark knew the county much better than she did, so she pushed the book over to him.

Perusing the map, Mark did little clucking noises with his tongue as he studied the map. "I think that's the old Parmelov place. But he died a couple of months ago. I know, because we have his car insurance, and his son called and canceled the policy last month."

Snapping his fingers, Mark excitedly said, "That's it! It must be an estate sale! Parmelov's wife died years ago, and his son and daughter don't even live in Texas anymore."

There was more excited discussion before Kenneth, his brow furrowed in deep concentration, suddenly raised his hand and began waving it like a student wanting to get a teacher's attention.

Mark, noticing Kenneth's waving, rapped his knuckles on the table, causing the excited babble to temporarily quiet down.

"Yes, Kenneth?"

"If I remember correctly, the rules in the book state that only *one* lost treasure at a time can be found! Yet there are *three* maps here!"

A momentary silence followed Kenneth's pronouncement before Mark, with a puzzled look, glanced over at Nick and said, "He's right. There are three maps and three locations."

Nick drummed the table with his fingers as he considered the maps and locations revealed to them by *The Book of Lost Treasures*. Kenneth *was* correct, at least on the face of it.

However, it came down to what he had confided to Abby: the *interpretations* of the simply stated rules were something they had no understanding of. What's more, they would only discover these nuances as they were revealed through experience by using the mysterious book. It was all the more reason to be very careful in what they wrote in the book.

"The request was singular and specific," Nick said slowly. "We asked for the location of any antique that might meet a certain criteria, namely that the antique be of a monetary value that equals or exceeds a thousand dollars and that the owner is unaware of its value. By producing three maps, this must mean the book can and will reveal multiple locations if they fall under the terms of the request."

"A lawyer couldn't have phrased that any better!" Mark said as he pounded Nick on the back. "Well, I don't know about the rest of you, but I'm ready to get started! Mr. President," Mark said, winking at Nick, "I move everybody who agrees to follow me!"

"So moved!" Nick cried, and with that, Mark led them to his SUV. Mark and Nick got into the front seats with *The Book of Lost Treasures* in his lap, while Patti and Abby sat in the back. Steve and Kenneth piled into Steve's car. The GTO gave a husky roar as Steve started it and began to follow Mark, who had already backed up and pulled out into the street.

The first official search of the Treasure Hunt Club began!

Chapter 21

It took only a few minutes to travel to Brook Street, a residential section of modest brick homes. As they turned and pulled onto the street, they saw a full-scale garage sale in progress at one of the houses on the block. Even at this early hour, cars were already parked up and down the block, and a throng of potential customers was examining the various items for sale. Mark was forced to park at the end of the block, with Steve parking behind him. They all got out and walked up the sidewalk toward the garage sale.

Racks of clothes lined the driveway, and a line of tables set end to end on the front lawn held boxes of knickknacks and other items. Inside the garage itself were larger articles for sale, and consulting the book, Nick led the club members there. Studying the book, Nick found the detail on the map to be amazing! Items for sale were actually catalogued by location, and it was a simple matter of following the route outlined by the map.

With his location represented by the moving red dot, Nick dodged a Hispanic couple looking at a small coffee table and stopped beside a stationary exercise bike that was for sale. Behind it was a wooden crate, and propped precariously on top of it was what looked to Nick to be an urn or large crock. Carefully, he moved the stationary bike aside and picked up the crock. It was extremely heavy, and Nick grunted as he set it on the ground before him. Light flashed from *The Book of Lost Treasures*, and glancing down, Nick had to shade his eyes as the words "*Treasure Found*" glowed like fire from the first map. Hastily, Nick closed the book before it drew unwanted attention.

"This is it?" Steve asked doubtfully as he and the others crowded around the crock. "It looks like a big clay crock my granddaddy used to store dried pinto beans in."

"Is it … pottery?" Patti asked.

"It's pretty heavy to be a pottery piece," Nick commented.

"There's something painted on it!" Mark said as he squatted beside the crock. A thick coat of dust covered the crock, as if it had recently been moved out of storage. Anybody got something I can clean it off with?"

Patti nodded and fished a couple of Kleenexes out of her purse, and Mark wiped the dust off. A scene, etched in a bluish paint, was revealed of a soldier holding a regimental flag and a woman dressed in a bonnet and hooped skirt.

Squinting at the painted figures, Mark said, "It looks to me like the soldier is wearing a Confederate uniform."

"Painting or not, it still looks like an ugly piece of pottery to me," Kenneth said, unable to keep the disappointment out of his voice.

"Look, if it was something obvious, like a great work of art, it wouldn't have been put out at a garage sale now, would it?" Nick snapped. "Besides, if the book revealed its location to us, it must be worth at least a thousand dollars."

"Let's buy it and then use the reference books to see if we can find something equivalent to it!" Patti chattered excitedly. All the club members quickly agreed, and with Steve picking up the crock, they went in search of the owners.

Rounding the corner of the garage, they quickly spied the garage sale proprietors. An elderly couple that looked to be in their late sixties or early seventies sat in lawn chairs behind a card table in the shade of their front porch. Each had a handmade nametag made of index cards pinned to their lapels, with the names "Roger" and "Mabel" neatly printed on them. A cigar box containing money rested on the card table in front of the couple.

As Steve hoisted the dusty crock, Nick asked, "How much?"

Squinting from behind a pair of thick glasses, the silver-haired woman named Mabel, peered at the crock, while her husband, also wearing glasses, did the same.

"My grandmother's stoneware crock!" she exclaimed. "I'd for- gotten I even had it until we cleaned out the attic!" Looking at it with a distasteful expression, she added, "It never was much to look at."

Rubbing her chin in concentration, Mabel glanced toward her husband before saying, "How about ten dollars?"

Nick readily agreed and quickly handed the woman's husband a $10 bill. "Can I have a receipt?" he asked.

"For that?" Mabel asked in disbelief.

"Well … I like to keep meticulous records of my … financial transactions," Nick managed to say.

Snorting, Mabel shook her head and scrawled out a receipt on a piece of notebook paper. As she handed it to Nick, he thanked her, and they hurriedly made their way back to their cars. Mark popped the door to the Expedition's cargo space up, and Steve carefully set the stoneware crock down into it.

While they were doing this, Patti had grabbed the reference books from the backseat and was furiously thumbing through them.

"Look!" she cried, holding one of the books before her and pointing.

As everyone crowded around Patti, she excitedly jabbered, "Here's a picture of a stoneware crock from around the Civil War era, and it looks identical to the one we just bought! *Its estimated value is between twenty-eight to thirty thousand dollars!*"

Gasps sounded all around, with everyone clamoring to get a closer look at the picture Patti was pointing to in the book.

Passing the reference book around, all the club members finally got to scrutinize the picture themselves, with all agreeing it looked just like the crock they had just bought.

"Let's move on to the next map and get the next antique!" Nick said, with no attempt to control his excitement.

In response, there was a rush to get into the cars, with Nick pausing just long enough to place the heavy crock between Abby and Patti in the backseat before jumping into the front passenger seat of the SUV.

Steve goosed the throttle on the GTO impatiently, the engine roaring, as Mark finally got the Expedition started and pulled out onto the road.

It took less than ten minutes to reach Edwards Avenue, which was another residential section. The homes here were older and were primarily wood frame houses of pier and beam construction. Unlike the garage sale on Brooks Street, this one wasn't nearly as busy, and Mark was able to pull up and park in front of the house. As before, clothes on makeshift racks were strung out on the lawn and driveway, along with all manner of items, large and small. Not bothering with tables, the couple putting on this garage sale, a portly middle-aged man and his wife, had simply put everything they were selling directly on their lawn or on their concrete driveway.

Consulting the map in the book, Nick climbed out of the SUV and made a beeline for one of the objects that had been placed on the driveway. It was a carved, wooden eagle with wings spread wide, and its talons were clutching a pale blue sphere, which was presumably the earth. This sphere rested on a platter-shaped base, which was also made of wood. The eagle had been painted a gold color, which had faded over time. Stopping beside the figurine, Nick squatted down beside it and studied it closely. It looked to be about two feet high and almost as wide from wingtip to wingtip. The faded paint was chipped in places, and the circular wooden base had a small crack in it.

However, the detail evident in the eagle carving caused Nick to give a low whistle in appreciation. Although it looked top-heavy, with the spread-winged eagle perched on the earth, Nick found when he picked it up and then set it down that it was perfectly balanced.

The second he touched the carved figurine, *The Book of Lost Treasures* flared brightly in Nick's hands. As before, the words "*Treasure Found*" had replaced the map on the book's page.

Stuffing the book in his satchel, Nick picked up the eagle figurine with both hands and examined it as the other club members crowded around. Turning it over, Nick saw the initials "JHB" carved into the circular wooden base.

Kenneth shook his head. "Don't tell me *that's* what the book picked as a valuable antique?"

When Nick nodded, Kenneth added, "But it looks like a cheap cigar store souvenir! No wonder no one knows it's worth anything!"

Nick, who obviously knew a thing or two about woodworking, couldn't have disagreed with Kenneth more. However, he bit his tongue and carried the figurine toward the front of the house. A large red and white striped umbrella, the kind you might see at a beach or beside a swimming pool, had been hammered into the grass and a large beefy man sat lounging in a lawn chair beneath it. Bald as a billiard ball with fleshy red jowls, the man had a metal tackle box sitting in his lap, which Nick quickly deduced held the garage sale money. The man's wife, a waifish woman, sat primly beside him in another chair. When Nick showed them the carved eagle figurine, the man gave it a bored look.

"Twenty bucks," he stated simply.

Although he knew he could have haggled him down, Nick wanted to take no chances and handed over a $20 bill.

As the money disappeared into the tackle box, Nick asked curiously, "Is there any, um … family history concerning this piece?"

With a shrug that caused his jowls to quiver, the man replied, "Been sittin' on a mantle at a fishin' cabin on Lake Texoma for years. My wife's uncle owned the cabin, but when he sold it, he gave us that eagle thing. She might be able to tell you more," he finished, jerking his thumb toward his wife.

Flashing a watery smile, the man's wife said, "Uncle Bert told me once that the eagle belonged to his granddaddy, which was my great-granddaddy. I believe great-granddaddy moved to Tulsa from Missouri way back in the early twenties. Does that help?"

Nick assured her that it did and thanked her. He then asked for a receipt, hoping he didn't get the same reaction as he had when he had asked for a receipt on the crock. Grunting, her husband produced a scratch pad from inside the tackle box and wrote out the receipt. Nick then carried the eagle back to the SUV. Feeling the curious eyes of the garage sale couple on him, Nick suggested they adjourn to one of the several city parks located in Pleasant Mountain. The others quickly agreed, and piling into the Expedition and GTO, they drove the short distance to the nearest park.

Pulling up next to a picnic table, Mark stopped and parked the SUV as Steve pulled up beside him and did the same. Nick opened the door and carried the carved wooden eagle figurine and placed it carefully on top of a cement picnic table. While he was doing this, Patti and Abby had carried the reference books to the table and were poring over them.

This time it was Abby who gave a sudden and excited squeak as she pointed to a picture in the book she was holding.

"I think I found it!" she cried.

Following Abby's trembling finger, Nick spotted a picture that looked quite similar to the eagle figurine they had purchased at the garage sale. Reading the information accompanying the picture, he saw that the carved and painted eagle figurine had been made by John Haley Bellamy (1836–1914) of Kittery Point, Maine. Something about that name jogged Nick's memory, and suddenly, he remembered!

Grabbing the figurine, he turned it upside down. There, as he had seen earlier, were the carved initials "JHB." That could only stand for *John Haley Bellamy*! Looking back at the picture in the reference book, Nick's breath caught in his throat as he saw the estimated value of the carved eagle figurine.

$50,000–$55,000!

"It's worth at least fifty thousand dollars!" he blurted out. Ignoring the gasps of his fellow club members, he quickly showed them the initials on the base of the figurine.

"That's … that's close to eighty thousand dollars or more on just *two* antiques!" Mark said in disbelief. Nick and Kenneth danced an impromptu jig. Changing partners, Nick grabbed Abby around the waist and swung her, laughing, round and round, while the rest of the club members clapped and high-fived one another enthusiastically. Finally breathless, Nick and Abby collapsed on the picnic table's stone bench.

"Eighty thousand dollars!" Steve said as much to himself as to the others seated around the picnic table. "I wonder what the last antique is worth?"

Nick looked across the table at Mark. Grinning, he said, "Let's find out!"

No one objected as Nick led a second rush to the parked cars. Grabbing the wooden eagle, he carefully laid it down in the SUV's cargo area before shutting the door. By the time he was finished, Mark already had the Expedition started, and the others were in their seats waiting impatiently for him.

With Mark leading the way, it took twenty minutes to reach the Parmelov house. Along the way, Mark told Nick what he knew about the late Anton Parmelov, who had been his father's client. Of Russian heritage, Parmelov's wealthy parents had immigrated to Chicago in 1917 to escape the upheaval resulting from the collapse of the Tsarist Monarchy and the onset of the Russian Revolution. Mr. Parmelov had been born in Chicago and had married his wife and raised his two children there. Tiring of the cold Chicago winters, he and his wife had retired and moved to Texas twenty-five years earlier, ultimately settling in Pleasant Mountain. His wife had preceded him in death five years earlier. Mark stopped his narrative as a winding, black, asphalt drive appeared to their left that led from the farm-to-market road they were on and to what proved to be a large ranch-style home. Turning, Mark drove down the asphalt drive and parked the SUV. A number of cars were already parked in the circular drive in front of the house, and a few had signs on the car doors advertising wholesale antique businesses, with some from as far away as Dallas, Texarkana, and Houston. As he got out of the Expedition and spotted the signs, Nick knew with a sinking feeling that they were now going head-to-head with professionals at the estate sale. These people knew their business, and unlike the garage sales they had come from, there would be no valuable antiques slip by unnoticed. Hoping they weren't too late, Nick pulled *The Book of Lost Treasures* from his satchel and hurried into the house. With the rest of the club members hard on his heels, Nick paused and looked around as he entered the house. A table had been set up by the front door, and a young boy, possibly eleven or twelve years old, handed Nick a piece of paper. As Nick scanned the paper, he saw it was printed with items that would be auctioned off at eleven o'clock that morning. An area had been set up in the large front den with a portable podium and about twenty or so folding chairs facing it. A tall spare man wearing a black Stetson, probably the auctioneer, was fiddling with the microphone on the podium. Obviously, this was where the auction would take place. Looking at his watch, Nick saw it was ten thirty.

"Is *everything* being auctioned off?" Nick asked the boy.

Shaking his head, the boy said, "No, just what's listed on the sheet I gave you." Dressed neatly in a white short-sleeved shirt and jeans, the boy continued, "My father said everything not on the auction list is tagged with the price written on it." Nodding, Nick hoped fervently that the piece the book led them to was one with a listed price and *not* one to be auctioned off!

As Nick opened *The Book of Lost Treasures* and studied the map within, it reminded him vaguely of the board game Clue. A maze of rooms, representing the layout of the Parmelov home, was detailed on the map. He half expected the names of Colonel Mustard or Mrs. Peacock to suddenly appear as they followed the map's directions! However, other than the glowing line that led to a room on the southeast side of the Parmelov estate and the usual meticulous details, no names appeared.

Motioning to the others, Nick quickly went to the room indicated by the book's map. They passed individuals and small groups, who were critically eyeing furniture, paintings, table knickknacks, and other items before furiously scribbling notes and appraisal values in the notebooks they carried. When they finally reached the room, it was deserted, except for Nick and his fellow club members. Apparently, it had been a study of some kind, which was empty now, except for a small leather couch, a bookshelf lining one wall and crammed with books, a roll-top desk that had definitely seen better days, and a small circular table with a large lamp set on top of it.

The directions in *The Book of Lost Treasures* led straight to the lamp, and as Nick approached it, he saw that it was painted a garish, metallic gold color. Tall and vase-shaped, the paint gave the lamp a cheesy quality that only increased as Nick stooped over to scrutinize it more closely.

The lampshade, a dingy white color, was actually patched in two different places, and a cheap gold braid had been glued to the outside of the bottom part of the lampshade, as if in an attempt to give it a higher quality it obviously didn't possess. Spotting a handwritten price tag dangling from lamp, Nick gave a huge sigh of relief.

"This is it," he told the others.

"How much?" Mark asked.

Picking up the price tag, Nick saw $50.00 written on it.

"Fifty dollars!" Mark blurted in disbelief when Nick told him the price. "For that? They ought to pay *us* to take it off their hands! Are you sure this is the antique?"

When Nick nodded, even Abby and Patti shook their heads as they looked at what had to be the ugliest lamp any of them had ever seen in their lives.

When Nick picked up the lamp to carry it, no flash of light came from *The Book of Lost Treasures.*

"Wait!" he said, putting the lamp hastily back on the table. Opening the book, he saw the map was still there. The words "*Treasure Found*" were nowhere to be seen.

"Something's wrong! The map is still in the book!" His face a mask of concern, Nick showed the others the book.

"What happened?" Mark asked Nick. "Why hasn't the book indicated we found the lost treasure like it always does?"

"I … I don't know," Nick confessed. "But this *is* the piece the map led us to, it has to be! Look!" Picking up the lamp with one hand, Nick held *The Book of Lost Treasures* open with the other. Walking slowly out of the room, the red dot on the map moved, as did the lost treasure indicated by the map. Both were located so closely together, as to be virtually one and the same.

"See! It moves along with me on the map! This has to be it!"

"Let's pay for it and figure it out later," Mark suggested.

No one objected. A short time later, they paid a handsome, middle-aged woman, presumably the mother of the boy at the door, for the lamp and left. This time, they received a receipt without asking, as the woman automatically handed them one. Placing the lamp on the hard surface of the circular drive, Nick studied it, a confused expression on his face.

"I don't understand!" Nick's face was twisted in frustration. "This has to be the antique! It has to be!" The others huddled around Nick, no one saying a word.

"What are we going to do now?" Steve finally asked.

"I don't know. Maybe … wait!" Nick said, his voice rising in excitement.

"This has to be the piece! Are we all in agreement on that?" Heads nodded all around.

"Good! I want to try something! Steve, you got a hammer or something in your car?"

"Yeah, I have one in my tool box in the trunk. Why?" he asked curiously.

"Just get it, and I'll explain later!" Steve trotted over to the GTO and popped the trunk. After rummaging around for a few moments, he produced a hammer and jogged back to Nick, handing it to him.

"What are you going to do?" Mark eyed the hammer in Nick's hand uneasily.

"Look how large the lamp is. Also, when I picked it up, it felt heavier to me than what it should. I think maybe the lost treasure is *inside* the lamp!"

"You mean you're going to *break* the lamp open with that hammer? Nick, are you *sure*?" Mark asked dubiously.

"Pretty sure!" Nick said, grinning. "Besides, what have we got to lose?"

"How about a valuable antique?" Kenneth blurted. "You could be destroying something worth thousands of dollars!"

What followed was an animated argument that raged back and forth until Nick finally called for an impromptu vote. With Nick abstaining, the final tally was 3–2 in favor of breaking the lamp open. Mark, Abby, and Patti voted for, while Kenneth and Steve voted against it.

"The *ayes* have it!" Nick declared.

Taking a deep breath, he eyed the lamp and, gripping the handle of the hammer, chose the bulging swell of the upper part of the lamp and swung. The sharp *crack* of ceramic breaking filled the air, and pieces of the lamp fell to the asphalt driveway. Dry sawdust cascaded from the inside of the lamp, and as they watched, Nick nimbly caught an object that fell out along with the sawdust.

Openmouthed, Nick stared at an enamel jewelry box. Gilded in silver, he had no time for other observations as bright light suddenly flashed from *The Book of Lost Treasures.*

Glancing in the book, Nick saw the familiar words "*Treasure Found*" glowing brilliantly. They had found the hidden treasure!

Standing and showing it to the others, Nick saw that a mounted figure, like that of a knight, was painted delicately on the hinged cover. Astride a massive war mount, the knight seemed to be studying a sign at a crossroads of sorts. Carefully flipping the lid open, they saw the jewelry box was lined with a rich purple satin.

"It's beautiful!" Abby breathed.

"I agree," Nick quipped, feeling immensely proud of himself for figuring out the secret of where the lost treasure had been hidden.

"Don't let your head get too big, or you won't be able to fit it inside the car!" Abby said, wrinkling her nose at Nick.

Nick had to struggle to keep a firm hold on the jewelry box as Mark, Steve, and Kenneth took turns congratulating him with hearty backslaps. Patti, who had been strangely quiet, was eyeing the box intently. Suddenly, she turned and ran back to the SUV and selected one of the reference books and ran back to the others. Flipping rapidly through the pages, she finally stopped, her face draining of color. Fighting to control her breathing, she placed her hand over her heart and leaned against Mark for support.

"Patti, what's wrong?" he asked, his face knotted in sudden worry.

"I've … I've seen a picture of that jewelry box before!" Waving her hand rapidly back and forth in front of her face as if she was experiencing hot flashes, Patti continued.

"It's a Fabergé!" she blurted. "It's a Fabergé silver-gilt and cloisonné enamel box! Nick, turn it over!" she demanded.

As Nick complied, she pointed with a shaking finger at some- thing etched on the base of the enamel box, "Look! There are the Fabergé and Imperial Warrant marks! According to the reference book, this jewelry box was made between 1908 and 1917 by the Russian imperial jeweler, Carl Fabergé!"

"You mean the guy who made jeweled Easter eggs for the Russian Tsars?" Mark asked with a puzzled expression.

"Forget about the history lesson!" Steve cried. "What's it worth?"

Looking around at each of the club members in turn, Patti took a deep breath.

"It's worth over *one hundred thousand dollars*!"

Chapter 22

The drive back to Mark and Patti's was done in numbed silence. They had discovered almost $200,000 worth of antiques in less than three hours work! *The Book of Lost Treasures* had delivered in a way none of them, including Nick, could have believed in their most fervent imaginings. Where they went from here, what was next, was on all their minds as Mark pulled the SUV into the driveway and parked.

Entering the house, Patti went straight to her laptop and logged on to the Internet. The others, drained by the day's events and the valuable discoveries they had uncovered, sat in the den talking quietly to one another while Patti surfed the Net. When finally she closed her laptop, she announced she had found an art and antiquities dealer in the Dallas suburb of Garland whose specialty was rare and unique antiques. She suggested they take the stoneware crock, carved wooden eagle, and Faberge jewelry box there and see what they would be offered for them. The others readily agreed, and a short time later, Steve and Kenneth left. Nick, restless and hungry, took Abby, and they went to Wendy's for a late lunch.

After dropping Abby of at Mark and Patti's and giving her an enthusiastic goodbye kiss, Nick walked to the Sprint, unable to keep a happy smile off his face. *And why not?* he thought to himself.

This had been the best day of his life!

July flowed into August, and the next several weeks went by as if in a blur. Much had been accomplished during that period of time. Nick had accompanied Patti to Garland, and when they had shown their pieces to the rare antique dealer, a pencil-thin woman in her late forties, she had offered them $150,000 on the spot! When they had hesitated, saying they had to think about it, she immediately upped the offer to $160,000. By the time they had called all the other club members on their cells to inform them of what they were being offered, the ante had been raised to *$170,000!*

They left the antique dealer's shop with the check.

A bank account and line of credit had been established at one of the local banks in Pleasant Mountain for the Treasure Hunt Club. They deposited the money earned from their discoveries there. In addition, Patti's law firm had agreed to handle all the club's legal affairs and was now on retainer. The coin dealer in Texarkana had offered them $3,000 for the coins Mark had brought him, and every weekend brought newly discovered antiques garnered from the various estate sales and garage sales *The Book of Lost Treasures* led them to as they expanded to nearby counties. There had been no more eye-popping discoveries like the first weekend had brought them, although they had found an eighteenth century mahogany three-tier stand at an estate sale in a nearby community. Paying only $25 for it, it had fetched them $8,000 from the Garland dealer. All told, they had realized around $30,000 in profit in the subsequent weeks of scouring the nearby communities and counties for "lost" antiques.

By the end of August, it became apparent the well had run dry concerning the search for valuable antiques in the immediate area around Pleasant Mountain. By specifically targeting rural areas and small towns, *The Book of Lost Treasures* had made the search and discovery of the antiques relatively easy. The club members, however, were loath to try the same tactics in larger cities for fear they would be overwhelmed by the multiple sites that could be produced by the book.

As Nick had pointedly reminded everyone, the book's rules made clear that no more requests could be made of it until *all* the lost treasures had been found and recovered! Therefore, Nick had called for a meeting on Tuesday night the last week of August, with the main item on the agenda concerning what to do next. Meeting again at Mark and Patti's, they started promptly at seven o'clock that evening.

"I call this meeting of the Treasure Hunt Club to order!" Nick declared as he put his glass of iced tea down on the coffee table next to him. Arrayed around him in the spacious den were all the club members, who looked at him expectantly. The minutes of the previous meeting were quickly approved, and Nick asked Patti for a treasurer's report. With over $200,000 in the bank, Patti had invested most of the money in short term CDs.

Interest accrued from the CDs had already earned several thousand dollars, and the club members applauded appreciably when informed of this. Although every club member was owed an equal share of the money, so far, everyone was content to leave it in the bank and let the money grow.

"Does anyone have any suggestions on the next request we make of the book?" Nick asked, after they had dispensed of all the old business.

Kenneth shot to his feet; his pudgy face a mask of animated excitement.

"The chair recognizes Kenneth!" Nick grinned at Kenneth's exuberance.

"Baseball cards!" he blurted.

"What about baseball cards?" Nick asked when Kenneth was not immediately forthcoming with an explanation.

"That's what we should try and find next … baseball cards!" Kenneth repeated, as if it all made perfect sense to him.

"Well … okay. Would you care to elaborate?"

Nodding vigorously, Kenneth launched into an explanation.

"Collecting baseball cards is a multi-million-dollar industry!" he gushed. "The older and rarer the cards, the more they're worth. I bet *The Book of Lost Treasures* can lead us straight to where some of these cards have been hidden or lost!"

"How much money are these baseball cards worth?" Steve asked as he took a long pull on the bottle of Bud Light he held in his hand.

"It depends. Like I said, the older and more rare the card, the condition it's in—it all factors in on the card's worth. The range could vary from just a few dollars to over a million."

"Million! Did you say million?" Steve spluttered, choking on his beer.

"Sure! A Honus Wagner card sold at auction just this past year for over two million dollars. In fact, it's these rare Honus Wagner cards I think we should go after!"

Seeing uncomprehending looks all around him, Kenneth sighed and, sitting down, spread his hands before him.

"Look. What I'm talking about is what is called the Honus Wagner T206 baseball card. This card is part of a series of five hundred twenty-six cards released in 1909 by the American Tobacco Company with Honus Wagner on them. There are only fifty to sixty cards even known to still be in existence, therefore, making them very rare, very *expensive* cards to collect. If there are any of these cards left that still exist that aren't already part of someone's collection, the book can lead us to them. Since they are so rare, we shouldn't have to worry about multiple sites or maps showing up in the book."

"I like it!" Mark said, looking at Nick.

Thunderstruck, Nick immediately tried to wrap his mind around the concept of a *million* dollars!

If Kenneth was right and *The Book of Lost Treasures* could lead them to even one of these rare baseball cards, it would make the money they had realized from the discovery and sale of the antiques look like chump change!

"What's your plan?" he asked eagerly.

Rubbing his hands together briskly, Kenneth said, "I've given it a lot of thought, and we will have to word our request carefully, but here's what I came up with."

Taking his Android, Kenneth scrolled to a document on it, opened it, and then read:

> Reveal the location of any hidden or lost 1909 T206 series Honus Wagner baseball cards that are not already part of any collection and on property whose owners would sign a contract, thus giving the Treasure Hunt Club exclusive ownership of any lost or hidden cards in exchange for ten percent of the card's value.

"Whew! That's a mouthful!" Mark exclaimed.

Shrugging helplessly, Kenneth said, "It is, but in order for us to follow the rules of the book and still get the desired result that we want, I had to word the request this way. However, I'm open to suggestions on how to improve the request."

"How do we even know the book will recognize the statement about the ten percent contract?" Abby asked.

"The truth is, we don't know," Nick admitted. "We won't know until we try including it for the first time on locating a lost treasure."

The discussion over Kenneth's suggestion carried on for another hour before Nick called for a vote. The final tally was unanimous to ask *The Book of Lost Treasures* to locate any of the rare baseball cards that might still be in existence and lost. It was also decided to use the wording proposed by Kenneth when the request was written in the book.

"Now, when do we want to do this and how?" Nick asked.

Beaming in pleasure over the club's endorsement of his idea, Kenneth waved his hand frantically to get Nick's attention.

This time, Nick couldn't help himself and laughed as he said, "The chair once again recognizes Kenneth!"

"The odds are if there are any of these lost baseball cards left, the map produced by the book will lead to a place a long way away from Pleasant Mountain. We need to be prepared to travel to another city and probably even another state. Since we don't know how far away or how long it will take us to recover the baseball card, it might take days. Therefore, we need to decide which club members are going to go and then time our request to the book around their schedule. Once we have done that, I would suggest they leave immediately upon a map appearing in the book. There's always the chance something might happen to the card that prevents us from recovering it if we wait one minute longer than necessary."

Nick nodded, impressed with Kenneth's logic. Apparently, he had given careful thought to his proposal, and Nick could find no holes in it. *Kenneth had certainly come full circle from being the Doubting Thomas of the club to now someone who eagerly gave suggestions on what to ask the book next,* he thought with some amusement.

"Okay, who wants to go?" Nick asked.

Suggestions were bantered back and forth until it was decided that Nick, Mark, and Kenneth should be the club members sent to recover any lost baseball cards revealed by the book. Furthermore, they would make the request of the book Friday morning so they had the weekend to travel and recover any lost baseball cards revealed by the book. Nick was an easy choice, since he had no regular job; Kenneth, since he was the baseball card expert; and Mark, because he had a more flexible work schedule than anyone else. Abby had nixed herself immediately since her classes at TAMU-Texarkana had started, and she already had tests to study for, while Steve and his garage band were playing a gig at a local bar for the next several weekends. Their course of action decided, Nick adjourned the meeting until Friday morning, and the club members drifted home one by one.

Nick was the last to leave, and he and Abby snuggled on the dark front porch for a while. Standing with his arms wrapped around Abby, they kissed and talked for about fifteen minutes or so before Abby told Nick she had to go to bed since she had an eight o'clock class the following morning. Disappointed, Nick managed to give Abby one final kiss before, giggling, she said good night to him and shut the door.

Nick's disappointment was only temporary. Walking to his car, his thoughts turned to the upcoming search for the rare Honus Wagner baseball cards. Were they really worth more than a million dollars? Were there any more still even in existence? To find even one would make each club member's share close to a half million dollars apiece!

Nick folded himself into the Sprint and started the little car. Pulling out onto the street, he wore an ear-to-ear smile.

He couldn't wait for Friday!

Chapter 23

At precisely six o'clock Friday morning, the Treasure Hunt Club reconvened once again at Mark and Patti's. Sitting at the kitchen table with *The Book of Lost Treasures* open before him, Nick copied word for word the request Kenneth had composed. As Kenneth held his Android before Nick with the text Nick was copying, the others held their collective breath. When he finally finished, beads of sweat had formed on Nick's forehead, and he wiped them off with the back of his hand.

At first, nothing happened, and Nick feared they had hit a dead end with this request. However, just as he was opening his mouth to tell Kenneth he was sorry but that it had been a good idea, a now familiar flare of light issued from the book. Astonished, Nick turned the page and was greeted with a series of three maps. The first map led from DFW International Airport in Dallas and went straight west before ending at Albuquerque, New Mexico.

The second map was a detailed city map of Albuquerque, with a golden glowing line leading from the city's International Airport to an address approximately ten to fifteen miles north- west of the airport.

The third and final map was a schematic of the interior of a split-level structure, obviously a home or house, with the brightly glowing words "*Here Lies the Lost Treasure*" indicating the location of the baseball card they were seeking!

An explosion of *whoops* and excited shouting erupted from the club members. By the very act of a map appearing meant there was at least *one* of the rare Honus Wagner baseball cards to be found and recovered! Dollar signs filled Nick's vision as he joined the others in loud celebration.

When the excitement finally died down, Patti ran to retrieve her laptop and immediately logged on to the Internet. Moments later, she was searching for flights to Albuquerque from DFW. While she was doing this, the others were discussing the maps that appeared in *The Book of Lost Treasures*.

"I've never seen maps like this appear before in the book," Nick said thoughtfully. "Its three maps, but they are all related to locating the same lost treasure."

"I wonder why the first map is obviously a route one would take if *flying* to Albuquerque?" Mark mused. "I mean, the book could just as easily have produced a road map from Pleasant Mountain to Albuquerque."

"I bet that whatever is the shortest and most direct route to a lost treasure is going to be on any map produced by the book!" Kenneth exclaimed.

"Who cares? Dudes, we are going to be rich!" Steve cried as he flung his arms around Mark and Nick. His face was flushed with excitement, and somehow, he managed not to spill any of the beer sloshing around in the Texas longneck he held in his right hand. Releasing his friends, he chugged the rest of the beer before setting it down with a loud *thump* on the kitchen table. Raising his hands above his head, Steve did an improvised Rocky Balboa imitation.

Although Steve's reaction had Nick grinning in amusement, a small thought had managed to creep in the back of Nick's mind. Was Steve genuinely excited, or was it the beer making him react in such a way? It seemed to Nick that Steve was drinking more than he usually did. In fact, this increased drinking seemed to coincide with the establishment of the Treasure Hunt Club. His train of thought along this line was interrupted as Patti, who had left to retrieve something from her printer, burst back into the kitchen.

"Here are your boarding passes!" she gushed as she passed them out efficiently one by one to Nick, Mark, and Kenneth. "Your flight leaves DFW at one twenty in the afternoon and arrives in Albuquerque at two fifteen in the afternoon. They are on Mountain Standard Time, so set your watches back one hour."

Nick, Mark, and Kenneth had already packed in anticipation of having to make an out-of-state trip, so it was a simple matter of throwing their bags into the Expedition and climbing into Mark's SUV. Mark kissed Patti good-bye, with Nick doing the same to Abby. As they backed out of Mark's garage and pulled out onto the street, the remaining club members waved at them enthusiastically as they drove away.

The quest for the rare Honus Wagner card had begun!

Other than the usual hassle of getting through security at the Albuquerque airport, the hour and a half flight to Albuquerque went by without a hitch. They had spent most of the time on the flight studying and discussing the third and final map in *The Book of Lost Treasures.* Apparently, the baseball card they were seeking was secreted *behind* something mounted on a wall. As to what that something was, the book's map, surprisingly, did not provide them with a clue. They wouldn't know until they got to the home or house. However, it meant they would need to make a trip to a hardware store to secure tools to excavate or pry whatever it was from the wall in order to get to the baseball card.

Once they arrived at the airport, they immediately collected their bags and went to the rental car section and rented a car. Getting a recommendation from the rental car clerk on a good nearby motel, they piled into the white Dodge Durango they had rented and set out to find the motel. As promised by the clerk, the motel was just a short distance from the airport. Pulling up to the front lobby of the La Quinta Motel, Mark got out to secure them rooms for the night. With him, he carried a debit card issued to the Treasure Hunt Club, as all their expenses would be paid for by the club. A short time later, he returned, and they trooped to their room on the first floor of the motel. Stowing their bags and belongings in the room, they left and immediately set out to find the location of the lost baseball card.

Getting into the Durango, Mark drove, while Nick sat in the passenger seat next to him, with Kenneth in the backseat.

With *The Book of Lost Treasures* open in his lap, Nick fed Mark directions. Other than stopping at a nearby Home Depot the motel clerk had steered them to in order to buy the tools they needed, they headed straight to the address indicated from the map in the book. As they followed the roads and streets outlined by the book's map, the expanse of the Rio Grande Valley stretched out below them to the west. A strip of bright green vegetation grew on either side of the meandering flow of the Rio Grande River, while, in contrast, the mesa that spanned the land north and west of the valley was a drab brown of desert grasses and cactus. To the east, the Sandia Mountains towered over the city of Albuquerque, its rocky peaks thrusting upward toward the blue azure sky.

Less than twenty minutes later, they crossed a bridge that spanned the Rio Grande River. Wide, shallow, and a muddy brown color, the Rio Grande flowed in a southeasterly direction toward its ultimate destination of the Gulf of Mexico. Looking up from the book as they crossed the Rio Grande, Nick curiously studied the muddy river so prominent in southwestern lore. He saw numerous sand and mudflats scattered throughout the river's basin, and a thick belt of cottonwood trees grew in profusion on either side of the river's edge.

Although he was slightly disappointed at having thought the Rio Grande was a much larger river filled with a much larger volume of water, he had to admit it was still an impressive sight!

Having crossed the river, Mark turned the Durango right on a broad avenue named "Rio Grande Boulevard." Traveling north, the map in the book indicated this road would lead them to their destination. Adobe houses and other structures, indicative of the southwestern architecture so prevalent here, appeared on either side of the road. As they drove further, the rural nature of the area became more pronounced, as fields of alfalfa began to appear. Irrigated by a series of ditches whose water was provided by the nearby Rio Grande, these patches of alfalfa dotted the land at intervals, along with the occasional barn, corrals of horses, and grazing cattle. Huge cottonwood trees grew everywhere, some with their massive boughs actually overhanging the road.

However, it was apparent to Nick, especially as they drew closer and closer to their destination, that the rural nature of the area was definitely in transition.

Small adobe houses existed side-by-side, huge, gated mansions. Expensive Mercedes, Lexuses, and BMWs appeared in the expansive multi-car garages of these mansions, while battered pickups and small fuel-efficient cars were parked in the blue-collar yards of the mansion's neighbors. It was an eclectic mix of rural and urban, rich professionals and working-class poor. There was not the slightest doubt in Nick's mind that should he pay another visit to this area in the next five to ten years, it would have been completely transformed into an upscale stretch of real estate, where only the very wealthy could afford to live.

"Is that it?" Mark asked, interrupting Nick's thoughts as he pointed to an adobe house on their right with the address of 12573 Balcones Southwest. Checking quickly with the map in the book, Nick saw that it was the same address on the map, and he nodded his head affirmatively.

Pulling into a dirt alley beside the adobe structure, Mark killed the engine and they all got out of the SUV. Checking his watch, Nick saw it was a little past four o'clock. Studying the house, he saw several of the large cottonwood trees grew in the front yard. The day was hot, and sweat trickled down Nick's face as he, Mark, and Kenneth moved in for a closer view.

A cracked concrete sidewalk snaked from a wooden one-car garage located beside the house and led to an open and spacious front porch. An old Ristra, or wreath of dried red chili, hung from a peg beside the front door. An ancient chain-link fence completely surrounded the modest front yard of the house, while the unfenced back of the house led to a large, open field. An old, Farmall tractor sat rusting away on the north side of this field and was canted to one side, due to one of the large rear tires being completely flat. Wild sunflowers grew in profusion within the field, their graceful stalks rising high above the hardy grasses and weeds that grew thickly on the ground beneath the sunflowers' yellow blooms.

Quickly stepping into the shade provided by the cottonwood trees, Nick saw a realty sign planted in the front yard. The name "Chavez Realty and Associates" was on the sign, along with the company's phone number. Nick looked over at Mark. He nodded that he too had seen the sign. Continuing on, they rounded the corner of the chain-link fence and came to a gate in the fence. Nick, Mark, and Kenneth filed through the gate and went up to the front porch. Peering through the dusty front window, Nick cupped his hands beside his head and attempted to look inside.

Although only dimly illuminated by the light coming through the windows, Nick saw that the inside of the house was deserted. There wasn't a single stick of furniture in sight, and even from his imperfect view from the window, he could tell the house had been vacant for some time.

Trying the front door, Nick quickly determined it was locked.

Looking over at Mark he asked, "Now what do we do?"

Shrugging, Mark replied, "We call the realty company."

Nick watched Mark take out his cell and punch in the phone number on the sign. After a moment or two, someone answered, and Mark spent the next five minutes chatting with that person. Finally, he smiled and said good-bye, flicking the cell phone shut and pocketing it.

"Well, I have good news and bad news," Mark announced.

"What?" both Nick and Kenneth blurted in unison.

"The bad news is this property has already been sold, and the new owners closed on it last week. The realty company just hasn't had time to take their sign down yet."

A collective groan immediately issued Nick and Kenneth.

"However, therein also lies the good news!" Mark continued, unperturbed. "It seems a developer bought this property with the intention of tearing down the house and subdividing the land into at least three lots. Since the house is going to be torn down anyway, I convinced the associate I talked with to allow us to search the house for, er, *things* of value. Naturally, I mentioned the ten percent contract we would offer his company for anything we find."

Nick gave a huge sigh of relief, immensely glad that Mark's quick thinking had turned a potential disaster into an advantage.

"Now, when the realtor gets here, let me do all the talking," Mark warned. "If he asks either of you anything, just play along with whatever I've been saying."

"You got it!" Nick stated, a sentiment echoed by Kenneth. With that, they settled down to wait for the realtor.

A single locust began to trill on one of the nearby cottonwoods and was soon joined by other locusts in a chorus of loud buzzing. Impatient, Nick walked around to the back of the adobe house. Wiping a film of perspiration from his face with his shirtsleeve, he stood with hands on hips as he surveyed the area behind the house. Trees and bushes grew thickly next to the field, with an old irrigation ditch running parallel to the property line. The Sandia Mountains rose in the distance, its majestic peaks now covered in a mantle of angry gray-black rain clouds.

From his distant vantage in the valley, Nick could actually see the sheets of rain that were falling on the Sandia's western slopes. As he stood mesmerized by the sight, he observed an occasional bolt of lightning flash through the slanting rain.

"Nick! The agent is here!"

Startled by Mark's voice calling him, Nick quickly gathered his wits and made his way back to the front of the house. He arrived just in time to see a young Hispanic man exit a black Cadillac Escalade. Slender and of medium height, the young man's face cracked into a friendly smile as he shook hands first with Mark, and then with Kenneth and Nick.

"Gentlemen, my name is Robert Mondragon. I'm a junior associate with Chavez Realty. What can I do for you?"

Mark introduced each of them to Mondragon and produced a business card, which he handed to the realtor. It had *The Treasure Hunt Club* embossed on its face, along with a list of the club's officers, business address (Mark's), and phone number (also Mark's).

"As I explained on the phone, we are in the business of finding and recovering antiquities and other unusual artifacts. We would like to search this house in hopes of finding something of value."

The realtor, his face a mask of confusion, said, "But the house is vacant and has been for months! There's nothing inside the house, no furnishings or anything!"

"I realize that, but our company has a rather extensive data- base, and this house was flagged as definitely having possibilities," Mark replied smoothly. "You see, some of our greatest discoveries came from places no one else thought to look. By the way, do you know anything at all about the history of this house or area?"

Mark's question had the effect of temporarily distracting the realtor from his line of inquiry. Seizing the moment, Mark started slowly walking up the sidewalk to the front door. After a moment's hesitation, Mondragon began to follow.

"As a matter of fact, my grandfather's house is just a block or two down the road from here. Back when my father was growing up there, this entire area was chili and alfalfa fields. Then about fifteen or twenty years ago, the damn Californians began to move here and decided this was a great place to live. Since then, the price of land has gone sky-high, and where adobe houses used to be, now there are multi-million dollar mansions! My grandfather is eighty years old and has lived in the same house for over fifty years. He can't afford the property taxes anymore and is going to have to put his house up for sale."

"That's the price for progress, I suppose," Mark said with a touch of sympathy in in his voice.

"Well, the commissions are good, and I'll make sure Grandpa will get a king's ransom for his little home!" Mondragon said, his dark eyes flashing in good humor as he fumbled with a set of keys in his hand. Finally finding the right key, he unlocked the door and pushed it open.

Motioning the others in, Mondragon closed the door once they had all entered the house.

The interior of the house was noticeably cooler, and Nick stood for a moment to allow his eyes to adapt to the gloomy interior.

"Sorry, but the electricity was turned off as soon as the new owners stated their intention to demolish the home," Mondragon quipped.

Nick pulled a small flashlight from a tote bag he had carried in from the rental car and switched it on. The tote bag also carried *The Book of Lost Treasures,* but Nick didn't want to risk using it in front of the realtor. Besides, he had already memorized the details of the map the book had produced. Nodding at Mark, he headed straight for a room at the back of the house.

Turning down a short hallway, Nick took a left and abruptly entered what must have once been a spacious family room or den. Stepping down onto a sunken floor made up of scarred hardwood, Nick looked around carefully. A fireplace made of adobe bricks was straight in front of him. Next to the fireplace was a sliding glass door that opened to the field behind the house. Dusty, floor-length curtains covered this glass door, only allowing a minimum amount of sunlight into the room. Looking upward, he saw square wooden beams that spanned the room and supported the ceiling.

Taking another step into the room, Nick shined the flashlight beam at the thick adobe walls. He was rewarded seconds later with the reflection of light off of a ceramic surface. Moving in for a closer look, he peered closely at what proved to be a large rectangular piece of tile roughly six inches by six inches.

"Mexican tile. A lot of the older homes around here have them," a voice stated from behind his shoulder.

Startled, Nick almost dropped the flashlight. Looking behind him, he saw the smiling face of Robert Mondragon. Arranged close behind him were Mark and Kenneth. So intent was he in studying the details of the room, he hadn't noticed them follow him in.

Seeing an opportunity, Mark quickly interjected, "This is exactly what we are looking for! The market for antique Mexican tile is red hot! Can we remove them from the walls?"

Mondragon hesitated for just a moment before shrugging and nodding. As Nick played the flashlight's beam around the room, he saw that the Mexican tile was spaced at regular intervals on all the room's walls. Fighting to keep the grin off his face as he realized what Mark was up to, Nick dug through the tote bag to retrieve the tools they had purchased.

"By the way, I'm fascinated with the architecture of these old, southwestern homes. I saw something in the kitchen as we were passing by that perhaps you could enlighten me on!" So saying, Mark steered Mondragon out of the room and led him back in the direction they had come from.

The second the pair had left the room, Nick quickly took *The Book of Lost Treasures* from the tote bag. Opening it up, he scanned the brightly glowing map of the house within it. It led straight to one of the tiles on the north wall of the room. Striding quickly to the tile on the wall, he placed the book on the floor and dug a hammer and small chisel out of the tote bag.

"We have to work quickly! Keep an eye out, and let me know if the realtor comes back this way!" Nick whispered to Kenneth. His chubby face quivering in excitement, Kenneth nodded and took up his post by the entrance into the den.

Tapping the chisel carefully into the grout cementing the tile to the wall, Nick began the process of removing the tile. The grout, brittle with age, cracked and fell in pieces to the floor.

Wedging the edge of the chisel behind the tile, Nick gently tried to pry the tile from the wall. Suddenly, it popped out, and Nick had to drop the hammer to catch the tile. A square hollow was revealed, its interior cloaked in darkness.

His heart pounding in excitement, Nick's shaking hands placed the tile and chisel on the floor. Picking up the flashlight, he aimed the beam into the hollow's interior. The light revealed a cardboard shoebox covered in a thick layer of dust. Pulling the shoebox from its hiding place, Nick placed it on the floor in front of him. Light flared brightly from *The Book of Lost Treasures*, and the now familiar words "*Treasure Found*" glowed in fiery letters. Closing the book and placing it in the tote bag, Nick swept the dust off the shoebox's cover.

A picture of a young boy and a dog was revealed on the cover, and "Buster Brown Shoes" was stenciled in large black letters below this picture.

Willing his hands to stop shaking, Nick removed the shoebox cover. Playing the flashlight's beam inside the shoebox, its light revealed a jumble of baseball cards crammed inside. Choosing one at random, he held it before the flashlight. A smiling picture of Lou Gehrig kneeling with a bat in one hand presented itself to his astonished eyes. Quickly searching the card, he found the year 1931 stenciled below the picture.

"They're coming back!" Kenneth whispered urgently before he could search through more of the cards.

Quickly putting the Lou Gehrig baseball card back into the box, Nick placed the lid back on the shoebox and lowered it into the tote bag. Just as he finished this task, Mark and Robert Mondragon swept back into the room.

"Well, was the tile what you thought it was?" Mondragon asked.

A grin split Nick's face from ear to ear. "Yes, it was everything we thought it was and more!"

Unable to see Nick's face clearly because of the room's gloomy interior, Mark and Kenneth nevertheless could tell from his excited answer that he had hit the jackpot.

The next forty-five minutes were spent dutifully removing all the tiles from the walls. If Mondragon noticed the hollow space in the wall from where Nick had removed the shoebox full of baseball cards, he gave no indication of it as he kept up a friendly banter the entire time they were involved in the process.

They learned from the real estate agent that the home's former owner, Eli Candalaria, had at one time been a semi-pro baseball player, who had barnstormed with his team, the Duke City Roadrunners, in the thirties, forties, and early fifties. He had died recently in an Albuquerque nursing home at age ninety-three. His heirs had quickly sold his home and land to the developer.

Shaking the pieces of grout and dust from their clothes, Nick and the others finally left the adobe house. Carefully stacking the tile in the cargo area at the back of the Durango, Nick shut the cargo door and dusted off his hands. Then he placed the tote bag carefully in the passenger seat.

Turning, he saw Mark take the club's 10 percent contract from his briefcase and give it to Mondragon to sign. The developer that had purchased the house had given Chavez Realty power of attorney, and the agent perused the contract briefly before signing it. Waving a friendly good-bye, Mondragon got into the Escalade and drove off.

Nick, Mark, and Kenneth scrambled to retrieve the shoebox from the front seat once Mondragon's SUV had disappeared from sight.

"Wait!" Mark said, breathing hard, as Nick pulled the shoebox from the passenger seat. "Not here! One of the neighbors might see what we are doing and get suspicious! Let's go back to the motel room and examine the contents of the shoebox there!"

Reluctantly, Nick and Kenneth agreed. The drive back to the motel was one of the longest in Nick's life, and he repeatedly fought the urge to rip the lid off the shoebox and examine the baseball cards inside it. When they finally pulled into the La Quinta parking lot, they practically sprinted to their room from the rental car. Impatiently, Nick waited while Mark used the room's card to unlock the door. Once the lock clicked open, Nick carried the cardboard shoebox to the nearest bed and dumped its contents into it.

Dozens of baseball cards spilled from the box. Mark, seeing the sheer number of cards, immediately suggested they split the cards into three groups, with each of them searching through their cards for the Honus Wagner. Nick and Kenneth quickly agreed, and each raked a small pile of the cards to where they were sitting on the bed.

Less than five minutes later, Nick heard a gasp and looked up to see Kenneth holding a card reverently before him in one trembling hand.

"It's … it's a T206 Honus Wagner card! Look, it has the American Tobacco Company name printed at the bottom!"

Kenneth's normally fish-white complexion had turned a ruddy pinkish-red, and his breathing came out in short, explosive gasps. If Nick hadn't known better, he would have thought Kenneth was experiencing a heart attack instead of a flush of euphoria at discovering one of the rarest and most expensive baseball cards in history.

The Book of Lost Treasures had delivered again!

Chapter 24

The events of the next few weeks rocketed by in a blur to Nick. Mark and Kenneth took the Honus Wagner baseball card to a well-known card and sports memorabilia dealer in Houston for authentication.

After carefully studying the card, the dealer agreed it was an authentic T206 Honus Wagner. With that, he offered Mark and Kenneth *two million dollars for the card!* When Mark had called to tell Nick and the others what the sports memorabilia dealer had offered, even the normally unflappable Mark couldn't contain himself as he gleefully shouted the amount over the phone!

Deciding that although they could probably get more for the baseball card at auction than the Houston dealer was offering, the club members decided the immediate offer of two million dollars was too good to pass up. After brief negotiations, Mark and Kenneth returned from Houston with a two-million-dollar cashier's check.

At this point, the club members decided their enterprise had grown too big to handle among themselves and that they needed expert help. In rapid fire order, Patti's law firm, already on retainer, assigned a senior associate to handle the club's legal affairs, an accountant was hired to handle the financial affairs, and a small office building was leased to house the club's headquarters.

Bigger and better times lay ahead for the Treasure Hunt Club!

"Where are you taking me, Nick?" Abby asked, giggling, her eyes closed.

"We're almost there! Keep your eyes closed!" Nick said as he pulled into a driveway and stopped the car. Getting out of the car, he opened Abby's door and helped her out of the car.

"You can look now!"

Still giggling, Abby opened her eyes.

"Ta-da!" Nick cried as he held his arms spread outward.

Surprised, Abby saw that they were standing in the driveway of a split-level condo. Constructed of brick and stucco, Abby saw immediately that the condo was brand new. Without waiting for Abby to comment, Nick ran up to the front door and unlocked it. Opening it, he waved impatiently for her to follow him.

"What do you think?" Nick asked happily as they stood in the middle of an empty den covered with thick, lush carpet.

"It's … it's … *nice*, Nick," Abby answered uncertainly. "Um, why … why are we here?"

"I've signed a lease on this condo, and I'm moving out of my trailer!" Nick cried. "I've finally got a place of my own!"

"But … but you already have a place of your own. What's wrong with your trailer?" Abby asked apprehensively.

"What? That dump? Are you kidding? The bathroom here is almost the size of my whole trailer!" Without waiting for Abby to respond, Nick excitedly grabbed her by the hand and began showing her each room.

Finally stopping in the middle of the master bedroom, Nick let go of Abby's hand and, standing, did a slow circle.

"Isn't it perfect?" he gushed.

"I … I guess," Abby said without conviction.

For the first time, Nick noticed Abby's lack of enthusiasm. With a puzzled look on his face, he asked, "What's wrong? Don't you like the condo?"

Shuffling her feet, Abby kept her eyes down. Finally, she looked up and said, "What I like or don't like isn't important, Nick. If *you* like this place, that's all that matters."

Now thoroughly confused, Nick took a step and positioned himself in front of Abby. "What … what is it, Abby? I mean, it's not like I'm moving to a whole new town or anything. I don't understand!"

Sighing, Abby pulled her hands from Nick and turned away. After a moment, she put her hands on her hips and turned back to face Nick.

"I guess I'm being silly, but that trailer you are so anxious to move out of is where I first met you. We chatted for hours in that little trailer, Nick, with each of us talking about our hopes and dreams. It's … it's where I fell in love with you, and I'm not ready to just put those memories so readily aside."

"Besides," Abby continued as she waved her arms expansively, "this place, it … it doesn't feel right. It's not you, Nick!"

Nick stared at Abby in disbelief. "You mean you prefer that hot, stuffy, sardine can of a trailer instead of this nice, roomy, *comfortable* condo?"

"Yes!" Abby stated emphatically.

"What? That's crazy!"

"You asked me, and I told you what I thought. If you don't want my opinion, then don't ask for it next time!" With that, Abby crossed her arms angrily and turned away from Nick.

Nick, agape, couldn't believe what was happening! What should have been a triumphant tour of his new condo was instead turning into the first serious argument between him and Abby. Shaking his head, he placed his hands on Abby's shoulders and gently turned her back toward him.

"Look, I didn't mean to say I didn't want your opinion. It's just… well it's just that I didn't get this condo only for me. I got it for *us,* Abby! And I guess I thought you'd be as excited about it as I was! If I hurt your feelings, then … then I'm sorry."

The angry look on Abby's face quickly melted away. "What … what do you mean you got the condo for us?" she whispered.

Nick's carefully laid plans to "pop" the question to Abby died a quick and sudden death. He had envisioned the condo tour to be followed later that evening by an intimate dinner at Porter's, all to set up what he wanted to ask Abby. Now he would have to improvise. *At least,* he thought bitterly to him- self, *I have a lot of practice at doing that!*

Taking Abby's hands into his own, Nick took a deep breath and said, "What I mean is that I love you, Abby. When I'm with you, I am happier than I ever thought I could be in my life. When we are apart, it's like a piece of me is missing, and I can hardly wait until we are together again. I would have asked you this sooner, but my trailer can barely accommodate me, much less the both of us. So … so what I'm asking you, Abby, is to move in with me. That's why I got the condo."

Abby's face, which had lit up in hopeful expression, now turned into disappointment at the last of what Nick had said.

"Oh," she said simply.

For the second time, Nick was baffled. For one brief moment, Abby looked joyful, the next like she had just lost her best friend. What was going on?

Feeling his own temper begin to rise, Nick dropped Abby's hands and stated sarcastically, "I'm sorry that telling you I love you is such a downer. I'll try to remember that next time I spill my heart out to you!"

"Nick, don't be that way. You … you just don't understand," Abby said quietly.

"Well, enlighten me then!" Nick shouted as he raised his arms in frustration. "What don't I understand? What am I missing? I mean, I thought you loved me too!" So saying, Nick began to pace about angrily.

Catching Nick firmly by the arm, Abby swung him around to face her.

"I do love you, Nick. And it's because I love you that I won't live with you."

Nick stared at Abby as if she had grown two heads where one had existed. Putting his hand to his forehead in exasperation, Nick said, "Ah, I know women are from Venus and men are from Mars or some such foolishness, but you aren't making any sense! *If* you love me as you say you do, then *why* would living with me pose such a problem with you?"

Sighing, Abby took a moment before answering Nick. "I … I thought you were going to ask me to marry you, Nick. But living together … that's not something I want to consider."

"Why, Abby, why? People do it all the time!" Nick said, his voice rising.

"Because marriage, even an imperfect marriage, represents *commitment*, Nick! Living together, it's … it's an arrangement of convenience for too many people. I don't want … I don't want *us* to be that way!"

"Considering how your first marriage with that jerk, Rob, worked out, I would think you of all people would certainly have a different philosophy, Abby!" Nick retorted.

Abby felt her cheeks begin to warm. "One bad marriage or relationship doesn't mean they all have to be that way!" she said hotly. "If that were the case, I would never have given you the time of day!"

Her face now flushed completely red, Abby continued and said, "Besides, let's face it, Nick, commitment to *anything* has never been a consistent part of your life!"

"Oh, so sleeping with me on our first date represents this … this *commitment* you're talking about, Abby? Here I buy a condo and ask you to live with me, and *I'm* the one with commitment problems? You've got to be kidding me!" Nick said, laughing harshly.

Nothing was said for long moments while both Abby and Nick stood silently fuming. Finally, sniffing back tears, Abby turned and faced Nick.

"I don't regret that night, Nick, and I'm sorry you have chosen to cheapen the memory of it, but let me explain something to you! Everybody, including *you*, wants—no, *needs*—somebody to cherish them! I thought I had found that person when I married Rob. As you have so … so *thoughtfully* reminded me that didn't work out so … so … " Abby's voice began to crack as tears began to flow freely down her cheeks.

"So I met you," Abby said in a tremulous voice, hoarse with emotion. "Someone who told me at a particularly vulnerable time in my life that, 'If I had been *his*, *he* would never have let me go.' You don't know how badly I needed to hear that, Nick. I needed to know that I was the center of some- one's universe."

Hitching her purse over her shoulder, Abby absently wiped the tears from her eyes before continuing. "From that moment, I knew I was falling in love with you, and I slept with you, Nick, not out of any pent up physical desire, but because I wanted to spend the night in the arms of someone who I thought truly loved me too."

"So as crazy as it sounds to you, I won't live with you, Nick. I love you too much to do that." With that, Abby turned on her heel and walked out of the bedroom and toward the front door. After a moment's hesitation, Nick followed, his mind a jumble of angry, confused thoughts.

They rode away in silence.

Chapter 25

Carter was looking at the monthly sales report when he heard the noise of raucous laughter coming from outside his office. Glancing up, he was rewarded with the sight of his personal secretary's firm derriere as she was bent low to replace a file in the bottom of a filing cabinet. With a tight black skirt that looked as if she had been poured into it, Tellie Brewster's outfit left little to the imagination. Licking his lips, Carter was momentarily distracted until a second round of laughter erupted. Curious, he waved Tellie over.

"Tellie! Go see what that racket is all about!"

Nodding, Tellie flashed a sensuous smile at Carter. Pausing with her hand on the doorknob, Tellie asked, "Are we still on for tonight?"

Grinning, Carter said, "Of course! Just be sure you wear that little number I bought you at Neiman Marcus in Dallas!"

Unbeknownst to Carter's wife, Tellie's job description also included that as his full-time mistress.

Hips swaying seductively, Tellie sashayed out the door. Moments later, she returned with a still chuckling Bobby Prather, the Cannon dealership's business manager.

"What's going on, Bob? You having a party out there?" Carter asked, smiling.

Throwing himself down in a chair beside Carter's desk, Prather shook his head and said, "You're never going to believe who just came in and bought a brand-new Jeep right off the lot!"

"Haven't a clue, Bob."

"None other than Nick Hollister! Who would have believed that fool could ever have afforded a brand-new car?" Prather said, slapping his leg and laughing. As part of the management team at the Cannon car dealership, Prather was fully aware of Carter's opinion of Nick.

"Hollister? You must be mistaken! A world-class idiot like him could never buy a new car!" Carter stated emphatically.

Shrugging, Prather said, "I've got the bill of sale right here. Paid cash for it too!"

Snorting, Carter snatched the sale folder out of Prather's hand. Rapidly, he scanned it, his eyes growing wide in disbelief.

"There must be some mistake! Are you sure this is *our* Nick Hollister?"

In response, Prather got up and went to the window in Carter's office that overlooked the car lot. Raising the blinds, he gestured with his hand and said, "See for yourself! The Jeep just came out of the detail shop, and Hollister's standing next to it."

Rushing to the window, Carter shouldered Prather aside and stared as Nick took the keys from the service attendant, started the Jeep, and drove off. Slowly, as if in a trance, Carter turned away from the window and trudged back to his desk. Falling heavily into his chair, he absently thrummed the top of the desk with his fingers.

"Not possible! There's no way he could pay cash for a new car!" he muttered to himself.

"Maybe he won the lottery or came into an inheritance or something," Prather offered helpfully.

Carter, frustrated, shook his head and said, "I guess nything's possible, but not with Hollister. He's the type of guy whose luck only runs in one direction—and all of it *bad*!"

Tellie and Prather looked at each other uncertainly as moments of thick silence filled the room. Suddenly, Carter slammed his fist down onto his desk with an audible *thump*!

"Well, I'm going to find out! Bob, if you'll excuse me!" Carter said, gesturing impatiently to the door. Taking his cue, Prather hurried out as Tellie closed the door behind him.

"Get me Jimmy Fitch on the phone!" Carter ordered Tellie. "He's just the man for a job like this!"

Leaning back in his chair, Carter steepled his fingers in total satisfaction. By the time Jimmy "The Sneak" Fitch got finished, Carter would know where every penny in Hollister's bank account came from, along with every detail of his miserable life he might want!

Carter smiled grimly to himself. Hollister should know better than to try to keep secrets in a town like Pleasant Mountain.

And what better person to teach him that lesson than Carter?

"What was Kenneth so excited about?" Nick asked Mark curiously.

"I don't know." Mark turned the wheel of the Expedition into the parking lot of a strip mall. "All he would say was that we needed to get over to the Radio Shack store as soon as possible. I mean, he was so wired, I could barely make sense of what he was saying over the phone!" Nodding, Nick sat back, mystified. What in the world had gotten Kenneth so amped?

Nick's musings were interrupted as Mark expertly pulled into an open parking space in front of the Radio Shack store. Along with Radio Shack, the strip mall contained an abundance of retail stores and several small restaurants. Located across the road from a Walmart Supercenter, the stores within the strip mall did a steady business, and even at barely nine o'clock in the morning, the parking lot was already filling up.

Nick and Mark barely made it out of the SUV before Kenneth burst from the store.

"Come in, come in!" Kenneth said, gesturing exuberantly with his hands. Grabbing Nick and Mark each by an arm, he propelled them rapidly through the glass door leading into the store. Nick managed to catch a glimpse of a sign taped to the door that said "Under New Management" before he and Mark shot past it.

Once inside the store, Kenneth abruptly halted them, and beaming ear to ear, announced, "I'm the new owner! What do you think?"

Nick and Mark looked at each other, completely dumbfounded by Kenneth's sudden revelation. "Er, ah, that's … that's great, Kenneth," Nick finally managed to say.

Nodding his head so rapidly that his jowls quivered, Kenneth could barely contain his enthusiasm.

"I've got it all figured out!" he exploded. "Now that I've got some working capital, I'll expand our product inventory, which, in turn, will increase our customer base! I figure I can double our sales within a year! The sky's the limit!"

Mark and Nick looked at each other a second time. Mark, clearing his throat, asked dubiously, "So, Mr. Parnell sold you his store … just like that?"

"Are you kidding me? He took the first offer I made him," Kenneth said giddily. "I mean, I've been suggesting to him for years to expand, but he just kept putting me off! Now that I own the store, I can finally do what he wouldn't!"

Kenneth put an arm around Nick and Mark. "I've always dreamed of owning my own electronics store, and I owe it all to both you guys. Especially you, Nick! I mean, you were the one who found the book that made all this possible."

Nick, at a loss as to what to say, simply shrugged. As Kenneth clapped them both heartily on the back and stepped away, Nick noticed for the first time that Kenneth was not dressed in his usual garb. Gone were the checkered shirt, high-water jeans, and black tennis shoes. Instead, he was nattily attired in a pair of dress slacks, held up by a Brighton leather belt. He wore a long-sleeved shirt and knotted tie. Gleaming black patent leather shoes covered his feet, while a perfectly fitted blazer hung from his pudgy frame.

But what really caused Nick's jaw to drop in surprise was not how Kenneth was dressed but how his hair looked! Rather than the usual wiry appearance, it had been styled into heavily moussed, tight ringlets!

"Kenneth, you … your hair … your clothes—" Nick started to say.

"You noticed, huh?" Kenneth blurted, interrupting Nick. "I've decided I needed a new image, especially if I'm going to be a store owner!

"Therefore, I've decided I need a whole new wardrobe, and I've hired a personal trainer and nutritionist! And here, look!" Taking a card out of his wallet, Kenneth showed it to Nick and Mark. "I've bought a membership at South Seas Tanning Salon. I'm going to be tan, fit, and in the best shape of my life! It's the beginning of the new me!"

Before either Nick or Mark could respond, a pouty voice from the back of the store called out, "*Kenneee!*"

A moment later, a pretty girl walked out and stopped in front of Kenneth. Blonde and curvaceous, she ignored Nick and Mark as she said, "I can't find those … those *thingees* you wanted."

"Thingees?" Kenneth asked, perplexed. "Oh! You mean the new shipment of iPods!

"Heh, heh. Candee just started working here," Kenneth explained to Nick and Mark. "She's still learning the ropes."

Flustered, Kenneth turned back to Candee and said, "Um, as soon as I've finished talking to my friends, I'll help you look for them."

Sighing heavily, Candee studied her perfectly manicured nails and said, "Okay, but I'm going to have to take my lunch hour at eleven o'clock instead of at twelve."

"But … but I have an appointment at eleven!"

"I know, but I really, really *need* to take off at eleven o'clock today!" Candee purred as she stroked Kenneth's hand.

An audible *urp* escaped Kenneth's lips, and his complexion turned a ruby red.

"Oh … okay," Kenneth finally managed to say in a strangled whisper.

Smiling prettily and patting Kenneth on the hand, Candee turned and skipped back to the warehouse section of the store to resume her search for the "thingees."

After a moment to control his rapid breathing, Kenneth led a bemused Nick and Mark to the door and waved as they drove off.

"Well, what do you think?" Nick asked Mark as they pulled away from the strip mall.

Shaking his head, Mark replied, "Working as an employee at a store is whole lot different than *owning* a store. I hope Kenneth knows what he's doing!"

Nodding, Nick said, "You want to go get some breakfast? I'm starved!"

Smiling, Mark said, "I'd love to, but Patti and I have an appointment with Dr. Shultz. Some other time maybe."

"There's nothing wrong is there?" Nick asked, his face a mask of concern.

"Oh no! It's just, well, you know Patti and I have tried for years to have kids, and with the old biological clock ticking, we have to start exploring our options before it's too late. We never could afford some of these options before, but now, since you found *The Book of Lost Treasures*, that's no longer the case."

"That's great! I'm happy for you, buddy!" Nick exclaimed.

"Yeah, it's all good. We're excited of course. It's just … it's just…" Mark's voice trailed off, and Nick looked over at his friend.

"What is it, Mark? What's wrong?" Nick asked, concerned.

"Well, Patti and I disagree over … over the *course of action,* so to speak."

Nick, who had never heard of Mark or Patti disagree over even such trivial decisions as to whether to super-size the fries at McDonald's, sat up and regarded Mark with a troubled expression.

"What do you mean?" Nick asked. "You two never differ over *anything*!"

Mark gripped the steering wheel so hard that his knuckles cracked and, with a voice edged with anger, replied, "Like I said, the biological clock's ticking, and we are running out of time to have kids. So I suggested that we go to a reputable adoption agency and begin proceedings to try and adopt a baby.

The process is expensive, and it sometimes takes years, but the adoption counselor I talked to said that with our profile, she could practically *guarantee* placing a child in our home within three years!"

"But … Patti doesn't want to do that?" Nick asked uncertainly.

"No!" Mark exploded. "She wants us to have our *own* baby! That means fertility drugs, possibly minor surgery, or even in vitro implants in her womb. All of this is not only expensive but it takes time, and *none of it is guaranteed to work*! So what happens if we go through all of this and Patti still can't get pregnant? We lose precious time we could have spent in adoption proceedings!"

"Why not do both?" Nick asked hopefully.

"I suggested just that, but Patti won't hear of it!" Mark said angrily. "She said it costs too much money and that if we pursued both possibilities, we could end up with two kids instead of one! I asked what's wrong with that, she said we would be first-time parents and that we would have our hands full with one child, much less two! She won't be reasonable, I tell you!"

Nick, speechless at his friend's outburst, sat back in numbed silence.

As they pulled up to a stoplight, Mark, as if sensing Nick's discomfort, glanced over at him and grinned sheepishly and said, "Sorry to lay all that on you, Nick. Patti and I will work it out. We always do."

Nick nodded, uncertain as to what he could say.

Anxious to change the subject, Mark said, "Are you and Abby going to Dusty's Watering Hole Friday night?" Dusty's was a local honky-tonk located on the outskirts of Pleasant Mountain.

"No. Why?" Nick asked curiously.

Mark shook his head and asked, "Don't you ever read your mail? Kenneth's not the only new owner in town. Steve bought Dusty's last week, quit his job, and is practicing with a new band. Their first appearance is this Friday, and Steve sent invitations to all his friends. We got ours two days ago."

Nick stared numbly at Mark. The sudden revelations of the day threatened to overwhelm him. Kenneth and Steve *owners*? Mark and Patti *arguing*? This, on top of what had happened between Abby and himself, was like trying to digest an entire elephant in one huge bite.

The light turned green. Mark pulled through the intersection, and he was left with an uneasy feeling that events were starting to spin out of control. What's more, it occurred to him that a common thread wound through all of what was happening in his friends' lives.

And that thread was Nick and *The Book of Lost Treasures*.

Chapter 26

Carter looked up as Tellie let a diminutive, weasel-faced man into his office. Quickly motioning for Tellie to close the door, Carter gestured for Jimmy Fitch to take a seat. It had been only three days since he had talked to "The Sneak," and he was anxious to learn what he had found out about Hollister's sudden good fortune.

"You work fast, Jimmy. What did you find out?" Carter asked, getting straight to the point.

While watching Fitch take a thick folder out of his brief- case, Carter reflected on what he knew of the man. He had worked for Carter's family since before the move from Atlantic City, and as his nickname, "The Sneak," indicated, he was very good at ferreting out information other folks would just as soon be kept secret. Possessed of a small stature and a personality that could best be described as unremarkable, "The Sneak" was constantly underestimated by those who didn't know him well—which, of course, was just the way Fitch wanted it. Little did they know he had managed to both obtain a law degree and become a Certified Public Accountant. He now ran his own business, Fitch & Associates Consultants, which specialized in financial investigations and, besides the Cannon family, had many other high-powered clients.

Dressed in a coat and tie, Fitch took a pair of glasses from his pocket and adjusted them on his nose. Clearing his throat, he glanced at Tellie and then questioningly at Carter.

Waving at Fitch, Carter said, "Go ahead! Tellie's my personal secretary and can be trusted."

Nodding, Fitch said, "You can read about all the details in my report, but in summarizing the main points, I can tell you that your boy, Nick Hollister, has been a very busy man. I went to his bank and posed as a potential depositor. Conveniently for me. I had the bank officer out of his office and obtaining a safe-deposit box key, his computer was still on. It took me only a few moments to hack into their client database, and I discovered that Hollister has over a quarter of a million dollars in his account."

"No!" Carter exploded in disbelief.

"Hey, you don't know the half of it," Fitch assured Carter. "I managed to do some more surfing through the bank's accounts and found out that there is a partnership account shared by Hollister and at least five other people. This partnership has liquid assets, whose combined worth is over *two and a half million dollars.*"

Carter's chair hit the wall behind his desk, rebounded, and fell to the floor with a resounding *thump* as he shot up out of it.

Leaning forward with both arms extended on his desk, Carter looked down at Fitch and managed to gasp, "What … what are you saying?"

Unperturbed, Fitch met Carter's steady gaze unflinchingly and said, "I'm telling you that Hollister and his friends have come into possession of a large amount of money in a relatively short period of time."

Carter staggered backward, perplexed, and ran a hand through his hair. How? How had Hollister managed to acquire so much money? He righted his fallen chair and sat back in it. Shaking his head, as if to rid it of cobwebs, he looked back at Fitch.

"What else have you got?"

Nodding, Fitch resumed his narrative. "My next stop was the law office that represents this partnership. After chatting up with one of the junior associates, I found out that the name of this business partnership is 'The Treasure Hunt Club.' The associate was very closemouthed about what exactly this … this *club* does, although he did let slip they had found some very valuable antiques."

Carter pursed his lips in concentration over what Fitch had discovered. His knowledge of antiques was limited, but he knew enough to know that for Nick and his friends to "accidently" stumble across over two million dollars of rare antiques was next to impossible.

"Anything else?" he said, glancing over at Fitch.

Shaking his head, Fitch said, "Only that the club recently leased a small office building on the north side of town and that they are advertising for a secretary." With that, Fitch handed Carter the folder and snapped his briefcase shut. Tellie showed him to the door, shutting it firmly behind him.

"What do you think?" she asked Carter.

With a perplexed shake of his head, Carter admitted, "I don't know. Fitch's report raises more questions than it answers. If, in fact, Hollister and his friends have been finding rare antiques, they have to been having help in finding them! They have to!"

Pacing about the office, a frustrated Carter said as much to himself as to Tellie, "But who or *what* is helping them?"

Stopping suddenly in midstride, Carter snapped his fingers, and a broad smile spread across his face.

Tellie, who had seen that expression on Carter's face before, asked eagerly, "What?"

"Tellie, you are hereby going to take a paid leave of absence from the Cannon Auto Group."

"Why?" Tellie asked, frowning.

In reply, Carter walked over to Tellie and pulled her toward him in a close embrace. Whispering in her ear, he said, "Because I can't expect you to work two jobs at once, now can I?" Seeing that the confused expression remained on Tellie's face, Carter released her and laughed.

"What? Didn't you hear? They're in need of a new secretary at the Treasure Hunt Club!"

The smile disappeared from Carter's face to be replaced by a determined glint in his eyes.

"And I know the perfect person to fill that position!"

The noise in Dusty's was deafening as Nick led Abby to the table where Mark, Patti, and Kenneth were sitting. The place was packed as Steve's band pulsed out rock anthems, which competed to be heard over the sounds of dozens of conversations, clinking glasses, and the scraping of chairs. Helping Abby into her seat and then taking his own, Nick looked around curiously. He hadn't been to the honky-tonk since the last time Steve's garage band had played there the previous summer. Other than expanding the small stage the band played on, the place hadn't seemed to have changed much.

Returning his attention to his friends around the table, Nick asked, "How's Steve's new band sound?"

Mark, who was nursing a beer, looked over, grinning and said, "Well, you know Steve. His music comes in two varieties: loud and *louder*!" Nick laughed at Mark's analysis and was soon joined by Kenneth. However, he noticed that Patti studiously avoided joining in the merriment. As he looked over at her, he saw a strained look on her face. It was not something that most people would notice, but for Nick, who knew Patti and Mark well, it was an obvious red flag. Apparently, they had yet to settle the issue of adoption versus fertility attempts in order to have kids.

As if to confirm his diagnosis of the situation, Nick looked questionably over at Abby, and she gave him a slight shake of her head. Since she was living with Mark and Patti, he was certain she knew something was going on. The irony of the situation was not lost on Nick, as he was reminded of their own recently strained relationship. Since their falling out at Nick's new condo, they not only had not been out together but they had had no con- tact, other than a few brief cell phone conversations. Nick viewed the invitation to hear Steve's new band as a golden opportunity to assess the damage that had occurred to their relationship.

When he had arrived to pick up Abby in his new Jeep, Nick wasn't sure what to expect, but Abby had greeted him with a kiss, and they had talked as they always did on the drive over to Dusty's. Although it had seemed "normal" to him at first, now he wasn't so sure. It wasn't anything he could put a finger on, but rather, he sensed it was as if their relationship had somehow been fundamentally altered and was now out of kilter. These thoughts caused him to glance again at Abby, and he was surprised to see her already gazing at him. There was a hint of sadness in her eyes, and with a jolt that went straight to his heart, Nick knew it was for *them* and not for Mark and Patti.

Nick was spared any further thought on the matter as Steve's band finished a set with a loud crescendo, and he joined them shortly afterward at their table. Gesturing at a waitress, he ordered a drink and then looked expectantly at his friends.

"Well, what do you think?"

"About owning Dusty's, or about your new band?" Mark asked.

Laughing, Steve waved his arms expansively, "All of it, of course!"

Steve's speech was somewhat slurred, and he giggled as if at some private joke he had just told himself. The waitress arrived with Steve's whiskey and Coke, and he downed it in one gulp before immediately ordering another.

Nick looked at Steve with concern and said, "Hey, don't you think you should slow down a bit? You've still got two more sets to play!"

Steve ignored Nick and gushed, "Isn't this the greatest rush ever? My own band and my own bar! Dreams really do come true!" Steve said this so loudly that those in the tables around them looked over curiously.

"Yeah, yeah it's great!" Nick said quickly before Steve could shout another comment.

Leaning forward, Steve whispered to Nick, "And I owe it all to you and your trusty book, my buddy, my buddy, my friend." This struck Steve as inordinately funny, and a fresh round of giggling erupted from him, interrupted only by the arrival of his drink.

Grabbing his glass, Steve stood up and said, "Well, gotta do some mingling before the next set. Drinks are on the house!" With that, Steve walked off, swaying slightly as he negotiated his way around patrons and tables.

"He's drinking way too much!" Mark observed apprehensively as he watched Steve's retreating back. Nick could only nod, his concern for Steve matching that of Mark's.

The sight of Steve staggering away placed a somber pall on the friends as they sat through another set by Steve's band. When the last ringing note squealed to an end, as if in one accord, they all stood up and waved at Steve before making their way out of the club. Saying their good-byes to each other, they got into their cars and drove away.

Nick drove slowly as Abby sat quietly in the passenger seat next to him. Neither seemed to know what to say, and they made the trip back to Mark and Patti's house in awkward silence.

Getting out of the car, Nick opened the door for Abby and helped her out. The touch of Abby's hand on his own seemed to galvanize Nick, and he suddenly pulled her toward him.

"I can't stand it anymore! I've got to know something!" The words tumbled from him in a rush. "Do you still love me?"

Abby hesitated for a moment before placing both her hands tenderly on either side of Nick's face.

"Yes. Yes, I'm very much in love with you, Nick," Abby replied softly.

Kissing him gently on the lips, Abby pulled away from Nick and made her way to the front door. Reaching into her purse, she retrieved her house key before turning to face Nick.

"But sometimes love isn't enough," Abby said. "Sometimes love can't survive unless it is allowed to grow." With that, she unlocked the door and entered the house, closing the door behind her.

Long seconds passed as Nick stared at the door. One moment he had been in euphoric heaven when Abby said that she still loved him. The next moment had brought it all crashing down. What did she mean? Did she love him or not?

Those questions occupied his thoughts all the way home.

Chapter 27

"Your resume is quite impressive, Miss … Miss …" Nick faltered as he searched for the name on the resume. They were sitting in the club's new office annex. The smell of fresh paint competed with the smells of the recently laid carpet. The new office furniture had not yet been delivered, and the furnishings were Spartan—nothing more than a dented filing cabinet, a few old folding chairs, and a card table.

"*Ms.* Brewster, but everyone calls me Tellie," Tellie said with a smile on her face. "As I indicated on my resume, in addition to typing eighty words a minute, I am quite proficient in Excel and PowerPoint." With that, Tellie chose to cross her legs, the action causing her skirt to ride higher. She had chosen her outfit carefully, deciding she must appear professional in her guise of seeking the secretarial opening, but at the same time, she wanted her other "assets" at least demurely displayed. Therefore, she had settled for a dark blue skirt that was not too short, but still short enough to display a tantalizing amount of her shapely legs. The white blouse she wore was cinched tightly to emphasize her small waist, and she had left it unbuttoned just low enough that a hint of cleavage was exhibited. Her long red hair she had arranged to simply fall about her shoulders, and she wore less makeup than normal, choosing to emphasize her brilliant blue eyes rather than her model cheekbones.

"Oh, okay … Tellie," Nick said, laughing nervously. "Er … if we were to offer you the job, when could you start?"

"Immediately!" Tellie said without hesitation. "I'm in between jobs, and I just moved into a new apartment. The rent is due at the first of the month, and while I have enough money to cover it, I won't have enough left over to buy food and gas."

Having been in just that situation too many times in the past himself, Nick nodded sympathetically.

"How about tomorrow?" Nick asked. They really didn't need a secretary until the following week at the soonest, but it sounded like Tellie was in a tight spot financially, and besides, the club could afford it.

"Tomorrow would be fantastic!" Tellie blurted out. Standing up, she shook Nick's hand and said, "You won't be sorry, Mr. Hollister! I'm a hard worker!"

Nick returned Tellie's handshake and said, "I'm looking forward to working with you, Tellie. And it's Nick, not Mr. Hollister."

Beaming from ear to ear, Tellie said, "Okay, Nick. I'll see you tomorrow!" With that, Tellie turned and walked to the door, pausing to wave at Nick before leaving. Nick, who had been appreciating the sight Tellie's backside had presented him, smiled guiltily and waved back.

Nick collapsed back in his chair with relief, glad that this was finally behind him and that they had hired a good secretary. Now the club could focus on future projects. Sighing, he leaned back in his chair and closed his eyes. With free time on his hands, he began to think of what they could use *The Book of Lost Treasures* to find next.

After driving a discreet distance away from the Treasure Hunt Club office, Tellie pulled over to the side of the road and retrieved her cell phone from her purse. Punching a cell number that only Tellie and a handful of others knew (and this did *not* include Carter's wife), Tellie reached Carter on the second ring.

"What have you got?" he demanded without preamble.

"I'm in," Tellie stated simply. "I start tomorrow."

"That's great!" Carter said, laughing harshly. "Now remember, what we are looking for is whoever or whatever they are using to find all these priceless antiques."

"I know, I know," Tellie replied irritably. They had been over all of this many times before.

"Can I see you tonight?" Tellie asked hopefully as she abruptly changed the subject.

"Baby, you know we can't be seen together. Even a dimwit like Hollister gets suspicious if he thought there was a connection between the two of us."

"It's funny, you never seem to share the same concern that your wife might see us together," Tellie pouted.

"Now, now, you know that's different! As far as my wife is concerned, you work for me, and we are very careful about our, er, *liaisons* so that she isn't any the wiser."

"That's just the point! I'm tired of hiding our relationship and meeting furtively like common criminals! I love you, Carter, and I want you to tell your wife about *us*!"

Caught off guard by Tellie's passionate outburst, Carter had to curb his first instinct to tell her what she could do with her demand. Instead, he took a steadying breath and said, "You know I love you too, baby. It's just that things are … *complicated* right now. I promise you, once you find out the secret to Hollister's success, we will take that next step, and I'll make you the happiest woman on the planet."

With that, Carter clicked off, leaving Tellie to grasp her cell phone rapturously to her breast. Did that mean what she thought it did? That Carter was finally going to tell his wife about the two of them and file for divorce?

The day seemed much brighter as Tellie put the car in gear and drove off.

Chapter 28

"I call this meeting of the Treasure Hunt Club to order!" Nick said, taking a small gavel he had bought at a trophy shop and rapping it on the surface of the recently installed table. They were meeting in the conference room of the club's new office annex, and six high-back, leather chairs were arranged around the table facing Nick. A tray containing a stainless-steel pitcher filled with ice-cold water had been set on the table along with glasses for the attendees.

"The chair recognizes Mark!" Nick continued. At that, Mark stood up and faced his fellow club members.

"I would like to propose that our next search using *The Book of Lost Treasures* be for these rare coins," Mark said as he passed out stapled sheets of paper containing the details of his proposal. Nick, who had already been briefed by Mark on what he had in mind, put his copy on the table absently beside him. As he observed his friends reading and digesting the information on the documents

Mark had prepared, he was struck by how much had changed in just the short five months since his discovery of the mystical book. What had started with such promise, with such giddy anticipation, now seemed to have lost much of its luster, and he didn't understand why! They were living the dream, all of them, with more money and potentially a lot more money than they ever could have hoped for in their wildest dreams! Now, as he looked around the conference table, he was dismayed to see the subtle and not so subtle transformation of his closest and dearest friends.

Patti, he observed, sat next to Mark, and she seemed distracted as she leafed through his proposal, a pinched expression on her face. This, the same Patti, whose gentle personality and warm smile never failed to lift Nick's spirits, regardless of how low he might be feeling, while Mark seemed to have morphed into all cold, hard business, rather than the man who would take a day off at the drop of a hat just to spend it with friends and family.

Turning his attention to Steve, he saw he was constantly pulling a bottle of Jack Daniel's from an Igloo cooler he had brought with him. Pouring it into a glass of ice he was sipping from. Dressed in black leather, rather than his customary jeans and T-shirt, he looked to Nick like the rocker version of Johnny Cash. Steve had even parked his beloved GTO and was now driving a black Porsche convertible he had bought off the lot in Longview. Kenneth, for his part, had a thick stack of invoices he was trying to look at while simultaneously trying to peruse the document Mark had prepared. A worried expression was on his face, and he was constantly dabbing at the beads of sweat forming on his forehead (which was a florid red due to numerous trips to the South Seas Tanning Salon). Mark had told him that

Kenneth's business was not going well. Whether that was from incompetent help, from Kenneth's lack of business expertise, or both, he didn't know.

Finally, Nick's attention settled on Abby. She had barely glanced at the document before her, and it seemed to Nick that her mind was a million miles away, as if she could have cared less about ever finding another valuable artifact.

Mark's clearing of his throat brought Nick's musing to an end and abruptly back to the matter at hand.

"As you can see, the coin or coins we are looking for are among the rarest and most valuable in the world. The Saint-Gaudens twenty-dollar double eagle gold piece was first struck in 1933, with four hundred forty-five thousand produced by the U.S. Mint in Washington, D.C. However, the gold standard was abolished shortly after that because of the Great Depression, and before these coins could be put into circulation, the Mint was ordered to take these coins and melt them. Only a few survived, two of which are now on display at the Smithsonian.

However, apparently not *all* the Saint-Gaudens were destroyed. At least ten have surfaced at various intervals since 1933, and in 2002, one was sold at auction for over seven and a half *million* dollars! I say we ask *The Book of Lost Treasures* to locate any of these lost coins that might still exist."

"I think I read something about these coins," Kenneth said, looking up from his invoices. "Isn't it illegal to own them since the government ordered them melted?"

"Not our problem!" Mark said, brushing off Kenneth's comment. "The coin dealers I've talked to said that private collectors, particularly overseas collectors, have a long history of buying coins under, shall we say, 'dubious' circumstances. Besides, if these coins are lost, we're not hurting anyone, especially the government, by finding them."

"You're talking about breaking the law!" Patti said as she stared at her husband in disbelief.

Flashing Patti an irritable glance, Mark ignored her and continued. "If we are fortunate enough to have the book locate any of these lost coins, we simply sell them to these collectors, and then it's *their* problem to settle the legality issues with the government."

"I like it!" Kenneth said. "I make a motion we accept Mark's proposal!"

"Shecondt!" Steve slurred.

Patti and Abby both looked angry, and when Nick called for a vote, the final tally was 3–2 in favor of Mark's proposal, with both women voting against it.

An uncomfortable silence settled over the room. Nick hastily suggested they immediately put the question to the book.

Seeing no disagreement, he pulled it from his satchel and placed it on the table. Mark gave him a printed copy of the exact words he wanted used when making the request. It read:

> Reveal the location of any lost Saint-Gaudens $20 golden eagle coins minted in 1933 by the U.S. Government Mint in Washington, D.C.

Nick carefully wrote the request word for word in *The Book of Lost Treasures.* As they all held their breath, a familiar golden glow immediately issued from a map that suddenly appeared on the following page.

"What's it show?" Mark asked as he, Steve, and Kenneth crowded around Nick.

"It's a map of Arlington, Virginia," Nick replied. *"Here Lies the Lost Treasure"* was pulsing within the city boundaries, marking the spot of the lost coins on the map. Nick turned the page, and another map showed the detailed location of a house, along with the street name and address.

"Looks like at least one coin exists!" Nick said as he turned to Mark, grinning. "But somebody must own that home. How are we going to play this?" he asked.

"Let me handle that. I'll think of something," Mark said in a determined tone.

The meeting quickly broke up after that, with Patti and Abby the first out the door. Nick was so enthused at the prospects of finding a Saint-Gaudens worth millions that he barely noticed their quick departure.

All of Nick's previous worries and concerns about his friends were forgotten as the excitement of the moment washed over him. It suddenly occurred to him that if they did indeed recover at least *one* Saint-Gaudens, they wouldn't just be rich.

They would be millionaires!

"Here are your tickets and boarding passes," Tellie said as she efficiently handed them to Nick and Mark. "You leave DFW at one forty, and your flight arrives in Arlington at five thirty in the afternoon, eastern standard time. You're booked at the Hyatt Regency, and I've included your confirmation number with your plane tickets. I've already arranged for a rental car at the airport, and you'll simply have to pick up the keys at the rental agency. Mark has the club's credit card, so there should be nothing more that you need."

Smiling, Tellie added, "Good luck!" although she didn't have a clue as to what Nick and Mark were leaving on their "business" trip for.

"Boy that Tellie sure works fast!" Mark said after they had left the office and were out of earshot. "You hired a great secretary, Nick!"

Nick couldn't have agreed more. After less than three weeks on the job, Tellie had far surpassed his expectations. She worked hard, didn't complain, and handled even the most routine jobs with zeal. In fact, she was rapidly making herself invaluable!

With that thought in mind, he got into Mark's car, and they drove for the airport some two and half hours away.

As soon as Mark's car disappeared from sight, Tellie called Carter. As she was the only one in the office, she didn't bother trying to keep her conversation low.

"They've left."

"Good!" Carter said. "I've got two men already at DFW. They'll shadow them all the way to Virginia, where another team will pick them up." Pausing he asked, "Did they tell you anything before they left?"

"No," Tellie said, shaking her head. "All I know is that it's something big."

Carter bit back a curse. Even with his men following Hollister and Chambers, they were still shooting in the dark. At best, his men might discover *what* they were looking for in Virginia, but that still didn't answer the *how* part! How were they able to find such valuable artifacts?

Tellie, as if sensing Carter's frustration, said, "I've got a plan that might finally tell us what they are using to find all these valuables."

"What? What is it?" he asked eagerly.

"I'll let you know after tonight," Tellie said. Knowing that he would grumble and demand to know what she had up her sleeve, Tellie lied and told him someone was coming and clicked off. Truth be known, Tellie's frustration matched Carter's and then some. *She* was the one stuck in this godforsaken office, running errands for some of the biggest nerds on the planet. Let Carter stew for a while since it was his plan that put her here!

Another reason she hadn't told Carter the details of her plan was because she wasn't sure it would work. However, she smiled inwardly to herself; she was pretty confident that after tonight, she would have the information Carter so desperately wanted.

Humming to herself, she began to plan what she would wear to Dusty's that night.

Chapter 29

Nick and Mark's plane touched down without incident as it touched the runway in Arlington. There had been no delays, and they had actually arrived a few minutes earlier than the 5:30 p.m. arrival time. Picking up their luggage at the baggage terminal, they stopped next at the rental car kiosk, where, as promised by Tellie, the key to their rental car was waiting for them. Their hotel was located just a few short blocks from the airport, and after checking in, they ate a quick meal at the hotel restaurant and turned in early for the night. Nick, who thought he would be too keyed up to sleep, fell asleep almost as soon as his head hit the pillow.

Waking up early the next morning, Nick and Mark skipped breakfast in their haste to locate the address of the home that might contain the lost Saint-Gaudens coins. Their rental car came with a GPS navigation system, and they entered the address in it that the map said was the location of the rare coins. Twenty-five minutes later, they turned onto a street containing modest, bungalow-style homes. It was immediately apparent that this was an older neighborhood, with junked cars resting in the driveways of several residences.

Mark stopped the car beside a house with an unkempt front yard, whose address matched that of the map in *The Book of Lost Treasures.* The address was painted on the curb beside the house, but it was faded and flaking so badly that they had to get out of the rental car and peer closely to make sure it was a correct match.

"Not one of the best neighborhoods I've ever been in," Mark commented sourly as they stood beside the curb.

Nick grunted in assent before his attention was captured by a sign on the front porch of the home that was partially obscured by an overgrown hedge.

"Mark, look!" he blurted, pointing excitedly.

As one, they both rushed to the front porch. There, leaning against the hedge, was a sign that said "For Sale or Rent by Owner." Below this was a scrawled phone number. From the weathered condition of the sign, it had apparently been sitting there for a long time.

Both Nick and Mark peered through the bay window on the front porch. The window was filthy and the interior dark, but they could still make out a small living room dotted here and there with the dusky forms of furniture. A gloomy sense of abandonment cast a pall about the house, and it was readily apparent that it had been unlived in for quite some time.

Nick and Mark turned to each other and, grinning, high-fived one another. By a fantastic stroke of luck, the coins were lost in a house that was for sale! Mark quickly took out his cell and called the number on the "For Sale" sign. After what seemed to be an interminable amount of time, someone answered the phone. Mark introduced himself and then asked about the house. After chatting for a few minutes, he said good-bye and clicked off.

"What?" Nick asked, unable to curb his curiosity.

"Well, the guy's name is Curtis, and I guess I woke him up. He was pretty grumpy until I asked about the house. Then, all of a sudden, it's like he's wide-awake and nice! Anyway, he's driving over here to meet us and said it will take him twenty minutes."

Nick nodded, and then he and Mark spent the time waiting for Curtis by looking around the old house. A fence with a warped wooden gate guarded the entry to the backyard. As Nick pushed it open, his ears were assaulted by a sharp squealing sound produced by the gate's rusty hinges. A five-foot high cinder block wall encircled the backyard, and as Nick and Mark soon discovered, it was just as overgrown as the front. Calf-high grass and weeds had turned brown in the late November weather and crunched loudly under their feet.

From their position in the backyard, Nick and Mark had a bird's-eye view of the surrounding area. Nick noticed that all the adjacent homes had what looked like large, earthen mounds in their backyards. Puzzled, as he peered more closely, he saw that these "mounds" were actually hardened concrete with rusty vent pipes poking from them.

"What's that?" he asked Mark curiously as he pointed at the mounds.

Following Nick's finger, Mark studied one of the concrete mounds. Finally, he gave a low whistle and said, "Well, I'll be! These houses around here must *really* be old! Those are bomb shelters, Nick! During the height of the Cold War in the fifties and sixties, everybody was building them in case of a nuclear attack."

Pausing, Mark looked around and said, "That's strange. This house seems to be the only one without a bomb shelter."

Indeed, as Nick cast about, he saw nothing that resembled the humped bomb shelters. After a few minutes of searching, he shrugged and gave up. About that time, he and Mark heard a car pull up into the driveway. Hurrying back through the gate, they arrived just in time to see a large man struggling to extricate himself from a Honda Civic. The car had definitely seen better times, as it had a bent front bumper and a thick sheet of plastic had been duct taped to where the missing passenger-side window had formerly been.

Huffing and puffing, the man appeared to be middle-aged, and he sported a huge beer belly, which a stained undershirt struggled to contain. Bloodshot eyes blinked at Nick and Mark, and a thick three-day stubble covered his face and double chin. Although the temperature was in the low forties and he was wearing only the undershirt and no coat or jacket, he was sweating profusely.

Hastily, he shut the car door and turned to walk toward Nick and Mark. As he did so, he lost one, and then the other, of a pair of green Crocs he had hastily jammed onto his bare feet. Cursing, he hopped on the cold concrete of the driveway and attempted to place them back on his feet. Finally giving up, he sat down on the driveway and put them back on his feet. It was from that position that he saw Nick and Mark studying him in bemusement.

Rolling to his knees, he managed to lever himself up and onto his feet. Then extending a meaty hand, he said, breathing heavily, "Curtis, Curtis Branson. You Mark, the guy I talked to on the phone?" he asked, looking at Nick.

Nick shook Curtis's hand before he pointed at Mark and said, "No, he is."

Curtis immediately switched his attention to Mark. "So, you interested in the house?" he asked eagerly.

Mark, who had already rehearsed in his mind what he was going to say, was deliberately noncommittal and said, "We're interested in acquiring rental property, but we'd like to see the inside of the house first."

Bobbing his head rapidly, Curtis pulled a set of keys from his pocket and hurried to the front door. Unlocking it, he motioned them in. Once inside the house, a stale, musty odor permeated the air. When Nick tried to turn on a light switch, he was unsurprised to see that it didn't work. Undoubtedly, the electricity had beenturned off for some time. Looking around, Nick noticed dark stains in the ceiling, evidence that the roof leaked and needed repair.

Making a show of studying the house, Nick and Mark went room to room before discovering the house contained a large basement accessed by a creaking set of wooden stairs.

Taking a penlight from his pocket and playing the beam about, Nick spot- ted an old boiler in a corner, along with various boxes, broken furniture, and assorted knickknacks, all covered with cobwebs and a thick layer of dust. If the musty odor was strong upstairs, it was downright overpowering in the basement.

Hurriedly going back up the stairs and exiting the basement, Nick and Mark gratefully gulped the stale air. A few moments later, they went out on the front porch.

"What can you tell us about the history of this place?" Mark asked Curtis.

Curtis took a can of Skoal from his back pocket and placed a healthy pinch under his lip. Spitting on the brown grass, he said, "Well, this place is owned by my aunt. She's been in a nursing home for almost five years now, and Medicare doesn't cover all the costs of her care. I'm the only family she's got left, and I help my aunt with her financial affairs. So I've been trying to sell the house to help pay her bills."

Nick detected a brief gleam of greed in Curtis's eyes, and he immediately doubted the veracity of his story. More likely, he thought, Curtis had "helped" to squander his aunt's money, and now he needed to sell the house.

Curtis paused long enough to spit again before continuing. "This residential area was one of the first mass-produced housing areas in Virginia, and they started building these homes right after World War Two. They knew how to build houses back then!" he said proudly as he gave the wall beside the porch a firm knock. Instead of producing a solid thump, a dull *thud* sounded. Hastily, Curtis pulled his hand back.

"Er, ah, as I was saying, my aunt inherited this house from her daddy when he moved here after retiring from the Mint. She lived here—"

"Her father worked at the *Mint*?" Mark asked excitedly as he interrupted Curtis.

"Well … yeah," Curtis replied, puzzled at Mark's reaction. "She said he worked there for over forty years."

Nick and Mark looked at each other, unable to keep the expression of triumph off their faces.

"How much do you want for the house?" they asked Curtis simultaneously.

Tellie sat by herself at a table near the stage at Dusty's, where Steve's band was currently playing. A vodka tonic sat untouched in front of her as she toyed impatiently with a gold bracelet about her wrist. She was wearing a black strapless cocktail dress with a plunging neckline, and since taking her seat at the table, she had fended off no fewer than ten men who had tried to pick her up. Ranging in age from those barely at the legal age to drink to men twice her age, she had firmly but politely turned down all offers. She was after bigger game tonight, and with both Nick and Mark out of town, the timing was perfect.

The band finished playing, for which Tellie was extremely grateful. The ringing in her ears had subsided somewhat as she spotted Steve walking off the stage.

"Steve!" she cried out waving. "Over here!"

Blurrily, Steve stopped and looked in Tellie's direction. A sloppy grin appeared on his face, and he turned and walked to her table.

Tellie patted a chair beside her, and Steve plopped into it.

"You sounded so *good* tonight!" Tellie gushed as she leaned forward, exposing her deep cleavage. "I had no idea you were so talented! Can I have your autograph?" And with that, Tellie pulled a pad and pen from her purse and pushed it toward Steve.

"You bet!" Steve said enthusiastically, his chest expanding proudly.

Tellie studied Steve as he jotted his name on the pad. His eyes were a bleary red, and she had no doubt he was well on his way to becoming drunk. Deciding to speed up the process, she signaled for a waitress.

"What are you having?" she asked Steve.

"Are you kidding? I own the place!" Steve said, tittering. With that, he ordered drinks for the both of them, failing to notice that Tellie still had a full drink before her.

An hour later, Steve's band went back on stage without him. As they began to play, he had his arm around Tellie and was regaling her with stories punctuated here and there with fits of inebriated chortling. Feeling the time was as right as it was going to get, Tellie put her hand on Steve's knee and leaned in close to him.

"You know, I've heard all sorts of amazing stories about you and the rest of the club members. Some of it is so fantastic, I just don't believe it could be true!"

Steve's breath had a tang of alcohol on it as he whispered conspiratorially to her, "Well it's true all right! Every bit of it!"

Tellie cast a doubtful glance at Steve. "I don't believe you!

You're just teasing me!"

Despite drifting in an alcoholic fog, Steve managed to look scandalized. "No, I swear, I'm telling the truth!"

Tellie ran her finger around the rim of her drink. Looking sideways at Steve, she said demurely, "Well … okay. But which parts are true?"

Sniggering, Steve held his finger up to his lips. Leaning in he whispered, "You have to keep all this to yourself, because we're not supposed to tell anyone." Tellie breathlessly assured him she would, and Steve proceeded to tell her all about the discoveries the Treasure Hunt Club had made, from the stoneware crock to their most recent discovery of the rare Honus Wagner baseball card. When he had finished, Tellie sat back in amazement. Thinking hard, she realized that while Steve had divulged where the sudden riches of the Treasure Hunt Club had come from, he still hadn't revealed the secret of their string of successes.

Lightly rubbing her hand alongside his inner thigh, Tellie nuzzled Steve's neck and purred, "But how are you able to find all those things?"

Steve grinned foolishly and made a show of looking about as if someone might be eavesdropping on their conversation. With the loud noise made by the band playing in the background, the prospects of being overheard were so ridiculous that Tellie had to stop herself from laughing.

Crooking his finger and motioning to Tellie, Steve leaned forward until their noses almost touched.

"That's a big, big, *big* secret!" he stated expansively.

Tellie looked at Steve with wide, innocent eyes. "I've never known anybody that had a really *big* secret before!" she breathed. "Oh, I wish you could tell me what it is! I promise I won't tell anyone—cross my heart!" Crossing her chest, Tellie saw Steve's eyes stop and linger on her breasts. As if a dam had broken and swept away his indecision, Steve turned and reached for his drink among the sea of empty glasses on the table. Chugging it quickly, he slammed it down on the table.

He hunched forward, whispering, "Okay, but you can't tell anyone!" Seeing Tellie vigorously nod her head yes, Steve continued. "Nick found a book in the back of a frame of an old painting, and the book is called *The Book of Lost Treasures.* Legend has it that the book was given to a sea captain by some mermaid princess whose life the captain had saved. Anyway, the mermaid told the captain that the book could find lost treasures and stuff. Well, when the captain died of old age years later, this book sorta disappeared until Nick found it."

Rubbing his hands together gleefully, Steve said, "And here's the best part: it *works*! The book actually works! You write down in the book what lost thing you want the book to find for you, and it produces a map that shows you where it is!"

"A map? Like a treasure map?" Tellie asked doubtfully.

"Yes! Exactly like a treasure map!" Steve exclaimed.

"X marks the spot and all that?" Tellie asked testily as she felt her temper rising. Surely, she hadn't wasted an entire evening being told a fairy tale by this drunken fool!

"Yes, it's true! I swear!" Steve said hastily as, even in his drunken state, he sensed Tellie's dubious change of heart. "I mean, think about it! How else could we have found a Civil War crock worth thousands of dollars at a garage sale? Or … or a Faberge jewelry box hidden in the base of a worthless lamp? Or … or … " Steve's voice trailed off, and his head drooped. The temporary rush of emotion, combined with the alcohol in his system, had finally overwhelmed Steve's synapses, and his nervous system began the process of shutting down. Within moments, he was snoring as his head rested on the table.

Tellie looked at Steve's unconscious form and considered what he had told her. As unbelievable as it sounded, she was certain Steve had been telling her the truth. The facts fit with what she knew about the club, and there was no other readily available explanation as to how they had acquired their sudden wealth.

A tingle crawled up her spine as she realized the implications of her train of thought. *If* such a book actually existed, and *if* it could actually find lost treasures…

Tellie got up abruptly and cast one more cursory glance at Steve. With any luck, he would not be able to remember any of their conversation when he finally awoke from his drunken stupor. Hurrying out the door of the bar, her mind was numbed by the possibilities of the riches such a book could reveal.

As she got into her car and drove away, she wore a triumphant smile. This book changed everything. It certainly gave her leverage in her relationship with Carter. The cow he was married to was soon to be history.

A new chapter was about to be written with her as Mrs. Carter Cannon!

Chapter 30

"Gentlemen, it is so good to meet you."

Nick and Mark looked down at a wizened elderly woman who was seated in a wheelchair. With hair as white as snow, the woman and her wheelchair were situated in a small courtyard located behind the Sunny Acres Assisted Living Complex. She was bundled tightly against the cold, and a thick book entitled *The Complete Works of Edgar Allan Poe* rested in her thin lap. Besides themselves and the elderly woman's nephew, no other Sunny Acres inhabitants were about.

Although they had quickly come to terms with Curtis on purchasing the house (which included his ludicrous claim that the moldering "furnishings" within the house vastly increased its worth), he had called them less than an hour later and said his aunt had insisted on meeting them before signing the deed over to them. From the tone of his voice, he had not been very happy with that prospect. Nevertheless, he had driven back to the house with all the legal documents needed to conclude the sale, and they had followed him to the nursing home.

The old woman shook each of their hands with a surprisingly strong grip, and after Nick and Mark had introduced themselves, she said, "My name is Claire, Claire Branson. My nephew says you are interested in buying my home."

As she said this, Nick saw that Claire was studying both of them with an alert intelligence that belied her age. Given the slothful nature of both her home and her nephew, Curtis (who was chewing on a hangnail, a bored expression on his face), the last thing Nick was expecting to see was the sophisticated and intelligent septuagenarian before him.

As if reading his mind, Claire smiled and said, "There is an old saying, Nick, that is as true today as when it was first coined: 'Never judge a book by its cover.' Take Poe, for example," she said while lifting the heavy book from her lap. "By all accounts, he *should* have been one of the most successful authors of his age. He had limitless talent and, in his relatively short life on this earth, produced some of the greatest works in the history of American literature. Yet, he died an alcoholic, penniless, and alone."

A glint of amusement appeared in Claire's eyes as she saw the looks of surprise on Nick's and Mark's faces. Chuckling quietly, she said, "I was a professor of English at Virginia Commonwealth University for many years. American literature was my specialty."

Opening the Poe book in her lap, Claire's expression turned businesslike as she retrieved a business card she had placed in it. Squinting at the card, she said, "You represent the Treasure Hunt Club. An odd name for a business, and one that certainly piqued my curiosity.

You'll forgive me if I ask what type of business you represent?"

Mark cleared his throat and said, "The club is actually a partnership. We are in the business of finding and restoring antiques and other valuables that are often considered junk by their owners."

"And you believe my house may contain such valuables?" Claire asked in a tone of disbelief.

"Well, not exactly. With the housing bust, we feel that there is an ideal investment opportunity to buy real estate cheaply, for the purpose of renting or selling at higher prices when the market finally recovers," Mark said, delivering the rehearsed line he had prepared carefully.

"I see," Claire said, tapping her forefinger thoughtfully against her lips. It was apparent to Nick that from the expression on her face, she wasn't buying the explanation, and a sudden fear that she wouldn't sell them the house leapt into his mind.

Moments later, this fear evaporated as Claire shrugged and said, "Not that it makes any difference to me what you want the house for." Gripping the wheels on her wheelchair, Claire turned it so that she was directly facing Nick and Mark.

"The *real* reason I wanted to meet you has a lot more to do with sentimentality than anything else. You see, my father, a man whom I loved and respected deeply, last lived in that house. Daddy died in 1975 at the age of ninety, and as his last living blood relative, the ownership of the house passed to me. I would sometimes stay there on weekends, but I lived the rest of the time in an apartment I kept near downtown."

Claire's eyes turned distant as she said, "My father was an extraordinary man. He grew to manhood on a farm and never had any formal schooling. Yet, he taught himself to read, and when I and my brothers and sisters were small, he would read to us every night from Dickens, Longfellow, Keats, and even Shakespeare. It was from him that I learned my love for literature."

"He worked for forty-eight solid years at the U.S. Mint in Washington, D.C., and he took great pride at being one of the longest-tenured employees in the history of the Mint. Upon retirement, they even placed his picture next to those of the Mint directors, past and present, an unprecedented honor at the time. Because my mother died when I was eighteen, my father lived alone, so when he retired, he moved here to Arlington to be closer to my family and me. The day he died was one of the saddest in my life."

Taking a Kleenex from her pocket, Claire dabbed at the mist in her eyes.

"I've lived a long, full life, gentlemen. I have experienced things that others can only dream of, and I was married for over fifty years to the absolute love of my life. I count myself extremely fortunate, which is why I can tell you the money you are offering for my house means nothing to me. That house is the last link to my father and to my past. To see who is buying the house provides an old woman with at least some closure. I hope you understand.

"Well, enough of that!" Claire said abruptly as she sniffed one final time and jammed the Kleenex back in her pocket. Signaling to Curtis, she took the documents he handed to her and signed each of them quickly. When finished, she gave them to Mark, who placed them in a large manila folder. He then handed her a bank draft wired from the club's bank in Pleasant Mountain. Claire barely glanced at it before handing the check to Curtis, who hastily stuffed it in his pocket.

Claire thanked Nick and Mark and then had Curtis wheel her back into the assisted living complex. Left alone in the open courtyard, they both stood silently for a few moments as a cold breeze suddenly brushed against them.

Looking guiltily at each other, Nick and Mark slowly made their way to their rental car. It was time to get to work.

Neither noticed the car that pulled out of the parking lot and followed them as they drove away.

"I don't understand! The book says the coins are *here*!" Nick said, frustrated, as he speared his shovel angrily into the ground. They were standing in the backyard, and holes where they had dug pockmarked the area.

"I don't know! Just keep digging!" Mark snapped. The sun was low in the horizon, and they had been digging steadily for over two hours.

Nick snorted and stepped on the shovel to drive it further into the ground. The shovel's tip shivered to a halt as it suddenly hit a solid obstacle.

"Mark!" he cried.

Mark rushed over, and together, they began shoveling dirt furiously. Within minutes, they had excavated a section of what looked to be poured concrete. Further digging did nothing but expose more of the pitted concrete.

Calling a halt to their efforts, Nick and Mark leaned exhausted on their shovels.

"We … we could dig all night and still … still not uncover this thing," Mark gasped. "It's going to take a bulldozer or a backhoe or something to finish the job."

Nick, too tired to answer, could only nod. As he stood trying to catch his breath, he glanced at the adjacent house next to them. In the waning light, he saw the oval shape of what he now knew was a bomb shelter rising from the ground. A thought suddenly struck him, and dropping the shovel, he ran to the cinder block wall that encircled the backyard. Squatting beside it, he looked back at where they were digging and made a rough estimate of the height of where the ground came up to the wall. Standing up, he leaned over the wall and looked at the other side to see how high the ground came up to the wall on the neighbor's property. It was lower. Much lower!

His exhaustion forgotten, Nick sprinted to the opposite side of the yard to compare the ground level on the wall there also. Peering over the wall, he saw it too was much lower on the neighbor's side!

"Mark, he covered it!" he crowed. "He brought in dirt and covered up the entire bomb shelter! That's why this is the *only* house in this whole area without one! It's been there the entire time beneath our feet!"

After Mark saw the difference in how high the level of soil came to the inside of the cinder block wall compared to the outside of the wall shared with the adjacent homes, he quickly agreed with Nick. Their enthusiasm was tempered quickly with the sobering realization that short of bringing in earthmoving equipment, they had no way of uncovering the bomb shelter and finding out what had been buried within it.

"It doesn't make any sense!" Nick said, baffled. "Claire's father went to a lot of trouble to cover up and bury that bomb shelter. He *had* to have a reason for doing so! Since the book says the coins are *in* this bomb shelter, he must have stored things he valued there. But if that's the case, how did he access the bomb shelter? He *must* have had a way of getting to it!"

"You don't know that for a fact, Nick," Mark said tiredly. "For all we know, he may have thought the bomb shelter was more of an eyesore than anything else and decided to cover it up."

"Then *why* does the book say the lost coins are located there?" Nick asked pointedly.

Mark had no answer and simply shook his head.

His frustration mounting, Nick decided to check the interior of the house again. They had unlocked the back door, so he opened it and walked in. The sun was setting, and Nick switched on one of the powerful halogen flashlights they had brought with them. He went from room to room, inspecting each one carefully. Mark joined him a few minutes later, and between the two of them, they scoured every inch of the home's interior. An hour later, they had found nothing that could give them a clue to the buried bomb shelter.

"Nothing!" Nick said in disgust as he and Mark sat in the living room. "We've searched everywhere! Now what are we going—"

Nick suddenly stopped in mid-sentence.

"Wait! There's one place we haven't checked. C'mon!" he cried at Mark as he got up and sprinted out of the room. Mark found him moments later going down the stairs of the basement. Reaching the bottom, he joined Nick, who was already playing the beam of his flashlight about. Due to the accumulation of junk and clutter crammed there, neither Nick or Mark had previously considered the basement.

"It's here, Mark! I can feel it!" Nick exclaimed. "The answer is down here somewhere!" Striding to the far wall, Nick pointed at it.

"This wall is adjacent to the backyard where the bomb shelter is located. Let's start here!"

The basement was pitch black, so Nick and Mark were obliged to coordinate the beams of both their flashlights to inspect the wall. Composed of red brick and crumbling masonry, it looked unremarkable to both of them, and besides an oval Mobile Oil sign that was bolted to the wall, it was featureless.

After their inspection of the basement wall revealed nothing to them, Nick and Mark stepped back to consider what they would do next. Something about the wall bothered Nick, and as he struggled to pinpoint exactly what it was, it suddenly came to him.

"Mark, didn't Claire say her father worked at the Mint for forty-eight years?"

"Yep. She said they even put a picture up of him along with all the past directors," Mark replied.

"Then why would a guy who worked forty-eight years at the Mint hang an *oil company* sign from his basement wall?" Nick asked pointedly.

"Yeah! Yeah, you're right, Nick!" Mark said excitedly. Together, they rushed toward the sign.

The background of the sign was white with Mobile Oil's logo, the red Pegasus, superimposed upon it. As Nick ran his fingers carefully over the sign, he noticed the eye of the winged horse seemed a bit larger in scale than the rest of its figure. Curiously, he touched it with his finger, and as he did so, he felt it give a little. Emboldened, he pushed the eye with his finger and was rewarded moments later when an audible *click* sounded from the wall.

Both Nick and Mark stepped back from the wall and played their flashlights on it. A fine crack had appeared in what had formerly been the solid wall of the basement.

As they moved in for a closer inspection, they saw that the brick and masonry had been set in such way as to cleverly disguise a door built as part of the wall. Excitedly, Nick grabbed the edges of the Mobile Oil sign and pulled.

A section of the wall swung outward, revealing a narrow passageway. It was only about six feet high, so Nick had to duck as he entered the passageway. Brick and mortar lined the corridor with thick wooden beams interspersed at regular intervals to support the ceiling. As Nick squeezed down through the corridor, it reminded him of pictures he had seen of mining tunnels.

Reaching the end of the passageway, Nick, with Mark hot on his heels, saw that it opened into a subterranean chamber. Playing the flashlight's beam in front of him, Nick spotted a narrow set of concrete stairs on the opposite side of the chamber that led upward before coming to an apparent dead end at the ceiling. With a start, he realized it was the buried bomb shelter!

As Mark entered the chamber, the light from their flashlights revealed a small wooden table and chair sitting in the corner of the bomb shelter. An old-fashioned oil-burning lamp sat on the table. Swinging the beam of his flashlight about to see what else occupied the cramped confines of the room, Nick noticed a dull gleam of light reflected off what he thought was one of the solid concrete walls of the bomb shelter. Puzzled, he took the few steps needed to reach the wall and ran his hand over its surface. Caked dust cascaded from the cool, smooth surface he was touching, revealing a pane of glass!

Mark heard Nick's excited shout, and within minutes, they had scrubbed the glass surface free of the accumulation of many decades' worth of dust from its surface. Peering closely, they saw what looked like a display case cleverly recessed into the wall. Two large panes of glass fronted this case, and both were set in tracks that enabled them to slide open or shut.

The back of the display case was lined with what looked like crushed blue velvet. But it wasn't the velvet that immediately caught Nick and Mark's attention. It was the row upon row of shining coins that were inset into the velvet! Sliding one of the glass panes open, Nick saw that the coins were arranged in groups of four by denomination and by year.

Four pennies were followed by four nickels, which were followed by four dimes, and so forth. Shining his flashlight on the first set of coins, Nick saw the year 1905 stamped upon them. He realized abruptly that that was probably the first year Claire's father starting working at the Mint. He must have collected four coins of each denomination for every year he had worked there! If that was true, that meant…

Nick aimed his flashlight at each set of coins, scanning the year on them as quickly as he could. His heart beat like a hammer in his chest as he followed the year each set of coins was struck. Reaching the end of one half of the display case, Nick hurriedly pushed open the other sliding pane of glass.

Skipping over several sets of coins, Nick spotted the year 1929, 1930, 1931, 1932, and finally, the year *1933*!

The shaft of Nick's flashlight wavered slightly in his shaking hand as he saw four large twenty-dollar gold pieces that reflected a golden metallic luster. Touching one of the coins tentatively with his forefinger, a bright glow of light emanated from the satchel he carried slung over his shoulder. Nick gave a shout of exultation! They had found the Saint-Gaudens double eagle coins!

He didn't need to look to know the words "*Treasure Found*"

were glowing brightly in the book!

Nick and Mark took only the Saint-Gaudens coins with them in their haste to pack up their things and get back to their hotel. Leaving all the other coins and sliding the panes of glass shut, they exited the cramped passageway and pushed the cleverly disguised section of wall back into place.

Once again, it resembled a featureless section of the wall. Collecting their tools, they threw them in back of the rental car, locked the doors of the old house, and left.

As soon as Nick and Mark had driven off, a pair of head- lights came on from a car that had been parked against the curb a short distance from the old house. Stopping in front of the driveway, the headlights were extinguished, and two shadowy figures exited the car.

Nick and Mark didn't know it, but a second inspection of the house was going to take place that night.

Chapter 31

Within days of arriving back in Pleasant Mountain, both Nick and Mark had driven to Houston to have the coins appraised by a coin expert, whose specialty included U.S. minted gold coins. He had taken one look at the Saint-Gaudens and almost fainted! Once he had recovered and had carefully studied the coins, he verified they were authentic. When asked their value, the dealer hadn't hesitated, saying each coin was worth a minimum of five million dollars, or as a set, twenty to twenty-five million dollars! He finished by saying his estimate was conservative and that at auction, the coins might fetch as much as five to seven million dollars more. Nick had almost started hyperventilating when hearing the estimate of the coins worth, while Mark wore a stunned expression on his face. They quickly thanked the coin expert, and as they giddily made their way back to Mark's car, they both shared a common thought.

They were multimillionaires!

Disgusted, Carter threw the report he had just read onto the top of his desk. It had been compiled by the men he had assigned to tail Hollister and Chambers, and as he had feared, it had added little to what he already knew. Apparently, Hollister and his "club" member had bought a house. Big deal! The house was a dump, according to the tail, and other than a bunch of holes that had been discovered dug in the backyard, a thorough search of the premises had revealed nothing out of place or unusual. Even assuming that Hollister had found something inside the house or had dug something up, his men had not seen them carry anything out. Therefore, he knew zippo and the entire enterprise had been a colossal waste of time!

To make matters worse, his headache, which had started out as a dull throb, was threatening to graduate into a full-blown migraine. Gulping three Advil, Carter had just washed the pills down with a cup of water when his cell trilled. Looking at the caller ID, he saw it was Tellie.

Answering, he growled irritably, "I sincerely hope you have some good news for me!"

"My, my! Someone woke up on the wrong side of the bed!" Tellie chirped.

In no mood for any kind of games, Carter barked, "Do you have something for me or not?"

Undeterred by Carter's abrupt manner, Tellie laughed and said, "Yes, I do have something. In fact, I believe I have exactly what you have been looking for."

Carter's headache fled as he gripped his cell excitedly. "You've found it! You've found what Hollister has been using to get rich!"

"Bingo!" Tellie cried happily over the phone.

Tellie then explained to Carter her trip to Dusty's and how she had managed to get Steve drunk and pump information from him about the Treasure Hunt Club. Saving the best part for last, she told Carter about *The Book of Lost Treasures* and how the club had been using it to find all the antiques and other rare items that were the source of their sudden wealth. At first, Carter was skeptical just as Tellie had been. However, as Tellie pointed out, they *had* found the rare antiques, they *now* had fat bank accounts, and they had found *too many* rare items to be coincidental! As Tellie talked, Carter felt his disbelief melt away.

"The only problem is that Steve never told me where they keep this book," Tellie finished.

"Oh, don't worry about that," Carter assured Tellie. "Why?"

Leaning back, it was Carter's turn to laugh. "Because I plan on finding that book and taking it way from Hollister!"

Nick turned into the parking lot of Porter's and, finding an open parking slot, pulled in and turned off the car. Getting out, he opened Abby's car door, and they entered the restaurant. He was in the mood to celebrate and, the day after arriving back from Houston, had called Abby and asked her out to dinner. After being seated, they had each perused the menu for a few minutes before handing it back to the waiter.

"I'll have the T-Bone, *rare*," Nick said.

"Um, I'll have the six-ounce rib eye, well done, please," Abby said a moment later.

"We'll also take a bottle of your best red wine," Nick added before handing the waiter their menus. Nick watched the with satisfaction. They were at Porter's, and the only thing that could have made the moment any sweeter was if it had been Tony that had waited on them. It had been two weeks since he and Mark had taken the rare Saint-Gaudens coins to Houston to be authenticated and appraised. Now they were in the process of deciding whether to auction off the coins or to bypass the auction houses and take bids directly from private collectors. The coin dealer in Houston had made some discreet inquiries on their behalf and said offers were already pouring in.

Now, as he sat in Pleasant Mountain's fanciest restaurant with Abby to celebrate the club's latest and definitely *greatest* discovery, Nick felt at peace with his life, and that at long last, his luck had finally turned. True, he and Abby still had work to do to repair their relationship, but all in all, the future looked bright indeed!

"You look like the cat that ate the canary," Abby said, smiling at Nick.

"Pardon?" Nick said as Abby's comment pulled him from his pleasant musings.

"I said you look like the cat that ate the canary," Abby repeated. "It's what my mother always used to say to me or my brothers when she would see a certain look on our faces. It's the same kind of look I saw on your face just a moment ago."

"Oh," Nick said. "I was just thinking about how perfect things seem to be working out."

The smile on Abby's face disappeared at this comment. The waiter then appeared with their dinner salads, and Abby picked at hers, while Nick attacked his with gusto.

"Do you really believe that, Nick?" Abby said as she continued to poke at her salad. "That things are perfect, I mean?"

Puzzled, Nick looked up, chewing. Swallowing, he said, "Of course! Once we sell those coins, you, me, and everyone else in the club are going to be rich!"

Perturbed, Abby hesitated for a moment before putting her fork down and gazing directly at Nick.

"Nick, have you looked around you? Do you see what is going on?"

Abby's tone of voice and the look on her face caused Nick's good mood to flee instantly.

"What … what do you mean?" he asked cautiously.

"Did you know that Patti and Mark are having serious marital problems? Did you know that Mark moved out last night and is living with his parents until he can find his own apartment?"

"Huh?" Nick said incredulously. Mark had never said a word to him!

"Did you also know that a couple of days ago, Kenneth called Patti and asked her if she, as treasurer of the club, would advance him some money to help prop up his electronics store? It seems a store employee, instead of ordering thirty radio-controlled cars to sell for the Christmas season, ordered *three hundred*!"

"Ken … Kenneth di … did that?" Nick stuttered.

"Yes! That's what I'm talking about! Things are *not* perfect—not for Patti, not for Mark, not for Kenneth, and not … not for *us*!"

As Nick sat there, openmouthed, Abby plunged on.

"All you can see, all you seem to care about, is that … *book* and the dollar signs it brings to your eyes!"

Before Nick had a chance to reply, a persistent trilling came from the cell phone clipped at his belt. Fumbling to retrieve it, he finally managed to put it to his ear and answer it. Moments later, his face went white as a sheet.

"Are you sure?" he finally managed to say. "We'll … we'll be there as soon as we can."

Stunned, Nick turned to Abby and said, "That was Mark. Steve's in the hospital, and he's in critical condition. I'm afraid he collapsed on the stage at Dusty's, and they had to call an ambulance to rush him to the emergency room. Mark said the emergency room doctor said he was suffering from acute alcohol poisoning." "Abby," Nick said, his voice cracking, "Mark said he might die!"

Chapter 32

Nick looked down grimly at Steve's unconscious form lying in the hospital bed. Tubes ran from his throat and nostrils, and the rhythmic hum of a ventilator pumping air into and out of his lungs echoed softly in the quiet confines of the room. Steve's arms were festooned with tubes leading from his veins to an IV bag. The other club members were all there, huddled miserably in the tomb-like silence of the small hospital room. Patti's eyes were red from crying, and she sniffled constantly. Mark and Kenneth stood in silent anguish, while Abby looked as if she too might start crying at any minute.

A nurse walked in and looked at the heart and blood pressure monitor mounted beside Steve's bed. Picking up a chart hanging from the end of the bed, she wrote something on it.

As the nurse turned to leave, Nick asked her anxiously, "Is he going to make it? Is he going to be all right?"

The nurse stopped and looked sympathetically at Nick and the others.

"It's too soon to know anything definite. However, I can tell you the first twenty-four hours are the most critical. We'll know more tomorrow."

Seeing the exhausted, anxious faces peering back at her, the nurse added, "Look, there is nothing you can do tonight for your friend. I suggest you go home, get some sleep, and come back tomorrow." With that, the nurse made one last notation on the chart and left the room.

The room was again silent as the friends contemplated what the nurse had said. Kenneth was the first to leave, as he turned and slowly made his way to the door. Patti followed shortly afterward. Abby hurried after Patti, and the two women clung to each other as if for mutual support, leaving only Nick and Mark in the room.

"I had to call Steve's parents and tell them what had happened to him," Mark said quietly, a haunted expression on his face. "He has no family left around here, and someone had to call and tell them. They're driving up from San Antonio, but it will take them five hours to get here."

Turning, Mark faced Nick and said, "It was the hardest thing I have ever had to do in my life. Steve's mother … she started crying, and I … I …" Mark's voice started to tremble, and he couldn't go on. Finally, after a few moments, he was able to regain his composure.

"Anyway, I'll stay here and wait for them," Mark managed to say. "Somebody needs to be here when they arrive, and there's no way I'll get any sleep tonight anyway."

"Are you sure?" Nick asked.

"Yeah," Mark said, smiling sadly. "Go home like the nurse said and get some rest."

Nick nodded and turned to leave. When he got to the door, he hesitated with his fingers on the door handle. After a moment, he abruptly pivoted and rejoined Mark.

Together they waited throughout the long night.

Nick awoke to the sound of a phone ringing persistently. He was disoriented as he looked about blearily before realizing he was on the couch at the club's office annex. The events of the night before started to penetrate the fog of sleep in his mind, and he recalled that Steve's parents had finally arrived at the hospital around two in the morning. After an excruciating few minutes, when Mark had to explain what had happened to Steve all over again, Nick and Mark had left with the sounds of Steve's mother crying anew, following them out the room. Rather than drive all the way to the other side of town where his condo was located, Nick had instead gone to the office annex.

Miserably, Nick sat up and made his way to the small bathroom adjacent to his office. Turning the cold water on, he scrubbed his face with the water until he felt somewhat revived. Drying his face with a paper towel, Nick looked at himself in the mirror above the sink. His hair was disheveled, and his eyes were red and bloodshot. As he was considering his haggard appearance, the phone began to ring again. Looking at his watch, Nick saw that it was almost 9:30 in the morning. *Where the devil is Tellie?* he thought irritably. She got to work at 9:00 and should have already answered the phone!

Opening the door to his office that led to the anteroom where Tellie's desk sat, Nick was greeted by an empty room. Hurriedly, he walked over to her desk to pick up the annoying phone.

"Yes!" he snapped.

"Mr. Hollister?" a nervous voice asked over the phone. "This is Brad Atwater from the bank. I'm sorry to bother you, but a situation has come up."

"What kind of situation?" Nick asked impatiently.

"Well … oh dear, this is all so disturbing!"

"Mr. Atwater, will you *please* tell me why you called me!" Nick said, exasperated, rubbing his eyes.

"Yes, yes, of course! I'm … I'm afraid a *lien* has been placed on the Treasure Hunt Club's account."

Any residual sleep that Nick might still have been feeling fled instantly.

"What?" he shouted. "Who … who would do that?"

"It's more like *whom,* Mr. Hollister," Atwater's voice stated. "A company called Chavez Realty and Associates claims they were defrauded by you and your business associates of valuable property. Their lawyer was in contact with our in-house counsel and stated that he had received an injunction from a judge to freeze all accounts and assets of the Treasure Hunt Club. No sooner had this conversation concluded than an official with the U.S. Department of Treasury appeared here at the bank and presented our bank president with a *federal* injunction to freeze the club's assets!"

Stunned, Nick's sleep-deprived mind struggled to process what the bank official had just told him. What did he mean about a lien? A federal injunction? What was going on?

Clueless, Nick knew he was over his head and said, "I'm going to contact our lawyer. Thank you, Mr. Atwater," and hung up the phone. Pulling his wallet from his back pocket, Nick was in the process of looking for the business card with Patti's law firm's phone number when two men wearing black business suits and sunglasses walked into the office.

Looking up, Nick asked, puzzled, "Can I help you?"

The two men conferred quietly for a moment or two before one of them asked, "Are you Nick Hollister, president of the Treasure Hunt Club?"

Baffled, Nick said, "Yeah, yeah that's me."

"We're agents with the U.S. Department of Treasury, Mr. Hollister. We would like to ask you a few questions about some property that was stolen from the U.S. Mint many years ago." With that, both agents took out their credentials and showed them to Nick. Nick gulped when he saw the words *Secret Service* stamped above each man's badge.

Nick's mouth moved but, try as he might, nothing seemed to come out. He was spared further embarrassment when the office phone began to ring yet again. Grateful for the diversion, Nick snatched the phone from its cradle.

"Hello?"

"They accused my father of being a thief," a voice said, thick with grief. "They said my father stole coins from the Mint when he worked there."

"What … what?" Nick stammered.

"They said they searched my father's house that I sold to you and found a secret cache of coins that were stolen from the Mint." As muffled sobs came over the phone, Nick realized that it was Claire Branson. But before he could say anything, another voice suddenly replaced Claire's.

"We're gonna sue you and everyone else associated with your little club! Those coins are the rightful property of my aunt!" Curtis's angry voice shouted over the receiver. With that, the line went dead as he abruptly hung up.

The rapid sequence of events, combined with only the few hours of sleep Nick had been able to grab, was threatening to overwhelm his already whirling mind. Realizing he was still holding the phone, Nick hung it up. Glancing over, he saw the two Secret Service agents looking expectantly at him. His shaking hand finally managed to pull the business card he was looking for from his wallet.

He placed the call to the club's lawyer.

The sun was setting when Nick and Mark finally emerged from the law firm's offices. They, along with Patti, Kenneth, and Abby, had been deposed by the Treasury agents with the club's legal counsel present, and the questioning, with the exception of small breaks, had gone on continuously for hours. From this questioning and the give and take that ensued between their lawyer and the government agents, a clear picture of what had transpired emerged.

The coin dealer that had authenticated and then done the appraisal for them on the Saint-Gaudens was bonded.

Therefore, unbeknownst to Nick and Mark, he was obligated to report the recovery of the rare coins to the proper authorities, and this information had eventually traveled up the ranks to the highest bureaucracy in the Department of Treasury. There, it had kicked up a mini storm of controversy, and an immediate investigation had ensued. The first people questioned were Claire Branson and her nephew, Curtis Branson. From the information provided by Claire and Curtis, it was a simple matter to concentrate the focus of the investigation on the house that the Treasure Hunt Club had bought from Claire.

Sophisticated, state-of-the-art equipment had been brought in, and the false wall in the basement had been quickly located, which, in turn, led the investigators to the buried bomb shelter, where Claire's father had secreted his coin collection. All that was left at that point was to put the pieces together, which had led the Treasury agents to Pleasant Mountain and the Treasure Hunt Club. The rest was history.

After the secret service agents had finally left, Nick and Mark had consulted with the club's lawyer. He was optimistic about getting a favorable judgment on the lien placed on the club's accounts by the real estate firm based in Albuquerque. The ten percent contract that the real estate firm's representative had signed should hold up in court, he assured them. As far as the federal government's claim that they were in possession of stolen government property, he was less sure.

This was not an area of law he was familiar with, but he thought the federal government's case was tenuous at best, based as it was on completely circumstantial evidence. There were no witnesses still left alive from the era that the coins were struck, and if the case ever went before a jury, he doubted the jury would find for the government, since it was claiming property that even *the government* didn't know had existed!

This had raised Nick's flagging spirits until the other shoe had dropped. Even under the most optimistic of scenarios, the lawyer said, it would take years and a mountain of legal fees to settle these cases against the club. In the meantime, their accounts would remain frozen.

He had then urged them to consider settling with Chavez Realty and the Treasury Department. Nick and Mark had told the lawyer they would talk it over with the other club members and get back with him.

Too tired and discouraged to talk, Nick and Mark had simply said good-bye to each other and went their separate ways. As Nick drove through the downtown area of Pleasant Mountain, he glanced at the Christmas decorations that adorned the light poles lining the roadside. The city always went to a great deal of trouble, he knew, to decorate the entire downtown business district at Christmas, but even the gaily-colored Christmas lights and ornaments failed to lift his spirits.

Almost without knowing it, he found himself parked in the driveway of his condo, the engine of his car still running. Staring sightlessly at the closed garage door lit up by his headlights, Nick tried to dredge up a spark of will to get out of the car and enter the condo. Finally, he leaned forward, his head resting on the car's steering wheel. Dry sobs began to shake his body as he thought of Steve barely hanging on to life, of Mark and Patti's separation, and all the other awful events of the past twenty-four hours.

After a few moments, Nick managed to compose himself, but rather than turn off his car and exit it, he backed slowly out of the driveway and put the Jeep in gear. With a determined look on his face, he drove away.

He knew where he had to go.

Chapter 33

Carter looked at the thin gray book in his hands and grinned in satisfaction. He was sitting in a comfortable recliner within the screened porch of his cabin on Lake Cypress Springs. The lake, located about fifteen miles west of Pleasant Mountain, was home to some of the most exclusive real estate this side of Dallas. The lake property was ruinously expensive, but that hadn't stopped Carter from buying up the lots on either side of his cabin. Thickly covered with trees, these additional lots ensured he would have more privacy. Now, as he sat studying the mysterious book, he was taken by the notion that if the book had half the capability Tellie said it did, he would be able to buy the whole damn lake! In fact, with Christmas just a few weeks away, he vowed that one day, that would be his Christmas present to himself!

Chortling, Carter lit a cigar and inhaled deeply. Exhaling, he let out a pungent stream of smoke into the cold air and thought of the events that had brought the book into his possession. He had begun the quest to find the book by having his men first search Hollister's trailer to see if it were there. They had hit the jackpot when, less than an hour later, they had found the book. Rather than store it in a secure place, like a safe deposit box in a bank, the weak-minded fool had hidden the book within a loose section of flooring underneath the cheap carpet of his trailer.

At first, Carter had been in disbelief that even someone like Hollister could be that dumb, but upon reflection, he figured that was par for the course. Common sense apparently didn't run in Hollister's family.

An evil grin split Carter's face. His initial instructions to his men searching Hollister's trailer had been to make sure they left things as undisturbed as possible so that if they didn't find the book there, Hollister would be none the wiser.

That had all changed when they had discovered the book. Then he had ordered his men to toss the place. He *wanted* Hollister to know someone had searched the trailer and taken his precious book! Laughing out loud, Carter could just imagine the look on Hollister's face when he discovered the book was missing. Wouldn't he love to be a fly on the wall when that happened!

"You seem to be in *much* better spirits today!" Tellie said as she slid into Carter's lap. She had come from inside the cabin, where she had fixed them both a drink.

"And I owe it all to you!" Carter said, beaming, as he took the proffered glass of bourbon from Tellie. Holding the glass out in front of him, he added, "Cheers!" and as Tellie's glass clinked with his, they both shared a final laugh.

Downing her bourbon with one gulp, Tellie delicately wiped her lips and looked down at Carter.

"You *do* owe me, Carter, and I know *exactly* how you can repay me."

"Anything!" Carter said, grinning, as he sipped at his bourbon.

Pushing herself off of Carter's lap, Tellie stood before Carter and, with hands on hips, said, "I want to be the next Mrs. Carter Cannon!"

The grin immediately left Carter's face. "But … but that would mean—"

"That you would have to divorce your wife," Tellie finished for him.

Carter's initial shock over what Tellie said quickly left him, and his lips curled into an ugly snarl.

"Are you crazy? I don't have a prenup with her! Her father is a full partner in a high-powered law firm in Dallas, and you can bet he would make *damn* sure she took me to the cleaners!"

"So what?" Tellie tossed back angrily at Carter. "With the book *I* got for you, you'll be so rich that you won't be able to spend all your money!"

Carter put his drink down with a loud *clunk* and stood up to face Tellie.

"You're not listening!" he shouted angrily. "I said I didn't have a prenuptial agreement! My wife would get *half* of everything I own! Half, damn you!"

"I don't care!" Tellie shot back, her chin thrust forward. "I'm not going to skulk about anymore. If you don't tell your wife about us, *I will*!"

Carter's reaction was instantaneous. He backhanded Tellie, sending her reeling to the floor.

"You … *bastard!*" Tellie hissed as she tasted the blood that dribbled from her mouth. "Once I'm finished talking to your wife, my next stop will be the sheriff 's department. I'm sure they will be very interested in the little breaking and entering job you ordered."

Two large men had silently entered the room upon hearing the commotion. Carter gestured to them, and they each grabbed Tellie's arms and dragged her upright. Before Tellie could say anything else, Carter drove a fist deep into her abdomen.

Gagging, Tellie would have collapsed if Carter's men hadn't held her up. Carter waited patiently as Tellie fought to breathe. When she was finally able to take short sips of air, he held her lolling head up in one hand so she could see him.

"You're not going to say a thing," he said pleasantly. "In fact, you're going to leave this town and never come back."

Bending forward so that his face was just inches from Tellie's, Carter's expression turned hard, and he whispered, "I can make you disappear anytime I want to, and you, of all people, should know that. But," he added, straightening, "just in case I haven't made myself clear or you have any doubt I won't follow through on what I said..."

Jerking his thumb toward the cabin's door, Carter said, "Take her in the back, boys, and work her over. Make sure she gets the message!"

Tellie's screams fell on merciless ears as she was dragged to the back of the cabin. Carter turned away, Tellie already out of his mind.

His attention was back on the mysterious book he held in his hands.

Nick slowly negotiated the Jeep around the ruts and potholes with practiced ease. When he cleared the last of the trees on his overgrown property and pulled up to his trailer, he was surprised to see another car already there. Blinking in surprise, he realized the car belonged to Abby. Getting out, he saw her sitting huddled in her coat on the broken cinder block step beside the trailer's door. The security light behind the trailer cast just enough light that he could see Abby smile wanly at him.

"I knew you would come here," she said, standing.

Nick began walking toward Abby, which quickly turned into a run. Reaching her, he pulled her to him, his breath coming out in ragged gasps.

Holding her tightly, Nick buried his head in Abby's fragrant hair. Gently, Abby stroked his neck. They stayed embraced for long moments before Nick finally straightened up, his face a mask of anguish.

"How can everything go … so wrong?" he whispered to her.

Abby just shook her head and said, "I don't know, Nick. But that *book* seems to be the one piece that connects all of the bad things that have happened."

At that moment, Nick happened to look up, and he noticed the door to his trailer was slightly ajar.

"Did you go into my trailer?" he asked Abby.

"No, why?"

"Because the door's open," Nick said, alarmed, taking the few steps it took to reach the door. In the dim illumination provided by the security light, Nick saw the door had been forced open, and the metal around the lock was bent outward. Quickly, he entered the trailer and turned on the light.

It was a scene of utter chaos, with drawers pulled out and their contents emptied. All of the cabinets had been opened, and everything within them was thrown onto the floor. The feather pillows on Nick's small bed loft had been cut open. The feathers were dumped out to join the pile of flotsam on the trailer floor. "What … what happened?" Abby asked over Nick's shoulder.

A sudden awful thought struck Nick, and ignoring Abby, he quickly got down on his hands and knees. Frantically, he pushed aside the debris on the floor and pulled up a section of the carpet, exposing a loose section of the floor. Levering up the piece of flooring, he immediately saw the space was empty.

"*No!*" he howled.

"Nick! What is it?" Abby cried.

"*The Book of Lost Treasures* is gone! It's been stolen!" Nick yelped.

"Are … are you sure?" Abby asked.

"Of course, I'm sure!" Nick said, throwing the piece of flooring down angrily. "This is where I hid it!"

As Abby was opening her mouth to ask another question, Nick's cell trilled.

Ripping the cell angrily from his belt clip, Nick clicked it on.

"Yes!" he bellowed.

"Well, I take it from your tone of voice you've discovered that your trailer has had some visitors. You wouldn't have anything missing, now would you?" a smug voice asked.

It took Nick a moment or two to recognize the voice. When he finally did, it took all his self-control not to throw his cell phone to the floor and grind it under his heel.

"Carter!" he spat. "What have you done with my book?"

"You know, you really should do a more thorough background check on your employees, JV. You might have discovered that the secretary you hired actually works for me … oh, and I think what you mean is *my* book!" Carter added, laughing. "I'm sure you've heard that possession is nine-tenths of the law and all that."

Tellie worked for Carter? All of a sudden, Tellie's eagerness to please, her hard work, the seemingly innocent questions she was always asking—it all fell into place with a deafening crash, and Nick knew with an awful certainty they had been had.

Gripping his cell so hard his knuckles turned white, Nick snarled, "It's my book, and you know it! You can't just steal it and say it's yours!"

Enjoying himself immensely, Carter replied, "I can assure you, JV, that I and my legion of lawyers can do just that! You've got no way to prove the book is yours. For every witness you produce that says the book is yours, I can produce four more!"

"You … you can't use the book!" Nick said desperately. "The rules say it can have only one owner!"

"Ah, yes. The rules," Carter said with the first subtle hint of annoyance in his voice. "Unfortunately, you may be right. Every time I erase your name in the book and replace it with my own, my name fades, and yours appears in its place."

"See! I told you!" Nick cried triumphantly.

Unperturbed, Carter continued. "All that means, JV, is that we will have to come to a suitable business arrangement. I think that an eighty-twenty split would be fair, with me, of course, getting the eighty percent. Oh, and naturally, I will be the one deciding what lost treasure the book seeks next."

It was too much. Nick felt white-hot anger and frustration course through him and boil over.

"Go to hell!" he screamed. Running to the trailer door, he pushed roughly past Abby and hurled the cell phone as far as he could throw it.

Abby, who had been following the conversation closely, grabbed Nick by the arm and attempted to calm him.

"Nick! Please! Get a hold of yourself!" she pleaded with him.

"That bastard! That slimy bastard!" Nick snarled. "He'll pay!

I'll make him pay!"

"Nick!" Abby shouted one more time as she pulled Nick around to face her. "There are things more important than that book! Let Carter have it!"

Nick looked at Abby in angry disbelief.

"Let him have it? Just like that. Let him have it?"

"Yes!" Abby said with her mouth set firmly. "Let him get whatever he deserves from that book."

Nick laughed harshly. Pulling away from Abby, he said, "That's easy for you to say! You don't know what it's like to have *nothing,* to never have any money, to have to ask friends for loans just to keep the electricity from being turned off!"

Turning on Abby, he snapped, "And you certainly don't know what its like to be bullied and humiliated by a piece of trash like Carter! I'm done with that, Abby. I'm through! I'm tired of being laughed at and made fun of! That book you so flippantly want me to forget about was my ticket to a better life! And I don't care what you say! If I have to move heaven and earth, I'm going to get it back!"

Abby stood still as Nick's angry words washed over her. Tears—slowly at first, then faster and faster—began to streak down her face. Finally, she quietly turned and slowly began walking toward her car. Opening the car door, she stopped and looked back at Nick's glowering form.

"You don't get it, do you Nick?" she said, her voice trembling. "I never cared about the book or any of the money it could bring. All I ever cared about was you." Starting the car, Abby got in and drove off. Nick followed Abby's headlights as they appeared and disappeared in between the trees and bushes.

Eventually, her headlights winked out completely, leaving him alone in the darkness.

Chapter 34

Nick stared at the slanting light of the morning sun as it streamed through the open doors of his workshop. Eyes red and bloodshot from lack of sleep, he had sat on the hard, floor, zombie-like, through the night, staring into the dark and brooding on all that he had lost. Cold and stiff, his mouth was dry and gritty, but still, he couldn't stir himself to move to even get something as simple as a drink of water.

Replaying the events of the previous night over and over again in his mind, he had seen the finality in Abby's eyes and knew he had hurt her irrevocably. When she had gotten into her car and left, he knew with a dreadful certainty she would not be coming back. The book had supplanted their relation- ship, and Abby had realized that it had become more important to Nick than her—something that Nick had steadfastly denied to himself, and something that he had allowed his anger and selfish desires to mask until he had seen the headlights of her car disappearing. He should have run to his own car then and there, chased her down, and begged her to forgive him. Instead, he had let her simply drive away.

Now it was too late.

Now she was gone.

A single tear slid down Nick's cheek. He had never felt so empty, so hollow. Abby's absence left a hole in his heart so large that no amount of money and material possessions *The Book of Lost Treasures* could produce would ever be able to fill.

It occurred then to Nick that his life had a bitter consistency to it. He had managed to bungle things up once again—this time with Abby, the one and only person that had ever loved him unconditionally, and the only person that he now knew he had ever really loved. By using *The Book of Lost Treasures,* he had found the wealth and security he so desperately wanted, but in so doing, he had lost something of far, far greater value. There was a twisted irony to it that caused him to laugh out loud, a sound that appeared to his ears as a dry, cackling chortle that echoed throughout the silent workshop. He began to laugh louder and louder until his laughter acquired a hysterical edge to it and tears streamed down his face. Still engaged in this mirthless laughter, he did not hear the car pull up to the workshop or the door open and close as someone exited the car.

A shadow fell across Nick as he gasped for breath. Dully, he looked up, finally realizing someone was standing there. Rubbing his gritty eyes with knuckled fists, he squinted upward, his eyes narrowing in recognition.

"You!"

Standing before him was Tellie Brewster. Struggling to his feet, Nick speared Tellie with an angry gaze.

"What are you here for? To gloat?" he snarled.

Nick had never hit a woman before in his life, but such was his rage that he took a step toward Tellie before he could stop himself. Fearfully, she edged away from him.

"Nick, please!" Tellie blurted in a trembling voice.

The pleading tone of her voice caused Nick to pause. With arms held stiffly at his side, his fists clenching and unclenching, he noticed Tellie's appearance for the first time.

She was wearing a short, tight pink skirt that displayed her long shapely legs. Black high-heeled shoes covered her feet, while a buttoned black blouse was tucked into the skirt, and she wore an abbreviated pink blazer over the blouse. But it was her face that drew Nick's attention. The dark sunglasses she wore could not conceal the black bruises beneath both her eyes and on one cheek. Normally full and sensuous, Tellie's upper lip was split, while her lower lip was puffed outward to twice its normal size.

"What the hell happened to you?" Nick demanded.

"It seems I had a disagreement with Carter and some of his goons," she stated simply. Under the circumstances, Nick found it hard to generate much sympathy for her.

"What do you want?" he barked.

"I … I wanted to give you this." Digging into her purse, Tellie took out a small oblong object and handed it to Nick.

Hesitantly, Nick took the proffered object from Tellie. He saw, to his surprise, that it was a jump drive.

"What's this for?" he asked suspiciously.

"It contains the code to open the safe in Carter's office. That's where he is keeping your book. There is also a schematic of the security system and the codes to disarm it. Finally, it contains the password to his personal computer. Carter has certain financial information he keeps on it, and … well, let's just say that I think you will find it *interesting*. It's encrypted, and I couldn't get that information, but if Kenneth is as good as everybody says he is, he should be able to decipher it."

"I see," Nick stated as he studied the jump drive. Abruptly, he looked up and held Tellie in a steely gaze.

"Why are you doing this?"

For the first time, Tellie smiled, a painful act considering the damaged condition of her lips.

"Oh, for the usual reasons, I suppose. Wrath from a woman scorned and all that. But … but there actually is another more important reason why."

Raising an eyebrow, Nick looked questioningly at her.

"You … you and all the other club members are good … and decent people, Nick. And that's saying something in a world filled with S.O.B.'s like Carter Cannon. You didn't deserve the treachery that I brought upon you. It's just that … that I loved Carter, and I thought … I thought he loved me too."

Tears had sprung to Tellie's eyes as she rummaged around in her purse until she produced a Kleenex. As she lifted the sunglasses up to dab her eyes, Nick got a brief look at them before she lowered her sunglasses again. One eye was swollen almost shut, while the flesh around the other eye was bruised to an ugly purple so dark that it almost appeared black. His anger toward Tellie drained from him as he realized what a savage beating she had taken from Carter.

"I realize now that Carter used me, that he never really loved me, and that he never *intended* to love me. So … so foolish and stupid of me, and I should have known better. But … I was blind." Tellie's voice cracked bitterly as she said this.

Composing herself, Tellie held herself up straight and forced the smile back on her face as she peered at Nick.

"I discovered last night, when I was hurting and crying and feeling sorry for myself, that there was only one thing left I could do."

Tellie moved closer to Nick and, grasping his hand, gently closed it over the jump drive.

"All that's left is to do the right thing … and this is definitely the right thing to do," she whispered in his ear. "Take this, and get your book back, Nick. Show Carter that he can't just run over anyone he pleases. And believe me when I say how sorry I am for my part in this."

Kissing Nick softly on his cheek, Tellie turned, smoothed her skirt, and walked purposefully out of the workshop. Moments later, he heard her car starting and the fading sounds as it was driven away.

Stunned at the rapid turn of events, Nick opened the palm of his hand and stared at the memory stick. Tellie's last words flashed through his mind: *"All that's left to do is the right thing."* His head jerked upright at the simple realization of what she had said.

The right thing!

Suddenly, it was all clear to him!

Running out of the workshop and to his trailer, he threw open the door and retrieved his old Walmart cell phone from off of the small kitchen table. Flipping it open, he began to make calls.

He knew what he had to do!

Chapter 35

"I call this meeting to order!" Nick said as he rapped his knuckles on top of the table he had pushed to the middle of his workshop.

It had taken some doing, and he had had to beg, cajole, and threaten to get the club members to agree to attend a meeting.

Now, two days later, he looked around and saw that all the Treasure Hunt Club members were present—all except one.

Conspicuous by her absence was Abby, an empty chair mute evidence of her truancy. Swallowing to rid himself of the hard lump that had risen in his throat, he studied his friends.

Steve, to everyone's relief, had regained consciousness in the hospital and, after another twenty-four hours of observation, had been released to go home. He had insisted on attending the meeting and, unable or unwilling to drive himself, had been forced to ride with Kenneth.

His face was abnormally pale and covered in a thin film of sweat. Normally dressed in his signature sleeveless T-shirt and jeans, Steve was bundled in a thick sweater and jacket as if he were chilled. His hands, finally free of a beer bottle or can, shook with tremors as they rested atop the table. All were classic symptoms of an alcoholic going through withdrawal, and sadly, Nick knew Steve had a rough road of recovery ahead.

Turning his attention to Kenneth, Nick saw his friend's hands twisting nervously in his lap, a worried expression on his face. Eyes darting like a trapped animal, Kenneth's stress over the management of his store and his personal financial troubles was clearly evident on his face.

His pen guard, minus its usual compliment of mechanical pencils, lay askew in his shirt pocket, and the checkered shirt itself had places where Kenneth, in either haste or distraction, had missed a button or two. However, the most obvious sign that everything was not right with Kenneth was that he was missing his utility belt, which carried his iPhone and computer tools. For Kenneth to be without his beloved electronic gadgets was, Nick knew, the equivalent of being naked.

Finally, Nick turned his scrutiny to Mark and Patti. Both had arrived in separate cars, and both sat with Kenneth and Steve between them. From their stiff postures and the deliberate way in which they ignored each other, he could tell that nothing had been settled between them. It was a heartbreaking sight, and Nick quickly turned away before he became undone by it.

Taking a deep breath, Nick began. Placing the jump drive before him on the table, he said, "You all know that Carter stole *The Book of Lost Treasures.* Well, Tellie paid me a visit shortly after Carter took the book and gave me this."

This caused an immediate stir among the club members, who looked curiously from the jump drive back to Nick.

Explaining what was on the jump drive and why Tellie had given it to him, Nick said, "I propose we use this information and get *The Book of Lost Treasures* back. And then," Nick said, steeling himself as he purposely leaned over and placed his hands flat on the table, "I further propose that we settle the lawsuits against the club, divide all the remaining shares evenly, dissolve the Treasure Hunt Club, and give *The Book of Lost Treasures* back to Hank Harper!"

An explosion of dissent erupted from Nick's friends.

"But why?" Kenneth protested, "Why dissolve the club and give the book back?" This sentiment was quickly echoed by the others, and Nick waited until the verbal tumult had calmed down before answering. Finally, taking a deep breath to fortify himself, he explained.

"I want each of you to look at one another. Then consider what's happened to you, to me, to *us*! Look at what we've become! The book has transformed us into something that we're not, something we were never meant to be!"

Pointing at Steve, Nick said, "As long as I've known you, you were the most carefree person I've ever known. You enjoyed working on cars, made a good living at it, jammed on weekends with your band, and liked to cruise in your GTO … oh, and you liked to drink beer! But now, it's like you're this big rock star and club owner with responsibilities and an image to keep up, and you traded your GTO for a Porsche and your garage band for a gig at the bar you own. What's more, you went from sipping beer to guzzling whiskey, and look where that has gotten you!" Steve couldn't meet Nick's gaze and looked away.

Next, Nick turned his attention to Kenneth. "And you, look what's happened to you, Kenneth! Happy as can be working at Radio Shack and fixing computers, doing *exactly* what you wanted to do! Yet, you had to change your image, had to change the way you looked and dressed, and ended up looking like the small-town equivalent of a street corner pimp! You bought the Radio Shack store you worked at without a clue as to how to run it, and now you worry all the time about money!"

Finally, Nick glanced at Mark and Patti. With eyes misting with tears and his throat tight with emotion, he whispered, "And my two best friends in the whole world, the happiest, most in love couple I've ever known, here you are now, sitting apart and *living* apart, not speaking to one another. I always envied you, always wanted someone to love me like you love each other. Now all you do is argue."

Patti and Mark looked guiltily at each other, their own eyes beginning to become moist with tears.

Nick, the tears now leaking freely from his own eyes, spread his arms wide and said huskily, "To each and every one of you, I want to say I'm sorry. It's my fault that things came to be like this. *I* was the one who found *The Book of Lost Treasures*, and *I* was the one who talked each of you into buying into it! If it hadn't been for me, none of this would ever have happened."

Swiping angrily at his eyes with the back of his hand, Nick looked pointedly at the empty chair Abby should have been sitting in.

"I found out the hard way that some things are priceless, that some things you can place no monetary value on. All of you, *each* of you, are my friends, and how many people can say they have four good friends? I cherish that more … more than anything, and more than any stupid book!"

"So before any more lives are ruined, before any more damage is done, let's get *The Book of Lost Treasures* back and take it out of circulation. Because … despite everything that's gone down, that's … that's the *right* thing to do!"

In the silence that followed, each of the club members began considering what Nick had said. The quiet was so complete that only the sounds of chairs creaking and shoes scuffling on the floor could be heard.

Finally, Mark slowly turned and looked at Patti. Their eyes locked, and a smile slowly grew on Mark's face.

Without taking his eyes from Patti, Mark raised his hand.

"The chair recognizes Mark!"

"I move we get the book back, return it to Harper's Antiques, and dissolve the Treasure Hunt Club!"

There was a scraping sound as Patti pushed her chair back across the concrete floor, stood up, and walked over to Mark. Standing beside her husband, she put her arm across his broad shoulders and hugged him.

"I second!" she said resolutely.

The motion passed unanimously.

Mark and Patti were the last to leave and stood arm in arm by the sliding doors of Nick's workshop, chatting with him. Kenneth and Steve had left after the details of the plan to recover *The Book of Lost Treasures* had been hammered out. Nick had waited until then to ask Patti about Abby. She had sorrowfully told him that Abby had come home, packed her things, and left. She had cried the entire time, and she had refused to talk to Patti or tell her where she was going. Nick told Patti he had tried calling her a dozen times on her cell, leaving message after message begging her to call him. Although she had tried to be optimistic, Patti's expression and body language revealed to Nick what she really believed.

That it was over between Nick and Abby.

Therefore, it was with a mixture of happiness and sadness that Nick stood in the cold night air and waved good-bye to Mark and Patti. He was happy that his dear friends were well on their way to repairing their relationship, but this was tempered with the awful realization that Abby was no longer part of his life.

Once their headlights had disappeared from sight, he trudged slowly back to the open doors of the workshop. With his breath billowing outward in white clouds in the cold night air, he stood for a moment before the doors and looked at the quiet interior of the woodworking shop, carefully pondering everything that had happened. He prayed that they could successfully pull off the daunting task of recovering the book from Carter Cannon, get it back to Hank Harper, and then go about the business of getting on with the rest of their lives.

Shaking his head, he switched the lights off, pushed the doors together, and locked them. Turning, Nick headed not toward his comfortable condo in town but to his Airstream trailer.

The final meeting of the Treasure Hunt Club had come to an end.

Chapter 36

Nick, Mark, Patti, and Kenneth squatted in the darkness behind a tall hedge of holly. The holly was planted beside the Cannon car dealership and ran along the property line for some one hundred feet or so. Planted by the unfortunate owner of the house next to the dealership some years earlier to provide some semblance of privacy from the bustle and light of the car dealership, the owner must have finally given up, as the house now lay vacant, a "For Sale" sign leaning at an angle from where it had been hammered into the front yard.

Taking a small penlight from his pocket, Nick shielded its beam with his hand as he checked his wristwatch. It was straight up at two o'clock in the morning—time to set their plan into motion.

Looking around at the huddled forms of his friends, they, like him, were dressed all in black. Black toboggans covered their heads, and black camo paint was smeared on their faces. Despite the gravity of the situation and the illegal nature of what they were about to engage in, Nick had to stifle the impulse to laugh at their SWAT team-like appearance. Kenneth, in particular, looked like some giant, black carapace beetle. However, there was no mistaking the determination in Kenneth's eyes as he looked expectantly at Nick.

A portable, lightweight mic and receiver was secured snugly to Nick's head, and he whispered softly into the mic arranged by his mouth.

"Zeppelin, the eagle is ready to fly! Do you copy?" Zeppelin, as in *Led* Zeppelin, was the code name Steve had chosen. Steve's responsibility was to provide surveillance for the front of the car dealership and keep them apprised of the movements of the security officer that patrolled the grounds.

"Eagle, roger that! Spread your wings and fly!" came Steve's muffled response.

Ending the transmission, Nick eased upward and took one more look over the hedge. It was a cold and frosty night, and the heaviness of the air presaged rain as Nick peered intently at the brightly lit dealership. Spotting his target, he spied the back door leading into the service area and garage bays. From there, they planned to enter the dealership's adjacent suite of offices and, ultimately, Carter's private office.

Having utilized the schematic of the security system on the jump drive provided by Tellie, Nick knew the exterior security cameras panned the area directly in front of the door they had chosen once every fifteen seconds. That should give them more than enough time to get to the door, open it, and hurry inside before the camera panned back across it. All exterior doors at the Cannon car dealership were equipped with slotted electric eyes that took scan cards to unlock, much like most modern motel rooms. By having the correct code to imprint on a card—the information provided, once again, by Tellie—it was child's play for Kenneth to prepare a scan card to unlock the door.

Squatting down beside the club members, Nick whispered, "Is everybody ready?" Seeing affirmative nods all around, Nick stood and led them to a narrow gap in the hedge. Taking a pair of portable binoculars clipped to a utility belt around his waist, Nick studied a security camera mounted on one of the tall light poles that illuminated the dealership lot. He knew this was the camera that panned the area and door they were headed to. Carefully counting in his head, he waited until the camera began to pan away.

Quickly clipping the binoculars back to his belt, he hissed, "Let's go!"

Leaving the dark shadows of the hedge, they charged across the brightly lit strip of ground they had to negotiate to reach the door. Within seconds, they had reached their destination.

"Kenneth!" Nick whispered with his heart pounding like a jackhammer.

Quickly, Kenneth pulled a plastic card from his pocket and inserted it in the card slot. They were rewarded with an almost inaudible *clicking* sound as the door unlocked and a green LED light flashed from where it was mounted atop the card slot.

As they were opening the door and filing in, a cold drizzle began to fall. Cursing, Nick quickly shut the door. They had taken turns for the past week observing the night security guards' movements and routines. Without fail, he always began his patrol on the hour, every hour. Unhurried, the guard usually took his time casually strolling around the sprawling dealership as he inspected the cars, property, and buildings. This took him approximately a half hour to do before he returned to the safety and warmth of the guard shack to drink coffee. Like security guards everywhere, it was a predictable and boring routine, and Nick had no doubts the biggest problem faced by the guard was staying awake. However, the falling drizzle might force the guard to hurry his routine so as to get out of the wet weather faster. If so, that meant they would have less time to crack the safe in Carter's office, retrieve the book, and leave before the guard came their way on his inspection routine.

Mark interrupted Nick's thoughts as he hissed urgently in his ear, "Nick, we've got trouble!"

"What?"

"The code to turn off the alarm isn't working! It's still beeping!"

The panic in Mark's voice was unmistakable as Nick hurried over to the keypad mounted on wall. A persistent beeping came from it as Patti tried repeatedly to punch in the number sequence that disarmed the alarm.

"They must have changed the code!" Nick whispered as he felt his own panic begin to rise within him. They had only seconds before the alarm went off!

"Move out of the way!" Kenneth ordered as he shouldered his way past Nick and Mark. Taking what looked to be a small flathead screwdriver from a tool pouch at his belt, he quickly popped the plastic cover off the keypad.

"Nick! Take your penlight and aim it at the keypad!" Kenneth ordered tersely.

While Nick fumbled to retrieve the penlight from his pocket and snap it on, Kenneth took two electrical leads with alligator clips at their ends, and as Nick flashed the penlight's beam on the keypad, he clipped them precisely onto the junction of two electrical circuits within the keypad. Next, he quickly attached the electrical leads to a port contained on what looked to be an ordinary handheld calculator that he pulled from his pocket. The "calculator" had a red LED screen, which now had numbers that scrolled by at such an incredible speed that they appeared to be nothing more than blurs of reddish light.

Beep, beep, beep went the keypad.

"Most of these security alarms have a thirty-second window to arm or disarm," Kenneth went on conversationally, as if they were discussing nothing more pressing than the weather, "and I'm going to estimate we lost at least ten to twelve seconds of that before I was able to intervene. Fortunately, I modified this calculator by adding a memory chip one-hundred-times more powerful than that contained in the most advanced calculators on the market. When combined with the decoding program I wrote and installed in this baby, it can do millions of calibrations and number combinations per second. It *should* be able to produce the correct code before the alarm goes off." Even as Kenneth spoke, numbers were being produced in red glowing light on the calculator's screen.

Beep, beep, beep.

Nick's stomach was churning, and he had broken out in a cold sweat as he listened to the persistent beeping.

Beep, beep, beep.

More numbers were produced on Kenneth's device.

Beep, beep, beep.

An itching feeling came from the small of Nick's back, an itch that seemed to travel farther up his back with each beep produced by the keypad.

Beep, beep, beep.

Surely the thirty seconds have passed and our time is up! Nick thought desperately. *Surely the alarm is going to go off, and we—*

Suddenly, the beeping halted as the flow of numbers stopped and flashed on the LED screen. Kenneth had then quickly punched "enter," and the keypad fell silent in mid beep.

Nick almost collapsed in relief, his breath coming in quick, ragged gasps as if he had just finished running a marathon.

"Good … good job, Kenneth!" he managed to whisper.

"Oh no problem!" Kenneth whispered back, his white teeth showing in the darkness as a grin split his black camo-smeared face. "I tried this on the security system at the store, and the most time it took to sequence the proper code was five seconds. Took a little longer here though … about six point seven seconds, I'd estimate. I'm going to have to make some adjustments, it seems."

Nick gave a low snort of laughter. Only Kenneth could be standing in the dark interior of a building they had just entered illegally and be more worried about the operating speed in nanoseconds of his code-breaking device than the act itself.

Kenneth unclipped the leads from the keypad as Patti hugged him, and Mark gripped his shoulder in grateful congratulation. Once he had stowed everything in his pouch, they immediately made their way to Carter's office, where they discovered another keypad was built directly into the door right above the doorknob.

Hesitating for only a few moments, Nick quickly began punching numbers on the keypad. This time, the combination worked, as the door lock clicked open. Wordlessly, they entered Carter's office.

Sweeping his penlight around the room, Nick studied the office's interior. An expensive, wide, wooden desk was directly in front of him, and a black, leather, high-back desk chair was centered behind it. A leather couch straddled the wall to Nick's left, while two plush leather chairs were set before Carter's desk. A bookcase filled with pictures, books, and other memorabilia ran along the wall to Nick's right.

Finally, a stainless-steel frame containing a large aerial photograph of the Cannon car dealership was mounted on the wall behind Carter's desk.

Making a beeline to the mounted photograph, Nick pulled gently on it. The frame swung silently open, revealing a safe built into the wall. The square gray metal facing of the safe had no combination dial mounted onto it and was flat and featureless, except for a chrome handle to pull open the safe door.

A computer rested on the right side of Carter's desk. It was a flat screen monitor/tower combination, and Kenneth turned it on as he sat down in the leather chair behind the desk. As soon as the computer booted up, Kenneth entered Carter's password. Fingers flying over the keyboard, he soon was studying a menu from a program that flashed onto the screen.

"Apparently, the safe can only be opened by a wireless command transmitted by Carter's computer. I've read about these 'smart' safes, but this is the first one I've ever seen," Kenneth commented thoughtfully. "There is no dial on the outside of the safe, because the locking and unlocking mechanism is built inside the safe's door and responds only to the computer's command. Also, the computer's programming causes it to choose a new, random number combination daily. The safe's 'brain' is mated to the same program, which, in turn, changes the combination to unlock the safe to the same number code selected by the computer."

"That means," Kenneth said, turning in the chair to face his friends, "the number combination Tellie gave us is useless. The combination has been changed!"

Nick shrugged and said, "So? What's the problem? Just get the new combination from the computer and have it transmitted to the safe, unlock the safe's door, and we can get what we came for. Simple!"

Kenneth rolled his eyes. He said, "You don't understand, Nick! In order to access the new numeric combination, I have to have Carter's master password for this program. It's not the same password we used to log in on Carter's computer!"

A hushed silence fell over the darkened office.

"Can … can you *get* the password?" Nick finally asked.

Kenneth gave Nick a look as if his friend had just asked him if water was wet.

"Of course, I can!" he retorted, shaking his head.

Unzipping his coat, Kenneth pulled a small laptop from an inner pocket within and placed it on the desk. Flipping it open, he booted up the laptop. His fingers were a blur of motion as they played over the keyboard. Seconds later, he gave a satisfied grunt and sat back patiently while he studied the laptop's screen.

Unable to contain his curiosity, Nick whispered, "What are you doing, Kenneth?"

Without taking his eyes off the screen, Kenneth replied, "I'm attempting to implant a 'worm' into the frequency the computer uses to communicate with the safe. If successful, the worm will travel along the frequency and embed itself in the computer's programming. From there, the worm will search for Carter's master password, and once we have that, we can access the changed code and open the safe. Normally, the antivirus software in Carter's computer would detect the worm and quarantine it. However, I've designed my worm to elude most standard anti- virus software. Unless Carter has a specially designed antivirus program on his computer, by the time my worm is successfully quarantined, it will already have given us the password."

Kenneth's explanation was interrupted as Steve's urgent voice suddenly sounded through the transmitter in Nick's ear.

"Eagle, the security guard is headed your way! He'll be there in just a few moments!"

Stunned, Nick hesitated for a few moments before reacting to the unwelcome news from Steve. Running out of the office, Nick dodged around several new car models displayed on the showroom floor before sprinting to an exterior window that faced the front of the dealership. Making sure he kept in the shadows, he peered cautiously around the window's edge. Row after row of new cars, trucks, and SUVs for sale were arranged facing the road that approached the car dealership. Suddenly, Nick stiffened! Fifty yards away, the security guard was hurriedly making his way through the drizzle straight for the office complex they were in!

The others had followed Nick's mad rush out of the office and were looking at him expectantly with equal amounts of curiosity and fear written across their faces. He was just about to open his mouth and tell them to run for it when Steve's voice once again came over the transmitter.

"Eagle! Hold a second! I'm going to try something!"

Moments later, Nick saw the security guard pause, then stop and look over his shoulder. Turning completely around, the guard began running in the opposite direction. Nick faintly heard honking coming from the direction of the frontage road that ran parallel to the dealership. Straining to see, he peered through the window and was rewarded with the sight of Steve's yellow GTO turning donuts on the road. Dark smoke rose from the squealing tires as Steve continued to honk and spin out.

Grinning, Nick turned back to the others and said, "Steve has diverted the security guard. We've got to work quickly! I don't know how long he can keep it up. How much longer, Kenneth?"

"Anytime now," Kenneth replied confidently. As if in response to Kenneth's comment, a chime sounded from the laptop in Carter's office.

Hurrying back to the office, Kenneth sat down at the laptop. A broad grin spread across his face. "Got it!" he quipped as he looked up at the others.

Fingers once again a blur as they played across the laptop's keyboard, Kenneth finally stopped, his forefinger poised above the "enter" key.

"Password acquired, and the safe should be opening … *now*!" Kenneth stated as he pressed the enter key.

An almost inaudible *click* came from safe. Nick hurried over to the safe and grasped the safe's handle. Pulling, the safe's door swung open easily on its oiled hinges. Snapping on the penlight, Nick swung the beam inside the safe. Stacks of bundled cash were interspersed with other documents that Nick pushed impatiently aside. He gave a whoop of excitement as his hand closed on a thin, gray book. Pulling it out, he flashed the penlight on the book and saw he held *The Book of Lost Treasures* in his hand!

"We got what we came for!" Nick whispered in delight to the others. "Let's go!"

"Wait a minute! I've got one more job to do!" Kenneth stated emphatically.

Puzzled, Nick looked over at Kenneth before saying urgently, "We've got to go! The security guard will be back anytime now!"

"No! You said Tellie told you Carter had some incriminating financial information that he kept on his computer. If we can get that information, we can use it against Carter in case he tries to get the book back!"

"What good will that do us if we are caught red-handed in Carter's office?" Nick demanded.

"Look, I don't know if any of you has thought this out, but I have!" Kenneth said with his chin thrust out stubbornly. "You know how Carter is! So we get the book back! So what? Carter will do everything in his power to get it back! This includes doing to us as bad or worse what he did to Tellie! I don't know about the rest of you, but I don't want to be looking over my shoulder the rest of my life. If we can get the goods on Carter, we're safe, and we're home free! He wouldn't dare touch any of us if we have evidence of illegal financial doings by him!"

Nick thought for just a moment before realizing that Kenneth was right. Carter would stop at nothing to get the book back if for no other reason than to assuage his ego over being outfoxed by people he believed beneath him—especially Nick!

"How much time will it take to retrieve the information?" he hissed tersely.

"Just a few minutes, that's all I need!"

"Okay. A few minutes are all you have! However, Mark is going to keep a lookout by the window. The second that security guard turns around and steps one foot in the direction of this building, we're leaving! Understood?"

Grinning, Kenneth gave Nick an informal salute. Then he pulled out a lanyard hanging from his neck. A flash drive hung from the lanyard, and Kenneth quickly popped it off and inserted it into a port on Carter's computer.

Humming happily to himself, he got down to the serious business of downloading Carter's secret financial information onto the flash drive.

As Mark took up a position by the window, Nick whispered into the mic, telling Steve what they were up to and asking him to continue to keep the security guard occupied as long as possible. Then he returned his attention back to Carter's office. Closing the safe's door, Nick used a handkerchief to wipe it down thoroughly to remove any incriminating fingerprints. Pushing the picture frame shut over the safe, Nick wiped it down thoroughly also. *We should have worn gloves,* he thought. He made sure every surface that might possibly contain their fingerprints was wiped clean.

Just as Nick finished wiping off the door handle, Kenneth raised both arms over his head, a look of triumph on his face.

"Done! I've downloaded every dirty little detail! It's encrypted, just like Tellie said it was, but once I get it home, I'll have the information extracted within an hour!"

Relief washed over Nick's face. Immediately, he spoke into the mic and said, "Zeppelin, we're out of here!"

Hoping that the security guard hadn't called the cops on Steve, he motioned urgently to the others that they were leaving. Waiting impatiently while Kenneth removed the flash drive from Carter's computer and popped it back on the lanyard, he tapped his foot until Kenneth turned off the computer. Snapping the laptop shut, Kenneth returned it to the inside of his coat, while Nick wiped down the keyboard on Carter's computer.

As soon as everyone had filed out of the room, Nick took one last look before shutting the door. Hurriedly, they made their way through the office complex before reaching the door that they had initially used to enter the building. Nick took the binoculars clipped to his belt and looked through an adjacent window at the camera on the light pole panning the door's exterior. When it began to pan away, he motioned the others, and they quietly opened the door before sprinting for the shadows of the holly hedge.

Nick was the last to leave, and as he firmly closed the door behind him and ran after the others, he was filled with a feeling of exultation.

They had done it!

They had recovered *The Book of Lost Treasures!*

Nick looked about the darkened basement. Taking the Coleman outdoor lantern he had bought, he turned on the gas and lit the wick. Quickly, it caught, and bright light filled the basement. Placing the lantern on an old suitcase resting on a moldering box of magazines, he got to work. He had flown back to Arlington by himself and had told none of the other club members what he was up to. He had one final important task to do before giving *The Book of Lost Treasures* back to Hank, and it was something he was unwilling to involve any other club members in. For all he knew, the Secret Service might still have Claire's old home under surveillance and arrest anyone on the spot who might so much as set one foot on the property! If so, then he was determined only he would be arrested. Besides, Nick reasoned, he had started all this, and it was his responsibility to try and fix the problem he had caused.

Twenty minutes later, Nick had cleared a path from the boxes and other assorted junk so that an old wooden file cabinet was revealed. Breathing heavily, he stared at it. The file cabinet was scratched and scarred and leaning precariously against yet another stack of boxes. Nick knew it was the middle drawer in the file cabinet that contained what he sought, so without further ado, he pulled on the rusted metal handle screwed to the drawer. The wooden drawer was warped and resisted Nick's initial pull until, grunting with effort, he was able to pull it open with a loud squeal of protest.

Looking inside, Nick quickly located a cardboard box of receipts. Praying that time and mildew hadn't erased the writing on them, he began to thumb through them. Thankfully, most of the receipts looked legible, and as soon as Nick's hand touched the first one, a bright light shone from *The Book of Lost Treasures* that he had placed beside him on one of the boxes he had moved. Smiling, he began to go through the receipts one by one.

"Package for you, Mrs. Branson!" the orderly called out to Claire as she wheeled herself to breakfast. Pausing, Claire stopped her wheelchair and looked back at the orderly.

"For me?" she asked, puzzled. Who would be sending her a package?

The orderly, a slim African-American man named Draymond, replied, "Yes, ma'am! It's addressed to a Mrs. Claire Branson, and you are our *only* Claire Branson!" Carrying it over to Claire, he handed her a legal-sized FedEx box and said, "See, there's your name. You want me to open it for you?"

Claire nodded, and Draymond ripped the slotted tab from the end of the box. Handing the box back to Claire, he walked off. Claire upended the box, and a smaller manila envelope slid from within it. Opening the envelope, Claire pulled out a series of receipts that were paper clipped together.

She immediately recognized the handwriting on the receipts as that of her father's. A typed letter was also within the envelope. Mystified, Claire pulled the letter out and unfolded it. It read:

> Claire,
>
> I am so sorry that the Treasury Department has accused your late father of stealing from the Mint. If we had simply minded our own business, none of this would ever have happened. However, given the description you had given us of your father and what a faithful and diligent worker he was at the Mint, it occurred to me that perhaps we were not giving him the benefit of the doubt due him. Therefore, I did some searching in the basement of your father's house, and I discovered these receipts. Please note the official stamp of the Treasury purser on each receipt and, more importantly, what your father was purchasing!

> You see, each year, he took some of his pay and bought coins from the Mint to add to his coin collection—the same coin collection found in the buried bomb shelter. He didn't steal them, and the receipts prove that! Also, pay close attention to the date when he bought the 1933 Saint-Gaudens gold pieces. The date on the receipt shows that your father bought the Saint-Gaudens three weeks *before* the decision was made by the federal government to go off the gold standard and melt all the Saint-Gaudens coins. That makes these gold pieces "legal to own!" So your nephew was right all along. You are the rightful owner of these coins. By showing these receipts to the proper authorities, you will not only clear your father's name but you will also be be able to claim ownership of the coins. I hope I have set things right for you. I tried my best.
>
> Sincerely,
>
> Nick Hollister, president of the Treasure Hunt Club

Claire looked up from the letter with tears of happiness in her rheumy eyes. The fond memories of her father, tarnished by the Department of Treasury's accusations, seemed to well up inside her, warming her soul. Hugging the letter and receipts happily to her breast, Claire closed her eyes and fixed the image of her father in her mind. Had Nick been around to see Claire's reaction to the letter and the receipts he had sent her, he would have known that he had succeeded.

He *had* set things right.

Chapter 37

Nick leaned against the Jeep and watched as, in the distance, several cars turned into the cavernous Home Depot distribution center parking lot and approached where he, Mark, Steve, and Kenneth waited for them. As the line of cars drew nearer, Nick could see that, like some cliché from a spy novel, they were all black Suburbans.

"Looks like Carter's bringing the cavalry!" Mark quipped in Nick's ear.

Nodding, Nick answered, "I didn't expect any less."

It had been two weeks since they had recovered *The Book of Lost Treasures* from Carter's safe.

As promised, Kenneth had decrypted the financial information retrieved from Carter's computer in less than an hour. He had printed a hard copy of the juicier parts for Nick, Mark, and Patti, and it hadn't taken long for them to see they had Carter by the proverbial short hairs. All that remained was to close the deal and make sure that none of them were ever bothered by Carter or his goons again; hence, the purpose of their meeting today.

When Nick had first called Carter to propose the meeting, he had immediately flown into a rage, and through much cursing and threats, he had demanded the book back. Hanging up on Carter in the middle of a particularly colorful harangue, Nick waited for five minutes before calling him back. Enduring yet more profanity and threats, Nick let Carter vent for a few minutes before hanging up again. This time, he took ten minutes before calling back. When Carter answered the phone, he was much more subdued, fearful that Nick would hang up again. It was then that Nick told Carter where they would meet and at what time. Carter had flown into another rage at the effrontery of Nick Hollister telling *him* what he was going to do! That was when Nick hung up on Carter for the final time.

He didn't call Carter back.

Nick had chosen their proposed meeting and rendezvous site carefully. It was on the northwest side of the huge warehouse complex encompassed by the distribution center.

Acres of open asphalt parking space were adjacent to the warehouse, while dozens of tractor-trailers abutted the loading bays of the warehouse, waiting for loading or unloading. It would be impossible to set up an ambush in such a large, open area, which is exactly why Nick had chosen this spot.

Nick's silver Jeep, Mark's blue Expedition, and Steve's yellow GTO were arranged in a semicircle in the parking lot. They stood in front of their cars and waited for Carter and his entourage to reach them. Kenneth, who had ridden with Steve, stood with them as they steeled themselves for what they all knew would be a *very* unpleasant meeting. Patti, despite her protestations, had been left at home at Mark's insistence. Besides, as he explained to her, someone would need to call the authorities if things went badly.

A cold February breeze blew across the gargantuan parking lot as the three black Suburbans screeched to a stop twenty yards in front of where the four friends stood. Immediately, men poured out of the SUVs, while Carter, in the lead Suburban, slowly got out and stood, a smirk on his face as he looked at Nick and the others. Nick counted a dozen men as they arranged themselves around Carter. The jackets the men wore did little to conceal the bulges inside their coats, and Nick swallowed hard as he realized they all were packing handguns.

For his part, Carter was dressed as if he were about to attend the grand opening of an art museum. Stylishly attired in a dark blue Armani suit and silk tie, his black leather shoes had been polished to a high sheen, and an expensive Burberry coat was draped across his shoulders. Snapping his fingers at one of his men, the man hurriedly produced a pair of sunglasses, which he handed to Carter. Putting on the sunglasses, Carter turned and began walking toward Nick and the others, his men trailing close behind.

Stopping ten paces from Nick and his friends, Carter surveyed them with a contemptuous stare while his men fanned out and effectively cut off any means of escape. Taking off his sunglasses, he let his gaze settle on Nick, his expression hardening.

"You stole something from me, JV. I want it back, and I want it back now! Since I am feeling particularly generous today, I'm willing to overlook the theft, provided you give me the book back immediately *and* cooperate with me in using the book to find the things *I* want to search for!"

Looking at the stone-faced men arrayed on either side of him, Carter effected a cruel smile before turning back and saying, "Otherwise, it's going to be a *particularly* bad day for each and every one of you."

Despite the fact that Nick expected threats and bluster from Carter, a thick knot of cold fear formed in his stomach.

Knowing he had to appear calm and unperturbed, Nick fought to choke back and control this fear.

Taking a deep breath and hoping his voice didn't crack as he addressed Carter, he stood up straight from where he had been leaning against the Jeep and faced his nemesis.

"We're not giving you the book back, Carter. Considering you stole it from *us*, I think you know what you can do with your request. In fact, what you and your 'sales associates' can do is get back into your cars, drive away, and never, ever, bother any of us again!"

Carter started laughing a short, barking, harsh laughter that left him momentarily breathless. Recovering, he wiped his eyes with a monogrammed, folded handkerchief. Placing it back into his suit pocket, he strolled forward until he was just a few feet from Nick.

"Now why should I do that?" he asked in a low, dangerous voice.

"Because you don't want to go to jail!" Nick managed to reply.

Laughing again, Carter sneered at Nick and said, "For what? The book? You can't prove a thing, and you know it! You'll have to do better than that, JV—*much* better than that!"

His expression turning hard, Carter took one more step toward Nick until his face was only inches away.

"Now, I'm only going to ask you one more—"

"I'm not talking about the book," Nick said, interrupting Carter.

For the first time, Carter faltered, as a look of uncertainty played across his face.

"What … what are you talking about?" he demanded.

Motioning to Mark, Nick held out his hand as Mark unsnapped his briefcase and took out a manila folder. Closing the briefcase, he handed the folder to Nick, who, in turn, handed it to Carter. Folding his arms across his chest, Nick steeled himself for the coming storm.

Mystified, Carter stepped back and opened the folder. Inside were a series of documents stapled together. Taking them out of the folder, he began to study the first page.

Nick watched Carter, as by degrees, his face began to turn pink, then red, and then purple with rage. Rifling through each of the pages quickly, his breath coming out in angry, explosive gasps, he finally looked up at Nick with barely controlled fury.

Crumpling the documents in one large fist, he asked through clenched teeth, "How … *where* did you get this?"

For the first time, Nick smiled. "It doesn't matter where we got the information, Carter. All that matters is that we have it."

"You're a dead man, Hollister! You and all your goofy friends as of this moment are dead! Do you—"

"Shut up, Cannon!" Nick barked. Blinking in surprise at Nick's sudden command and at a momentary loss of words, Carter closed his mouth.

"Now, just in case you still don't fully appreciate what's in that folder, let me spell it out for you. It shows that you moved cars and inventory from your dealerships so that they wouldn't be counted as taxable assets. Like a shell game, you moved new and used cars from one dealership to another and then cooked the books to cover those moves. Once the coast was clear, you moved the cars again, selling cars that, according to the inventory, *didn't even exist on the lot.*

"But here's the best part! Because your family happened to own dealerships in Arkansas and Louisiana, you moved your cars, your inventory, *across state lines.* That's what they call 'interstate commerce,' which, of course, makes it a federal offense. The FBI would be *very* interested in the Cannon family of car dealer- ships, don't you think?"

Silence descended on the distribution center parking lot as Carter digested what Nick had revealed to him. Finally, he looked up at Nick, his eyes bright with hatred.

"What's to stop me from breaking every bone in your body, Hollister, until I have every paper, every document, you and your pathetic collection of friends have?" he hissed.

"I'll let my good friend, Kenneth, answer that," Nick said, unperturbed.

Pulling his iPhone from the clip on his belt, Kenneth activated the screen and scrolled down, and then, facing his friends, said, "Gentlemen?"

"Mine's an Android!" Mark said, pulling his cell phone from his pocket and holding it high.

"Mine's an Android, too!" Steve said, holding his cell phone aloft.

"I like to call mine a *thingee,*" Kenneth said, grinning, as he held the iPhone up before him. "But the important thing, regard- less of their make and model, is that all our cell phones have Internet and e-mail capability. So I forwarded an attachment that contained all the illegal financial information downloaded from your computer to everyone here. At the press of a key, this e-mail attachment, with all the incriminating evidence you have in that folder, can be sent by our cell phones to every regional FBI office in the southeast."

"Isn't the information age wonderful?" Nick quipped with a broad smile on his face.

The rage so evident on Carter's face slowly bled away to be replaced with a look of resignation.

"What do you want?" he finally asked dully.

"I've already told you," Nick said. "We just want to be left alone, and as long as you do that, this financial information will never see the light of day."

"How do I know you won't turn this in to the FBI the moment you leave here?" Carter demanded.

"Well, Carter, I guess you're just going to have to trust me on that," Nick stated with a thin smile on his lips.

Opening his mouth to provide a retort, Carter quickly closed it as he realized he had no choice but to believe Nick.

"Oh, and Carter? If any of us, you know, meet with some sort of *unfortunate* accident in the future, we each have a complete hard copy and disk containing all of your interesting financial transactions in safe deposit boxes in the bank, which are to be opened upon our demise. Kenneth also has loaded a program on our home computers and laptops that any one of us can activate that will trigger the release and transmission of this stuff to the appropriate authorities. He tried explaining to me how it works, but you know me. I never was much of a computer expert."

Shoulders slumped in defeat, Carter stood silently for a few moments. Finally, he made an almost imperceptible motion of his head, and his men turned and slowly started to walk back to the black Suburbans.

As Carter turned to join them, Nick stopped him.

"Carter, there's one more thing."

"What? What is it?" Carter snarled.

Poking Carter hard in the shoulder, Nick said, "I want a piece of you before you go!"

Mark, who had heaved a sigh of enormous relief at seeing Carter and his men begin to walk away, stood up quickly at Nick's sudden pronouncement, alarm written all over his face.

"Nick, what are you doing?" he cried.

Turning to face his friend, Nick held Mark in an unflinching gaze. "I've got to do this, Mark. I've got to settle this, or at least try to settle this, between Carter and me.

He's bullied and humiliated me since junior high, and it's time I finally pushed back."

"Nick, no! We've got what we wanted; there's no need to do this!"

Nick reached out and grasped Mark gently by the shoulder. "You don't understand, Mark. This isn't about the book, and it's not about you, Patti, Kenneth, or Steve. It's all about me. I've run away from things all my life every single time things got tough or uncomfortable. I look back now, and I see that it's eaten a hole in me that I'll never be able to fill—at least not until I finally stop running."

"But Nick, Carter's bigger and stronger than you! He's at least fifty pounds heavier! There's got to be a better way!" Mark said, pleading with Nick. Steve and Kenneth, who had overheard the entire conversation, walked over and joined in loud agreement with Mark.

Sighing, Nick smiled crookedly at his friends. "Don't you see? I've got to make a stand or … or I'll just keep running. For once, I've got to face my fears. Besides," he said, winking at them, "I've got a plan."

Mark met Nick's gaze with his own. Shaking his head sadly, he finally nodded before slowly backing away. After a moment's hesitation, Steve and Kenneth joined him.

Carter's expression had gone from dumbfounded amazement to one of pure joy. He quickly motioned to one of his men and handed him the Android and his suit jacket.

Loosening and taking off his tie, he began to roll up the sleeves of his dress shirt.

"I've got to hand it to you, JV. You had me over a barrel, and you could have just walked away. Instead, you've proven to me, once again, what I've always believed about you—namely that you are the biggest fool I have ever met! Losing the book is a small price to pay for kicking your ass!"

Ignoring Carter, Nick took off his own jacket and handed it to Mark. With his back turned to Carter, Nick reached into his pockets and handed his keys and wallet to Steve. His thin frame shivering in the cold breeze, he turned and faced Carter.

A semicircle of Carter's men and Nick's friends formed around the two combatants. Carter, grinning in anticipation like a child on Christmas morning, began dancing and feinting around Nick. With his arms and fists held up before him awkwardly, Nick tried to follow and anticipate Carter's moves.

"I know a good orthodontist I would be happy to recommend to you, JV," Carter said as he continued to prance and feint. Enjoying himself immensely, he continued, "Because when you wake up in the hospital sometime tomorrow, not only will you be eating soft food for a month, but you're going to need total dental reconstruction."

Before Nick could supply a retort, Carter's fist darted in like a snake, clipping Nick solidly on the chin. Staggered, Nick took a step backward away from Carter. Before he could shake the cob- webs from his head, Carter closed in again, a left jab also landing on Nick's chin. Although Carter was pulling his punches so as to prolong the fun, the second blow almost sent Nick to his knees. Groans of dismay came from Mark, Steve, and Kenneth, while Carter's men laughed and hurled insults at Nick. Dancing back, Carter waited for Nick to recover.

Nick's jaw felt as if someone had hit him with a hammer. Through the haze of pain, he again considered the plan he had conceived to take Carter down. It all hinged on Carter becoming overconfident and leaving himself open to one punch, a single punch that would effectively take him out. The problem with this strategy was threefold: first, Carter would have to be lulled into a sense of complacency that would allow that one blow to land. Second, Nick had to stay on his feet and remain a punching bag long enough for Carter to become overconfident. And third, it would be thin, skinny Nick throwing the "knockout" punch, and there was no guarantee he could land a punch with enough force to do the job.

Although Nick could see immediately that the over confidence part wasn't going to be a problem, remaining on his feet and conscious would be problematic if Carter ever stopped pulling his punches. As for the one blow that Nick so desperately needed an opening to throw, unbeknownst to the others, he had supplied himself with an advantage to help with the force of the blow. He prayed fervently that he would get the opportunity to use it before Carter lost interest and put him down for good.

Circling each other, the fight went on, with Carter providing almost all the damage to Nick. The minutes seemed to stretch into hours for Nick as he was pummeled relentlessly. Landing only a few awkward blows, Nick kept up the charade as best he could while looking for the opening he sought. Bleeding copiously from his mouth, his right eye almost swollen shut, and a goose egg-sized bruise on his left cheek, Nick was a pathetic sight. Twice, Mark tried to intervene to stop the fight, and both times, Nick had waved him emphatically off.

Carter, sensing the end was near, now wore a disappointed expression on his face. Like a cat that had tired of playing with the mouse it had caught, Carter moved in for the kill and threw a double combination of a right jab to Nick's jaw and a left jab to his stomach. Nick dropped like a rock to the hard asphalt.

Gasping for breath, he tried to get back to his feet.

"Nick, for the love of God, stay down!" Mark pleaded, tears in his eyes over the beating his friend was taking. Steve, his jaw clenched in anger, moved to interpose himself between Nick and Carter.

"Stay … stay away!" Nick gasped. "Ma … Mark! Make him stay away!"

With great reluctance, Mark held his arm up and blocked Steve's progress. Together, they watched Nick stagger to his feet.

Carter watched Nick struggle to stand up with a mixture of amusement and for the first time since he had known Nick, a grudging *respect.*

Standing before Carter, swaying on his feet and his arms hanging limply by his side, Nick tried to focus his eyes on Carter. Grabbing a handful of Nick's shirt, Carter held Nick stationary as he sized him up. As if searching for the best possible place on Nick's face to land the final punch, Carter grimly studied him.

With Carter roughly grasping Nick's shirt with one hand and the other held casually by his side, Nick realized abruptly through the fog of pain that the moment he needed had finally arrived.

Carter had left himself open.

Nick's right hand tightened into a hard fist. His knuckles turned white with the effort, and as he prepared to take his one, his only, and his best shot at Carter, memories suddenly flashed before his eyes.

Carter booby-trapping his school locker.

Carter dumping a bowl of mashed potatoes and gravy on his head in the cafeteria. Carter dunking him headfirst into a toilet in the locker room. These and so many other insults, humiliations, and embarrassments, all suffered at the hands of Carter Cannon, thundered through Nick's mind. Then suddenly, there was one final memory—it was of Abby, of their fight, and her driving away while he simply stood and watched. Anger coursed through Nick, and adrenaline surged through his veins.

With knees flexed and his weight distributed on the balls of his feet, Nick put every ounce of energy and strength into the right uppercut that rose from the fist clenched by his side. Like a freight train, his fist gathered speed as it rushed toward the vulnerable bottom part of Carter's jaw so prominently displayed.

Nick's fist crashed into Carter's jaw.

As if watching the whole thing in slow motion, Nick saw Carter's head snap back violently, his teeth giving an audible *click* as they smashed together from the force of the blow.

Releasing Nick's shirt, Carter staggered back. Standing for a moment, a look of vacant befuddlement on his face, Carter's eyes seemed to focus and lose focus. Then they rolled back in his head, and Carter collapsed onto the ground, out cold.

Nick stood gasping as he looked at Carter's prone form lying on the hard, unyielding asphalt. Although he hurt in a dozen places and could barely stand himself, all he could think about was one thing.

He had done it; he had knocked out Carter Cannon!

He had finally faced his fears.

Nick and Mark stood side by side in the now deserted warehouse lot. Carter's men had picked up his unconscious form and loaded him, without a word, into one of the Suburbans before driving off. Steve and Kenneth, once they had determined Nick wasn't seriously hurt and in need of immediate medical attention, had been practically delirious in their joy and congratulations of Nick knocking out Carter. They had left moments earlier, leaving Nick and Mark alone.

"You took a big chance! A huge chance!" Mark admonished Nick. "Carter was right when he said you just might wake up in a hospital. If you hadn't landed that lucky punch, well … who knows what would have happened?"

Grinning through swollen and split lips, Nick said, "I told you I had a plan, and besides, that punch wasn't so lucky. I had a little help!"

Eyeing Nick suspiciously, Mark asked, "What do you mean?" "I've always had big hands, and when I handed you my coat and Steve my wallet and keys, I took this out of my pocket and held it concealed in my fist." Holding his right hand out, Nick opened it.

Mark's eyes widened as he saw a roll of fifty-cent pieces tightly bound together in plastic. Nick had been holding them when he had knocked Carter out. Unlike brass knuckles that would have been impossible to conceal, the hidden roll of half dollars had provided Nick with the heft and extra solid weight to land a more devastating punch. Mark grinned as he realized that Nick had indeed planned ahead.

Laughing, the two friends made their way to their cars. This chapter of their lives was finally over.

It was time to go home.

Chapter 38

Hank was dusting off and rearranging some table lamps when he heard the pleasant tinkling of the door to his shop opening. Wiping his hands off with a rag from his back pocket, he hurried to the front of the store. It was a cold, blustery day, and he felt the blast of cold air from the open door long before he reached his destination. A tall, thin man in a beige down jacket was standing with his back to Hank by the store counter. There was something vaguely familiar about the man, even turned away as he was.

As Hank opened his mouth to greet his customer, the man turned around, and Hank immediately recognized him.

There was a sad expression on Nick's face as he reached out and shook Hank's hand.

"Hello, Hank. Things don't look much different than the last time I was here. Business been good?"

Pumping Nick's hand, Hank gave a hearty laugh. "Better than I expected, Nick. It keeps me pretty busy."

"That's … that's good, Hank. That's real good."

The way Nick said this last statement and the peculiar look on his face caused Hank to pause and study Nick intently. It was then that he noticed the pale remnants of bruises around Nick's eyes and cheeks.

"What is it? What's wrong, Nick?" Hank finally asked.

Sighing heavily, Nick lifted a satchel he was carrying. Placing it on the counter, he took a thin book with a gray binding out of it and held it before him. Hank's eyes widened as he saw it was *The Book of Lost Treasures.*

"I came to give this back to you, Hank."

Speechless, Hank stared at the book for long moments. Finally, he said, "But … but the book belongs to you. You bought it fair and square along with the painting."

"Yes, I know, but I don't want it anymore. So I am returning the book to its *rightful* owner!"

"I don't know what you mean, Nick," Hank said with his jaw thrust forward obstinately. "The book belongs to *you*!"

Tired of holding *The Book of Lost Treasures,* Nick placed it on the wooden counter next to the satchel. Turning back to face Hank, Nick squared his shoulders and gazed directly into the diminutive storeowner's blue eyes.

"I've had a lot of time to think about the book and all of the circumstances by which I acquired it. And you know what I think?" Pausing for just a moment, Hank finally asked pensively, "No, what do you think, Nick?"

"I think it was no accident that I happened to find *The Book of Lost Treasures.* I think I was somehow … I don't know … *chosen* to possess the book. Which, if true, would make *you*, Hank, some kind of … *keeper* of this book, some kind of arbiter, who decides who gets the book next."

"Nick, do you know how crazy you sound?" Hank asked with his arms spread helplessly.

"You mean as *crazy* as an old, forgotten book that reveals maps to lost treasures, Hank?"

Hank's arms dropped to his side, and he made no attempt to respond. A resigned expression appeared on his face.

"The clues were always there, I just didn't take the time to piece them all together. I was too busy trying to get rich using the book. I mean, the all *too* familiar way you described to me the legend of the book, some of the comments you made to me, and, of course, the *convenient* way you led me straight to the painting that held *The Book of Lost Treasures*!"

Other than to lick his lips nervously, Hank made no response, instead preferring to hear Nick out.

Continuing, Nick said, "But the kicker—the clincher, if you will—was the painting itself. The sailboat in the painting was named *La Princesa Sirena*, which is amazingly similar to *La Princesa de las Sirenas*, or *Princess of the Mermaids,* that was part of the legend concerning the book. Quite the coincidence, don't you think? Or, more likely, the painting told a story you already knew by heart!"

A grim smile covered Hank's face as he asked, "What is it that you want, Nick?"

"I've already told you, Hank. I want to give the book *back*!"

"Everybody around town knows that you've suddenly come into a lot of money, Nick. I can only assume, as *you* say, that the book has somehow been responsible for this. Why would you want to give it back?"

A loud *thump* came from the counter as Nick's clenched fist struck it.

"Because I don't want it anymore!" he cried, his face suffused red with rage. "Because the cost of owning the book is more than I can bear! Because, because …" Nick's voice tapered off as his anger rapidly drained away, leaving him feeling limp and empty.

"Because you were right, Hank," he finally managed to say in a low whisper. "Our most precious treasures *are* right before us, in plain sight, and I was too stupid, too greedy, and too blind to see it until it was too late."

Standing straight and with eyes blurry with unshed tears, Nick reached over to the counter, picked up *The Book of Lost Treasures,* and, once again, held it out before him.

"So I'm asking you to *please* take the book back, Hank."

Hank eyed the book sadly for a moment before reaching up and taking it from Nick.

Relieved, Nick said simply, "Thank you, Hank." Giving Hank a farewell wave, Nick zipped up his coat, picked up the satchel, and turned to leave.

Hank watched Nick as he walked toward the door. His eyes flicked onto the mysterious book he held before he looked up once again at Nick's retreating back. Nodding to himself, as if he had come to some sort of conclusion, he cried out, "Nick, wait!"

Surprised, Nick turned to see Hank running toward him as fast as his short legs could carry him.

Puffing from the effort, Hank took a moment to catch his breath as he stopped before Nick. Puzzled, Nick looked down at Hank.

Finally, looking up at Nick, Hank said, "Mind you, I'm not admitting anything concerning your outlandish theory about this … this book and its connection to me, but *if* the legend of *The Book of Lost Treasures* has any validity, I feel a duty to point out something to you that you might have missed."

Folding his arms across his chest, Nick said, "I'm listening." Grinning, Hank's blue eyes sparkled.

"It occurred to me that part of the problem with the *use* of *The Book of Lost Treasures* is that it is misinterpreted!"

"What do you mean?" Nick asked curiously, despite himself.

"I mean a *lost treasure* doesn't have to be money, jewelry, gold, or something of a tangible value! It can be something completely different, something that has value only to the *heart*!"

For a moment, Nick stood stock still, as if his feet were rooted to the floor. The wave of realization of what Hank had said roared through his mind like a tsunami. His heart leaped, and a look of hope slowly grew across his face.

Dropping the satchel, he asked, "May I borrow *The Book of Lost Treasures* one last time, Hank?"

"Of course," the diminutive shop owner said, chuckling.

Taking the proffered book, Nick considered carefully for a brief moment. Then, without hesitation, he wrote something in the book. Light flared immediately from one of the pages, and Nick studied it intently. A smile creased his face as he handed the book back to Hank.

"Thanks, Hank. I've … I've finally found what I've been searching for."

Hank studied Nick's face intently before, finally, his own smile tugged at the corners of his mouth.

"Yes. Yes, I can see that you have."

There was nothing more to be said, and the two men gripped hands one more time before Nick turned and with a stoic purpose walked out of the store.

Cold air blew in as Nick opened the door, but Hank didn't notice it.

The warm glow he felt inside more than compensated for the chilly wind.

Chapter 39

Eighteen months later

Nick sat in his car and studied the apartment on the first floor of the gated apartment complex. It was the latter part of May, and the temperature was already warm at ten o'clock in the morning as spring marched into summer. He had left Pleasant Mountain at five o'clock that morning to drive to Rowlett, a suburb east of Dal- las and just the other side of Lake Ray Hubbard. He had arrived at the apartment complex a little before seven o'clock and had been waiting and watching since. For the hundredth time, he rehearsed in his mind what he would say and how he would act as he worked up the courage to approach apartment number 154 and knock on the door. His heart hammering in his chest, a heavy sigh escaped from his lips as he gripped the door handle resolutely and opened the Jeep's door and stepped out.

It was a Saturday morning, and as such, many of those who occupied the apartment complex had taken the opportunity to sleep in. Nick's lonely walk to number 154 was therefore observed by no one except a solitary mockingbird that chirped and whistled in a nearby live oak. Reaching the apartment's door, Nick hesitated. Looking around, he saw two pots of red geraniums flanking the door along with a gaily-colored welcome mat set between them. Twice, he brought his hand up to knock, and twice, he instead let his hand fall to his side. Finally, jaw set and teeth gritted, he raised his hand and knocked firmly three times on the door.

"Just a minute. Be right there!" a familiar voice called out from behind the door.

Memories came flooding back into Nick's mind at the sound of the voice, and it was only with great difficulty that he was able to push them aside. He needed a clear mind to do what he had come here to do.

The door suddenly opened, and Abby stood facing Nick. "Yes, what do you—" The words caught in Abby's throat as through widening eyes she saw Nick standing before her. Long moments passed as Nick and Abby stood looking at each other. Abby was dressed casually in a pink American Eagle T-shirt and beige shorts. Her long hair was piled haphazardly on top of her head, held there by a hair clip, and she was barefooted. Nick swallowed hard as he drank in the sight of her.

Finally, Abby was able to clear her voice. "Nick! What . . . what are you doing here?"

"I need to talk to you, Abby. May I come in?" Nick asked softly.

Abby stood frozen for a few seconds. Finally, she moved aside to let Nick in. Shutting the door behind him, Abby, still holding the doorknob as if for support, slowly turned and looked at Nick. Finally letting go of the doorknob, she leaned against the door and folded her arms across her chest.

"I don't hear from you or see you in what, a year, year and a half, and now you want to talk?" Abby asked incredulously, her face twisted in anger. "I … I don't think this is a good idea. In fact, I would like you to leave! I should never have let you in!" Hot tears began to fill her eyes as she finished.

"I deserve all of that … and more," Nick managed to say through the lump that had risen in his throat. "But … I had a reason, Abby. If you'll just hear me out, I swear I'll never bother you again."

Wiping the angry tears from her eyes, Abby was forming a retort when she saw the expression on Nick's face. He had the desperate look about him of a drowning man trying to make one last grab at a life preserver that was just out of reach. Forcing herself to reign in her emotions, she finally man- aged to still her rapid breathing.

"Okay, Nick. Say what you came here to say … but it won't change anything between us!"

Nick nodded gratefully and took a moment to look around the apartment while he composed himself. Papers to be graded were piled haphazardly on a table in the small kitchen, evidence of Abby's student teaching at a nearby elementary. She would make a great teacher, he knew. She loved kids and had the heart for it. With great difficulty, he turned back to her.

"I … I need to show you something. But … in order to do that, I need you to come back to Pleasant Mountain with me."

Her jaw dropping in surprise, Abby managed to sputter, "What? Go back to Pleasant Mountain? With you? No! Not in a thousand years!"

With bitter sadness, Nick shook his head. "If I were you, I'd feel the same way, and I don't blame you for not trusting me, Abby. I was the one who screwed up. I was the one who let the best thing in my life slip through my fingers. But then, you've always been a better person than me. And I'm hoping that because of that, you will come back with me to Pleasant Mountain. I have to … no, I need to show you something! If you'll just let me do that, as I said earlier, you'll never be bothered by me again!"

"Don't … don't you do that!" Abby said as she pointed a trembling finger at Nick. "Don't you dare make me feel guilty so that somehow I'll go with you!" Tears were now falling freely from her eyes.

"Do you know what my life was like after we broke up?" Abby cried. "My heart was ripped in two! In my wildest, most feverish dreams, I never thought I could be hurt again as badly as Rob had hurt me when we divorced. Yet, not only was it as bad with you, it was worse! It was like reliving a nightmare all over again!"

Collapsing on a nearby couch, Abby buried her face in her hands and sobbed as Nick watched helplessly. Finally, he walked over to the couch and sat down next to her. Wanting to hold her so badly and comfort her that he had to force his arms to stay clasped in his lap, his own heart threatened to break as he listened to her unrestrained weeping.

"It was never you, Abby. It was all me. You have nothing to feel guilty about," he said in a voice cracking with emotion. "You have no obligations to me, none whatsoever. But despite that, I'm asking, begging, you to please come with me this one last time."

Nothing more was said as Abby's sobbing eventually died away. Finally, she turned her tearstained face toward Nick.

"All right, Nick. You win," she whispered. "I'll go with you. But understand, after this, I don't ever want to see you again."

Standing abruptly, Abby walked unsteadily toward her bedroom and shut the door. Fifteen minutes later, she exited, dressed in blue jeans, sandals, and a simple, white, ribbed blouse. She had brushed her hair back into a ponytail, and with eyes still rimmed red from crying, she had put on a minimum amount of makeup.

Slinging her purse over her shoulder, she said coldly, "Let's go!"

Locking the door behind her, Abby followed Nick to his car. He opened the door for her, and she slid into the passenger seat Nick got in, started the car, and began to make the journey back to Pleasant Mountain.

Once they had exited onto I-30 traveling east to Pleasant Mountain, Nick tried to talk to Abby. He told her that Steve had successfully finished his rehab, had joined a local chapter of AA, and had gotten his old job back at Dock's Auto Repair. He also told her that Kenneth had managed to talk Mr. Parnell into buying back the Radio Shack store, and now they were partners in running the business. Mr. Parnell kept up with the store's finances and the inventory, while Kenneth ran the store. Kenneth was happier than he had seen him in months, he assured her.

Finally, he told Abby that Patti was pregnant. She did not need a special procedure or fertility drug, and the pregnancy had come as a complete surprise to Patti, Mark, and even Patti's doctor. She was due sometime in December, and both Patti and Mark were practically walking on air they were so happy. This elicited a small smile on Abby's face, the only indication she had heard a word he had said.

They drove the rest of the way in silence.

Almost two hours later, Nick turned onto the road that led to his workshop and trailer. Only, instead of the rutted dirt road, a paved black ribbon of asphalt greeted Abby's eyes. As they turned onto the road and made their way past the clumps of pine trees and sweet gums, Abby suddenly sat up and gasped! There, in front of a neatly trimmed lawn where Nick's Airstream trailer used to be, was a large, two-story farmhouse! An expansive, elevated porch wrapped around the house. Ceiling fans, spaced at intervals, turned lazily above the porch. Rocking chairs were interspersed along the length of the porch, and a wooden love seat hung suspended from two chains fastened to the porch ceiling. Azaleas, begonias, and impatiens had been planted beside the base of the porch and provided a pleasant contrast of red, pink, and white flowers.

Her mouth still open from surprise, Abby heard her door open as Nick beckoned to her. Enthralled, she stumbled out of the Jeep. Holding her arm, Nick steered her gently toward a set of wide stairs leading up to the porch. A pair of large front doors welcomed them at the top of the stairs, but instead of opening them, Nick led her on the porch to a corner at the back of the house. A decorative wooden railing followed the contours of the porch as they walked. Approximately four feet in height, it had been painted a glossy white. Each of the circular wooden rails was fitted expertly into the flat wooden top of the railing. With sudden inspiration, Abby knew Nick must have built the railing. Stopping, Nick pointed at a lake approximately five acres in diameter some one hundred yards away. Wildwood ducks swam in the muddy water of the partially filled lake, and a wooden pier ran from the shore to a point less than halfway into the lake. The land around the lake had been cleared. A riot of colorful wildflowers was growing. Texas Bluebells, Indian paintbrush, and yellow sage grew in wild profusion. Located nearby was a covered pavilion. Delicate latticework formed the outside walls of the pavilion, and Confederate Jasmine had been planted next to the latticework. Already, the slender vines of the jasmine were growing up the pavilion walls, their small white flowers filling the air with a sweet aroma. A stone bench was set inside the pavilion facing the lake.

Her hands placed beside her mouth in amazement, Abby removed them and managed to say, "How, why …?"

"Someone not so long ago told me this place had possibilities, remember?" Nick said with a wane smile. "C'mon. Let me show you the rest."

Walking beside Nick in numbed silence, Abby noticed the oversized picture windows that flanked the front doors. As Nick unlocked and opened the door, her curiosity was piqued, and she eagerly stepped into the house.

She gasped for a second time as she saw the home's interior. A sizable den occupied the first room she saw. A hardwood floor had been polished to a glossy sheen; large throw rugs were placed strategically within the den. A brick fireplace, framed by an antique wooden mantle, was built into the wall to her right. Great pains had been gone to so that the original luster of the antique mantle had been returned to its wood. A long couch, end tables, a round coffee table, and a pair of over-stuffed lounging chairs were tastefully appointed within the den. However, the room was dominated by a magnificent painting mounted on the wall above the fireplace mantle. As Abby moved closer to study it, she saw it was of a sailboat on a lake at night. A couple, dressed in clothes of a bygone era and with their arms affectionately around each other, was on the deck of the sailboat. The scene tugged inexplicably at Abby's heart, and it was with reluctance that she turned away to continue the tour of the house.

Leading her deeper into the house, Nick showed her the kitchen. Squares of rose-colored porcelain tile covered the floor, while a breakfast nook had been built next to the kitchen along with a large walk-in pantry. Deep wooden cabinets made of oak had been built on either side of the large stainless-steel kitchen sink. A beautiful dining table dominated the formal dining room adjacent to the kitchen. Made of cherry, two drop leaves were located in the middle of the oval table, and the wood had been stained and finished to a warm dusky-brown glow. A cut-glass chandelier, obviously an antique, hung from the ceiling above the dining table.

Exiting the kitchen, Nick led her back to the den, where a set of wide, winding stairs led to the three bedrooms upstairs.

Taking the stair, Nick led Abby up to the second story and into the master bedroom. Thick amber-colored carpet covered the floor, while a king-sized four-poster bed was set against the wall to her immediate left. A delicate canopy was stretched above the bed on the four posters. To her immediate right, Abby saw sunlight streaming through a set of tall French doors, which led to a small balcony. Stepping out onto the balcony, Abby saw that it gave a magnificent view of the lake and grounds behind the house. A white wrought-iron table was nestled to her left on the balcony. The tiny table was flanked by two wrought-iron chairs, and Abby could see it would be a perfect place to sit and drink coffee or tea early in the morning and watch the sun rise.

Gently touching Abby's arm, Nick motioned for her to follow him back into the bedroom. Reluctantly, she turned and followed Nick into what proved to be the bathroom. A marble counter with two inset porcelain sinks ran the length of the bathroom.

A mirror stretched from the marble counter to the ceiling above. Located behind the counter were two sliding doors framed completely in mirrored glass. Sliding the doors open, Abby saw they led to a pair of large walk-in closets. Sliding the doors shut, Abby turned back to the bathroom and spied a beautifully restored antique, claw-foot tub that stood next to a glassed-in shower. The fixtures were all of a soft, golden brass.

"It's … it's beautiful!" Abby whispered. "It's all so beautiful." Turning to Nick, she asked, "How much of this did you do?"

Grinning ruefully, Nick replied, "I built all of the furniture, the cabinets in the kitchen, the rocking chairs on the porch, and I installed the hardwood floor in the den. The rest I subcontracted out. Oh, and I also built the porch railing and the pavilion."

"Nick, this is so amazing! You did a wonderful job!"

Shrugging, Nick said, "It's not so hard when you have a good teacher like Papa Bill … and inspiration." The last he said while looking directly at Abby. Abby held his gaze for a moment before turning away.

Not wanting Nick to see the conflicting emotions registered on her face, Abby remained with her back to him as she asked softly, "Why … are you showing all this to me, Nick?"

"Let me show you one last thing before I answer that … please," Nick replied.

Nodding reluctantly, Abby let Nick lead her back down the stairs and out of the house. From there, they walked the short distance to Nick's workshop. Pushing the sliding doors open, he flipped on the light switch and beckoned her to follow him.

If Abby had been surprised to see the house and what was in it, she was totally unprepared for the sight before her.

When last she had seen the interior of Nick's workshop, it had been a jumbled mess, filled with tables, chairs, stools, and other furniture all in various stages of completion. The one thing they had had in common was that none of them had been finished! Now, arranged in neat rows were chairs, tables, stools, and bed frames, and all of them were complete! A display area of sorts was set up beside the entrance of the shop, and examples of the furniture Nick built were placed there. In addition, the entire shop was neatly and efficiently arranged. Tools hung in their proper place along one wall, while stacks of pine, oak, and cherry were placed advantageously beside one another, and Abby saw that Nick had even taken advantage of the space beneath the false second-story platform and built a small office there.

As they went deeper into the shop, Abby saw a lone table and two chairs had been placed in an open area roughly toward the middle of the workshop. As they reached the table, Nick bade Abby to take a seat in one of the chairs. Sitting down, Abby spied a tiny wooden jewelry box, obviously an antique, which had been placed in the center of the table. Made of hand carved mahogany, light reflected from its wood in a rich, warm luster. Taking his own seat in the chair next to Abby, Nick cleared his throat.

"All of this—the house, the lake, even what I've done with my workshop—I've done for you, Abby … for us. You … you were the first person to believe in me, even though I was clueless as to what it was I wanted or needed."

"Nick, you don't have to explain anything to me. You … you don't have to do this," Abby quickly interjected.

"Yes, you deserve an explanation, Abby, and given the hell I put you through, it's the least I can do. It's something I have to do!"

Seeing Abby raising no more objections, Nick continued, "When I discovered The Book of Lost Treasures, I thought my prayers had been answered, that I had finally hit the big time. I was going to be rich! Yet, it was as if each discovery we made using the book came with a price, a price that I discovered too late wasn't worth the cost it made upon me, my friends, and ultimately … you."

Standing up, Nick paced beside the table. "Stubbornly, I continued to blame all the problems, Steve's alcoholism, Kenneth's bad business sense, the fighting between Mark and Patti, even our breaking up, on bad luck, bad karma—whatever you want to call it. But the night you left me, the night we broke up, it finally dawned on me that the book simply mirrored the priorities of its owner … me! I had let my own selfish desires blind me to what was going on around me. Worse, the things I should have counted as extremely important, I relegated to minor insignificancies. All I could think of was the next big lost treasure and all the money it would bring. In the process, I lost almost everything I hold dear." Nick's voice had sunk to a low whisper. "I wanted you back, Abby. Believe me when I tell you I'd trade everything, every penny, if I thought that would bring you back to me. But given how badly I knew I had hurt you, given my well-deserved reputation for screwing things up, for never finishing what I started, and finally, for my almost pathological aversion to commitment, I knew you would probably never believe anything I could tell you. Therefore, I had to show you! So I cashed in all the shares I had left when the Treasure Hunt Club dis- solved and took the money to do something productive for the first time in my life! I drew up the blueprints for the house, had it built, and then finished every stick of furniture I had never got around to completing. I enrolled at the community college, and I will have my associate's degree by next May. Finally, I took your advice and began trying to sell the furniture I made. It's amazing! I sold a rocking chair to one of the subcontractors I had hired to build the house. He liked it so much, he ordered two more. He told one of his suppliers, and now this guy wants me to build a kitchen set for him!"

Sitting back at the table, Nick gazed at Abby. The silence between them was thick as Nick let Abby ponder what he had told her so far. Finally, he reached over and took Abby's hand gently in his own. She did not pull away, and he knew it was time to reveal the final and main reason he had brought her here.

"I love you, Abby, and deep down, I'm desperately hoping and praying that you still love me too. I can't change what happened, and I can't change the damage I've done. But I swear to you, if you take me back, I'll dedicate the rest of my life making sure you never regret it."

Tears had sprung into Abby's eyes. The feelings she thought she had successfully banished concerning Nick came rushing back with such force, they threatened to overwhelm her.

Fighting for every ounce of self-control, Abby tried to quell the raging emotions inside her. She found she desperately wanted to believe Nick; that despite everything, their relationship could still have a happy ending. But even as she realized Nick was right—that she did still love him—that same love reminded her anew of the incredible pain she had struggled to survive.

"I asked you once if I would always be the most important thing in your life, and you promised me I was. You didn't tell me the truth then. How can I believe you now?" Abby whispered as she sniffed back tears.

"Because I can prove it to you, Abby," Nick replied softly. He pushed the small jewelry box to her. "Please … open it."

Hesitantly, Abby picked up the jewelry box and slowly opened the lid. Nestled inside the jewelry box was a wedding ring. It was an unpretentious ring; a simple band of gold topped by a single modest diamond. Finding it hard to breathe, Abby lifted the ring from the box with a hand shaking so badly, she almost dropped it. Wrapped securely around the base of the ring and tied by a white piece of thread was a narrow strip of paper.

"I gave The Book of Lost Treasures back to Hank Harper, but before I did, I made one last request of it. On that small piece of paper is exactly what I wrote."

Untying the thread, Abby removed the paper and spread it out flat. In Nick's precise handwriting was a single sentence. It read:

> Reveal to me the location of my heart's greatest treasure.

"What appeared was a map leading me straight to apartment number 154—your apartment, Abby."

Time seemed to stop for Abby as she held the ring in one hand and the thin strip of paper in the other. Warring emotions raged through her in a contest every bit as fierce as that fought by soldiers and armies.

Turning her head, she looked at the ring in her left hand.

Turning right, she looked at the slip of paper in her other hand.

The battle raged, it's outcome uncertain …

Epilogue

Hank Harper showed his last customer out of the shop. Waving a friendly good-bye, he locked the door and, whistling tunelessly, made his way back to the cash register. Stepping up onto the platform behind the worn wooden counter, he rang the antique register open that rested on top of it and began to carefully count the day's receipts. As he was in the process of separating the paper money into different denominations, a bright, golden glow suddenly appeared through the cracks of a locked drawer located beneath the counter. Puzzled, Hank pulled a set of keys from his pocket and, choosing the proper key, unlocked and opened the drawer. The Book of Lost Treasures lay at the bottom of the drawer. Even though the book was closed, light emanated from all around its edges. Slowly picking the book up, Hank opened it. There, glowing in an intense golden light, were the words "Treasure Found."

A broad smile slowly grew across Hank's face. Sighing in satisfaction, he closed the book, placed it back in the drawer, and locked it. Whistling happily, he returned to counting the day's receipts.

Coming Next

A Stunning New Novel
By Michael Scott Clifton

The Janus Witch

Chapter One

The cart rolled to a stop.

Wooden wheels squeaked and grated while settling on the dirty, uneven cobblestones of the village. Canvas-covered ribs formed a pitched oval around the back of the cart, its interior cloaked in murky darkness. A line of buildings stretched into the gloom of the night, their only consistency being no two structures were exactly alike. Ranging from single story to several stories high, more than a few leaned precariously on their foundations as if ready to collapse at the first puff of wind.

Here and there a torch sputtered casting a weak illumination. The flickering light revealed a deserted, narrow thoroughfare along which the haphazard collection of shops, taverns, and dwellings were located. Stone gutters, overflowing with refuse and debris, ran alongside the road. The sulfurous, rotten-egg reek of rotting garbage, competed with the equally potent smell of human waste thrown out of windows to spatter onto the cracked and stained cobblestones.

Warped from wind and weather, a wooden sign hung unevenly from a rusty iron pike bolted to the side of a nearby tavern. Two rust-spotted chains held the sign to the pike as it swung, creaking, in the evening breeze. The cracked and peeling paint on the sign revealed the picture of an enormously fat soldier, his belly spilling over his belt. The soldier held a pike beneath which was etched, *The Potbellied Pikesman.*

A cloaked figure studied the sign from the padded bench of the cart below.

"You know how to pick'em, Morganna," a voice called from the back of the cart. "Why must we always stay at pigsties and hovels in every village?"

Morganna ignored the comment and continued studying the sign. Blood-red lips were pursed in concentration, as she tapped the cart bench with her forefinger. A long, scythe-like nail grew from the appendage. Deep in thought, Morganna scored grooves in the wooden cart bench with the razor-sharp nail. As if reaching a decision, she abruptly threw back the cowl of her cloak revealing long, raven-black hair. A pair of dark eyes glanced back to the canvas-covered interior of the cart.

"Get out. We finish our business here tonight."

Groans greeted her command.

"Why here? Why must it be at this pestilent flophouse? Why can't we at least stay someplace where the bed lice aren't the size of rats?"

Scowling, Morganna replied, "I've told you before, we must keep a low profile. We cannot afford to bring attention to ourselves or our activities. The last thing we need is to give the Hunters a trail to follow."

The hinged back of the cart banged open, and two figures climbed out. A brace of flickering, smoking torches bracketing the scarred door of the tavern revealed two women of breathtaking beauty. One had hair the color of spun gold and eyes of deep blue, while the other had rich, burgundy-colored hair and emerald-green eyes.

Identical lockets were draped about each woman's neck. The chains holding the amulets were made of highly polished silver, and inset into each locket was an opal as black as night—as if no light was reflected or received by the gem. The surface of each opal appeared to ripple like water.

The three women stopped in front of the tavern door. Each stood taller than most men as they conferred with one another.

"Let me guess. Whores again?" quipped the blonde.

"Of course, Argatha…and stop complaining before I turn you into a marsh toad!"

Tittering and cackling erupted from the women before Morganna finally brought it to a halt by chopping her hand.

"Enough! Tressalayne, get our implements from the cart. Argatha, follow me."

The burgundy-haired woman turned and began rummaging in the back of the cart while Morganna and Argatha approached two scrawny horses hitched to the cart. The lathered horses, underfed and with ribs protruding from tightly stretched skin, were still heaving from the exertion of pulling the cart.

Nodding at Argatha, Morganna touched the nearest horse. Immediately, a bright green light enveloped the animal, and when it subsided, a man appeared. Gaunt and naked, he was on his hands and knees.

"Stand!" Morganna ordered.

The man stood unsteadily onto his feet, the leather harness falling from his emaciated shoulders. His eyes, vacant and blank, stared sightlessly, while saliva dribbled in a thin rope from the side of his mouth.

Using her scimitar-like fingernail, Morganna quickly drew it across the hapless man's jugular. Blood spurted in a crimson stream from the severed throat which Argatha nimbly caught in a chalice tossed to her from Tressalayne. Chased in arcane symbols, the amber-colored chalice never overflowed despite the torrent gushing into it. Within moments, the fountain of blood slowed to a trickle. Eyes rolling back into his head, the man died, toppling face first into the hard cobblestones. His limbs were still twitching when Morganna repeated the procedure with the remaining horse-faux-man. The bottomless chalice welded by Argatha once again caught the hot, crimson stream.

Morganna picked up both bodies as if as light as straw, and carried them to a dark, filth encrusted alley running beside the tavern. Rats scurried away from the witch, disappearing in moldering piles of rotten food and garbage. With an effortless heave, she sent both bodies flying down the narrow lane where they landed with a graceless *thud.* Wiping her hands on her dress, Morganna turned back to Argatha and Tressalayne.

"Another advantage of staying in these seedy taverns is that dead bodies rarely draw much attention. A couple of dead men with slit throats in a back alley is more likely to elicit a yawn than any kind of investigation. I'll wager they'll lay there until they become so ripe the smell forces the tavern keeper to remove them."

Quickly changing tack, Morganna asked, "Tressalayne, do you have the changeling powder?"

Tressalayne nodded and handed Morganna a corked bottle whose contents glimmered in the weak light from the torches.

With practiced ease, Morganna pulled the cork from the bottle while muttering words in a harsh, guttural, language few if any in the village, county, or even kingdom would recognize or understand. Arranged at arm's length from one another, Argatha and Tressalayne stood while Morganna tapped a minute amount of powder in her hand. Blowing a portion of it from her cupped hand, first on Argatha, then the next on Tressalayne, Morganna re-corked the bottle and waited.

At first nothing happened. Only the mournful creaking of the tavern sign relieved the quiet of the night. Then, like embers or ash from a slow-burning fire, sparks began to fall from both women. Sluggish at first but building in intensity until with a crescendo, the sparkling fire completely enveloped both women. With a *pop* the sparks disappeared, and in their place were two shorter, scantily-clad women. Argatha wore a stained, blue gown that opened to her navel and barely covered her straining breasts. Of a light, transparent material, it left little to the imagination. Tressalayne wore a torn and patched green gown. The gown contained a slit that traveled to mid-thigh exposing milky skin and shapely legs, while her breasts threatened to fall out of the loosely-laced bodice. Cheap jewelry in the form of rings and bangles flashed from both women's hands and wrists.

Scrutinizing them, Morganna, nodded, satisfied. Handing the bottle of powder to Tressalayne, she said, "My turn."

Tressalayne stared at the bottle before comprehension began to sink in. "You mean…you mean—"

"Yes. You are ready. You have earned the right," Morganna said smiling.

"But you haven't even let *me* try transmogrification and I am older and more experienced!" Argatha protested.

"True," Morganna conceded, "but then Tressalayne is already more skillful than you and I have no doubt, more powerful. Now shut up and let's get on with it."

Argatha opened her mouth as if to supply a further protest, but a steely glance from Morganna caused her to quickly swallow the comment.

Fumbling with the cork, Tressalayne almost dropped the bottle. Fighting to keep her hand steady, she spilled some of the powder into it while repeating the spell spoken moments earlier by Morganna. Finally, she blew the powder onto Morganna.

Time passed and nothing happened. Argatha began to chortle and Tressalayne despaired that she had incanted the spell incorrectly. Just as she was about to ask for a second chance, sparks dripped from Morganna's figure. Building into a roaring, twisting tornado of sparkling light, with a *bang*, it winked out.

Morganna stood before them, a shorter and plumper woman in a worn, wine-red gown. Clinging tightly to her voluptuous figure, the gown was low cut exposing the deep valley of Morganna's enormous bosom.

Examining herself with a critical eye, Morganna nodded in satisfaction. "A little overboard with the tits, but otherwise well done." Turning to Argatha, she said, "Go get our 'guests'." Cackling, Argatha returned to the cart.

Looking into the back of the cart, Argatha commanded, "Come!"

Immediately, two figures climbed out of the cart and stood at attention before Argatha. One was a young man. Tall and slim with thick, curly hair falling to his shoulders, the handsome youth was clothed in an expensive tunic and riding breeches. The other half of the pair was a young woman. Lustrous blonde hair fell halfway down the woman's back and framed a face of flawless perfection. A shimmering, light-blue dress clung to her youthful curves, the tightly laced bodice molded to her modest bosom.

Both the man and woman stared blank-eyed and unblinking.

Reaching into the back of the cart, Argatha grabbed a canvas bag and tossed the chalice in it. Then, pulling a wand from her sleeve, Argatha tapped the cart three times. Shivering like a leaf in the wind, the cart began to shrink and continued shrinking until it was a hand-sized object resembling a child's toy. Placing the tiny cart next to the chalice in the bag, Argatha closed it and motioned to the young couple. Walking with wooden, jerking motions, they followed Argatha as she returned to Morganna's side.

Taking a last look around to make sure they had been unobserved, Morganna turned the iron handle of the tavern door and they walked in.

Unlike the quiet of the darkened street, the common room inside of the tavern was a maelstrom of noise, light, and commotion. A cacophony of dozens of voices assaulted the witches' hearing, some bellowing for more ale, others raised in argument.

In one corner, a half-dozen men in the rough, worn and stained clothing of drovers, herdsmen, and farmers were engaged in a game of dice. Boisterous shouting erupted as one bald, grizzled farmer threw the dice, the roar from the winners mixed with the groans of those who lost. Moments later a fight broke out over disagreement on the payment of wagers.

In another corner, a group of men were throwing darts at a chipped and pitted dart board. A gap-toothed barmaid in an ale-stained apron struggled to negotiate her way through the knot of men. Slapping and in some cases, punching, at the rough men whose groping hands attempted to pinch her ample backside, the barmaid went about her business of pouring ale and picking up empty leathern jacks.

The smell of sour ale, smoke, and unwashed bodies was overpowering, and Morganna, Argatha, and Tressalyne had to stifle their reflex to hold their noses. Morganna's sharp eyes spotted the tavern keeper wiping a worn and age-darkened wooden bar a number of paces to their left. The rag the tavern keeper was wiping the bar with looked little worse than the clothing he wore. A sweat-stained leather apron covered his wide girth, and a thick growth of grizzly chest hair erupted from the top of the bib like a shock of wheat. Jug-eared and balding, the tavern keeper warily watched the three women approach.

Stopping before the bar, Morganna purred, "We'd like a room for the night."

Running a critical eye over Morganna and her companions, the grizzled tavern keeper took his time answering. Finally, he said, "Ten coppers."

Morganna bit back a retort knowing that five coppers would be more than a fair price at such a backwater tavern. Reaching into the canyon between her breasts, she took out a small leather purse.

Before she could flip the coins to the tavern keeper, he thrust his chin toward the young man and woman standing behind the three witches.

"And five more for your clients."

It took every ounce of self-control for Morganna not to cast a strangling spell on the fat tavern keeper. Her plan of smoothly arranging for lodging and exiting the common room was in jeopardy. The longer they lingered, the more attention they would garner…the last thing she wanted.

Already some of the men in the tavern were pointing to the women. Others were staggering to their feet, no doubt to inquire as to the price for a night's companionship. Quickly, Morganna took a silver coin from the purse and pitched it to the tavern keeper. Deftly catching it in midair, he bit down on the coin. Satisfied, he reached under the bar and produced a sturdy iron key. Smirking, he handed it to Morganna.

Turning, Morganna led the entourage up a creaking staircase some ten paces to the left of the bar. Impatient, she waited at the top of the steps slapping the iron key in the palm of her hand. She was anxious to get started.

There was much work to do.

Here are the ways
you can remain connected
with Michael Scott Clifton.

Twitter -
https://twitter.com/michaelsclifton

Facebook -
https://www.facebook.com/michaelscottclifton/

Word Press Blog -
http://www.michaelscottclifton.com